A Pennyweight More

The Life of
Margaret Todd Wilson Johnson Pugh
(1823-1905)

By
Charlotte Dasher Hutchens

The dates, places and people are real and as historically accurate as I could keep them. Some events and dialog are a fabrication of probabilities reconstructed from a framework of real and known events, from historical documents and researched history of the State, County and family and friends.

*Dedicated to my Children and Grandchildren
that they may know at least one ancestor
as a REAL person.*

Chapters

Foreword

This is a story about the life of Margaret Todd Wilson Johnson Pugh. The years 1823-1905.

Daughter of pioneers in Illinois, a pioneer herself to Wisconsin and Kansas. Lived through a marriage, separation and death of her husband, the loss of two children, the Civil War in Illinois. She remarried and had a second family of children, pioneered in Kansas (1871).

Her son moves into Osage County with the Indians. After living in a soddy, working for her brother, and baking and farming for a living, she opens a boarding house in Winfield, KS.

She fights against discrimination of Negros, for women's rights and education, and the injustices of women having to prostitute because of not having other jobs available to them.

She was not a popular woman, at times, but respected enough that when she died her obituary ran on the front page of the Winfield newspaper.

The title means, Margaret was not famous and did nothing spectacular but by ordinary outspokenness at every opportunity given her, she lent her pennyweight more to the building of America and to the benefit of her causes.

Preface

Charlotte lived in Colorado and I in California. She was good about writing letters but after the babies came I most appreciated hearing about the things that they did because I was unable to visit very often.

I have always encouraged Charlotte to write because I saw from her frequent letters she had a knack to make us laugh and cry with her discriptive pictures. After a letter about the children I felt as if I had experienced a visit.

She has published articles for Nursing magazines. Having traveled extensively, mother of five children, grandmother of nine, great-grandmother of three, a nurse, very involved in various organizations and married for fourty-four years I thought she would have lots of material of interest to the public. It came as a surprise to me that she would go so far into the past for a story and yet it is an appropriate extension of her genealogy work.

When I read "A Pennyweight More" I was impressed because I was so interested in the story I forgot that Charlotte was the author and that Margaret was my great-great-grandmother.

Geraldine (Mills) (Dasher) Spellaza

Acknowledgements

Every book is dependent upon a certain amount of research, and one based on a genealogy is entirely indebted to historians and record keepers of all kinds.

I hesitate to name anyone for fear of omitting someone important. It has been years, and the memory is busy with more current events, but I will try because they are so deserving and apologize if anyone is left out.

My gratitude is extended to all of the helpful County Clerks and records keepers; To my great aunts, especially Leona Johnson Herrington and Sylvia Johnson Rogers Irwin; to the Richland County Illinois Genealogical Society, especially Joan Doane, Neil Galleghar and (cousin) Clessie Bagwell; to the Historical Society and museum in Cedar Vale, Kansas; to Mrs. H. H. Johnson (Jane) and her sister Mrs. J. C. Johnson, Jr. (Helen) (granddaughters of Jarome Willson); to Florence Gilchrist Pugh of Winfield, Kansas (daughter-in-law to Jacob Pugh); and to James Joseph Gilliland, Jr. of Leon, Kansas who generously shared his grandmother, Josephine Alta Meldrum's, DAR and genealogy papers that found Margaret in the first place, (Josephine was a grandchild of George, brother to Margaret); and to the Daughters of the American Revolution who lovingly promote and preserve our heritage.

Chapter 1

Courtship and Marriage

Margaret swayed gently and rhythmically in her seat as the train waddled along, gaining miles, bringing her back to her family in Olney, Illinois.

It might have been an exciting event for her and the three small children except they were exhausted, both from the trip and the stress of events that seemed at once unreal, and yet so raw and painful as to be a physical hurt —so unreal that it could have happened a million years ago—so painful as to be happening over and over again.

Margaret reminded herself that it did happen, and now they had to go home. Was it three years? Yes, three babies ago. She recalled her early years, and Ezra.

Margaret was the oldest daughter of John R. Wilson, a Virginia gentleman, and Elizabeth Heap from Washington County, Ohio, of a well educated family of some financial means.

Her mother, Elizabeth, had been raised on the frontiers of Ohio. She never quite overcame the feeling that her family and her children were just a touch better. She expected them to live up to their background, which included a grandfather who had fought with Lafayette, and supported the American Revolution with his ships. He had left a legacy of education for boys and girls, public service, and a sizeable estate in Carlisle, Pennsylvania.

Elizabeth wanted Margaret to marry well, but instead she watched the strong willed girl grow up with a restlessness, to leave her family, and go out to claim lands never before cultivated. She grew up with talk about overnight cities, instant millionaires, gold, Oregon. While Elizabeth cursed the day she had to leave Ohio ten years ago, coming to the Illinois wilderness, Margaret could not wait to find just exactly the right person to marry so she could go further away.

Elizabeth was sure that their lifestyle had influenced her children. She and John were just getting established in Ohio when they had moved, leaving their children without peers, friends and family. These frontier people did not hold to the old standards she liked.

Margaret smiled as she watched the countryside glide by, remembering her mother schooling her and her brothers on protocol, table manners, and other social graces. "Never pay a call to anyone without first sending a servant over with your calling card and announcing yourself." Margaret often wondered why anyone would work as a servant when they could own their own piece of land. Servants were usually single women. Would that now be her fate without Ezra?

Margaret was tall for the times. Five foot six inches, and she had a very pale complexion, camouflaged somewhat with light brown hair. She walked with her banker father's regal bearing. He had reminded her often of her intelligence, and how beautiful a tall girl could be if she did not slump.

She had rejected all of the planned marriages her mother had made for her. What Mother didn't know was that Margaret was looking for her own brand of man who would love her like she had read in a forbidden novel. She wanted someone who would not just

2

appeal to her eye, but someone who would also dream of going West. Margaret never dared to express any of this to her family, and while she was spirited and questioning, she was for the most part a loving and fairly obedient daughter who flirted outrageously with Ezra Johnson.

Ezra Johnson was three years younger than Margaret, big and full grown at nineteen. He lived with his sister Angeline (Johnson) Newell since she had married. Margaret had watched him grow up. They had attended the same school. After the death of his older brother, he had been responsible for helping out on the farm and developed muscle and grace beyond his years. Five sisters and a younger brother lived on the farm with his father, Joshua, and his stepmother, Lydia. His little brother, Edwin, was thirteen.

His mother, Mary (Gardner) Johnson, known by everyone as Polly, had died on June 13, 1844, laid to rest beside her son Bill, out on the Jordon Lake property. Joshua remarried two years later to Lydia Eckley, the doctor's daughter, and they had since had a son Harvey. Ezra's half brother followed him around like an adoring puppy. They all made quite a crowd at meal time in the two room cabin, but then it was no less than most folks hereabouts. Ezra's sister, Frances, was eighteen, and she did a big share of the work, too, both in and out of the house.

There was mutual dislike between the Wilsons and Johnsons. The Wilsons thought Ezra crude and uneducated, even unclean. Elizabeth doubted he even knew how to eat with tableware. And Josh Johnson thought of Margaret as a spoiled rich girl without gumption to pull her weight. It would be a burden on any man to keep her in clothes and a house like she was used to.

3

Margaret and Ezra had begun to meet on a regular basis at the school house while waiting on the younger children to be dismissed and taken home. Margaret's brother George was the school master this year, but Margaret would make excuses to pick up the children anyway. She would wait by the well, always the first to arrive. She would thrill seeing Ezra ride up on his bay at a gallop, dismount with a graceful step and a grin. They would flow into easy conversation and she found that the attraction was magnetic and the dreams were shared. He even smelled good. Was it soap? Vanilla? She could not quite distinguish it, but she liked it!

Ezra talked about the frontier, his own place without family around to boss and tell him to do work this way and that because that is the way it is always done. As he saw the light in Margaret's eyes kindled, his dreams seemed possible and started to form images that knew no boundary. Margaret dreamed with him.

It was only when they spoke about their bond and desire to marry that cold reality would sober their minds. Neither of their parents would consent.

Margaret's parents, of course, wanted a "higher class type" for her. A businessman, a banker perhaps. Joshua did not suspect more than that Ezra was "sowing his oats." But Ezra knew his father thought very little of an educated woman. He had heard him say many times, "Marry them young and raise them right! They's only really happy cookin' and tending babies. Teach 'em to read and they get high notions and are restless, making their man strive for what he don't need!"

Lovers' depression would sweep over them and drive them into each others arms for comfort and make them struggle to overcome being denied.

A plan formed gradually. They would marry at the courthouse and just announce it to their parents after the fact. It would raise a ruckus, but that would just have to be that.

One afternoon, in the fall of 1850, Margaret and Ezra met in town and marched courageously down into the basement of the church that served as the courthouse, nervous and determined, but suddenly very shy of one another. Emotions on fire, they fidgeted, sitting in the office, waiting for Isaac Hoffman. Isaac looked every bit the German clerk. With spectacles on his nose he stood over them, waiting, peering over the top of his glasses at the youngsters before him. He asked, "Do your folks know you are here?"

They didn't lie. They stared at the floor. He went on to say, "Margaret, you may be of age, but both Mr. Wilson and Mr. Johnson would drag me over the coals if I were to issue you a license to marry. I know that Ezra here is not twenty-one and the law says I must have a release of bondage from his father. Do you have that?" His tone was firm but gentle. "No? Then come back and if I cannot persuade you to wait until Ezra has a better means of supporting a wife, I'll issue you your license."

Their joy wilted into disappointment and hopes dashed in the face of so close a victory, making them leave angry. In spite of his gentle tone, they were not only angry with Isaac, but angry with themselves for not thinking it all through. They had acted foolishly in front of Isaac Hoffman.

They walked around to the front of the school house. The children were gone for the day. It was already common knowledge that they were a "pair," albeit, a forbidden pair. They had had several verbal clashes with their parents already. Each would have

5

had them separated if it were possible. The forlorn couple sat on the steps and planned again. How could they find a way?

"I'll leave my family, dowry, and home and make a complete break from them. We'll go off together and never come back." Margaret was ready to do whatever it took to fly off with the man she loved! She would have, too, except for the sobering thought that for Ezra, it would be illegal. Not just because he wasn't yet twenty-one, but he was working out a team of horses that would one day be his to start his own place. At nineteen he was a full grown man, doing the work of a man, and a horse, too, on occasion. Yet, deep down, overcoming his passion for Margaret, a strong tug of obligation pulled at him. He and his father worked right alongside one another, and his father had tried so hard to keep the family together. Edwin was only thirteen and it would be three or four years before he could replace Ezra.

Darkness folded about them and as they snuggled together against the autumn coolness, talking on and on, sorting out possibilities for a future they had hoped would have started that day. Suddenly, Margaret knew what to do about it! She decided against sharing her revelation with Ezra, just in case it didn't work out her way. She kissed him on the mouth to his surprise and excitement, right there in the school yard lit by the moonlight, seen by those interested in looking. She held his hands.

They walked home, reluctant to part, each heart throbbing in unison. Their arms moved carefully around one another's waist. On the porch, Margaret, knowing that her parents would be watching, stood on tiptoe and leaned her body fully, sensuously against Ezra's and kissed him once again passionately, fully on the

6

mouth! His surprise almost caused him to bolt from the porch, but instead, he was unable to move as passion controlled his thoughts. He wanted her so very much, but he was fearful of the scandal it could create upon Margaret. He didn't know whether to run, or stay, floating on this cloud they had created for one another. Kissing him again, lingering in the full enjoyment, she said softly, "Goodnight my love," and pointed him gently towards the steps. Ezra left, too puzzled to understand her motives.

Inside Margaret was greeted with silence. A grim faced set of parents scowled at her defiant posture. They knew they had exhausted their arguments about this farm boy. A boy who could, at the very best, end up as a laborer on his father's farm, and perhaps inherit a small third of the 160 acres, forevermore grubbing out food and sustanence as the weather and nature dictated!

Margaret pronounced softly to her parents, "Mr. Johnson and I have been married, spiritually . . ." with a raise of an eyebrow, a slight etheral glance to the ceiling and a seductive sigh, "If you know what I mean."

Her mother gasped the cry of a hurt bird, and clenched her breast. Father's jaw dropped at seeing a side of his daughter he had never seen before. Margaret had often been defiant, bold, angry, opinionated and even unladylike, but never sensuous. He recoiled from the realization that perhaps it was time to get her married! The shock Margaret had factored subsided sufficiently to allow him to speak "Where have you been with that boy? Did he . . .?" But what if she doesn't even know what I'm talking about or alluding to, he thought. Even though she was his daughter, he had not the slightest idea how she thought and what she knew. He was so confused it made him angry with being at a loss for words and frustrated with being so inarticulate before the females of his family. Margaret knew full well the impact her statement had made. She looked demurely to the floor, not answering a word, letting her statement about Ezra's and her's "spiritual" relationship conjure, undoubtedly, numerous imaginations in their minds.

Her father paced the bedroom that night, trying to sort out the whirlwind of emotions. Should he duel the bastard? His father would have demanded satisfaction for dishonoring a daughter, but this was 1850, and this younger generation is growing up so fast these days, and so independent! Arranged marriages are considered archaic by the young people. With land available, and the government pushing for settlement and expansion, some of these youngsters were going off without even the benefit of a legal document. Slapping his fist in his hand, gritting his teeth determingly, he declared aloud, "But by all that is holy, that won't be the case with my daughter!"

Elizabeth had been brooding silently in the bed, and his declaration attracted her attention. "John," she said pensively, "perhaps we should let them get married."

He whirled on his heel and looked at her, disbelieving, but with hope that she might, too, see that consenting to their daughter's marriage was the solution to salvaging a difficult situation wisely. She held up her hand, "John, hear me out please, and then you can decide of course." This meant she had decided and would let him take the credit or blame as the case may turn out!

"Margaret has exhausted me. She is getting on in years, and has been bent on turning down every eligible man in the country. Well, perhaps we should give her the dowry and her hope chest. They would just have to make do with that. You could go over there tomorrow and find out that rowdy's intentions, and if he has any decency, he will do the right thing. It would stop the gossip." Then, making it sound as if it was an after thought, she said under her breath, "Maybe they will go West?"

"I'm tired of worrying," she added in a nobler tone, "I won't interfere. We'll provide a decent wedding, as far as we can with that bunch." Tears came and her voice tightened, "Oh, John . . . I do think she deserves so much more." She held out her arms for his comfort.

"I think I'll just shoot the bastard and be done with it!" said John, looking past his wife's arms out the window.

"John! You have never dueled, and you are aware it is illegal now!"

"You wouldn't know it by all that goes on around here," he countered. "It's even expected sometimes."

"Margaret would hate you all of her life. What if I had Brother George go talk to him?" she said.

"No! By damn, I'm her father. I'll find out his intentions and if he's honorable, he'll marry her, and if he refuses, I'll shoot him!"

"Come to bed John," she said, smiling with the satisfaction that they were in agreement about their daughter's future. "It's cold." She snuggled deep into the feather bed. Elizabeth was still a handsome woman at forty-two, and desire often stirred in them. However, John's anger rendered him dispassionate and indifferent to Elizabeth's overtures tonight.

"Damn these children sometimes," he grumbled.

As he saddled his horse the next morning and rode south the four miles to the Johnson place, John was still not sure what action he would take. He promised himself to act respectful, and demand the same from them. If it didn't turn out that way, then he would treat it as a problem between him and Ezra.

Joshua Johnson had seven brothers and seven sisters. Everyone declared he was related to half the United States! Descendants had spread out every direction, from Vincennes, Indiana, and the old man James Johnson had brought most of them with him when he moved to this area, and they, too, all had big families. There were some Wilsons in town, too, but except for James they were not related to John. Certainly there were not enough Wilsons to match guns with the Johnsons in a full blown family feud. This confrontation had to be handled with care and integrity or it could get out of hand.

He thought about how the town had grown since they had come here. Elizabeth pretended it to be such a crude place at first, but this crudeness apparently cried out for her social and cultural leadership, which she was so skillfully prepared to do. The Wilsons could afford the Eastern fashions, and lived in one of the more substantial houses, on one of the more pleasant streets, within a short distance of the influential business area. Olney was populated by emigrants, people who were self reliant and hard workers who had few servants, and none had slaves. There were new ideas and new social guidelines that often shocked John and Elizabeth. Children picking out their own mates! What was the world coming to? John had had time to mellow slightly by the time he had reached the Johnson farm.

Josh Johnson was drawing water from the well at the back of the house, Ezra was tossing shocks of corn to the hogs. Edwin was on his way into the house with a pail of milk. Noises of the other children were coming from the two room log house. Chickens were running loose. Hound dogs, too busy sunning themselves, ignored him as he rode in.

Surprised by such an early visitor, Josh handed his bucket to Ezra and put his hand out in greeting. John stepped down from his horse, shook the hand and said curtly, "I'm here on business Josh, serious business with you and your boy, Ezra."

Josh looked at Ezra, searching for a hint of what his young son had been up to now. Had he been drunk and disorderly last night in town? He hadn't taken the horse out to race? What could it be? Out loud he said, "Well, come in and have some coffee and grits and let's talk. My Lydia is getting to be quite a cook."

John knew of Josh, but had never had any social dealings with him and had never been to his house before. It appeared to be clean enough, and at least the children were all up and about doing chores. That showed industriousness. The kitchen was crowded with barrels of flour, meal, potatoes, all stored by for winter. Firewood was stacked in a box by the back door. A basket of apples hung on the wall, with sacks of dried fruit, jerky and ham sharing space with coats and sweaters on pegs with various other garments. Under an oil paper covered window was the wash bench. Smooth wooden bowls and spoons were being dished up with steaming grits and the fresh milk was being strained through a cloth from the pail into a pitcher by Frances, Ezra's oldest sister. She was barely able to finish before the younger children dipped into it with a ladle, filled their bowl and took a place along the bench at the table.

Seeing the stranger with Papa, the children were suddenly quiet and stole a look around at each other to see what tone the visit would take. Mr. Wilson did not

11

appear too pleased to be here. Lydia, as lady of the house, offered coffee in one of their few pottery mugs. John took it with a Virginia gentlemen's bow, saying, "Thank you, Mrs. Johnson, for your hospitality." He now knew all possibility of a duel would be out of the question as he was inside their home and partaking. He remained standing, declined breakfast, but insisted that the children continue to eat . . . which took no encouragement from him.

"Josh, if we could talk outside . . ." They met Ezra as he was coming in. Their eyes met, "Good morning Mr. Wilson. You're about early today, sir." Sarcasm dripped from John's response, "You were out and about late last night, Ezra Johnson!"

Ezra averted his eyes, cleared his throat, bumped his head on the door post, portraying the anxiety he was feeling about facing Margaret's father. I'm a man, he told himself, I've done nothing wrong and I'll stand my ground to her father, or mine!

"Is your business with me, sir?" Ezra asked, standing tall, his shoulders squared.

"Yes, and no, but stay and declare yourself. Mister Johnson, I believe your son has been toying with my daughter's affections and I need to understand his intentions. Since he is not of age, I have come to ask you."

"Is this true Ezra? You dilly dallying with Mister Wilson's daughter?"

The crude remark brought John and Ezra both to defensive attention.

"No, sir," Ezra exploded, "My intentions and my actions are honorable and my feelings are deep for Miss Wilson, and if a way can be found . . . I was going to ask . . . We went to the court house . . . I need a leave of bondage, Father. I know you need me here till Ed is

12

older, but Margaret, well we don't just know how to work it out!"

Ezra anticipated John's thoughts before he could ask. "Nothing happened, Sir! I swear, it was nothing dishonorable! We talked, and night surprised us, I escorted her safely home. That was all, I promise."

John was beginning to appreciate the boy's discomfort. He had seen the two kiss and knew in his heart Margaret had been the aggressor, yet this apparently honest boy had to take the blame. He softened while Josh bristled defensively.

"You did not kiss her on the mouth?" John demanded sternly.

"No, sir, well, yes sir, you see, sir. . ."

Josh broke in, "Boy, you owe me for that team over there, and you don't have nothing to offer a female but your ass and your hands! What in God's creation are you thinking about, courting around like your doing? Do you think you are going to bring home another mouth to feed? Where do you propose to put her? On a nail?"

"No, Father, we want to go West!" Ezra had blurted out his dream before he thought.

"West! You got the gold fever, maybe? Let me tell you most of those poor devils came back in rags or left widows. Not one in a million of 'em ever found a nugget!"

"No, Father, not gold fever, land fever. We could go north. Up in Wisconsin people are pouring in. There is a boom opening up that new state. There's timber, coal, furs, shipping, now with new ports opening, even fishing. I've heard grandpa talk about it. The first in line get the biggest slice of the pie!"

Seizing the opportunity, Ezra turned to John, "I'll

marry your daughter, Mr. Wilson and provide for her well . . . with your permission, sir."

Josh broke in, "With my permission first, boy. You're not of age."

John suggested, "I believe we can solve our problem here, Mr. Johnson. Young people are so independent these days. Let them get married, but stay and work out what they will owe you. They can build a cabin, which will be left for your use when they leave for Wisconsin. Margaret has a dowry, and I must say, I believe they have what it takes to make it a go."

Josh considered John's plan with silence. It sounded good to him, much better than forcing a horse whipped boy to the preacher for dilling a girl. He didn't believe that nothing had happened, after all he'd been young once and nineteen. Now, here was this Mr. Wilson being generous as to offer a dowry to boot. "Done," he pronounced, "and I'll throw in a wagon with the team!" With a second thought, "If Ezra here will stay home until the team is full grown and broke to pull."

Ezra couldn't believe what he was hearing! He let out a whoop and threw his fist into the air, shook Mr. Wilson's hand vigorously, and slapped his father's back until Josh said, "Hesh up there boy. You'll make the neighbors think we're having an Indian raid!"

Things progressed rapidly once the plans were announced at church Sunday. There was so much to do in so short a time! They wanted to be married and in their cabin before winter and here it was already the middle of October. Ezra called out his neighbors to help him raise a cabin and bargained with Mr. Lutz and Mr. Connor to help build a table, chairs and a bedstead in exchange for a hog. Once the logs were downed, it only took three days to put up the twelve foot by twelve foot log cabin. It took another week to make the fireplace and they threw a big chinking party. All the children and adults except for Elizabeth who begged that she had a dress to finish, gathered at the cabin that was going up right next to Joshua's.

Dressed in their worst worn out clothes they started to stir the mud and grass straw in a slew box. Laughing at the freedom of getting as dirty as they pleased, the children raced back and forth with handfuls of mud, throwing and patting and poling it into the holes between the logs as high as they could reach. When they needed to go higher they climbed on each other's shoulders. Soon everyone was smeared and covered with more mud than was on the house. They dumped the last on the roof slats then sprinkled it with rye seed that would sprout and hold it in place. They all raced for the creek when they finished to wash up in the cold fall water. The two families were well acquainted by supper time.

Lydia, step-mother to Joshua's brood, had started supper with hot apple cider so no one would get colic. They had smoked ham and sweet potatoes, and it vanished quickly into the very tired bunch.

Mr. Huffman lived next door to the Johnsons and he was a good neighbor and silversmith. He came one day to present Ezra with a pair of silver wedding rings.

The leave of bondage was filed on the 11th of November giving Ezra his "freedom one year hence" and the wedding took place on the 14th in the Methodist church which was also the school house . . . and the court room when court was in town. It was one big room with an iron stove in the center.

Margaret was a beautiful bride and breathtaking in her satin white gown with the lace taken from her mother's wedding gown. Ezra had on his father's suit, but he was so unaccustomed to wearing formal clothes he was ill at ease even if it did fit perfectly.

It was a cold day and they had stoked the fire in the stove. It was a good fire and the room was warm. Reverend Benjamin Coates stood with his back against the cool wall while Margaret and Ezra's backs were to the stove. Their backsides burned as they listened to the preacher's wedding sermon. Those gathered for the occasion stood toward the edge of the room and had begun to fidget when little Harvey noticed Ezra sweating and said loudly, "Ma, why do they get 'em so hot when they're gettin' married?" There were snickers throughout the room and even the preacher couldn't stifle his smile.

At the reception in the Wilson home, Elizabeth, was determined not to show her disappointment at Margaret's choice of a husband, and resisted expressing her discomfort with the cut of Ezra's borrowed suit, but did comment to them, "Ezra, I'm so hopeful you can provide for Margaret. Her family is educated and she is accustomed to certain refinements that are not easily attainable at such distances from the centers of art and culture." Ezra, bolstered by his new status as husband and the help of the spirits spicing the punch, responded, "We Johnsons may not have had the time to become refined, but we have provided well for our families by using the tools of God and nature for three generations out here on the frontier. My Scottish grandfather fought with the great General George Washington, was educated, brave and elevated to the rank of lieutenant colonel in the Great War. My daddy fought the Indians and the British out here at Fort Vincennes, and we have all worked and fought to make this area safe for the latecomers like you. We have scant education, Ma'am, but we know our manners such as sparing a man's feelings and pride." Elizabeth declared the conversation closed by excusing herself.

The house was a buzz of activity as the whole town had turned out to wish the newlyweds congratulations. Everyone was related in one way or another. Ezra's sister, Angeline, had married into the Newell family and his father Josh had married Doctor Ephriam Eckley's daughter, Lydia.

Margaret's mother was a Heap, and together with all the Johnson kin of Gardners, Horrells, Andersons, French, Turner, Wallace and Shelbys the town was well represented, and the county to boot. Those not related had that special bond of friendly unified efforts making a civilized settlement. They had all fought Indians, British and renegades together.

Boards were being laid on the ground for a dance floor and the fiddlers were warming up, while the young people squealed with the delight of building a bonfire in the plowed field next door. The older people cautioned them to keep it small so they wouldn't burn down the whole town. Grandpa Johnson was passing around some of his famous Scotch and everyone stayed warm and happy till the wee hours of the morning.

Margaret and Ezra stole away in a borrowed buggy during the merry making, off to their new home out on Calhoun Prairie, next door to Joshua and Lydia.

They were ecstatically happy and excited about each other, and having a space of their very own for the first time in their lives. The twelve foot by twelve foot cabin felt huge after a lifetime of sharing living space with siblings and grandparents, travelers, and various relatives. It was the way of life to share any small space with anyone who needed it.

The secluded, sweet and passionate honeymoon lasted two days and nights, until Joshua and Lydia returned from their stay with Angeline in Olney. There was no longer any privacy. With the cabins so close it was immediately claimed as an addition to the main house. Margaret never knew how many would be at her table or who would be asking to sleep with them at night.

Ezra's little sisters wanted to see if she could cook. They were especially curious to try on her dresses. She had always had a stove to cook on at home, and cooking over the open fire made many things not only cook quicker, but taste different. She didn't know how to regulate the heat in the wall oven and things would bake mostly too slow, so gradually they started taking all their meals together. The food was stored together in the smoke house and most of what was there was there from combined effort including the lard and the soap. Vegetables had been grown and dried from the garden Ezra had helped make and care for in the summer, and many items were gifts from the wedding. Most folks had given food, seeing as how it was late in the fall and the newlyweds hadn't anything "laid by" for winter.

They settled into the routine. The women folk would wash on Mondays inside the wash house, which was actually a shed built around a fire pit with iron kettles hanging over it.

They had one kettle for rendering lard and another for making soap and washing clothes. The water was heated, the clothes boiled then lifted with a stick into another tub of cold rinse water. After they cooled a bit, they were inspected for spots which were then knuckled scrubbed away, sloshed and wrung and taken to the creek for a final rinse to get out all the soap. The white cottons were laid out to bleach in the sun on the fence, grass, or trees, whatever was out of the dirt. The

18

wools were washed in the first rinse water that had become soapy from the other clothes. There were a lot of clothes for the ten of them, even though it was then the custom to wear one dress all week. A light apron outer cover was changed more frequently. Everyone had a Sunday outfit that did not have to be washed every week since it was removed and hung up as soon as possible after getting home. Those who failed to do this caught Holy Ned if it should become soiled or damaged.

There were still undergarments, stockings and nightdresses and of course men's shirts, and the bed linens. Tuesday was ironing day and the day the beds aired. Wednesday and Saturday were baking days, and so it went. Spare time was used knitting, crocheting, tatting, spinning yarn and thread. Lydia even had a loom, although now a days it wasn't used much since cotton yardage was available. Lydia enjoyed working up a shawl or a piece of yardage for a skirt or breeches once in a while.

Time flew by and it was soon evident that Margaret was in "the family way." Ezra was torn with mixed emotions. He was delighted with the thought of a little Margaret, but he had planned to leave for Wisconsin as soon as possible after the crops were harvested, and a baby wouldn't allow them to travel. They went on with preparations for the trip anyway. Margaret was determined that nothing would stop them, even if she had to have her baby on the trail.

Margaret and her mother quarreled about "going into confinement." Elizabeth declared that "decent young ladies come home to live the last two months of their pregnancy so they won't have to be seen in public!" Margaret's reply was a steadfast "I'll not be pinned in a jail and hide. When the baby comes I will

19

be in MY home with MY husband." Elizabeth cried at each encounter. Margaret did not know if it was love and concern, or pride. She felt guilty but resolute.

On the 20th of August 1851, little Mary decided to arrive while a fierce rainstorm buffeted the cabin. When Ezra called for Lydia and Josh to help, all the children came too, in spite of being told to stay in bed. The room became a chattering bedlam, then turned into a tea party as cakes were found. The baby arrived into the warm and cozy cabin and her cry produced a hush of wonder and awe. They all kissed Margaret and the baby, and sat in sleepy reverie with them until morning.

Josh, by now, realized Margaret had spunk. Spoiled or not she would work. He never told her that, but he watched her with admiration as she milked the cows, hoed the garden and helped with the butchering. She had also birthed that baby without a scream. She'd do, he thought.

Chapter 2

West to Wisconsin

Ezra had worked hard training his team to plow, pull, and even ride. His wagon was finished and he had built an "outboard" for it. It was like a cabin inside the wagon but extended out over the side about a foot. With the extra room, a bed could be made across the end. When they arrived where they were going, they could remove the whole thing and live in it. It would provide temporary shelter and free the wagon for work.

Margaret was getting excited. Wisconsin was not exactly her dream of "west," but it was new country and a means to an end. She had learned from her father about business opportunity. She had a plan of her own she did not share with Ezra or her family because she did not want anymore opposition than she had already. Josh was still bitter about losing another son and discouraged Ezra at every chance about going anywhere, yet he didn't make anything sound very attractive around home. It sounded like he needed a farm hand and someone to take care of him. Ezra was sorry he had put off the trip another year, and pitied Edwin, who would be left behind. His advice to him was to get an education and leave the farm, too.

The crops and the baby had come about the same time. Collecting a winter's supply of food into the wagon made Ezra wonder if two horses could pull it all!

21

There was some room between the sacks and barrels for Margaret's trunks she had filled with linens. She had spent the summer begging old linens from her aunts and cousins. They had no idea they were playing into her secret plans.

Against family advice, the trip finally started in September. They kept a fairly fast pace since they were headed north this late in the year and could possibly be caught by a snow before they arrived. They started with the same spirit much like the rest of the Nation in that year of 1851. Expansion was the by-word everywhere. It was nationally agreed that everything between both oceans belonged to America, and officially or not, they would claim it by occupation.

They used good sense about preparing for the trip, and knowing it was a winter trek, they had the local shoemaker make each of them a pair of oversized boots. They packed wet wool under and around their feet and walked all day, vigorously, all about the farm until the wool packed and dried into a felt liner about 3/4 inch thick. It was an uncomfortable process for a day, but the warm felt boots would not only feel good but save them from frostbitten feet as well.

They lived off the land as much as possible and enjoyed the freedom and the fall beauty as they slowly moved through the gentle hills and across open stretches of plains alive with brilliant colored forest. They were safe from Indians as long as they stayed east of the Illinois River.

Fall mornings were cool, but the day warmed up quickly. The road to Effingham was rough and bare, no more than a trail, but the road to Matoon was wider and better traveled.

It was along this road that they met some other travelers going to Chicago. Not much talk was exchanged until evenings when they would camp together. Game was found quicker with two to hunt, and it was pleasant to share talk around the fire while cleaning up from the evening meal. William and Hannah Crider had been in St. Louis. Before that they had lived in Tennessee. Before that, they had crossed the Natchez trail from North Carolina! They would get the "itch" and just load up and move. Margaret didn't know how Hannah had kept her sense of humor living such a Gypsy kind of life but she was intrigued with her story anyway. Hannah joked, "Shucks darling, when my house gets dirty I don't clean it, I just talk Mr. Crider into moving!" She shook all over when she laughed. Her children had all chosen to "stay put" at various places along the trails they had traveled and Hannah didn't mind. She said, "It's like seeding the country. Besides, I never thought I'd live to see them all grown, but I did, and now we're off to do as we please. Not that we haven't always done that! 'Sides, living on the road isn't much different than living in a house 'cept you meet more people!"

Other wagons often joined them, leaving them at turnoffs or towns. At Kankakee a storm came up, wet, cold, and windy. The canvas of the wagon flapped and defied tying down. They huddled cold, damp, and miserable inside. Water condensed inside the canvas toward morning and dripped as if raining inside. They dug out some dried plums for breakfast and decided not even to attempt a fire because of the soaked wood. When the rain let up, Ezra learned not only to tie the canvas better, but to double it with the spare for winter protection. Experience is a very good teacher. They also collected some small wood, made a place for it inside the wagon so they would not have to go through that again.

Arriving in Chicago was exciting. Neither of them had ever been to a city larger than Olney, and had never seen a lake with no visible opposite shore. Margaret was fascinated with tides and waves and ships in the harbor. They were awed at the size of the vessels. Surely they couldn't have been smaller than the ones that plied the great sea to Europe.

A boarding house was found with a bath out in back. Gladly they paid for the pleasure of bathing and soaking in a tub of hot water. Ezra stayed with the wagon and baby while Margaret bathed, then it was his turn. She had kept the laundry done daily by washing the baby diapers and small linens every morning. The wash hung across the back of the wagon on a line and would be dry when they stopped.

Margaret was fascinated by the boarding house. She made mental notes about the traffic, the way food was served by a plate from the kitchen. Watched as the landlord let out rooms to as many as could crowd into the bed and sometimes added a featherbed on the floor. The mistress handled the kitchen affairs while the master collected fees, gave directions and orders to lackeys and the bath attendants out in the wash house. It was not a large place and was easily run by the family. Hardly more work than cooking for a large family or a harvest team, Margaret thought. A woman had to cook three meals a day anyway. Things she noticed found a place into her private plans for her own business.

Ezra was leery of traffic and strangers. The folks back home had spent the winter warning him with stories of mischief and evil that might befall them. The tales about pickpockets, thieves, cut throats and kidnappers at work in the city were the worst. There apparently were those that would drug a man and haul him off to the ships for forced service. They'd take his wife, too, and sell her. They'd lower their voice and squint a warning, "People of evil and there's no escaping them!" The talk did not change his mind but kept him very defensive. His hand never strayed very far from his rifle.

With hugs, their traveling companions left them after finding out the way to Milwaukee. The coast road was the best and most traveled, but not necessarily the safest. The master of the boarding house overheard them and said if they'd stay a few days they could make up a group in no time, since migration these days was pretty steady.

When Ezra asked about work he got a variety of reports indicating coal mining was good as was timber. Those new steamboats and railroads were needing both. Why, if they kept up that modern transportation like that between the two they will soon burn up every tree on earth!

"Might find dray work as a teamster with your wagon young man." Another man broke in, "Yea, every buck in the country tries to do that. Makes such competition among the teamsters it gets a might fierce." Another agreed with the first. "Vicious sometimes just going between here and there!" Still optimistic Ezra and Margaret pulled their wagon to the edge of town, bedded down and talked into the night about how to proceed until lovemaking, followed by a sound sleep, obliterated the city noise.

By evening of the second day in Chicago they met two families traveling together to Milwaukee that were happy to have another wagon join them. It was never wise to travel alone and the more the better, but Mr. Higgins explained that he would decide the route and the stopping places, which suited Ezra since the gentleman seemed to know his way around.

William Higgins was originally from Kentucky. His wife was Priscilla, who came from Illinois, and they were traveling with their children, Harrison, 13, Rosanna, 11, Catherine, 9, William A., 8, and John M., 6. The other travelers were the Grants. Samuel Grant and his wife Betsy had met up with the Higgins on the trail in Indiana. They had decided to head out for Wisconsin looking for opportunity and land like most everyone else. They had hoped to make some cash money to withstand the first years of homesteading. The Grants had no children with them but told about a son who had finished school at West Point and was in the Army. Mr. Higgins had followed a friend out here after he had received a letter explaining how a person could work in the mills in the winters and in the timber summers. With a wagon, a man could hire out hauling supplies and even timber or lumber. It was dangerous work, seven days a week, daylight to dark. No days off unless you got hurt, and then it was no pay and get out. The opportunity was attractive because it paid cash money, daily. When you had earned enough you could move on. Mr. Higgins said his dream was to homestead and raise horses on the Big River. A good stud was costly.

The group of three wagons moved out with the first daylight. North winds, cooler each morning, blew off Lake Michigan. Even at that early hour, laborers were placing rails and hauling freight, building what would become the world's largest freight yards. Following the coast road eight days later, they arrived in Milwaukee. Traveling as a group had been slower since Mr. Higgins liked to stop people along the way to glean information about what lay ahead. Thanks were given daily that they had not been robbed or suffered illness.

At Milwaukee the first stop was on a slight rise at the edge of town. Unlike Chicago, Milwaukee was mostly docks, warehouses and a main street. Residences scattered in a wheel shape, and farms dotted beyond them as patches cleared in the forest.

They journeyed on down to the heart of town where they found the general store and the fur trading post to inquire about a letter that was supposed to be there from Higgins' friend to describe directions to the timber camp. Tired as they were they agreed to press on, even though it was another fifty miles due west.

Margaret was getting more weary by the day. They were pushing hard to travel while the roads were passable. Fall rains had already made deep washes down and across the trail that was called a road. The lumber wagons had left a trail open but the traffic had cut deep ruts and dug outs where wagons had been stuck. They even passed an abandoned wagon so buried it was broken apart. The little group had to push, pull, and walk to help the horses make a few miles a day. It was a great relief to crest a hill only four days from Milwaukee and see a small clearing with a camp.

They learned that this had been the main camp of the timber operation and when it was abandoned by the loggers as they moved west, these people had taken up residence. They were squatter/traders. The cabins were still rough log affairs and a look around showed no great amount of planning. The largest structure was a general store. There was a barber shop and a bath house next door. Across the way, off on an angle with the trees between them, was a blacksmith shed and in the center of the clearing, as if proclaiming it was here first, was a saloon and a "female boarding house."

The saloon porch was crowded with six girls wrapped in quilts against the cool wind, but they quickly disappeared inside when they saw there were women in the wagons.

A large, hairy, muscled, red-eyed fellow introduced himself as Jake. He was friendly and feeling no pain. He occasionally sucked a jug sitting by his chair while he basked in the sunshine on the step in front of the general store. He watched the three wagons lumber up. The blacksmith looked up to hello them. Jake welcomed them to the saloon and introduced them. "This here's Mr. Benjamin Franklin Moore, proprietor of our barber shop and the saloon."

Mr. Moore was leaned back in a chair by the pot bellied stove. He was a smaller man than Jake but also muscled in a wiry sort of way with a moustache comically waxed and curled like a dandy. "You folks are a long way from home," he declared, a statement as much as a question. He passed the jug around and Ezra, Will and Stan all took a polite sip, not knowing or guessing what it might be, but not wanting to offend their host.

Ezra hung back as Will passed pleasantries. The ladies had found a place to sit on a bench in front of the stove, in the most part ignored as the men conversed. After awhile, Will inquired of Jake, "How far is it to the Main Timber Camp?"

"About four more days by horse back, but you don't plan to take your women out there do you?" Jake answered with a sneer. "They won't be allowed to stay, and they'll hurt your chances to stay as well!" The men looked at each other, puzzled. The thought had never crossed their minds. They had supposed in this day and age American women had proven they could endure frontier life.

Jake went on, "No, now you don't understand. It's like on a ship. Women is bad luck. They takes a man's mind off'n his work." He pointed to his right foot and they noticed for the first time it was a peg leg. "Lost it up there with a careless swing of my ax and there wasn't much left for Mr. Moore here to cut free. He staunched it, and stitched it with a flap so I could wear a stump and get around. He used to be on the ships you know, yes sir, saved my life he did, but no more logging for me." His voice almost cracked and he pulled long again on the jug. He didn't pass it around this time.

Ben spoke for the first time and he sounded sober. "Gentlemen, you'd best be advised to return your families to Milwaukee or Chicago, and if you want to see a woman when the weather's too bad to work, and that's not too often under this company's rules, then you can come here to . . ." He glanced at the ladies, and added "I'd be fearful for my women's safety."

Seeing the men beginning to ponder about leaving the women where it was more civilized, Margaret became angry and determined. She stood up and addressed them in a measured steady voice that left no doubt about her conviction, "My grandmother was born and raised on the frontiers of Pennsylvania. My mother was out in the Ohio and then the Illinois. I myself was raised on the fringe of civilization in Illinois. Ezra's grandmother was one of the first families to pole the Ohio River and go up the Wabash to Vincennes and his mother helped his father cut roads into Howard County. And if that is not enough they did the same in Richland County. We are pioneers, and I'll have you know, sir, that we go with our men, shoulder to shoulder. We can use guns or axes just as well and

29

as for women causing bad luck, they'll just have to learn that women are people, too." The men stared at their feet not knowing how to react at the outburst, but Ezra was proud that she had said she wanted to go shoulder to shoulder with him, no matter where. She had proven her worth several times along the trip. Jake and Ben shrugged, unsure whether to dispute Margaret to her face. Hannah and Priscilla had nothing to add to Margaret's remark, but nodded in agreement. Finally Jake said, "I'd better bring in more wood, it's getting a mite cool in here now."

Ezra, Will and Stan were uneasy. They really wanted their wives with them, not left behind to God only knows what in the City. Margaret took Ezra aside and whispered fiercely, "I've come too far to go back now. If they don't allow women in the camp we'll live outside it. We can live in the wagon, make a teepee or what ever, but I'll bet we can build a squatter's cabin. This place is squatted rights, and we can do the same, only closer!"

They stayed the night in the wagons making camp as they always did. Each couple discussed the problem late into the night. Morning came and they had all come to the same conclusion. They packed up and moved on to the logging camp.

It was another nine days before they reached the main camp. With nothing but hills and valleys of cut timber, little cover was left for game. The weather had stalled their trip for two days. Fortunately it was cold, the ground froze solid and the snow was not too deep. They had to dip into the grain barrels to feed the horses and into their reserves for their own meals.

The timber camp looked much the same as the one where Jake had squatted except the log buildings were surrounded by tents with fires glowing through the canvas, making it look from a distance like a dozen lanterns shining in the dark. Smoke from the chimneys sent out a friendly but deceptive look. Being forewarned, they did not want a confrontation in the dark, so the little group decided to make their own camp up on the hill for the night and approach the loggers in the morning. They retreated to where they had found a swift running creek that would delight any homesteader. The ribbon of silver behind the main lodge down below must be where their stream went on into the forest.

It was difficult to sleep. The anticipation of what was going to happen had everyone's nerves on edge. Would they have to return without work? It was very cold. Could they survive in the wagon all winter? They had doubled the featherbed and wool blankets and it was barely enough and this was only the first of November.

The men planned to unhitch and ride horseback into the camp, hire on, and not mention the women folk until later. At the road on the way to the camp they could hear a commotion of yells and screams echoing loudly in the timber. Reaching the crest of the hill where they had seen the camp the night before, they saw two blazing tents and men running half dressed, passing pails of water from the creek, trying to douse the flames of burning men and tents. Others were beating and pulling at the canvas and cots. Galloping in, dismounting quickly, they placed themselves in the water line, passing pails from hand to hand along to the blaze. Closer now, they saw the injured. The leader yelled, "Let it burn. We got 'em all out. Damn it all to hell! What a way to start the day! Get those guys inside and see if you can revive 'em! Shit Fire! Now we'll be short handed."

Will had followed the angry stocky built logger onto the porch waiting for him to notice the three extra hands, not sure if they'd be welcome or not with the present state of affairs. The leader wheeled around to survey the damage from his porch when he saw them now in the early light of morning. "Where the hell did you come from?" Will, always the spokesman, said "Heard you needed some hands. We came to hire on. I'm Will Higgins, this is Stan Grant, and Ezra Johnson." He offered his hand, "I'm Richard Turnkey. How did you bastards know we was going to have to replace the six men that got burned? Any of you doctors? I can use you to log in their place but no place to house you."

Inside the cook was smearing lard on the burns and passing the whiskey. One man was dead. Ezra's stomach turned at the sight and smell of singed hair and flesh. Other loggers nonchalantly sat nearby at the long table eating breakfast preparing to go to work. Rich yelled out, "You guys there, team up with these boys and show them what needs to be done. They'll be filling in." Turning back to Will, "We'll worry about you a place to sleep after work tonight. Get some grub, you won't get any more till night unless you can stuff some pancakes in your pockets."

Rich had a wagon hitched up and provisioned for the burned men to be sent back to Jake's camp. Remembering the last nine days they had endured Ezra asked, "How can they survive the trip? The road was so bad it took us nine days and it had turned colder since then." Rich shrugged and sneered, "They're lucky to get transportation. They don't work, they don't eat and they don't stay. I'll be needing extra hands now and Bud can drive them out and bring the new hands back. Got any objections?" Ezra burned under his glare, but being a head taller, he leaned down and stared back at the squinted, red eyes. "Yes sir. My wife could tend to these men, bring them back to health and they would not have to endure the trip nor the cold. You'd have your working hands back without a trip to Milwaukee and you'd be spared your driver, wagon and horses as well." It took a second for the words to register then Rich exploded! "Your wife! Your wife? You ass hole, You brought a WOMAN here? No wonder we had a fire! A woman in camp is bad luck!"

Murmurs of discontent stirred all around the crowd and Ezra restrained his instinct to punch the cocky Rich where it would hurt him most! He clenched his fist and teeth as well and said in a firm, quiet tone, "My wife had nothing to do with the damned fire! She knows some doctoring, learned from my stepmother. She is camped near here with a small baby and any Jack-a-lope fool enough to disturb her will die by my bare hands, if she don't get 'em first. Now," as he backed away, "we can be of service to each other or we can spend the day hollerin' at each other. Which will it be?"

Rich suddenly liked this big boy who was making some sense. But a woman in a logging camp could mean trouble. "Where you camped?"

"In the clearing at the creek east of here and we'll stay up there if you'll leave us be."

Tension eased as Rich grabbed a pancake and paced around looking at the groaning, burned men while he ate. "I'll have to charge them for board if they stay, and we'll have to raise a tent just for them, no . . ."

Ezra broke in, "Pitch the tent up by our wagon, my wife and I will stay in the wagon and these men in the tent." Then he quietly added, "There's two other

33

women and six children up there—my wife will be safe."

Rich reared back his head and let out a roaring laugh, "You bastards! You sly bastards!"

Margaret hardly knew what to think as a wagon load of blanket wrapped men drove toward the small camp. Ezra was not in sight and her heart raced. Hannah and Priscilla came from their side of the camp fire to stand beside her. The children, previously schooled, scrambled into the wagons and passed out loaded firearms to the adults. Harrison tried to stand real tall beside his mother with one of the rifles in his hands as well.

The teamster, seeing the arsenal he faced, stopped with a hail to the women, "HALLO, HALLO! Injured men here!" he called, "We need help! No one will harm you!" They relaxed a little but did not lay down their weapons. As they approached Margaret could see the blistered faces and the bandaged hands. The driver jumped down and rolled out a huge bundle from the back of the wagon. "I'm John, ma'am," he talked as he worked. "Sent to set up a tent here for these five men that was burned this morning. Your husband sent them and said you could doctor them till they could work again." He looked around for a place to pitch the tent. "You goin' to live in these wagons all winter?" Without pausing for an answer he said. "Boy," motioning to Harrison, "come help here. Stretch out that canvas over there." Deftly the tent was up in no time and the cots unfolded. The men in the wagon sat there in a semi-stupor, numb with pain and whiskey, afraid to move. Only a low moan or cough proved they were still alive.

The children had come out to watch now and the women were busy putting more potatoes into the cook pot for soup. The men were helped one by one to a cot where they lay almost touching each other it was so crowded. John started to hand a kerosene lamp from the center pole and two men began to cry a feeble protest. The fear of fire starting was greater than their cold. He took it down then handed Margaret some old sheets that the loggers had gathered for bandages, "This is the best we could do, Ma'am. I got to go, happy to make your acquaintance." He touched his brim and left hurriedly.

Dumbfounded the ladies could say nothing and only wonder at the circumstances that had brought these five burn victims to them to nurse.

Margaret broke out some of Ezra's Scotch whiskey for the men who suffered the most, spooned soup into those that could keep it down, and encouraged water into all of them. Toby, Joe and Jim were burned on their hands and faces and began to heal quickly without complications, but Bret and C. J. were burned along the back and legs as well as the hands and face, and both developed infections. Over Hannah's protest, Margaret sent them to the creek each day to "clean out the infection" with the cold, swift water, did away with the lard treatment, and rewrapped them with sheet strips that she had boiled clean from the previous day. After a week of this they looked better.

C. J. got chills and Margaret thought he would die. His breathing was tight and he had a constant cough with a putrid phlegm. Hannah feared she was killing him by sending him to the creek, but Margaret persevered and Hannah couldn't protest too loudly because of her own rattling cough. For C. J.'s night chills Margaret mixed a potent mustard plaster and had the children warm cloths for hours by the fire and run them alternately to her to place on his chest over the plaster. He was wrapped in a featherbed which she doubled to try to make the fever break. It took about twelve hours before she succeeded, and when it did, he went into a normal sleep.

The children were a lot of help, carrying water and soup to the patients and by the second week the men were up, trying to help each other. Toby was the least injured having burned only his hands. He would attempt anything he could to help, and Margaret was fussing at him about causing damage to his hands, but he was a big help getting Bret and C. J. out of bed to the latrine. In their impatience and pain, they cursed one another, rehashed the events of the fire, and the damnable circumstances that put them out of work, but there were no complaints about the ladies. As they slowly mended, they began to joke and realized they were fortunate they had not had to endure the fifty mile trip in a cold wagon, which they probably would not have survived. As rough and strong as they were, their instincts told them it was God's blessing for sure that sent these women out to this wilderness to feed and care for them. Even having Hannah preach her Bible to them every day was at first endured, then appreciated.

As they healed, time began to drag. Toby took over the chore of boiling the bandages, and since Margaret had wrapped each finger separately he was beginning to move them and help feed the others. He only wished he could relieve the ladies chopping wood. Because of the men they were using three times as much as they would have otherwise. Margaret was firm about any of them damaging the "new flesh" before it healed, even when her own hands were getting calloused and rough. She required them to air their beds and walk and those that could, came to the table to eat. Movement was necessary to the healing.

Tired as they were at night, Ezra, Will and Stan had built a log table and benches. It was a luxury from working and eating on the ground. The tail gates of the wagons were too busy a place while they lived in them.

Hannah's feet swelled more and her cough worsened. She became slower and slower. Margaret noticed her grey color. "Hannah put your feet up today, we'll do the chores." Hannah started to cry, "You all think I'm old and can't pull my weight?"

"No such thing, dear, you work twice as hard as we do and it's time for you to rest. Please take care and get better and don't push yourself till you drop over!"

Hannah reluctantly returned to her wagon. Priscilla whispered to Margaret, "I think she is dying Margaret. She is over fifty, you know, she can't live long like this!"

Snow fell during the night and she thought perhaps the men would not work but Ezra explained that when the ground is slick it is easier to slide the logs away for more cutting. They move the logs down to the stream to where it meets the river, then in the spring they are rolled into the river and floated to the mill nearer Milwaukee. "For now, all we do is cut. There will be days when it is too bad to cut and I'll stay home, but not today.

He looked at Margaret and exclaimed, "Home, Oh God, Margaret this isn't home. What have I done to you, to us?"

She kissed him hard, "Hush up, Ezra, I told you I wanted to 'go west.' I got just what I asked for, didn't I?" She thought to herself that she'd be more careful about what I ask for next time! Ezra dressed and left

37

the wagon, she followed, steeling herself to face the cold. She made a "nest" for little Mary to roll about in the featherbed.

A blizzard came in and for two days fierce winds buffeted the small group whose only option was to huddle in their featherbeds and try to keep warm. The men in the tent had a small fire pit to huddle over, taking turns stoking the flames while the others shared body heat. Most of the time they wrestled with the canvas to keep it from blowing away even protected as it was with the wagons and trees. Branches broke, sounding like rifle shot, making them aware of a new danger. Their meals consisted of jerky and snow eaten from their hands. The main camp fire went out.

The second day Ezra braved the storm to check on the horses and take them some grain. He returned quickly to the wagon. The third day dawned very cold, clear and still. Ezra, Will and Stan were up before daylight to shovel the snow from the camp fire site and the wood pile. Ezra split some wood, passed it to Will who started a new fire with his flint packet. Stan told them Hannah was worse, swelled like a toad and breathing heavy. "I have to get her to a better shelter. I hadn't looked real close at her for a while, and last night it hit me—we've got old."

Will said matter of fact, "You can't leave now, Stan, and even if there is a spring break, it'll only mean mud. Reckon you're here for a while, like it or not."

Margaret struggled into a second wool dress and a cape after she fed the baby. She came out, brushed snow off the table and started stirring up cakes. She breathed in the cold, crisp, pine scented air and said "Ah! What a relief to get out of the wagon! *And it came to pass!*"

"What are you talking about, woman?" Ezra looked admiringly at his wife, out of bed before anyone else.

"Why Ezra, that's my favorite Bible passage. 'And it came to pass.' That verse tells me everything passes, storms, pain, wounds heal. Anything can be bad, but it will come to pass!"

Before the men left for work Stan said, "I can't recall just what day it is, I lost track, but work or no, I declare it Sunday. I'm asking for prayer before we do anything else."

They all nodded agreement. It seemed fitting as the sun pecked through the trees. Priscilla gathered up the children at the tail gate of her wagon and she climbed down to join Margaret. They all assembled around the fire and even Hannah moved up closer to look out and listen as Stan read the 23rd Psalm and lead the singing of praise.

Soon after the children were spilling out to eat and enjoy the dry, powdered snow. Harrison and Li'l John went off to hunt rabbits for dinner. Sunday or no, fresh meat was needed.

Margaret's dream was to build a boarding house. She had the linens and dishes, but no house. She had not planned or dreamed she would have a hospital instead! Something had to be done soon. Little Mary was needing larger clothes and she did not have the time to sew. She pondered how to improve things when a piercing scream interrupted her worry. She turned quickly to see the boys breathlessly running into camp with the branches crashing behind them. Instinctively she grabbed the loaded gun as the boys ran behind her. A huge brown bear raised on his hind legs to survey the camp that surprised him. Blood was flowing from the blown away jaw where Harrison had first shot. Margaret took careful aim at his throat and squeezed the trigger. The blast reeled her around and she stumbled behind the wagon. The bear, unable to roar, gurgled out, spurting blood over the fresh white snow covered camp. Toby, hearing the commotion had his gun ready now and also pulled off a blast before the beast could come any closer. As it heaved and died there was complete silence and they all fearfully looked around to see if it had arrived alone or with cubs. Priscilla quickly checked to see if everyone was safe and accounted for. Little John began to cry in his mother's arms, and Margaret cried too, with relief.

Toby pounded his rifle butt on the ground and proclaimed. "We've got to have a cabin! There are more bear out there, and wolverines and such, to say nought of the weather!" In the tent he prodded, "Joe, Jim, you rowdies put on extra mittens. You're going to go to work today." Over Margaret's protest they began to plan.

Figuring they owed the ladies a lot for nursing them, they pooled their money, borrowed one of the horses and sent Toby to the main camp. He approached Mr. Turnkey with the confidence of his righteousness. "I'll be needing logs for a cabin Mr. Turnkey. We are paying."

"Who's going to build a cabin? If you all are that well, then come on back here to work."

Toby responded, "We can't handle the saws yet, but we can ax a little as we are. May take awhile, but those women up there are something to see and they deserve better, if we can do it." He told about their healing care, the blizzard and the bear. There's even a baby. "Come on boss, just enough logs for a cabin and we'll pay."

Rich grumbled. He was paid on commission for all the logs that got to the mill. If he sold a few here, well, who would know? Besides these new men were good

40

hands and had saved him from fetching more. "Fine, I'll sell you the logs if you haul them and raise the cabin. Don't know how you plan to get 'em up there. You figure it out and they're yours."

The deal done, Toby went back to the camp partly satisfied. Horses could pull the logs up the hill, but it would take some time and as he reflected about the needs of the group, he realized they needed a fair sized place to house eleven adults and seven children. Sleeping space alone would take a lot of room. They didn't have a lot of strength nor much time before another storm, but little by little they would start, and they would do it!

Word got around about the plans. The cook at dinner time passed the gossip. The men at the main camp had lost their fear of having the women around since they were not actually in the camp and nothing too bad had happened. Murmurs went around the tables like a gaggle of geese until all of them were in unamity. Their spokesman, Moose, stood up and called across the room, "Rich! We're goin' to wobble! We ain't a gonna stand aside while them women haul logs and build a cabin. Our buddies up there ain't fit yet. An iffn we take one lousy day we can raise the sucker 'fore the next storm!"

Rich reacted, "You no good ingrates. I give you an all-winter job and you go soft and want to wobble. Son of a bitch, I knew these women were bad luck! I do a favor, give them logs, and that's not enough? You can't do this, come to your senses!"

Moose walked back slowly toward Rich while he was talking, towering head and shoulders over his boss, "We are going to wobble one lousy day and if you want another tree downed this winter, you keep the peace. You foul mouth jackass, get that in your head.

41

We ain't askin', we's telling. 'Sides, we know you got paid for them logs and one day won't break you."

Back at the small camp they discussed moving the logs. It looked like a long process since there were so many other chores to do just to survive. They would need lots of logs and big ones. Also a fireplace. Jim knew of a bank of clay down by the river, and that too would have to be brought up on a sled about a mile. It was too cold now, fingers would frostbite in a minute if they were wet. Margaret said cooking over an outside fire was not so bad and Priscilla had a parlor stove for heat, so they would leave the fireplace until spring. Then they could gather rocks and build a proper one. They dreamed of having a warm space to walk in, and work in, and children to play in, just to be able to get out of bed and stand up and stretch would be a luxury for Margaret.

As Ezra started for work the next morning he and the two others saw the men at the main camp harnessing horses, coiling rope and heading for downed trees instead of the timber. Even Cookie was wearing his work clothes and boots.

Rich, given the night to think on it, had joined in. They were not half as surprised as the women were when they heard the commotion and saw what looked like an invasion of horses and loggers! It took a while to sink in but what a joy when it did!

With eighteen men from camp, two women to run and fetch tools, the building went up as fast as the logs arrived. Skilled as they were with saw and ax, they even put in a floor.

The virgin timber was tall and a thirty foot building was no problem, although Rich protested some about the crew's choice of his prime trees. Some trees were felled at the site, but these were not used because they were too green and would warp badly. What they used were not fully seasoned, but were better than new cut.

By noon, beans were cooked. Hams and cornbread came from the Dutch oven and roasted potatoes from the coals. Almost reverently the loggers came by and accepted food from the ladies. Even Hannah attempted to serve by sitting on a stool close to the fire. It progressed so well they decided to make a second floor ceiling. It would not take much more work or logs. Rich, of course, had to protest. They put up three more logs above the ceiling and started hauling the roof beams. At a 45 degree pitch, it would keep off the snow and form part of the wall. A rope with knots in it would suffice for the stairs tonight, delighting the children who could now escape the adults and have the whole upstairs to themselves. There was no clay or pitch to seal the roof, but pine boughs were lashed together and made to do until spring, and shakes could be peeled with a froe. Wagon canvas could be stretched over the beds to keep drips off the sleepers.

Margaret stood inside and cried with joy. Tomorrow they would move in and add finishing touches. Night fell and the loggers began to depart, shaking hands and receiving hearty pats on the back. As the light of a candle outlined Margaret through the canvas as she sat in the wagon nursing her baby, the voice of one of the younger men began to sing, "Silent night, holy night," and Rich said, "Oh yes, yes it is Christmas. I had forgot about Christmas."

Chapter 3

First Boarding House

Hannah died in the spring, just as the crocus were breaking through.

She had taught Margaret so much, even during her weakest days with consumption. Her spiritual strength and philosophy was an inspiration. Margaret learned from Hannah that certain things are worth fighting for. These would be such things as children, freedom, and personal dignity, while other things were not worth a glance, such as material possessions, fashions, and rigid rituals. Margaret and Priscilla felt like they had lost a sister. They all grieved heavily at her passing.

Stan now wanted to go home to Jo Davis County, and the Higgins felt that they had enough of a stake and wanted to go, too. It was decided that after spring breakup, when the roads were passable, they would travel.

It was late April when the supply wagon from Milwaukee came in. They packed up to return with it. Parting was melancholy. Margaret and Ezra had become attached to the children and would miss Priscilla's female company. Little did they dream at that parting that forty years later their children would have fought a war together and their grandchildren would be 1000 miles from here, married to each other.

The once cozy house now seemed huge, lonely and rather empty. With Ezra gone all day the baby was a delight but much work had to be done yet. By making a papoose sling, Margaret spent the now warm days gathering rocks for a fireplace. Using a small sled left by the children she could pull several at a time to a growing pile beside the house. What a luxury it would be to cook indoors, and they would need it for heat as well this fall.

One day at the creek Margaret was dreaming of "the west," thinking how wonderful it would be to find gold just by sifting sand in a pan right at your back door. She even spoke of it to Ezra that night and they laughed.

Their goats, sheep and chickens came with the second supply wagon. Margaret was delighted to have fresh milk again and wool to spin. Now they would have sweaters, milk, eggs, cheese and perhaps a kid in the spring. Ezra paid for the animals and exchanged news with the freighter. He also inquired about hiring his rig to haul freight, too. He laughed when he remarked about how he might ought to "keep it here to haul out the gold my wife is planning to pan." A casual joke.

His rig wasn't hired, but back in Milwaukee the drunken freighter repeated Ezra's remark about the gold. He was asked, "Where is this fellow?" The freighter shrugged and replied, "Grubbing out a sawyer's wage at the logging camp about fifty mile west of here. Name's Johnson. His wife must make more than he does!"

The news spread, and the next day a virtual caravan had headed down the trail to the camp. Gold fever was the same in Wisconsin as it was in California. Those on horses led the way and would not even be discouraged by Jake and Ben as they passed by, insisting it was a new strike found since Jake had worked there.

45

Margaret thought the noise she heard was loggers' wagons, but looking up from her cook pot she saw half a dozen men with pack horses. Frightened by their rowdy appearance and nervous eagerness, she scooped up Mary, placed her inside, reached for the rifle and met them as they halted at her fire.

"You must be Mrs. Johnson. Is this Johnson Creek? You got a deed?" Margaret refused to answer the questions and held the rifle ready on her hip aimed at the leader's midsection. "No need for that, Ma'am. We've come here to pan the creek and this must be the place see'un as there's only a woman here like we heard." He ignored the gun, mounted his horse, gave a hand signal and rode through the trees to the creek.

Puzzled, Margaret didn't try to stop them but continued nervously to watch from an upper window the frenzy of activity on the creek below the house.

That night the campfires could be seen and voices heard which frightened Margaret because these men had seemed belligerent.

Ezra came home and she lingered in his embrace with a tear of relief. She explained what had happened.

"Panning?" asked Ezra, "For gold? Fool's gold, most likely. Probably won't bother us if we don't bother them. Stay locked in the house tomorrow. Keep an eye out. I'll tell them at camp."

Margaret hated staying indoors and eating cold bread. Besides, she reasoned, the goat had to be milked and the chickens let out and fed. All this was difficult enough while watching the baby, but to carry a rifle and watch out for intruders, too, was a juggling act. The baby was too big for the papoose sling now. She was crawling and pulling at things, and worse, putting everything in her mouth. Margaret had fixed her a

46

cleared area surrounded with rocks to pen her in while she milked or cooked, and now Mary was even climbing out over the barrier. She had to be watched every minute! What she wouldn't give to have one of the Higgins' children back! She hurriedly milked and gathered the eggs and ran back into the house. As she ran back outside her heart froze to see one of the men reaching for her baby. The rifle was against the porch, just out of her reach.

"Here, you! Don't you touch that child!" She fearlessly charged out and snatched Mary away, and with a swoop of skirts she whirled to grab the gun, but a large hand crushed over hers painfully.

"Leave the gun down, Ma'am," he said quietly, "No harm meant."

"No harm?" Margaret screamed, fearful now. "You come sneaking up here without even a 'Hallo' and you say no harm?"

"I was watching you milk. I didn't want to alarm you and get a bullet for my visit, so I waited till you left your gun. Where's your man?"

"He'll be here soon and you and your rowdies had better be gone 'cause there's a passel of loggers who won't take kindly to your messing up the water above their camp."

He snarled, "How much gold have you stashed away, Ma'am? Heard you was mining quite a strike!"

"Are you crazy? Gold? Does that creek look like it has been mined? All I've ever fetched from that creek is water, and that's enough work for me! Do you think my man would be logging if there was gold at his back door?"

Confused by her statement he took her rifle and let her go. She backed away a distance, and seeing he was not going to pursue, she dashed for the house and bolted the door. He walked off with her rifle.

It was late morning when she heard steps on the porch. Her heart pounded fast. Mary was asleep and she had loaded another gun to stand watch. With relief she heard Ezra call, "Margaret, it's Ezra, let me in."

"You fool! I almost shot you. What are you doing home in the middle of the day?"

"The loggers are mad as hell. The water is foul at the cook house and they saw the squatters from camp. We've made a posse and we're running them off."

"Well, one of them has your rifle, and that only leaves us three guns. I poured fresh bullets and filled extra pouches with powder. Here's your wads. Ezra, let the loggers get 'em. You're a family man. I can't have you getting killed. Can't they be talked to? One was here and he left me alone except to take the gun."

"Do you think a bastard that would steal a gun from a woman is honorable enough to talk? No Sir! I'll not tolerate them threatening my home! I'm joining the others. You barricade yourself upstairs."

Margaret could not see Ezra or any of the other loggers and only part of the men on the creek. Frontier fashion, they had spread out quietly moving from tree to tree to advance on the miners.

Rich, however, advanced in a friendly fashion and hailed them. "Hallo. I'm the camp boss, gentlemen, and came to inquire if you're looking for work." Laughter greeted him from all sides. He stopped a little distance away. The miners slowly put down their tools and pans and gathered to see if they were challenged.

Rich went on, "I don't know what you're looking for in this here creek, but the only money here are wages earned at the camp and right now you men are fouling our water. Thought if you was aware of that fact you'd move on."

Again laughter, but nervous this time as they sensed the warning tone of his voice. They had caught a glimpse of movement in the trees and knew they were targets of at least a couple of rifles. "We heard there was gold in this creek. How come you're not panning? Got yours already?"

"No gold here gentlemen, and I'd know because I've been back in here nigh over four years with nothing to do 'cept hunt, fish, and ride herd over loggers and timber. Don't know how you got ahold of the rumor, but that is all it is. Sorry you made the trip. You'd better get back to where you come from and warn the others. This creek has no gold, and if it did, it belongs to the company logging here, and you're trespassing!" He warned, "Don't be foolish, gentlemen, we mean business."

Rich knew that they were aware of the gunners. His voice remained quiet and measured, giving the miners no cause to anger and a peaceful way out. Some backed away and picked up their tools and knapsacks, but the leader turned red with anger. He had not come so far and dreamed so big to be run off *his* stake. His anger turned to action as he went for his gun in a body roll behind a rock, taking a shot at Rich. One of the loggers' guns caught him as he reloaded, and the others dived for cover. Cookie came out firing. It was his cooking and cleaning water being polluted. He was inexperienced at fighting and standing exposed, one of the miners shot Cookie down. All became quiet as quickly as it started. Even gold fever can become secondary at the sight of death of human beings.

The miners threw down their weapons and packed their gear. Satisfied they were leaving, Rich called the loggers off. Each group claimed their dead comrades and packed them away.

Margaret saw the miners packing their horses, mount and leave. Her heart was in her throat since hearing the gun fire. She then heard the horses thunder past the house about an hour later, unaware that Ezra had guarded her and the house from Mary's little barricade out front.

Rich approached Ezra the next day about Margaret becoming the cook for the loggers. Of course they could not have her in the camp, but if she had a proper fireplace and stove, perhaps she could cook for them on the hill (as they had come to refer to Ezra's place). Margaret liked the idea, especially when she was told she would be paid and also have the Company stores available to her. Her dream of a boarding house was materializing, although not in just the way she had visualized in her plans.

A day of feverish work by the loggers completed her beautiful and very large fireplace. They also moved the supplies up from the camp, including the tables and benches as well. Margaret continued to cook outside for all of them for another week while a very small fire slowly cured the rock fireplace mortar. It was hectic getting used to and planning for the voracious appetites, but time began to fly by.

Supply wagons began to come regularly and word was out that they had a "civilized" camp with a woman there at last. A few men came to sign on and brought their families. Before fall, a small village calling itself Johnson Creek, came into being.

When winter arrived the usual exodus to leave did not take place. Garden produce had been stored away, cabins had been made snug and a supply house (later the general store) had been stocked with winter supplies. This winter was to be a far cry from last year's.

The company allowed the settlement, figuring that as the logging moved, a supply base would be closer at hand. They even helped survey off lots and sold them to the newcomers. Ground already cut, after all, was of no use to the company and was a prize for the farmer.

The next March, the March of 1853, Margaret gave birth to another baby, a girl they named Saphronia. Her neighbor, Mrs. Clay, assisted with the cooking while Margaret spent a few days recovering from the delivery of her child. She was cautioned that working too soon could cause her to lose her milk, but Margaret did not have time to slow down. Her body was hard with firm muscles made by hauling rocks, lifting pots, carrying water and a baby. Labor was long and gradual, and the birth swift. Recovery was almost immediate.

With two salaries their little nest egg was mounting even after spending some for material for clothing and grain for the animals this winter. Margaret began to dream of new and better things for the future.

Summer was hot. Margaret moved the kitchen outside again as some days were unbearable indoors. The blacksmith built her a grill for the outside fire. Once in a while her neighbors would all bring baskets of food, a fiddler would play and they would enjoy an evening of singing and dancing. Adults and children alike would join in. As the little ones got sleepy they would go to the wagons and sleep while the party continued.

Work as they did, seven days a week, nothing could make them work on the 4th of July! That one celebration was paramount and representative of a fierce basic, and now ingrained love of freedom, especially out here on the Frontier. It was felt so keenly it bubbled forth in a gigantic celebration. Speeches and dances, parades and picnics, all filled the day (sometimes the week) of every American from coast to coast, no matter where or what the circumstances. Johnson Creek was right in there doing its share.

Margaret was beginning to get homesick. She was troubled with that primitive urge to bond her babies to her family. She yearned to have them held and made over by their grandparents and aunts and uncles, to be made part of the family. Only this had she longed for, because Ezra had made her happy in every other respect.

However, it was not meant to be. As the end of the season came, Margaret guessed she was pregnant again, so she would be unable to travel. They stayed on another winter.

This year the snow was frequent, and deep and confining. The loggers had made the old cook house into a bunk house, and some had rented space in Ezra's house so the little family was once again crowded during those non-working days. Once in a while Margaret would learn a new word for her vocabulary but only because of a slip in the loggers' conversation. She always had received the utmost respect from her boarders, although, understanding human nature, she was aware that even her maturing figure no doubt might harmlessly fulfill a lonely logger's untold fantasy.

The camp celebrated with Ezra at the birth of his first son that came in late May. He was named William Lindsey Johnson. Lindsey being for both Ezra's father and great-grandmother. William just because she liked it.

Now Margaret really yearned to return home. Her dreams had progressed to education for her children, a family foundation and support groups, and oddly enough, she was thinking of good marriages for them among people she knew and respected. She thought how much she must sound like her mother! Now she realized what her mother had meant.

"We could open a boarding house in Olney, Ezra! Even a hotel. We have a stake. Please take us home," she asked.

The problem was, Ezra didn't want a hotel. He disliked the intrusion of strangers into his home, demanding his wife's attention, and now with children, it was precious little notice he was getting! Now if he had a farm, but he would need more money to purchase land in Olney. His father's place would be too small, and one more year here could solve his needs.

Ezra had spent the past four years working seven days a week, daylight to dark, and had not had time to think about his future. He had to save enough money for a farm, stock, and a house with furniture from back East. He was obsessed with his dream, his way. It had not dawned on him that Margaret would not agree or see their dreams in her mind just as he did in his. He did not want his wife being "looked" at by these boarders. He did not want his wife being around other men all the time! His jealousy caused him stress each time a meal was served or a compliment was given Margaret by one of the loggers.

Ezra began to drink to relax at night and quiet his tormented mind. Then he began to imagine Margaret's physical needs were wanting because his fatigue from too much work, combined with his drinking, would not always permit him to satisfy them. He began to imagine she wanted another man.

It was lonely for Margaret, but it was tolerable as long as they shared a dream, worked together for the future and found strength in mutual tenderness. However, lately there was no tenderness and Ezra's moods changed to suspicious looks. He refused to talk about a hotel or boarding house, and his nightly drinking numbed his mind until Margaret could not get a straight word from him about what he did plan to do. Little did she know that Ezra's mind played a game of private conversation, permitting him to *think* eloquently about his plans and hopes for all of them, while aloud, he could only communicate fears caused by imagined suspicions and resentments, and unrealistically criticize Margaret and the children for what he imagined as their shortcomings.

Events became public as Ezra began accusing various loggers of coming to the house too early for dinner, insinuating they had intentions toward his wife. Margaret was aware of Ezra's accusations and their relationship became more strained. It was then she began to seriously think of going home, even if she had to go without him. She could not tolerate Ezra in his state of mind. If it did not stop, she would have to leave, alone.

Tension mounted as Ezra refused to set a date to leave and they argued more each night. Margaret had proven she could support herself if need be, and she wanted to go home so badly that it verged on an obsession. He was never home with the children anyway, she reasoned. She could not continue to face this angry person Ezra had become. If she could only destroy all the whiskey stills! she thought. Why did people drink?

When the ultimatum finally became a reality, Ezra didn't really believe she would go. It was just one of her mood swings and would pass. Even if she did mean it, his manhood and position in the family demanded that he take a firm stand. "I'll not let you leave, we will stay and you shall say no more about it!" Ezra declared lividly. Margaret, her relationship with her husband challenged, choked back tears of anger and hurt.

Chapter 4

Returning Home

The next morning there was no conversation between Margaret and Ezra as the men ate and left for work. When Ezra returned that night the hearth was cold and the house empty. Margaret had packed the wagon and left. Hurt and ashamed, but too proud to follow her, he put together a meal for the men himself. He'd show them he didn't need her! Secretly, he was worried sick about how she would survive the trip all alone to Olney. Instead of following her, he got drunk again.

The road to Milwaukee was much improved since they had crossed it three years ago, and two days out, Margaret caught up with Mr. Clay and his boy who had left two days before her to go after supplies. They had been delayed with a broken wheel. He had it fixed and was ready to head out when Margaret came upon them. He welcomed the company, but was sad to see the young couple separate. Margaret's tale about this being just a visit home did not have him fooled. He knew Ezra would not have willingly allowed her to travel so far alone.

In Milwaukee, Margaret was surprised to see the train lines had extended from Chicago. It was there she decided to send the wagon back to Ezra via Mr. Clay's son and take the train home.

As they neared Olney, she grew more fearful of the reception she would receive.

The conductor announced their arrival at Olney, and Margaret began gathering babies and belongings while at the same time, steeling herself for the family encounters. As they came closer to the station she became more and more aware of her appearance. Her old hat had been too moth eaten to bring back so she was forced to wear a small, homemade one of mostly ribbons that did not match her dress. Her dress was at least new, but without fashionable hoops. Hoops in a logging camp? The thought made her laugh. Her shoes were her main embarrassment. She had worn out all but her boots and had not had the time in Milwaukee to have a pair made. If she walked slowly perhaps her long skirt would cover them. At least the children were presentable with the shoes they had handed down by the Higgins children. They were worn, and a little big, but passable. Hannah Grant's words came back to her, "Fashion is only good as long as it serves a purpose." Well, she was doing with what she had.

Her head held high, she stepped from the train, children trailing and clinging to her skirt. Mary was awed by the large, yellow depot, and the traffic and activity, the likes of which she had never seen. Margaret recognized her father on the platform but he did not recognize her tanned face and filled out muscles until she was close. She wanted to fall into his arms so very badly, to be comforted. It was a physical strain to hold back and restrain her emotions, but she would not embarrass him in public. Instead with a big smile and tears on her cheeks, she said,"Papa, please meet your grandchildren. This is Mary," she pulled the little girl from behind her, "This is Saphronia," the toddler was sitting on the ground now and John picked her up. Leaning forward, he opened the quilt in Margaret's arms, "And this is William Lindsey," she said.

John cleared his throat, "So good to see you looking well, my dear. These are fine looking children. Yes, very fine looking children." He avoided her direct gaze. Thoughts whirled in his mind and had tormented him ever since the telegram had come with the cryptic message, "Coming home, Tue. train, Margaret."

They loaded bags into the rig and paid a jitney to deliver the trunks to the house, and went home. She waited to give any explanations until the initial greetings were made at home. John had sensed this and had asked no questions.

Her mother was ecstatic, and all her brothers and sisters were there except George who had married Elizabeth McCulley and moved to St. Clair County. Her brother Joseph, and sister Elizabeth had also married, but were living in town. Still at home were her sisters Sarah, Emily, Samantha, and Amelia.

It was a festive supper and she even got Mamma to laugh about her boots. She clumped about the living room in mock high step, "Give me an extra berth Mr. Conductor, I may need to remove my shoes tonight!" and "No sir, I don't need more room for the baby. I'll just stash him away inside my boot here!" It was like old times, except behind all the gaiety was the unasked question. They all gathered around and became quiet and expectant. It was time to tell her story.

She brought them up-to-date about their lives in Wisconsin then added, "I just had to see my family, but I may have lost my husband."

They all became quiet as if she had announced a death. "Papa, I won't be a burden. I have a stake and I plan to open a boarding house." A glance toward her mother, "A respectable boarding house. I can be quite self-sufficient if I can negotiate a loan from the bank for the building. Ezra may, or may not return, but I am prepared for either eventuality. I think I can manage a mortgage if we find a suitable place."

Her father interjected, "Several items are being manufactured here now and all sorts of salesmen are coming through, and workers have been attracted who need temporary housing. You may have an idea for a favorable venture." He was impressed with Margaret's business acumen and industry.

The next months were busy and exciting as they found a large stable near the train depot, negotiated the loan, and began remodeling it into the boarding house with fourteen rooms upstairs, four downstairs, besides her very own apartment, large kitchen and dining room, and a parlor. Even unfinished she collected a waiting list of patrons, so her fears of being unable to repay were eased.

She had visited the Johnsons and led them to believe that Ezra would come home when he had his "stake." She didn't want to be thought of as a divorcee or even "separated," and she did not want to face the recriminations and condemnations of Joshua, who had never believed Ezra had the brains his deceased brother had.

It was only on awakening sometimes in the night to an empty bed that she would be filled with regret and dare to admit how very much she missed Ezra. She cried silently and explained her puffy face the next morning as having slept too hard. One did not discuss emotions. A strong person handled things alone.

She thanked God for her family's help in caring for the children. Furnishings had to be ordered and shipped in, food stocked and stored, curtains made, and she was quite proud that each room had a window. She had to ignore some of her old childhood "friends"

59

who gossiped about her "boarding house" being run by a "lady." Eyebrows raised when they saw Margaret physically helping with construction. Her body needed the physical activity.

A hundred details required attention, but with three years of mulling them over and over, mentally planning each and every aspect of running a boarding house, she was fully prepared to make each decision. Her father was amazed at her complete self-confidence. She hired a housekeeper and an assistant cook. She, herself, would do most of the cooking. Dinner would be at noon so the leftovers could be used up for supper. Then the kitchen was cleaned and closed by 7:00 P.M. What a nice change from the late suppers at the logging camp.

Pumps were installed inside the house. One for the kitchen and one upstairs near a boiler stove for hot baths.

Ezra's sixteen year old brother, Edwin, asked to come work for her after school as bath boy. All that was left was to hire a discriminating gentleman to let the rooms, help with luggage and keep order if need be. She had even made a deal with the jitney drivers to bring their fares to her lodge, or recommend it highly, and they would be reimbursed for each guest delivered. She would have competition from the Hotel Saloon downtown since she would not be serving liquor.

Business was brisk from the beginning and almost more than she could handle until a young man of eighteen came to her for a job.

He was small of stature but wiry and muscled. He was smart with figures and had a good sense of humor, too. Her father had wanted to hire him at the bank, but had no position for him at this time. He told Margaret that he had known Bennett Pugh and his family ever since they had come to Olney a few years ago. Satisfied Margaret gave him the job of letting rooms and soon everything was working like an oiled machine.

Much of her business was from salesmen stopping over. One gave little Mary a miniature sad iron from his sample case.

Routine problems came up, such as bad weather delaying the return of the laundry and they had to air the bedding, turn it over and reuse it. Unexpected guests for dinner or supper sent Margaret hustling to the kitchen to make noodles to stretch the soup. Weevils got into the flour and she had to hand-sift two-hundred pounds before baking that day! Train schedules changed, and some guests requested dinner in the evenings as they had missed the noon meal. But all of this and other crises only added spice to the adventure. As long as Margaret was making payments and paying her help, she could handle everything else.

There was little time to miss Ezra except for fleeting moments when she would see him in the children. She wasn't getting rich, but she was comfortable and in the evenings she liked to sit in the dining room just off the parlor, sewing and listening to the men's conversations.

She heard talk about the underground railroad, and approved. Listening to the pros and cons of slavery and how the economy would collapse without slaves. Margaret mulled that over. She ran a business without slaves, why couldn't everyone? They said the price of sugar and cotton would skyrocket, and besides, blacks wouldn't know how to work for wages and take care of themselves if they were turned loose. Why? Margaret asked herself. Sometimes she and Bennett would discuss these questions if they had a chance. He was anti-slavery too. Slavery was never a personal problem for her. John Wilson had left Virginia at a very young age and no slaves had been brought along. Black people lived in Olney, but they were families who lived on the creek and they stayed at their business and never mingled. What did these white men fear if the slave was unshackled? Retaliation? A take over? An uprising? The conversation was clear, however, that no matter which side of the slavery issue you were on, no one wanted the races to intermingle by marriage.

One night as Margaret was finishing supper a knock came at the back door. It was a black man, "Good evening ma'am. I was told I might find a meal here, I'll pay, of course." He was clean and neatly attired. Not a farm hand by his looks.

Margaret quickly said, "Yes, you can wash up over there at the wash bench." Pointed to a basin and bucket sitting on a bench there by the back stoop. As he washed and came into the kitchen for supper Margaret was a little nervous at her first encounter with such a situation. He did not move into the dining room, but sat as a matter of course at the kitchen table.

"Thank you, ma'am." he said as Margaret served him hot soup, cheese and bread then put out a plate of sliced beef roast. The girls serving the other supper guests, gave surprised glances at the sight, but made no comment until they were in the dining room. At the side board pouring water, Sue whispered loudly to Kate. "Wonder where the darky came from?"

A burly peddler from Richmond overheard the remark. Already drunk when he arrived he had sobered little even after eating. He jerked his head around and snarled, "What did you say girl?"

Sue giggled, "A black, dark as the ace of spades, is eating in our kitchen!"

Spoiling for a fight the peddler jumped to his feet, snorting something about, "Not under the same roof with me!" He staggered and plowed the air with his arms toward the kitchen door, like a bull defending his territory. Intimidated by his display no one looked up from their meal. Bennett missed all this as he had gone upstairs to prepare a room.

The red faced rowdy banged the door shut behind him, glowering at the black man and then at Margaret and shouted, "What the hell is a nigger doing eating in the same house with white folks? You one of them nigger lovin' white trash, helping 'em escape their rightful owners?" He took a plate in his big paw and turned it upside down with a slam onto the table, juices and soup spilled out across the table and into the negro's lap causing him to jump up to avoid it.

Margaret charged over to the mess with a towel saying, "Mister, you'd better clear out of here. I'm the proprietor and I'll decide who will be served, and for your information, I'd rather serve this gentleman than a drunken rowdy like you! Now get!" She pointed to the back door.

With an amazingly swift move the drunk grabbed her outstretched arm and flung her out the door, causing her to sprawl full length, face down on the packed hard ground. Just as fast, he jumped astraddle of her, yanked her skirt over her head and kneeling on them, secured her arms to the ground in spite of her struggle. Now terrified, she wriggled and fought only to have the breath knocked out of her when the lummox sat on her back full weight. Then she felt the chill of a cold steel blade slide under the waist band of her pantaloons.

Unable to call out with her breathing almost exhausted, her chest crushing with his weight and expecting the knife to cut her next, his body fell the full length of her, unconscious. She tentatively rolled and then heaved out from under him struggling to get her dress down and regain her breathing. She could barely see her benefactor even as he knelt close to her helping her. "Are you alright, ma'am?"

"Yes, yes, I think." Looking fearfully around, she saw the meat cleaver in the man's back and sickened from both what she saw and what might have happened. "I'm so grateful. I don't know what I would have done! I don't know what he might have done! Oh, God, thank you!"

She leaned on the negro's shoulder and felt his nervousness. "Ma'am I gotta get away from here now. If I'm found, they'll hang me no matter why. I'm in a fix now 'cause I killed a white man. They'll twist this and say I done it all, so if you're alright, I gotta go."

He stood her on her feet and started to leave. Margaret whispered breathlessly, "Wait! You don't need to run. I'll take the blame, credit, for this, I promise with all my heart. I'm so grateful, I could never put you in danger."

Seeing his frantic face, she relented. "Go with God and my gratitude!" She whispered, "You were never here. But you will be welcome back any time!" He slipped away and she never knew his name.

Come to think of it she didn't know this big ox's name, either. Her knees weak, she sat back on the ground and started to shake and cry, she called, "Bennett! Bennett!"

Bennett looked out from the upstairs window and blanched at the scene. He bound through the house and to her side, the boarders followed him. After hearing nothing more from the kitchen, they had all assumed the barbarian had left and all was well, and they had ignorantly finished their meal.

Margaret sobbed out the story, but not in full detail. She only said that the negro had fled from the outrage of the white man, and the rowdy had turned on her and somehow, with strength from above, she had been able to hit the man between the shoulders with the cleaver. It was years later that she ever confessed the true events to Bennett. Her story was accepted, although many privately questioned how she had been able to get hold of the cleaver and hit the man from behind. They later learned that he was an overseer from South Carolina, using peddling as a disguise to spy out places giving refuge to escaped slaves.

If Margaret had ever had any indifference about negro issues, she now had fewer doubts about her convictions. It appalled her to know the black man who saved her could take no credit for his heroic rescue and, indeed, would have jeopardized his very life by defending her.

She soaked at length in the tub that night trying repeatedly to remove the drunken odor left by her attacker. She didn't sleep at all that night but kept a vigil beside her babies, the attack playing over and over in her mind, her self-confidence shaken to the core. What was she doing here? No husband, three children and living in a house filled with men, most of them strangers. God only knew when another drunken customer might turn on her or the other girls. Her strength had been useless against her attacker, caught as she was by surprise. What could she have done differently? No answers came, only melancholy for her aloneness.

Little Linzzie, (they had nicknamed Lindsey and used this name until he was grown) woke at his usual time to nurse. The immediate chores of being a mother partly roused Margaret from her depression. Her breasts were so bruised it was painful to nurse the infant, and this morning every muscle in her body ached as she moved to dress and get ready to fix breakfast.

Anger began to well up about this whole business, thinking as she cooked, keeping an eye on the children through the adjoining Dutch door, so when the ice man came, she was barely civil. All day she snapped at everyone, not looking into anyone's face and repelling any sympathy offered with, "It didn't bother me! He was just scum." The sheriff made an inquiry for the record. Nothing further was mentioned of the affair in Margaret's presence.

It did not hamper business and the talk in the parlor continued about slavery, slave states and states rights vs federal laws. Elections were coming next year and speculations about political figures where aired. Buchanan was clearly the Democrats' choice because with all his experience, perhaps he could settle the issue and keep the nation together. Stephen Douglas was sure to go back to the Senate. He was for state's rights. Someone asked "Why have a state government, if it is only supposed to be a rubber stamp for the Washington bureaucrats and Congress?" Another said, "If they'd just leave folks alone instead of passing all these laws, we'd be better off!"

Margaret's grandfather had known the Buchanans back in Carlisle, Pennsylvania. Fine people, her mother said, but they were Democrats.

Bennett confessed to Margaret one evening as she sat in the dining room listening to the banter, "Mrs.

66

Johnson I feel terribly guilty that I didn't stop that madman from attacking you. I should have been down here, keeping an eye out. Instead you had to fight him all alone." His hand covered hers protectively. "I would have died myself if any harm had come to you."

Extracting her hand gently and patting his, she said, "Bennett you're a comfort and so much help. You could not have possibly done any more than you did. Past is past, and I appreciate your concern, and welcome your protection."

Life went on, Ezra's little sister Mary, married Mr. Pulliam. Little Lindsey had his first birthday (25 May 1855) and Grandfather Heap died. Grandmother Heap had passed on the year before. Margaret renewed her commitment to the Methodist Church, doing whatever she could. They were raising funds to build a new building.

The new year was bright and cold, but not much snow. Business was slower. Even with train traffic people instinctively stayed put in the winter. One day in February, a wagon pulled in and Bennett went out to meet the customer.

"Staying the night, mister?"

"Yep, sure will."

"Room and board both?"

"We'll see about that after dinner."

Ezra put a coin into Bennett's hand for stabling the horses and parking the wagon across the street.

Ezra stood inside the vestibule looking the house over with admiration when Margaret came in from the kitchen with a load of dishes for the side board. She thought she was dreaming at first, then a cry caught in her throat. She almost dropped the load as she slid it on the table, running to Ezra's arms. She wept, laughed and hugged him fiercely as they rocked in each others arms. Without a word Ezra knew he'd be staying the night, but would not need to rent a room.

He reacquainted himself with the children, drank coffee at the kitchen table while he talked with Margaret, busy cooking, and they caught up on all that had happened since she had left.

Ezra explained how grievous her leaving hurt him, made him drink all the more until he could no longer work timber. He couldn't even cook, or keep himself clean. A group of friends confronted him and spelled it out for him. Drink had caused him to be a risk to them at work, and a pest at home. He had to get off the jug or leave. Finally he spoke quietly, "I wasn't able to make it up there alone Margaret." He looked around, "Guess you didn't need me."

She turned to him, took his face in her hands, "My love. I've needed you all this time, and need you still, more than you'll ever know!"

Their lovemaking was delicately passionate after so long. It was almost like the first time. For the first time since having the boarding house, Margaret did not want to get up in the morning.

Ezra's reunion with his father was cool. Lydia had died leaving little Harvey and Harriet. His sister, Frances, had stayed home caring for them, but that was little comfort with Edwin off living in town with Angeline and going to school. Ezra felt his father was blaming him.

Joshua growled, "Don't suppose you'll be moving back out here now that you're a hotel man." He pulled on his whiskey jug, a constant companion now.

"The hotel is Margaret's venture Pa. I'm made for outdoor work and always will be. I don't quite know how to work out the living arrangements yet, but if you'll have me, I'd like to farm again with you and maybe buy out another farm 'round here someday."

Joshua's face softened and his eyes lit up, "Sounds passable, son."

Ezra toured the farm and its stock and saw the need for lots of work. In fact, he spent the rest of that first day repairing a fence at the pig pen that an old boar had crashed through. The boar laid sunning itself, indifferent to their efforts until some corn was poured into the trough. Repenned without incident, Ezra knew from his size it would only hold him until he wanted out again.

Spring could not shake the cold and snow, giving Margaret and Ezra days together that otherwise would have been spent in work. Ezra was living at the boarding house and riding the four miles horseback to the farm every day. Planting season, however, meant working until dark and by then he was so tired he would sleep down in the "bunk house" that had once been their home.

By the Fourth of July, Margaret knew she was pregnant again. Both were delighted, but Ezra wanted Margaret to sell the boarding house and come out to the farm to live again. He reasoned that it would give them enough profit to buy their own place.

Margaret, on the other hand, could only envision the extra work of tending a garden and animals plus cooking as she was now, and there would be the ordeal of building yet another house, digging another well and moving another time. "No thank you, sir," she repeated with every discussion of the subject. "This boarding house is simple by comparison and it does make more money."

The more money was the part that was sticking in Ezra's craw. Some of his old friends fled their burdens frequently by patronizing the local saloon. Pa had better whiskey, but it wasn't enjoyed like the shared pint downtown.

Margaret wouldn't let him into their apartment when he came in drunk. She'd shove him into one of the small downstairs rooms if there was one empty. One night the house was full and she tried to sober him up at the kitchen table, but he'd have none of it. He wanted to make love. She wrestled him around until he slid to the floor, one arm and his head hanging out the back door. Margaret just left him there. When she came down in the morning, he was curled up in a tight ball in the corner by the stove trying to keep warm. He looked at her with recrimination and asked, "You would have left me there to freeze, wouldn't you?"

"Yep," was all she answered and went on with fixing coffee. She didn't nag, but she didn't sanction his drinking with intelligent conversation.

Christmas was especially good. The children were old enough to enjoy the tree. They were three, four and five. They talked about presents, and learned the Christmas carols. Lindsey was a handful, getting into everything, especially bothering his sisters who tried to make him be their baby and he wouldn't cooperate anymore. They would then turn to Sarah Jane, who had been born the month before. A tiny, fragile child, Margaret would not encourage them to hold her. It took small, frequent feedings to make her thrive. Margaret's little sister, Samantha, had come over to stay a while and help with the children.

Ezra had to spend a lot of time the next spring out at the farm helping with the lambing. The weather was nasty and the flock was large. He asked Margaret, "Remind me never to raise sheep when we get a place of our own." Margaret felt sadness, knowing if she would give up her place, he could have his place.

Margaret bought fresh kitchen produce from Frances and other farmers about the country. She had given up her chickens and was buying all her food, so expenses were up a little. Her life was running smoothly except for Ezra's occasional bender, but he was so good compared to most men that Margaret didn't complain. Bennett looked on with sympathy for Margaret, and jealousy over Ezra's casual visits. He didn't feel Ezra properly appreciated Margaret.

The church basement was finished that year and little Mary started to the school that was held there. The county had made a contract with the Methodists to also use it for county offices and court trials until the court house could be finished. This helped with their building fund as well.

October was typical, with cool nights and warm days. Most of the garden was gathered, dried, and stored. The corn crib was full to overflowing next to the hog pens. Ezra was fixing the pen for the tenth time this year when one of the weaning pigs squirted through to freedom.

Ezra would have ordinarily let it go, but because it was already fed, it would be hours before it could be coaxed back inside with feed, and Ezra wanted to get home early. Besides, the children were outside and would chase it to exhaustion. Ezra sneaked around the well where the pig had found a puddle in which to cool. He pounced, caught a leg and hung on, with the pig screaming at a piercing screech. Harriet and Henry ran around the house to see Ezra and the pig wrestling, Ezra laughing loudly at the fight, but they froze in their tracks as the sow charged through the loose

71

fence. Ezra never saw her coming. She hit him in the back of the neck with both front hooves. Powerful jaws closed swiftly and his body went slack. She continued her attack furiously, striking and biting. The children ran for Frances, who found her brother mauled and chewed, the old sow calling her pigs to join her to eat the carcass.

Frances, faint from the sight, tears streaming from her eyes, walked in close, fired the rifle point blank, dropping the sow and scattering the pigs. She turned away to vomit, steadied herself on the well, screamed for little Henry to "run for Daddy, hurry and don't look back!"

She ran with dull sobs to the pen to barricade the opening. There was no need to look for life in Ezra's poor torn body. Joshua ran from the field, drew up short by Ezra, and whispered a choking scream squeezed from his mouth, "No! God, No! No! No!" He dropped to his knees, trying to deny this mangled flesh was Ezra.

Henry and Harriet were sent to the Huffmans with a request that they ride into town and break the news to Margaret and Angeline.

Mr. Huffman came into Margaret's kitchen, and Margaret sensed immediately that something was wrong. "There's something wrong?" she asked.

"Yes, Ma'am, something terrible wrong. Your Ezra is dead."

Unable to move, Margaret's mind tried to reject what she had just heard. She could not speak. The children, crying nearby, permitted her to instinctively grasp a reality she could manage, and she slowly turned to attend to them.

Mr. Huffman had passed word on his way through town, and the news had spread like wildfire. John Wilson went home with the news to Elizabeth and together they drove the rig over to pick up Margaret. Friends and neighbors came immediately, some to offer help and comfort, and others just to hear the grizzly details from Harriet and Henry. They hugged and petted the youngsters, squeezed and sympathized over them, big people passing them around until they cried to escape the well meaning clutches.

Bennett, Kate and Sue assured Margaret the children would be cared for and so would the boarding house and to take all the time she needed.

As the carriage drew close to the farm a group of Josh's neighbors were crowded around the small log house. They had helped Joshua and Frances set up boards between two chairs and lay the body there.

Mrs. Frazee and Mrs. Van Meter shooed Joshua and Frances outside and matter of factly went about their neighborly duty to clean and "lay out" their friend, lovingly remembering Ezra as a child and a young man, and how they had done this for his mother and stepmother, and his brother.

They put a clean shirt on him and covered him with a quilt, then joined the mourners outside, directing this one and that to bring food tonight and tomorrow. Some of the men were already unloading boards from a wagon, from which they would construct the coffin. Death was no stranger in young America and everyone knew their proper role and duty.

Margaret dazed, but outwardly composed, stood at the door. When she approached Ezra she resigned herself to the finality that he was indeed dead. He smelled of lye soap. He was clay white. He was cold.

She wept as she ran her fingers through his hair. She embraced him. Her mother, her father, Joshua and Frances were sitting against the wall keeping vigil, and wordlessly she embraced them also, and joined the receiving line, each person there having his own memories.

He would be buried tomorrow, next to his mother Polly, and his brother, William. It was 24 October 1858. He was 27 years, 8 months, and 7 days old.

Margaret took on chores others were most willing to do for her, but she wanted to keep busy at all cost. She had managed alone before, and she could do it again. It was difficult when she remembered often that Ezra would not be coming home this time. The black dresses the children had to wear reminded her every day and made her more angry than sad. "Mama, where is it written that we have to wear black for a year? The other children shun the girls, and that hurts. People are kind, but they are too condescending or avoid me!" She yanked at her own dress. "These widow's weeds!"

Quietly Elizabeth assured her, "That is just the proper way it is done. You must remain in mourning at least a decent period of time. This gives you time to grieve, and people give you distance so you can get your wits about you again. Besides, it gives a reminder to men that you are not yet available. Surely you don't want to be approached before a year!"

"Mama, I don't mind for myself, but I'm not going to dress the children in black anymore! Christmas morning they are going to have some colored dresses and I think, a bright blue coat with red mittens and scarves!"

"Margaret! You wouldn't put red on a child! Mourning or not!"

74

Margaret laughed and gave her a wait and see look.

Elizabeth confided in John, "Margaret is acting peculiar, John, I wish you would have a talk with her. You know, grief has a terrible effect on the mind sometimes. She is working too hard, too."

John talked to his daughter, but not about the red mittens. He let her know instead that her family was prepared to support her both emotionally and financially if she should need them. She was not going through this alone. That meant a great deal to Margaret.

Chapter 5

The Big Boarding House

Bennett did more and more work at the boarding house, and found reasons to linger after supper to talk to Margaret.

His exposure to people from all walks of life had made him outgoing, and as he acquired knowledge of other's customs, kept abreast of news and politics, he developed a self assurance. He also expressed a sense of humor, and had an easy way with people. He matured quickly by taking over some of the responsibility of the boarding house from Margaret. He admired her so much. He would pass on the news to her, as well as some of the clean jokes he had heard and make her laugh. He loved to do that.

Bennett was seven years her junior and they could relax socially without tongues wagging. Bennett would play with the children, too, and patiently talk and explain things to them. They turned to Bennett more and more when they had questions.

Mary and Saphronia spent much time with their grandmother. She remade clothes for them, taught them table manners. They learned how to properly pour tea and they would play wedding and receptions, dressing in Grandmother's old clothes.

Lindsey wanted none of that. His favorite play was in the dirt at the back of the house where he plowed and made corn fields with sticks, gathered twigs and whittled logs for houses. He had corn cobs for horses and cows, then made a scraper to make little roads. He dug a "mine" in a mound and tried to engineer it so it would not collapse. Another day he would pretend he had a train on his twig made tracks. He sure would like a toy train! Margaret knew at train time Lindsey would be at the depot watching the belching monster come in and load and unload and afterwards run to tell her all about what happened there today. Sometimes he would ride out to Grandpa Johnson's and go hunting with him and little Henry. Out there was everything anyone wanted to eat, deer, turkey, but he didn't like the white squirrel. Grandpa explained, "No place else had white squirrels. They were edible, but no one liked 'em. The Indians were superstitious about them, and while the white men denied any belief in their legends, they still avoided the squirrel too."

Agitation and a hurried pace seemed to grip the Nation. People were busier somehow and restless. There was lots of building, traveling, and anyone not producing was looked at as a slacker. Talk was all about joining the oceans by rail and filling the Oregon territory. Just crossing the Rocky Mountains had been a dream of a few years ago, and now they talked of a railroad speeding through there? All fascinating, but it seemed unrealistic just now with all the other pressing issues of holding the Nation together! Secession was on everyone's mind. Illinois would probably follow Indiana, but it was not certain, and this issue affected everyone.

Grandparents reminded them of the Revolution, the hard times, building a viable government, a monetary system, trade, and the border disputes that went on with England for forty years after the Declaration of Independence! Arguments were made that we should use the system to elect people to resolve the dispute, we didn't need to split. Others argued that the rebellion had to be physically squelched. It came to be that anyone with a gripe about the government enlarged it to include it as a "North-South issue," and talk about secession.

O. P. Morton over in Indiana was generating high feelings. A charismatic, brilliant lawyer who was previously pro-slavery, was now turning around and demanding that the secessionist be beaten down with force. He had aligned himself with the new Republican Party and was one of the first to advocate force against the South.

Abraham Lincoln had gained national attention after running against Stephen Douglas for the Senate in 1858. Although he lost then, his Republican party was gaining popularity and the emotions were on the rise against incumbents. Mr. Lincoln was in Olney seeking support for the presidency among his many friends in Richland County who he had served with in the Black Hawk War back in 1832. Mr. Beck, at the Olney Times, was the first newspaper in the United States to propose Abraham Lincoln for President.

While the Lincolns were in town, Margaret attended a tea her mother gave for Mrs. Lincoln. John Wilson was Mary Todd Lincoln's cousin, Margaret's middle name was Todd for the family. Abe Lincoln's Uncle Dennis was married to Ezra's cousin Elizabeth.

While the men held their conference in the parlor, Abe Lincoln discussed his convictions and good sense. The others agreed that perhaps here was the rational captain needed to ride out the gathering storm.

Margaret only felt sickening chill when these discussions occurred. Rallies for compromise were being held and the people wanting peace at any price were holding demonstrations at every political gathering.

It was at one such demonstration that O. P. Morton declared, "I am not here to argue questions of state's equity, but to denounce treason!" His words gathered weight when, as Lt. Governor, he moved into the Governor's chair as Governor Lane resigned to enter the Senate. He became more and more militant, but was campaigning for Lincoln in both Illinois and Kentucky.

By the inauguration they knew Lincoln could not make any compromise as seven states had already seceded. The elections had been the most highly charged events of the century.

Bennett teased Margaret about going to the White House now that her "cousin's" husband was President.

"Sure," she laughed, "I'd be welcomed as the beggar relative I am. Cousin Mary is in her glory and wouldn't recognize me now." With a mock dance she said, "I'd hoop my homespun and impress everyone with my 'earthy appearance!'"

They laughed and Bennett joined her in her dance. Their hands grasping, sent an electric feeling that brought their eyes to rest on each other. Desire swelled in both of them and frightened Margaret.

Bennett was just a boy, she reminded herself, but the strength in his hand told her differently, that he was a man. Kate burst through the door, "Do you want these curtains to go to the laundry or will we wash them ourselves?" she asked, looking first at Margaret then Bennett, wondering what they had been doing to make them act so awkward.

Fights in town broke out daily now, and Margaret and Bennett had to separate guests and ask them to leave their differences outside. As word came of the start of hostilities, certain young men and sometimes entire families moved south down the Mississippi, or over into Missouri. Some Illinois towns were more sympathetic to the South, but Olney's majority was staunchly Union.

It was rumored that Confederate and Union recruiters were working almost side by side some places. Olney didn't wait for recruiters. An exodus of men answered as soon as the poster went up at the depot telegraph office. It said state units would be kept together where possible when the men enlisted together. Special bonus would be paid to those who brought their own rifles and/or a horse. Most thought they would be home in three months.

Activity was the order of the day. People remembered other wars and warned the youngsters to stock up on shoes, material, food, anything you could store and afford. The tanning yard and shoe factory put on extra help and started making thick soled boots, hoping for an army contract. They too were stockpiling for the future. Even the banks were doing a brisk business as people deposited their money rather than carry it off with them to war or leave it behind to be stolen from a defenseless wife. Olney was still rural enough that almost every family in town had chickens, a cow, and a garden. No one really worried about shortages except for sugar and coffee, which was brought up from New Orleans. It was quickly hoarded and everyone had to make substitutes early on.

So eager to serve their country, old men shaved their beards to appear younger and youngsters lied about their ages so they could go with their fathers, brothers or uncles. The band played and speeches were made at the court house steps and it fired people up with patriotism. Others had private reasons for going. Either a nagging wife, or a chance to be more than a menial worker at a dull job, and the pay looked good. It was food furnished and cash money and no where to spend it. It was also rumored that there would be land bounty for veterans like they gave after the Revolution and 1812 and Mexican wars.

They gathered at the depot at dawn one morning, Margaret's brother John M. Wilson and Bennett Pugh, Wes Treadway and his brother-in-law Tim Webster, Dan Bryan and Joshephus Naylor and Ezra's little brother Edwin Johnson, George and Henry Houser. Dozens more Margaret had grown up with, knew, and was probably related to, all stood so proudly while the Sergeants took inventory of their belongings, horses and rifles, which they loaded onto the box cars and the men joined other recruits from east of Olney on their way to St. Louis.

The real goodbyes had been said at home, but families could not resist seeing their loved ones for as long as possible. They gathered on the depot platform to watch their departure. The band played, but its ranks were sparse with so many members now carrying rifles instead of horns. Tears spilled despite all efforts to hold them back as they deeply felt the reality that this could be the last time they would see these young men.

When Margaret's brother, John M. announced he was going, Elizabeth had a fit. "John, go to that recruiter and tell him Little John is needed to finish his education! That boy is barely 21! Please it is urgent! Use your influence!"

John talked to Little John, but decided the boy was a man enough to make up his own mind, and besides it might be good for him. He explained to Elizabeth that the discipline and responsibility may be just the thing the boy needed to mature and round out his education. Elizabeth was furious! However when the day came for him to leave she had packed a sack (he had already warned her they would not take trunks) of extra clothing, boots, sweaters and food.

John laughed at his mother's doting, "Mother they won't let me take any of that! They issued me a knapsack, and I can only take what fits in here!" It was pitifully small. "The Army will provide everything we need." She stuffed in a sweater and some cheese anyway. As the train was pulling out, she ran up to Bennett who was hanging from one of the windows, and handed him a picnic basket heavy with food, "For the Olney boys!" she yelled. Little John was teased, but they all enjoyed the vittles.

Margaret stood waving goodbye and bitterly thought, "Old men who want power, plan the wars, and the young men have to fight them. Why?" Anger made a bitter taste in her mouth. She felt no patriotism, only deserted and lonely, and the train wasn't even out of sight.

Back home she threw herself across the bed and wept uncontrollably. She realized now that Bennett was more than a friend, and now he was gone, perhaps lost to her forever. The children woke and cried too, not knowing why, but frightened because their mother was.

Margaret washed her face, went to the kitchen and made up the biggest breakfast she could dream up. The house was almost empty of boarders today.

Hopes were high that they would all be home soon, but Elizabeth's brother, Ben, wrote from Cambridge, Ohio, that the steel mills in Pennsylvania were gearing up for a long duration. Sentiments were high in the East. He had visited Washington City and the fighting had begun. Travel by coach or train was near to impossible. With so many on the move it was impossible to pick a safe route through the battle zones or bandits. The bandits and thieves were taking advantage of the citizenry left unprotected by law officers and the fact that they could be shot by the army without trial was no deterrent. He went on to report that the Army itself was a menace, as they were conscripting horses and food stuffs everywhere.

Bennett wrote to Margaret, but not frequently. Paper and stamps were in short supply. They were encouraged by their officers to write optimistic letters home and Bennett complied, saying he was having a fine time with his comrades. He tried not to complain, but would betray conditions by saying, "I long for evenings by the fire, dry and warm." He said the Ladies Aide sweaters had arrived and were so welcomed fights broke out over them. Some may have been confiscated by thieves and sold. Even food was being gathered up in the warehouses, but was not getting to the men in the field. They had hard tack and coffee and somehow certain ones always had whiskey. He also complained that their officers had been elected from the ranks and didn't seem to know much more than he did about soldiering.

Bits and pieces of news came in from other sources. Obituaries were banned from the newspapers for the duration of the war, but the casualty list was posted once a week at the telegraph office. The newspaper tried to report only the victories so morale could be kept high at home. The truth came home via the wounded returning. It looked dark for the North. This war, now everyone knew, would not end quickly.

General Grant camped his troops on the fair grounds west of the Olney Depot while he stayed at Margaret's Boarding House. He was in Illinois on his way to Cairo and Corinth, Mississippi. They had never met, but his parents had told him about Margaret and Ezra and their Wisconsin adventure and that his father had kept in touch.

At dinner he told Margaret about little Johnny Higgins joining up. "Fine lad, good people."

Margaret asked about his family and he said they were well, "Last I saw of them." She then asked, "How long will all this fighting go on?"

He sadly replied, "Mrs. Johnson, the bitterest war is between families, and our American family is in bitter disagreement. Even West Point, a National school of military training, using the same tests and techniques, and I thought the same loyalties, is split asunder. Divided down to the last man. We face an enemy as knowledgeable and capable and as convinced of his right as we are. It will not be a quick nor easy war." Margaret's heart beat with pity, both for him and her country. More of the town's men left with the General the next day.

The Ladies Aid Society was formed and the Methodist Church basement became a virtual factory. Yarn was spun and dyed blue. Cloth was woven for bandages. Ladies took home the dry yarn to knit. Margaret could turn out a sweater, cap and mittens every week. She didn't do socks, but others did. Even the very small girls could knit scarves and caps. Cloth bandages were made in strips and rolled and wrapped into bundles of ten. The Society contributed a great deal to the physical needs of the soldiers, but their main benefit was the moral support they lent each other.

Josh was raising more sheep but his whiskey was more in demand than his wool.

As the wounded returned home, or were brought into town, the hospital was filled. Dr. Brewer one day approached Margaret about taking a couple of men to care for. She did not hesitate, thinking "what if this were Bennett in a strange place?"

Everyone's work load had increased to take up the slack. Margaret did very well to get her wood cut, but she had to split it herself. There were so few horses that there were no jitneys to bring customers from the train. Lindsey would go down to meet the train and advertise the boarding house with a sign. He would then try to assist the passenger with the luggage to the boarding house. Margaret hired two girls to help. One took Edwin's place in the bath room, pumping water into the boiler on the stove, building the fire and heating water for baths. The patrons would dip out the water with a bucket and fill their own tub, but Susie had to drain it down a spout drain which dumped into the alley ditch, and then clean the tub for the next person. She also had to tote out the slop jars to the "back house" and clean them.

Women all over were filling in for their men, as clerks, accountants, teachers, shopkeepers, farmers, and even teamsters. Paid less, of course "to help the war effort."

Prohibition was still on the books in Olney, but had never been effective except to keep saloons from doing open business. They moved from Main Street to the back rooms of hotels and theaters, and the back packs of men.

Joshua still made two kinds of his Kentucky recipe, corn and grain, both in demand. When Lindsey was about eleven he weny out to visit Grandpa Johnson with his cousin, Jarome Wilson (George's boy), who was eight. They were supposed to be helping out, but they played and snooped around mostly. It was a fun place to play soldiers. Josh was trying to mend the corn crib the horse had kicked in.

85

Lindsey asked, "Grandpa, why is that cellar door blocked with the rock?"

"Cause it bangs in the wind."

"What do you do when it storms?"

"Move it, I reckon."

"Don't you need to get in there for your victuals?"

"Nope, Frances don't leave much out here at a time anymore, so I don't have victuals in the cellar. Now get outta here so I can get this done."

The boys ran off towards the house and detoured toward the curious cellar.

"I haven't been in here since I was a little kid," Lindsey informed Jarome. "Come on, Rome, help me roll this rock over."

The two strained with all their might without luck. Finally Lindsey remembered leverage. His curiosity getting more persistent as time gave his imagination a workout. What would the door reveal? A pit of snakes maybe! A buried Indian! A company of captured Confederates!

Jarome dug a small hole under the rock for the toe hold for the long oak pole. By laying a log near the rock under the pole the two boys pulled their weight down on the pole and the rock heaved over. The door could now be opened part way. It was dark inside but immediately obvious that there was nothing there but barrels, whiskey barrels.

Lindsey saw a chance to sample the forbidden juice. Who would know? He sent Jarome to fetch the dipper from the well. He pulled the bung loose and filled the dipper, splashing over onto his clothes and the ground as he fumbled to replug the hole.

They sipped and gagged and coughed. "Jarome, that is a man's drink."

"Yeah," Jarome gasped as the hot liquid burned down his chest and stomach. Lindsey noticed the warm, relaxed feeling, and the sensations in his arms and legs. He sat down on the cool, dirt floor. Rome sat beside him and they learned they didn't have to cough if they just sipped slowly instead of chugging it down. They giggled and sipped and ceased to care if they got caught.

"I feel sick," Jarome slurred.

"Good Lord Rome, not in here!" Lindsey shoved him toward the door. The sudden movement caused a heave in his own stomach. He was dizzy, and the sudden light hurt his eyes. He didn't see Grandpa Josh or anything else from his hand and knee position. The whole world was spinning around and he was trying hard to hold on.

"Damn it boys, what are you up to?" Josh's voice seemed to come from far away. Jarome tried to run, but was sort of glad Josh caught him because it kept him from falling down. Josh grabbed both by the suspenders and supported them into the house.

The house was a mess now that he batched there alone, but he found a clean dipper and made the boys drink water until they were sick again. Then he said, "Both of you lay down on this pallet on the floor so if you are sick again you won't make a mess on the bed." As they slept he cleaned up, chuckling to himself. "Initiation! Gotta happen sooner or later."

Margaret never knew. Lindsey explained his whiskey clothes by saying Grandpa was doctoring a cut on a horse's hoof.

Fatality reports were not believed. They were too gross to be accepted, and the call for more and more draftees was loudly protested. People could not comprehend the magnitude of Vicksburg and Shiloh. It would take yet another generation to absorb the facts and numbers. All people knew then was the immediate world around them and reports brought to them by returning soldiers, who would not or could not describe the horror they had been a part of.

These stories of misery gave rise to emotional indignation of the women of this country who pressed the Sanitary Commission to investigate the conditions of the hospitals, camps, and food services. They found that half of the casualties were from poor sanitary conditions. Typhoid, food poisoning, and pork parasites were rampant. Soldiers were foraging and cooking for themselves while warehouses of fresh produce either rotted or was sold off in the black market because there was such poor logistics system of distributing the foodstuffs to the troops. Utilizing the Ladies Aid Societies, physicians, merchants, and civic leaders, an outcry was heard by Congress forcing them to reorganize the entire military medical system.

By the end of 1862 the hospitals were no longer under the general line of command. Medical officers answered only to the Surgeon General of the United States. They could procure food stuffs for their own needs, and no longer had to watch patients fail to recover because of a diet of hardtack and coffee. Also, for the first time in history, a soldier could get a medical discharge from a physician or convalesce as a support person such as nurse, orderly or cook. He could even cut hair, sew or anything else useful until he could be fully prepared to return to fight or go home. It was under this directive that a medical team came to Olney to set up a hospital. First as an aid station, then as a convalescent station.

The local doctor's residence, which served also as Olney's hospital, was too small for their needs. Because Margaret had already taken in a few soldiers, they turned to her place. It was close to the Depot, roomy and had staff.

Margaret was overwhelmed by the invasion. She was adequately paid for the rent of the building and her salary as cook. Her girls would be trained as nurses aides, but the house suddenly took on a new air.

The medic in charge was not a doctor, but acted as if he owned the place. She had no say as to who or how many were placed in a room. The three nurses were quartered in Margaret's apartment, making it frightfully crowded.

The wounded began to arrive and gave her no time to think. They had received field treatment for the first time in any war, and with the general overhaul of the system, more and more were surviving to come back, but some were so crippled Margaret wondered how they would survive. They would now be a burden to their families and lose their pride and independence.

The furniture factory started turning out crutches, peg legs, hooks and braces, and wheel chairs, which Margaret had never seen before. She was to embark on an education, not just about nursing, in which she was fairly well versed, but in rehabilitation. Also the inventive process was in full swing all across the country and there was a growing confidence that people can do anything if they put their minds to it.

The medic was called Dr. Hall and was very good with the men. He encouraged them daily and it was only the civilians to which he was so abrupt and demanding. Margaret soon found that it was his way of protecting and procuring supplies for his men that made him appear so callous. She soon liked him in spite of his general unpopularity.

To ease the living quarters situation, Margaret moved into her parent's house. They were not that pleased, but willing to do it for the war effort.

Margaret had little time to keep track of Lindsey and knew the boy had some difficulty at school, but she figured he knew how to read and cipher and he would be able to learn all the other things when they could get a male teacher back. He knew how to get his way with her, too. She would scold, and he'd look sufficiently repentant and say "I love you anyway Mother, you're the best mother I ever had." He would hug her, even after a spanking, and say something sweet. She just couldn't manage to be too hard on a boy like that, especially her only son, and without a father.

In the school yard, little Martha Houser, two years older than Lindsey, watched the boys play mumbletypeg. None played better than Lindsey Johnson. Good as he was at games, he was always getting in trouble with the teacher. Martha's daddy said it was because he didn't have a daddy to discipline him. He said Margaret made a big mistake not getting married by now to give those children a "head of the house" so he could set the family into proper order. He was sure that correct discipline was the answer to any family situation.

When his children strayed from righteousness, they were promptly, swiftly, and sternly returned to the straight and narrow. He believed most in that part of the Bible that referred to sparing the rod and spoiling the child. Martha was afraid to sass the teacher or skip school like Lindsey did. He'd tease her sometimes but no more than any of the other girls. She was two years older, but she had always been small for her age so Lindsey was already much larger.

He liked to play with his lariat. He challenged boys to rope anything that moved since stumps and stationary objects had become too easy. They roped dogs and chickens, cats and even rabbits. For the most part he had gotten so good that the other children would gather and watch rather than compete. Once Martha was his target as she was running to answer the bell for class. He caught her and the sudden stop dropped her to her fanny. Lindsey thought it was hilarious until she jerked off the lasso and ran straight at him, instead of running to tell the teacher. He was surprised when she knocked him to the ground and started whipping him with his own rope.

"Hey," he screamed as he tried to shield his face and dodge the next blow, but she caught him with four or five licks anyway.

"I'll teach you to bully me, Lindsey Johnson, I'm not a play toy!"

"Hey, Hey!" he yelled and caught the rope at her hand. He jerked it away. "I was just teasing!"

"Well, tease somewhere else."

"You gonna tell now, I suppose?"

"I don't tattle tale. I can take care of myself. You just steer clear." Something about the sparks from her eyes filled him with delight. He had never teased a girl before that didn't cry and go tell. She had a lot more spunk than he realized. Guess it was from living with three older brothers.

Martha's fight had been seen by Michael, her third brother, but he didn't tell on her because she was in the right and Daddy would have made him take it up, and there'd be a big to do over it all.

Henry Houser had moved here with all his children from Springfield, Ohio where he had met and married Elizabeth Slaugh. They had three sons first, George,

Henry, and Michael, followed by four daughters, Catherine, Susan, Martha and Sarah. He came West at the beginning of 1859 when the war rumors began to get serious. They were originally Pennsylvania Dutch and had moved into the Ohio with their families, which was now very crowded, and land prices high. Henry took his part of his inheritance, moved his family out West and made a nicer life for them and was hoping to be safe from the war.

The railroad made the move easier and opened markets for any and everything. He had heard about Olney from others who had emigrated out to Richland County, and it sounded like you could grow anything from orchards to beef. There were large settlements of Germans and Swiss already here so the customs were not too different from what they knew.

At forty-three, Henry didn't volunteer to go to the army when the war came. His sons, George and Henry did, but he elected to stay and joined a civil defense militia for the home front so he could protect his still young family. Sarah was only five. He raised food enough to sell to the army and lent his support in that way. Before it was over, little Michael would go away to soldier too.

In 1864 news came of his son Henry's death. He developed a strange look in his eyes, and withdrew to within and no one could enter. His body became paralyzed and he, too, died September 25, 1864.

Three long years had dragged by and there was no end of the conflict in sight. At least the men who came through the hospital were now able to be discharged or reassigned as cooks or orderlies, and soon there was nothing for Margaret to do in the kitchen.

Dr. Hall was even more efficient in procuring food. She began spending more time with the nurses. They directed the bandage changes and sanitation. Margaret fell into the position of what in later years would be called a physical therapist. She began keeping progress notes to encourage the men, documenting progress for him to see. It was rewarding work but it bothered her that so many sat despondent and hopeless with no interest in living. Their minds had been too exposed to the gore of battle, and the death of friends and families, and even enemies, and the relentless command for them to go on and on to kill more and more was more than they could stand. Some were despondent that they were spared while others had died. They could not understand why they had not all died.

Margaret racked her brain daily to find a new way to fill these war torn minds with something to hope for. Surprisingly, children's games helped a little. Lindsey showed off with his lariat and even taught a one armed soldier how to lasso. Others took up the challenge from wheel chairs. Mumblety-peg and marbles were played, as well as chess and checkers. They found comfort and familiarity by reliving some of their childhood experiences.

The Ladies Aide came once a week and served a tea, but they left their daughters at home and forbid them to visit. Soldiers were rowdy enough and these were not "proper men," being maimed and all. "The old hypocrites," Margaret thought. "They make me so mad." She knew that some female company would raise her patients' spirits more than anything. Dr. Hall was a straight jacket, and ran a tight rein on both the nurses and the men. She knew he would never approve of her plan, so she didn't ask.

She took a few days to think it through and get up the courage because her reputation could be damaged forever if word got out.

Margaret first explained to the nurses that she could arrange for them to all have a night off, but they would have to be together in Clarmont. She would get volunteers to work in their places. Dr. Hall could come too, as escort. They were delighted, but explained that they could only go if it was through a night shift 7:00 p.m. to 7:00 a.m. and nursing procedures would not be attempted by the uninstructed relief crew. These must be handled by professionals. Margaret assured them everyone would benefit from a break in routine.

Margaret then arranged for Mrs. Balmer to have the nurses over for recreation one night a week. The sweet lady was more than willing to do her part for the war effort, especially if Dr. Hall was coming, too. She had a daughter that would like to live the life of a physician's wife.

Margaret's next move took her downtown, alone. Carefully she scouted the boardwalk for anyone who might see her, then slipped down the alley between the hotel and the furniture store. They were closed and she was hoping that she had timed her arrival before business hours. She went up the back stairs. Her first timid knock produced no results, but her second knock seemed almost too loud. The door opened. A woman stood with her robe opened, and seeing who was there, she explained. "You have the wrong door, honey, we don't do women and we don't need any help." She started to shut the door.

"Wait, I have a request. Please listen, Mrs. Dean."

"How'd you know my name?"

"Reputation, I guess."

"Step in. What is it you need here?"

Sue Dean was a plump, rough spoken, German blond. A working madame with eight working girls, who, it was said, were clean and honest. She threw them out if they weren't. She drank, but didn't abide drunks or brawls. Because she had kept a low profile her business had been tolerated by the townsfolks.

Margaret was very uncomfortable but she spelled out her plan.

"If you and your girls could come up to the hospital just once a week or so to give the nurses a night off . . . and Dr. Hall," she emphasized so Mrs. Dean would know all obstacles would be out of the way. "It would contribute so much to the war effort and the rehabilitation of these poor boys." She leaned over to whisper although they were alone, "Most of these men just don't feel like men anymore."

Mrs. Dean nodded knowingly.

"Trouble is," Margaret continued, "I can't pay you for this except your supper. The nurses think I'm bringing volunteers from the Ladies Aide Society."

Mrs. Dean burst out laughing! Margaret snickered too.

"Those old biddies won't come and be alone with the men at night for fear of their precious reputations! Will you, Mrs. Dean?"

"Honey, that's the best idea I've heard in a coon's age. You take care of Doc Hall and we'll take care of the rest!"

They decided Thursday night would be best because it was a slow night for Mrs. Dean.

Promptly at 6:30 the next Thursday, "The Relief Crew" arrived. Three ladies dressed in proper grey linen, scrubbed clean and groomed, the nurses nodded approval. They gave them a long list of instructions. Supper at six, help those who could not feed themselves, orderlies would rend up the dishes. If anyone bled or died send a message to Margaret over at the Wilson's. Anyone suffering could have a dose of laudanum. An orderly could give it. Lights out at 9:00 p.m. Then clean the lamps, trim the wicks, open the windows for fresh air. It was made plain that all other duties would wait for the nurses' return the next day. Gaily they departed for their first day off in months.

After supper Mrs. Dean asked the men if someone could play a French harp or a fiddle. Two said they used to. The new nurses began to circulate applying their bold touch. The other girls arrived and the singing started and the girls danced showing more than an ankle. Word spread and the soldiers who had despondently remained in their beds upstairs came to see what was going on. The drapes were drawn and the show began. Bawdy songs led to a strip tease and the boys by now knew what was what. Before it got too loud Mrs. Dean made the announcement that this all had to be kept quiet or the fun next week would be cancelled. If they wanted their "relief crew" they'd have to keep it secret. Girls kept up the entertainment in the parlor while other girls kept up the entertainment upstairs.

At dawn the girls left and the nurses returned to thank Mrs. Dean for their night off.

There was a different spark about the place but never a hint was dropped about what happened either from Margaret or the soldiers. They all tried hard not to appear tired. The nurses were pleased that the relief crew had not had to use much laudanum and everyone was in good spirits. "It must be that they were as tired of us as we were of our work. The day off really was beneficial!" Everyone agreed. Dr. Hall's ban on camp followers had been bypassed and gave the soldiers the feeling of having outwitted the brass. Margaret felt a little of the same.

It did become difficult some weeks to get all the nurses away. One wanted to stay home and catch up on her sleep, but Margaret convinced her that the relief nurses would feel they were not being trusted and would have their feelings hurt if anyone stayed to check on them.

Christmas of '63 looked bleak with so many boys away. Some would never return. The winter was bad here at the beginning of December. Margaret looked up to welcome a new arrival on crutches and exclaimed "Bennett!"

He managed a grin, but she could see he was not only wounded, but ill. As soon as she could she went to the bed he was assigned. She kissed him, which brought whoops and whistles from the others.

"What happened, Bennett?"

"Caught a Rebel slug. Sorta messed up my knee. See."

He took a 1 1/4 inch lead ball from his pocket. She held the distorted and flattened hunk of metal in her hand trying to imagine the force that it took to smash it, and the pain and suffering he must have had endured having it removed by a field surgeon. Her heart squeezed and tears streamed down her cheeks.

"Don't cry, Margaret. I was lucky it didn't hit something vital! I'll be up and outta here in no time."

He didn't sound too convincing as he broke out in a sweat and sank back onto the pillow.

Margaret could smell the infection. She also knew by now that the military took the quickest cure as the best cure and would take off the leg the next time the surgeon visited. She acted swiftly and with the help of Bennett's father, and her own, they convinced Dr. Hall to make room for others by letting Bennett go home.

Trying to remember all of Hannah's instructions and getting a few ideas from the nurses, Margaret made a poultice of chicken fat and salt. She soaked Bennett's wound open, then packed it with the poultice, wrapped it air tight, and forbade it to be opened for three weeks unless it putrified above or below the bandage.

The stink was awful. A fever made Bennett delirious and more than once Margaret had to "sweat him" until it broke. She knew both procedures were dangerous, but so was fever and so was gangrene. She stayed with him day and night giving him all the water and soup she could get down him. She forgot the hospital, the nurses, the relief crew and everything else.

New Year's Day 1864, the bandage was removed. The maggots swarmed hungrily, looking for something putrid to devour. There was nothing for them. Once washed thoroughly the maggotts, feeding on the poultice, had permitted the leg to heal, leaving it pink and clean and healed. The wound would have a wide scar but it was free of any infection.

She wept at her success, and Bennett pulled her to his side, to sit by him on the bed.

"Margaret, I've aged a hundred years out there in this damned war and I vowed if I got home I'd get on with life instead of death. I need to make the most out of this life I have left and I want to start now. You are all I could think about while I was there. When I thought of home it was you that filled my mind. I love you Margaret . . . Marry me?"

"Oh yes, Bennett."

On the February 2, 1864, Margaret Wilson Johnson became Mrs. Bennett Pugh. It was a quiet wedding befitting the times and the fact that she was marrying for the second time, but it didn't dampen the joy. She felt like a new bride, and was as shy about her wedding night as she had been with Ezra.

In the dark, peaceful, seclusion of their bedroom, Margaret unleashed a passion with uninhibited abandon that pleased and surprised Bennett. Each time their mutual exploration discovered new ways to bring pleasure and exhilaration almost beyond endurance. Totally satisfied with the frequent and passionate responses, it was a delicious, private world reserved only for the two of them.

Chapter 6

Lincoln and the War

John and Elizabeth were showing their years. John had taken a few falls for no apparent reason. He blamed it on being tired and overworked since his clerks were all gone to the war. That, and the stress of doing "patrol duty" in the neighborhood. There was also the unwanted but necessary job of enlistments of young men to fight. How hard that was when there were already so many new graves filling the cemetery with friends and kin. It broke Margaret's heart to see them age before her eyes. Without a place of her own now it seemed logical for Margaret and Bennett to move in with John and Elizabeth.

Bennett was reassigned to the hospital until his enlistment was up. Margaret returned there to volunteer as well. She had forgotten about the relief crew in her involvement in Bennett's life. She was delighted that the relief had continued without her. Mr. Balmer came for the nurses on the usual day and Mrs. Dean would come to the hospital. It had even evolved into something beyond their original intent! The Crew began to appear one at a time, to do bonafide volunteer duty and learn to be nurse's aides. They didn't fill Dr. Hall in on their backgrounds and he didn't have time to ask. Some of the town's people recognized them but they didn't dare say they knew the girls were prostitutes or they would have to explain how they knew. The girls were efficient and above reproach except for an occasional whispered word. Morale was never better.

Bennett would not talk about his war experience. All Margaret knew was that he belonged to the 66th Illinois Infantry called the Sharpshooters. Of course she knew he had seen action from the awful wound he had. At first she watched him at the hospital as he tended the new patients. He always asked, "Any news of the 66th Illinois?" and "Were you at Shiloh?" If they said yes nothing more was said, they would hold hands in silent understanding. Tears welled and there was a bond of battle between brotherhood. Once in a while, a veteran would reminisce about funny experiences, usually at a rookie's or officer's expense.

Gradually Margaret learned bits and pieces from Bennett and others that had marched with him. That fall of '61 they had boarded the train and went out to Benton Barracks near St. Louis, Missouri. They were issued Demmick American Deer and Target rifles and training began to make them snipers and sharpshooters. These western boys were already good hunters by necessity and General Fremont was counting on that. They joined up with the 14th Missouri Volunteer Infantry. They were hardly in service when they saw action. It was Christmas Day that they had their first casualties at Silver Creek. It was John Kile, he was in Bennett's Company, a youngster. They had been fighting two weeks in a foot of snow and it was so terribly cold. The winter was brutal.

They had left Camp Benton on the Northern Missouri Railroad back to St. Louis where they boarded a steamer called the Belle Memphis. Down the Mississippi to Cairo, up the Ohio to Paducah, Kentucky and up the Tennessee and moved into Ft. Henry which the Rebels had vacated a few days before they arrived.

There were skirmishes all along the way, but Bennett would say nothing about them and he would clam up when probed to tell anything more.

She knew he was at Shiloh. It was from others that she learned his "Birgies Sharpshooters" were commended for gallantry at the capture of Ft. Donelson. Three days of intense fighting there and then they had moved on to engage in the bloody battle of Shiloh on April 6 and 7, 1862. It would be years and years before the count, 25,000 dead, would be made public. This seasoned company went on to Corinth, Mississippi. They had to fight every step of the way, and stay there to face the fierce animosity of the population. They made camp, called Davis, and spent the next year in skirmishes all around. The Southern feelings of hatred were never quelled, just overcome.

Bennett did brag that their Illinois Governor Yates had made a big fuss about "his boys" being called 14th Missouri Infantry and had Secretary of War Stanton change their name back to the Sixty Sixth Illinois Infantry. He also told about a gal up at Hamburg, Tennessee (near Shiloh) that shot her own brother because he sold his hogs to the Yankees. Her name was Wardlow. Yes, feelings were sure hot down there. There would never be any sparking of one of those southern girls!

The Kansas Jayhawkers relieved them at Camp Davis and they pushed into Alabama as the advance Company under General Sweeney. It was in a skirmish near Lexington, Alabama that Bennett was shot. He was treated at one of their new field hospitals, put on a steamer and sent back down the Tennessee, Ohio and up the Mississippi to St. Louis and then the train home. All that time there were no bandages for changing, or relief from the typhoid that was one of the worst killers of the whole war! He could not march because of his injured knee, so he came home on the first available space on a train.

"It makes me so tired to think about it, Margaret. Them Rebs believe as fierce as we do that they are right. We'd be friends if we had on the same color coat! Now don't that beat all? Killin' 'cause the feller has on the wrong color coat!"

Margaret would make no comment as she watched the pain in his heart twist up his face. Bennett knew the real issues they were fighting. It was not her place to remind him.

She patiently cradled him in her arms after his nightmares. Sometimes he would wake up and they would make love and it would help bring him back from his mental battle. Sometimes his lovemaking would have a forcefulness that frightened her. Although he never hurt her, it momentarily showed Margaret that his experiences had hardened him terribly. Thank God he refused all liquor, saying he had learned from seeing others destroy their lives trying to block out the war pain. He said, "I have been delivered out of that carnage to live, not to drown in a bottle. At least when you feel pain you know you are alive."

News trickled back about the 66th. Those who lived had a leave for thirty days in Chicago, regrouped at Joliet and went back to Pulaski, Tennessee, on to Atlanta and joined Sherman's March to the Sea. The 66th was disbanded in July, 1865. They never knew if any of the original volunteers were still with the Sharpshooters when they were discharged. It is doubtful because of the many battles in which they had engaged.

Chapter 7

Martha

Raised in a strict German home, the intensely curious and physically active Martha Houser was continuously in trouble, especially for asking details about "Things that don't concern you yet."

At 9 1/2 years old, she wanted to know more about the opposite sex. She knew there were things going on that were kept from her, and she was bubbling over with curiosity.

Elizabeth Balmer and her sister, Catherine, were getting letters from her brothers, George and John Arnold Houser. When a letter came Catherine would weep, then smile, and weep again and Martha didn't understand. Catherine would only say, "I'll be in heaven when he gets home!"

There was no one to ask. School was an off again, on again thing since all the schoolmasters were off fighting in the war and everyone else was needed on the farms, so there weren't any children to talk to except at church. Father was even careful not to let her see certain things around the farm! Oh how she would like to know! There was a church garden planted for the widows and orphans which everyone tended when they had the time. Perhaps she would meet someone there she could talk to.

When Margaret and Bennett married, Martha tried to obtain information from Mary and Saphronia as to how they would make a baby. She had seen them kiss at the wedding. "Would they have a baby now?" She wanted to know. Mary clucked, "Really, Martha!" The girls were so embarrassed that their mother would get married again at her age they were not going to discuss the fact that she slept in the same bed with a man in a night shirt! Besides Grandmother Wilson had told them that it was unladylike conversation.

The fact was they didn't really know how married people got babies either. All they knew were people were building on rooms just for private sleeping quarters now. Mary and Saphonia knew boys were different from girls because of examining their baby brother, but such things were not touched, nor acknowledged in general conversation. Martha didn't have a baby brother, so she didn't even have a mental picture of such things.

Martha liked boys. They were always doing things like climbing and digging, games and things girls weren't "allowed." They were also more curious than girls and she liked it especially when Lindsey teased her, although she'd pretend to get mad and shove him. But if he ignored her she would pick up his marbles and run until he caught her and wrestled them away.

Martha's brother, Michael was sixteen and if the war went on much longer he'd be drafted. As it was, he worked from daylight to dusk helping Papa farm. They tried to grow everything they needed and have a cash crop too. With two boys gone it was very hard.

Catherine, Susan, Martha and even little six year old Sarah had to help. At daylight they went to the barn to milk. The three older girls each had a pail and each had two cows to do. Papa and Michael would climb up the ladder to the hay loft and throw down hay to the cows while they were being milked. They would pour a little grain into the manger to enrich the milk and make the cows contented so they would not "sour the milk", or hold it back. The men would carry the buckets to the hogs, pour out a little for the cats and give the rest to the pigs. One bucket would be taken to the house and the girls would strain it through a cloth into a clean crock. After breakfast the crock would be tied to a rope and lowered into the well to keep it cool. Sarah was expected to feed the chickens and gather the eggs. She would cry, and try not to go sometimes because the hens would flog her if they were still on the nest. She received no sympathy from anyone because they had all taken their turn at the chore.

Papa and Michael fertilized the fields by shoveling compost from the manure pile beside the barn onto a sled. The manure was cleaned from the barn every morning and added to the heap. The sled was pulled by a horse up and down the field until it was all shoveled onto the ground. The next process was to plow it under then break the clods with a harrow, make furrows and then plant the seed.

After all of that came cultivation, constant weeding with which they all helped and if the rain came in correct amounts they would then reap, and put up, wheat, barley, corn, oats, rye as well as the vegetables from the garden. In the fall Papa and Michael would butcher and render the lard but the girls would help make sausage by stuffing a clean gut with the ground and seasoned meat. Of course all this was extra to the everyday chores of cleaning, washing, sewing, knitting and weaving. If there was any extra time they had their "hand work" of embroidery.

Mamma was spotlessly clean. In the German tradition the dishes were not done until the stove was also washed, the wood box filled, the fire banked, and the floor swept. There was not much time to be bored.

Very little time to play. That was allowed on Sundays after church as long as you didn't soil your clothes. It was no wonder they jumped at the chance to go to school when it was in session. However as soon as the girls learned to read a little, Henry thought that was good enough. Now Martha's only chance to see Lindsey was on Sunday.

At church one Sunday, while her parents visited, Martha visited the outhouse. While sitting there she noticed a crack that had been chinked over but the plaster was loose. She heard someone enter the other side and just couldn't resist. Carefully pulling the piece out so as not to make a sound, she pressed her eye to the hole and saw Lindsey digging in the front of his pants. He pulled it out and directed the stream which came forth from it into the hole, all the while standing up! Martha was astounded. She had never seen such a thing. Her thought was, "How convenient!"

Lindsey apparently could feel someone watching and turned around to see the eye staring at him.

"Hey! Cut that out!"

He was embarrassed and turned, the stream going astray. Turning his back to the eye, he pulled his clothes together. He ran out and waited for her. For the longest time she wouldn't come out, but she finally thought it was safe and peeked out the door. Lindsey yanked the door wide and she fell out with a scream.

"Lindsey Johnson, quit it!"

Michael came over to defend his sister, he grabbed Lindsey's shirt and tore it by accident, but the fight was on.

Papa Houser and Bennett ran over to break it up and Lindsey hollered, "She peeked at me and he tore my shirt. Ain't my fault!"

107

"He knocked Martha down, 'tis too his fault, not gonna treat my sister that way!"

Martha would have disappeared into the grass if it were possible, she didn't dare say anything. The boys were made to shake hands and apologize. Martha caught the stern look her Papa gave her and knew she was in for it when they got home.

"Go cut a switch," was all Papa said. The rest of the family all looked at him puzzled but he gave no explanation. They knew better than to ask. Martha knew and he knew why the whipping was coming and that was sufficient. No one questioned Papa, not even Mamma. It wasn't too bad as far as whippings go. He had let her hold her dress down and it didn't sting so bad through the material. It also didn't dampen her curiosity.

Catherine was either in a mood of ecstasy or agony. She became so hard to live with Martha avoided her. Father would lapse into German to scold her. She was too old for whipping except for extreme transgressions. Susan would sympathize and swing her loyalty from Catherine, then to Martha, trying to make peace in the family. Little Sarah was staunchly loyal to anything or anyone Martha was.

Margaret's brother George arrived home in March of 1864, and they all celebrated. Mamma made funnel cake and everything. With him came John Arnold who had been writing to Catherine Houser, and before they knew what was happening both had weddings in the same week.

What a whirlwind of activity. Dinners to give, dresses to make, and friends to notify. The bonds were announced in Church three Sundays and then the weddings. April 7, 1864, George Heap married Elizabeth Balmer, and on April 10, Catherine Houser married John Arnold. Tongues wagged about Catherine being so young at sixteen to be getting married but she ignored it and soon concern died out when she failed "to show." Martha learned by paying attention to the gossip. Also, young Catherine could not resist imparting her new, adult wisdom to her little sisters. She didn't want them to be as unwise and innocent as she had been. What she told them dampened any desire they may have had to marry young. The wedding night stories, alone with Papa's reaction when he was asked for her hand, made the girls decide to wait until they were at least twenty-one.

1864 went on with weddings, births and brother Henry's death on the battlefield. Papa, too, was a casualty. The stress was too much for his heart. Michael Houser ascended to the head of the family.

Chapter 8

Tension

Most people were almost certain Lincoln would be nominated and re-elected this year. It wasn't wise to change horses in the middle of the battle. Just after the June nomination, John Wilson heard from his cousin again. Mary Todd Lincoln had so many cousins her notes were brief and mostly non-informative.

Once, Mary, wrote to inform them her son died in 1862. Little Willie had been a cute tyke, a surprise coming from that tall, rugged Lincoln. But it was just an announcement and that was all. Now she wrote her delight that they would be going back to the White House and she would not have to move. Apparently she loved what Washington social life they could have during the war. But she disliked the weather, and she was sure that in summer she would be back in Springfield. They had no idea the melancholy that she and the President were covering up.

John said, "My mother said she was a flighty girl, I hope she has finally found a position that keeps her busy. That husband of hers is getting some things done I suppose, but this war has to be ended.

"Why doesn't he just let the South have what they want! We don't have to have slaves! Let the States decide!"

"Papa!" Margaret exclaimed, "I'm surprised at you! So many have died and fought. It can't be in vain!" She was glad Bennett was not here to hear this.

110

"Southern boys have died too. Did they fight in vain?"

"Well, it cannot be at the expense of the Union!"

"I'm tired, Margaret. Your Uncle Ben and Isaiah Heap's boy, Ben have both been called up. One is too old and the other too young!" His voice getting higher pitched as he reached a crescendo, "What will it be next, women and children? Will they have it out when all the men are gone? Are we going to annihilate the entire country?" Margaret noticed the veins protruding on his neck as his anger mounted.

She changed the subject. "I'm going to the hospital Papa, you rest up a while before going back to the bank. The girls will read to you." She motioned to Mary to get the Bible and read to him.

John fumed and argued politics more and more with no apparent point to be made except he was fed up with the war. In November, Lincoln was re-elected with Andrew Johnson as his Vice President. John liked that because he was from the "West" (Tennessee) and that last Vice President was from Maine. At least the fellow had the decency to join the Army for three months. "Guess that will look good for him to run for office again." John remarked bitterly.

It was a wet and miserable winter. The hospital work was slacking up as the fighting moved east and finally orders came for them to close it and nurses and medics to move to Savannah, Georgia, Dr. Hall told Bennett, "I think we'll be near your old outfit, the 66th."

"If anyone is left that remembers me, tell them God's speed." Bennett answered solemnly.

The move was orderly as most all military moves are but the house was much worse for the wear. Paint was too scarce to consider. All of the furniture needed

111

refinishing. They finally sand papered the woodwork and furniture painstakingly, piece by piece, and then refinished with a mixture of linseed oil and turpentine. Good strong lye soap was used to wash the walls and scrub the floors. There was no floor wax to be had but at least they were clean. The varnish was gone from all the wear. Margaret brought her dishes and furniture back from her parents' house. A few doilies were put out and chairs recovered with quilted scraps making bright cushions. It wasn't needle point, but it would do. A few guests began to come in. Business was not good. Margaret continued to stay with her parents and go back and forth to cook at the boarding house.

Without the Army rent and pay, Margaret was getting worried about funds. Bennett solved her problem by going to work in the furniture factory which Mr. Fry managed. His work was slacking up, too, but with all the young men gone, he needed help none the less. Bennett liked the work and could do some of it sitting down and keep the strain off his knee. Mr. Fry had a horsepowered lathe and drill. Leather straps appeared to turn all over the shop, this one and that one turning the next one. Lindsey loved to go down and watch.

They had tried to get Lindsey back into school but had little luck. He played so much hookey and created such a disturbance when he was there they decided to change the course of action. Bennett would let him "help" in the furniture shop and Mr. Fry was pleased to have a free pair of hands, as long as the boy didn't hurt anything.

Other days Grandpa Wilson would take him to the bank and tutor him in banking skills and in the process, throw in mathematics as a way to make money. Other days he would go out to Grandpa

Johnson's and help with the farm. He was really in his element out there. Horses, cows, pigs and chickens were work; but just horses and cows, now that was good business.

The Faulks had moved in next door to the Wilsons and they had children just a little older than Lindsey. They all went to school but that didn't impress Lindsey one whit.

On April 10, the newspaper announced the end of the war! The news had been telegraphed and printed and the celebration was greater than any Olney had ever seen. A group of horsemen were gathered to ride to all the farms around and tell the good news. Soon wagons came from every direction filled with families who had dropped everything to come to Olney. They flocked to the churches with food and rejoicing.

Olney did not have an official charter yet, but many prominent men of the town spoke to extol the occasion. The veterans paraded through town to the park at the creek, and food was spread out for a picnic although the weather was cool. Fiddles appeared and games were played and prayers made for the safe return of all who had been gone so long, some had not been heard from since the beginning and mothers and loved ones had no knowledge if they were living or dead, and no way to find out.

All of this celebration made the news that arrived on April 15, all the more unbelievable. A special edition was being hawked on the streets, all trimmed in black with the boldest print available, THE PRESIDENT IS DEAD! *Shot at the theater the night before.*

Again horsemen rode to inform the neighbors, and again they gathered, but in a somber, unbelieving state of shock. John had railed against Lincoln and his policies, but now he had high praise for the man who

113

saw the nation through a terrible time and was unable to live and see the nation heal. He wasn't at all sure that Andrew Johnson could do the job. He had heard that no retribution was to be made against the South. Would they rise again? Bennett thought they might, considering the strong feelings he remembered in Mississippi. News came now, and again the South had been scorched and brutally beaten. If the reports could be believed and why not? It was in the paper, wasn't it? John and Elizabeth sent their sympathy to Mary Lincoln and offered assistance if needed.

Margaret's brother, John M. Wilson, came home along with the other Olney men. No one could call them boys any longer. He was full of ideas to put things back "Right with the Country." Father would argue for the sake of argument these days and no more had the news of his arrival wore off than he was at it with John M. It wasn't very serious, they both enjoyed the exchange and debate. They would seek out each other to hone a new point. It wasn't long before John M. was apprenticed to the newspaper and with backing from the bank, he bought it. He eagerly learned all he could, from the delivery to the editorship, and with help from the previous owner began making it a going thing. He pushed for a Town Charter, for bricking the streets, and installing street signs for the names of the streets.

Buildings started going up in Olney again, and this time they were smooth lumber, tongue and groove grand clapboard siding, just like ones back East, gingerbread and all. There was still a shortage of labor (so many men did not return from the war). But there was a boom from the people migrating West, as if to move would change their fortune. All roads led through St. Louis they said and Olney was on that main road.

Some never went on, Olney was West to them.

Weekly, the older men in town gathered in front of the newspaper office to discuss politics and decide the fate of the country, its problems and what should be done about them. Likewise, these things were re-hashed after every dinner at the boarding house, which kept Margaret better informed than most women about current affairs and political feelings.

Some of the discussions were about the resettle-ment of the Indians in Oklahoma. That was supposed to be a final solution. There were so few now they could all be put on reservations in one place to be surrounded by Americans who could keep them in control. There was fear of an uprising if they were forced into yet another location and there were the Indians out in the Rocky Mountains that were still rebellious. The big question was, what to do about them? Some argued that they would all die off soon anyway or assimilate with the rest of the population as soon as they became "civilized." No one knew much about them except they were savages that attacked, without provocation, the innocents that wanted to travel in peace across their territory. Indians were just nomads that did nothing with the land, so why did it bother them to see hard working men plow and plant and make the land productive?

Kansas had become a state in 1861, and Nebraska had petitioned to be admitted. The government would be granting homesteads out there soon to help finance the transcontinental railroads and link rich California and Oregon and Nevada to the rest of the country. Something had to be done about the Indians. They had always tried to take the side against the Americans and during the Civil War had sided with the South, so some argued that they had to be "subdued and corralled." There were arguments that putting them on the reservations would make a safe haven for them. After all whites didn't like being ambushed and bothered as they traveled and would get trigger happy and scared just at the sight of an Indian. At any rate, the land fever was once again popular, and people were ready to not only change their locations but their lives to "settle out west".

Directly after the War, in 1865 and 1866, there was a period of indecision about the government. Andrew Johnson disagreed with Congress over everything, and the Union wanted the Southern states to change their Constitutions and give the negro not only his freedom, but the right to vote! This rankled the southern states and years went by before the issue was settled and they were readmitted into the Union.

Negroes were turned out to their own devises. Without any decision making experience they were wandering the country trying to find a way to earn a living. They were fleeing the South for fear that this may be their only chance to get away from the bonds of slavery. It didn't quite seem real. Yet, many stayed with their masters because they simply knew nothing else and didn't want to change.

Everyone in the country learned that change was painful, even good changes. There were still skirmishes, duels and hard feelings. Fights were frequent everywhere. Missouri was being raped by Quantrell who refused to admit the war was over. So the urge to move had to be tempered with prudence and much thought went into preparations.

Margaret had never abandoned the idea of pioneering West. She read everything she could about it. Pictures were getting popular now and pictures of the

116

West, Indians, mountains, hunters, herds of buffalo, elk and deer looked so enticing.

Photographers were called "artists" and went about the Country giving lectures about their adventures. Margaret never missed one. If one had free land, what a jump. People created a town on free 160 acre sites by selling it off in town lots! She had Bennett excited about it too, until her precious, fragile Sarah sickened and died of pneumonia the winter of 1865. The tiny nine year old was laid to rest next to her father out at the Jordon Lake property. A wooden marker was engraved by Bennett since no stone cutter was in town anymore.

Margaret was crushed with despair. She could not work and didn't want to. She didn't care if the rooms were rented or cleaned or if the children were fed. She sat by the hour in her room in the dark, barely eating what they brought her. Mary and Saphronia, at thirteen and fourteen, took over the household duties. William Lindsey at eleven and closest to his sister in age, was puzzled and disillusioned. He was surprised that death could cause such pain. He longed for his mother's comfort, and she had shut them all away from her. Bennett tried to comfort the boy but they were not father and son yet, and his efforts were colored by his war experience. Lindsey was not able to understand that one must pick themselves up and go on with life.

Elizabeth and John felt that she needed to be alone and that was because they, too, wanted to be alone. After the funeral they had offered their condolences, then, they too retreated to their home. Friends and neighbors had the usual feast and condolences, but Margaret didn't seem to hear them.

Christmas was dismal and almost unbearable. The children made a feeble attempt to make it an occasion. There were no guests in the boarding house so Mary attempted to cook a ham for dinner. She stoked the fire too hot and it burned on the bottom. The meat was saved but there was no grease for a gravy. She had forgotten to buy butter and since Grandmother and Grandfather had gone to Uncle George's for Christmas, she didn't feel there was any place to ask for some, so the bread and the potatoes were eaten plain. The plum cake fell and was more like pudding. Lindsey made a remark about it "sure tasted slick!" Mary cried. Margaret stayed in her room.

One day in February a spring-like day dawned, it was warm the sun was out and it was dry. The air was sweet and even the birds sang and worked about in the yet bare tree branches. The white squirrel came out to run and play and everything seemed fresh and alive, except Margaret. Bennett had been patient enough all through this experience, but he had had enough. He feared Margaret would die or lose her mind completely if this went on. He was desperate. He went into her room, raised the shades and drapes. He took Margaret by the hand and forced her to the window. "Margaret, today you are going out, you are going to work, you are going to get tired from physical labor and you are not going to sit in this room another day. I forbid it!"

Margaret stoically looked at him barely apprehending what he had said. He fixed a tub of water.

"You are going to bathe and put on a fresh dress today, if I have to do it myself." His voice was like that of an old sergeant. Margaret looked into his eyes for the first time and allowed him to undress her. As she stepped into the tub, it was Bennett who stopped in his tracks.

"My God, Margaret, you are pregnant!"

He caressed her and tenderly bathed her. He

118

shampooed her hair and combed out the tangled mattes. Some had to be cut out, but he would worry about style later. He was saddened at the mess she had allowed herself to become. Guilt filled him for allowing it to go on, but she had always been the strong one, now he had to start acting like the head of the family, not like one of Margaret's children.

"Good grief," he thought, "she is thirty-eight years old and she is going to have my baby. It's been ten years since she gave birth. Will it kill her?"

As he worried he dressed Margaret in her Sunday frock and it hung about her thin shoulders, but her pregnancy filled the waist. Margaret's hand went to her belly as it jumped and pulsated, and a faint smile spread across her face.

"I'm pregnant," she said quietly. She looked at Bennett and said, "Sarah has come back, I'm pregnant".

"No!" Bennett commanded, "That is Not Sarah! Sarah was Ezra's child, this one is mine! I won't allow you to live a delusion any longer. Face the facts!"

Margaret's eyes flashed in sudden dark anger, "Get out! Get out!"

Instead Bennett embraced her tightly and allowed her to cry. In awhile he again washed her face and took her out of the room. The children were stunned at their mother's appearance. They had seen her very little in the last four months and then only in the darkened room. They snuggled her and kissed her, and she instinctively, tenderly responded. She had not felt anything for so long. She said she was tired now and would go back to bed, but instead Bennett lead her out of the house.

"We are going for a walk. Put on your hat and cape." He handed them to her. She did as she was told.

119

They briskly set out down the board walk toward town. Margaret was reluctant to see anyone and she was very pale. People did stare, but they tipped their hats and said a "Good day, Mrs. Pugh, Mr. Pugh!" Bennett kept the pace brisk so they would not have to stop and talk, tipping his hat and passing on with a smile. He felt wonderful. He was going to be a father. And Margaret was out of the house!

He didn't pay any attention to the ragged way Margaret looked until they reached a store front with a glass window.

Margaret caught a look at herself and cried out, "Oh, Oh Bennett . . ." whispering, "Is that me?"

She was so thin, pale and her hair standing out all over from under her hat. She looked wild! Cringing she whispered, "Oh, I can't be seen looking like this, please take me home!"

Without hesitation or comment he whirled her around and they just as briskly walked back to the boarding house.

Margaret was genuinely tired but her day was not over. Bennett determined to keep her busy, demanded dinner. The girls could help, but he wanted Margaret to cook. He stood by her and praised everything she did until it was ridiculous. She finally laughed. It surprised them all, especially Margaret who felt that sound was gone from her life forever. The food was good. The fried chicken beckoned the diners, and the children were gathered already at the table in anticipation of a good meal. The gravy was special because that was something neither Mary nor Saphronia could make well. After dinner they asked Margaret to read to them, while they did the mending, and after that, supper. Bennett finally allowed her to go to bed, but he went with her.

120

Very gently they made love in spite of her pregnancy and it was good. The next morning Bennett woke Margaret with kisses but pulled back the covers and raised her to her feet.

"Darling, you can never again go back to bed or stay in your room. I cannot control how you feel, but for the sake of your sanity you must leave this dark room." Urgently he chided, "You have always been so strong, so full of wisdom, so helpful to others, you must not let the death of your child take you away from the rest of us. Life is a gift, to be appreciated and used for God's Glory. It is a sin to waste it!"

Margaret nodded and said, "I know that, but I can't feel that, Bennett, I'm so tired. I know now what Papa was thinking and feeling during the war. A person can only endure so much."

"Please Margaret, try. At least keep busy and see if it doesn't get better."

The next few weeks did get better. School opened again and they went back to church, a few customers came to stay at the boarding house and Margaret had to cook. The children's clothes were deplorable, either worn out or out grown, so the sewing became a priority. Margaret fixed her hair. She had to cut it, but camouflaged the length by twisting it up to the top and securing it with a ribbon. She began to eat and her figure became that of a healthy mother-to-be. Spring came early and she felt joy gradually coming back with little things.

In late April she felt the first pangs of labor. She was frightened. She was remembering all the possibilities about late motherhood. So many "late" babies caused the mother's death, or worse, were born with defects. But she had tried hard over the past weeks to think positively. Only good can come of our love.

121

Her faith was returning and she felt strong enough within her faith to bargain with God. "If this baby is well, Lord, I'll never doubt you again." Silently she prayed for a little girl to take Sarah's place. Lindsey had run to get Bennett, Bennett had run for the doctor, the girls had run for Grandmother who was visiting the neighbors, and they all arrived about the same time. Margaret had been in labor for the past few hours, so it was getting closer to the time now.

Newspapers were spread thick on the bed, pillows propped her back and she pulled hard on the belts looped into the headboard. Quickly came the squall of a blue, wet, wrinkled baby boy. Bennett thought it was the most beautiful sight he had ever seen.

Margaret knew. "It's not Sarah. Sarah was here. We loved her. Sarah is gone now." She was finally able to accept the reality of Sarah's death. Her tears spilled for Sarah, and tears spilled for joy. With that brought the celebration of this new life. She smiled and held out her arms to her new son, Jacob.

Life resumed its natural pace. The older girls helped with the boarding house, Lindsey was working at the stables, Bennett was working at the furniture factory and turning out some beautiful furniture. He was able to buy some wholesale and soon the boarding house looked handsome again. They painted and made new curtains. Business picked up.

Two years later, in May 1868 little John was born. Saphronia and Mary had suffered embarrassment from their mother being pregnant, although their grandmother told them some facts of life, and that it was perfectly natural and legitimate for married people to have babies! But they did not want to admit that their mother did that sort of thing, although they were beginning to feel a stirring in their bodies for the opposite sex. Perhaps that was what bothered them so much.

Mary had started courting Bennett's brother, Preston. Margaret was upset at first, Mary was only seventeen and Preston was her family. Bennett had to remind her that it was not blood relation and even if it was, cousins sometimes married. So a year later on April 5, 1869 Mary had a wedding at the Methodist Church. The church was finished now and a big reception was held in the basement. Grandmother Willson (After the Civil War they started spelling the name with two L's) had put the whole affair together, since Margaret was once again pregnant. Even grandmother thought that this time it was a little too soon, but held her tongue.

The newlyweds moved into the boarding house apartment.

Little George . . . they had to have a George, Elizabeth said (for generations Heaps had been named John, George, John, George in succession) was born premature but was so fat and sweet. But something was not as it should be. His color was pale and his skin was almost transparent. His cry was weak. He had to be wakened for his feedings and seemed to tire before he began. When the doctor came he said he had a weak heart. And in five weeks little George was dead.

This time Bennett feared Margaret would break completely. They all watched with fear. Their own grief had to be held in check for fear of what it would do to Margaret. Bennett once again took charge and made excessive demands on Margaret. Clothes needed washing, mending, sewing, house cleaning, baking, he would even leave the wood splitting. Even though she had just given birth, he had no mercy on her and relieved none of her chores. He himself went into a work frenzy at the factory and it helped. He had two fine sons and he had to make a life for them and Margaret's children.

Chapter 9

Lindsey

Bennett was worrying what the future held for them. He was hearing some glowing reports about the West. It wasn't all Indians and scalping. It sounded exciting to be among those starting a new town and being in on the ground floor.

A fellow named Marsh went out to Kansas with a family named Baird and they started a store out of a wagon and made a big profit, staking them out a town on their homestead. It wasn't much, but they wrote to their friends and told them about the railroad planning to come through. Out there they said the bluegrass grows as tall as a horse and makes a fine hay, and grows natural without planting. There is very little forest to clear. Down on the river, where they made the town, was a tall cedar tree forest. Good wood to make good fences that would last a lifetime. Bennett could see an opportunity to manufacture furniture, too.

Ezra's father, Joshua, died in the fall of 1869, and so did his sister Angeline. A terrible flu came thru the town and took about ten people before spring. Almost everyone was sick with it.

In the summer of 1871, as Margaret was getting ready to go back to the boarding house to prepare supper, neighbors came to the house with a wagon. The doctor was following behind in his buggy. They gently pulled her father out on a canvas and took him into the house. They explained that he had gotten real angry

125

and upset at work and had an apoplectic fit. He was paralyzed on one side and couldn't talk.

Dr. Wright followed them inside and had the men go upstairs and disassemble a bed and bring it down to the parlor. Elizabeth was distraught, over John's affliction most certainly, but she didn't like sudden decisions and this invasion of her property was too much.

"What are you doing to my house? Take John to bed upstairs! What is wrong?"

Dr. Wright announced calmly, "John has had apoplexy. He will need constant watching and care, and if he lives, he will need it for the rest of his life. You had best make a room on the ground floor or you'll be needing a bed beside him and others to do the waiting."

Margaret and her mother clung to one another and consoled each other. All of Margaret's sisters had married now and were gone from home. Some lived here in Olney, but some had gone to St. Clair County nearer brother George.

Dr. Wright was correct. John did need intensive care. He could not eat even the most liquid food. His eyes pleaded to be left alone when attempts were made to feed him because he realized he would choke and could not cough it up.

His most private needs had to be taken care of, to Elizabeth's embarrassment. "Oh Mother, you would do it for me. What is so wrong about me doing it for father? If you don't sleep I'll be taking care of both of you!" She would shoo Elizabeth off to bed. She wasn't sure how long she could last at this. With two small children, and Lindsey and Bennett, and the boarding house, she was getting worn out quickly. John Willson obligingly died in 14 days. "Another stroke," Dr. Wright said.

After the funeral Margaret's brother George came and assembled all the family together. "All of you girls are married and John is a bachelor, still apprenticed, but ambitiously running for mayor, and Mother has no means of support. As the oldest son I am suggesting to you that mother come live with me."

A heated conversation followed, each making a similar offer for this reason or that reason, but George Heap Willson, in the Willson fashion, took charge and said that it was decided. Elizabeth didn't want to move but was proud to have a son that wanted her and would care for her and perhaps now as the man of the family, knew best. She would go.

He also decided to sell the house. Bennett and Margaret did not want to buy it, although it was roomy enough, but it was not what they would want permanently, so they moved back into the boarding house, making another apartment across from Mary and Preston. Mother's fine furniture was divided among the nine of them.

Elizabeth didn't seem to mind, "As long as it stays in the family, I don't care. Some of these things came from Springfield, but others came from Carlisle, and even from Great-great-grandfather in Philadelphia."

Margaret did not relapse into depression, but it was hard to endure so many deaths, plus the loss of her mother by moving, and her daughters by marriages.

Her memory became short and she often had to concentrate hard on what she was doing. Her thoughts would wander and she would shift from the past to the present uncontrollably. She wondered if she was losing her mind. Bennett comforted her, "I've seen that happen after a battle, Margaret. Death affects us even when we don't know the dead, and when we do, it can prey on the mind if you let it."

127

Brother George had told them while he was home, that he bought a large tract of land in Kansas. Then came his letter to explain,

"Expansion is the key to prosperity, you know. Buy early while it is cheap and sell later. Property can sit for generations and then can be sold at an opportune time. Bennett, it is a good investment. Perhaps you and Margaret should think about it, too? It's still available. Let me know and I'll see what I can do for you."

Margaret knew such a purchase was way over their heads even if they sold the boarding house.

George went on to write, "I'm taking Jarome out soon to look it over and make some plans to develop. My friends Marsh and Baird have even laid out a town. Now that is enterprise! That is where the money is!"

Bennett had heard about Marsh's town. His friend, Hank Horrell, wrote about the new settlement called Cedar Vale out in Kansas. He said the Bairds had opened a hotel of sorts, and the trade was fantastic. Even the Osage Indians would come and trade with them. He urged Bennett to come and bring everyone he could gather up. There was land for everyone and great opportunity. He assured them that the Osages were just as friendly as could be. Some even spoke English and were getting right civilized as long as you didn't get them drunk. They still wore blankets but wouldn't hurt anyone.

A new treaty was being negotiated and soon all the Indians would be moving south, to Indian Territory, where the Government was going to put in schools and civilize them! Bennett read the letter over and over to everyone who would listen.

William Lindsey was beginning to earn enough money to do some hell raising in town. He was trying hard to be grown up and independent and got his share of black eyes and hangovers in the process. "Just sowing his oats," Bennett would say, but Margaret was dismayed at his behavior change. He had been so industrious and attentive to his family, and now he was girl chasing and drinking. He had even started wearing a gun. When Bennett read Lindsey's letter from Cedar Vale, and of his excitement he could talk of little else. He was thrilled with the stories about pioneers taking all their worldly goods and treking off into the wilderness, getting scalped, the ones getting through making new settlements. And the money they could make by making a new town! And the importance of the people who did it! You could have a town named after you! The Indians were going to be all corralled in Indian Territories now, and that would make the whole of the land from one ocean to the other open for settlement.

Kansas was offering free homesteads, big open spaces, no forest to cut, maybe a few water problems, but creeks and rivers ran everywhere.

Margaret found her interest in settling in the new country growing. She was getting older, though. Did she want to give up her security, her boarding house, her friends, family? The answers came almost as fast as the questions. They could have another boarding house, with the boom in Kansas even a better one. As for friends, she was cultivating fewer and fewer as old ones left, some died, and some had turned on her because of Lindsey's behavior. As for family, she mentally counted the graves and sadly admitted they were dead or moved away, or so it seemed to her.

Olney was actually doing quite well in this postwar era. Many Easterners had moved "West" to Illinois. Apple orchards were in full production, and a cider and vinegar plant was opened. Cotton was plentiful and a fiber and garment factories opened as well. The community was becoming more stable and there was much talk about incorporating the area into a town with a mayor and officials. Still, Bennett's mind was on George's letter.

Margaret and Bennett stopped talking about if they would go, but when and how. They planned to sell the boarding house. Ship their beautiful furniture by rail to Parsons, Kansas. A large and sturdy wagon would transport them and their necessities and valuables not entrusted to the shippers. Lindsey could help drive the team, and of course, manage the cow and chickens. They would take horses for each of the men, plus two extra.

One problem stood in their way. Lindsey had been courting Martha Houser. She was nineteen now and quite changed from the little bouncy girl that used to tease him in school. Martha's father had died in 1864 and she and her sisters had all worked out in people's homes to support her mother. Her older brother, Michael, would hear to none of her talk about marriage. He insisted that even if she was twenty-one, she would not be given consent to marry Lindsey Johnson.

Michael Houser not only disapproved of Lindsey and his wild reputation, but did not like this talk about going west either. His father had sought out a land that would, in his mind be the land of destiny for his family, and Michael insisted that they should stay there. Lindsey would have to prove himself in many ways to win Martha's hand, even after she became twenty-one.

Lindsey had to court Martha at a distance and he yearned to just be able to look at her. There was no desire for any other. He began attending her Lutheran church. He would catch her eye and they would smile. He would ache, and even shudder in her presence and at every thought of her, and he would wonder how he could possibly endure three more years without having her. He would watch her small slender figure coming down the church steps and she would look straight into his face with her big chocolate brown eyes that pierced his very soul. All the wisdom of all the ages he could imagine were seen deep in those eyes! She didn't giggle with the other girls. Her laugh was mature and full. It was also silent when her brother was around. She tried to find a way to see him, to meet, to touch a hand, to speak, but brother Michael was keeping an eye on his little sisters. All Lindsey could do was watch them drive away in their buggy and wait for another chance to see her.

Margaret and Bennett were involved with the sale of the boarding house, the little boys, buying necessities, but Margaret did notice the change in Lindsey. "Son," she asked one night after supper, "what is bothering you?"

"Oh, nothing, I just wonder if I should go with you out West."

"Why, that is all you've talked about! You are the one that got the whole idea started! Now you want to back out?" She saw his face, "Who is it?"

Lindsey blushed. He had never confided anything about any of his "companions" but this was different. "Ma, I want to marry Martha Houser!" He blurted out the statement that had never been voiced before.

"Well?" Margaret urged.

"Well, she won't be of age for three years! Her family would never accept me even if she was twenty-one! I don't have the prospects, in fact her brother

Michael hinted that they had their eyes on cousin Jarome Willson!"

"Son, go with us. Make a place for her, and if she is the right one for you she will wait. During the war many a lass did not wait, but this only proved to the young man that she could not be faithful and therefore would not be a good wife. A hard thing to learn but better now than later." Her words made sense but did not console Lindsey.

Bennett's nephew, Jesse Pugh, came over the next day and talked to them about going along. He was not married. He was four years older then Lindsey and they all welcomed his company for the trip. With Mary and Saphronia both married and the little boys so young it appeared to be an ideal time to make the move.

Lindsey talked to some surveyors who had just returned from Kansas. They were full of details about the great things being done out West. "Why, it will only be a short time until this whole country will be laced with railroads! Since the wedding of the rails in '69, railroads have gone everywhere! Cattle can be shipped right from the farms! Well, not yet, but soon."

They went on to tell about wild cattle herds being brought up from Texas and fattened on the bluestem grass of Oklahoma and shipped out of Kansas. If you couldn't round up wild cattle, there were plenty of ranchers down there willing to sell herds as the heat dried up the grasses in the summer. Cheap! The thrill of adventure and challenge returned in Lindsey and he planned a way to see Martha and ask her to wait. He would have to be very direct. That meant he would have to face her family.

Lindsey cleaned up as he had never cleaned before. He bathed, trimmed his moustache, washed his hair, cleaned his boots. He was too large for Bennett's suit, but he put on a freshly ironed shirt and sweater-coat, all the while tried to work up his courage. He was tempted to settle his nerves with a good strong draw on the whiskey jug, but thought he had better not smell of spirits when he went to the Houser farm. It was a short ride, but Lindsey almost turned back several times in the distance. He was there, and Michael was on the porch getting ready to go out after dinner to work in the garden. He said nothing as Lindsey dismounted and hitched his horse, brushed his clothes, took off his hat and smoothed his hair back.

Lindsey cleared his throat, "Good day to you, Mr. Houser."

Michael Houser grunted and took the offered hand briefly.

"Fine day for gardening."

"Da, I suppose." He waited for an explanation for Lindsey's visit.

"May I talk to you, sir?" Lindsey asked while looking over his shoulder to see if he could see any sign of Martha.

"Da." His mouth was set in a firm line.

Lindsey fidgeted with his hat and wished he had a draw from a jug. "Sir, we are going out West, to Kansas. Guess you've heard about the sale and all, well I was wanting to speak to Martha before I left . . . I ah, well . . . I." He looked painfully into Michael Houser's eyes which had not changed from the inquisitive stare. Neither looked away for a long time.

Lindsey knew this was hopeless and tears of frustration and failure began to well in his eyes. He could not let these tears be seen. "Well, sir, I'll go." He pulled his hat down over his eyes and turned toward his horse, mounted, sniffed his runny nose, and as he

133

turned he said, "There is a farewell party for my parents Saturday, at the Methodist church. You are all invited to come." His tears visible now on his defiant jaws, "I want to say good-bye to Martha then." He turned quickly and rode off in a gallop.

"Who was here, Michael?" Susan and Martha both appeared on the porch wiping their hands on aprons.

"Johnson boy," he said without looking back at the girls. He moved off to the garden.

Martha ran from the porch to call Lindsey, but he was out of hearing. She whirled about and ran to the garden. "What did you say to him, Michael? What did you say? Why did he leave like that?"

Her brother turned to her with a sharp piercing look, "I said, NIEN! And you do not raise your voice to me!"

Martha pleaded, "Michael, tell me why Lindsey left! PLEASE!"

Her tears and the boy's were too much for him. Even Herr Houser could feel sympathy. "The boy asked us to the party Saturday." He went back to his hoeing.

Not daring to ask, Martha ran back to the house in hopes they would attend if she could enlist the aid of her mother and her sisters. "We're going to a party!" She announced as she went into the house. Susan and Sarah joined her in the excitement as they planned what to wear. They would go over and tell Catherine so she and her husband, John Arnold, could come, and maybe even brother George and Elizabeth could be there too. Martha secretly hoped Michael would not go. He was trying so hard to be like Papa that he had become ten times more strict! She must speak to Lindsey.

Michael did not want to go, but by evening it was a

foregone conclusion. Dresses were brought out to be retrimmed and refitted, shoes repaired and matching bows put on them. Skirt looped up over other skirts made a bustle effect. Michael had refused to buy real ones as they were too provocative.

On Saturday, Mamma helped them with their hair. Susan and Martha could have theirs brushed into an upsweep and fixed with combs because they were of "courting age," but Susan was too young. At thirteen she could only tie hers back with a ribbon. "Makes me look like a peeled onion!" she pouted.

Finally they were all ready and into the wagon. Michael was on the seat driving the team. The girls sat on benches in the back. It was warm for spring, but they brought comforts for the ride back home.

Michael had said nothing about not talking to Lindsey, so he was the first person she looked for as they arrived. He was talking to the fiddler when she caught his eye. Her tight lace trimmed bodice with rosettes of matching brown linen on her shoulders, and the gracefully looped cream color lace edging draped around her hips, made her an elegant woman that took his breath away. He had never seen her hair brushed up in a bouffant crown and her brown curls atop matched her eyes.

Lindsey found himself beside her and without asking, danced her away to the music. She barely came to his shoulder, but dark eyes twinkled as she looked straight into his. He felt a strength in her that surprised him. She was so petite. He had imagined her fragile and breakable, but as they danced, he felt muscle and warm flesh that begged him to embrace her. She will do, Lindsey thought. She was not only desirable, but would make any man a good pioneer wife.

135

"I'm going to Kansas," Lindsey blurted as they paused between dances.

"I know." Martha replied quietly.

"Will you come with me?"

The question shocked Martha, even though she had known Lindsey was pursuing her, she had no idea his feelings had developed so far already. When she didn't answer, but gave him a questioning look, he continued rapidly, "I'm going to prove up a piece of land, a hundred and sixty acres. We can raise cattle and horses and all we can eat. You'll never want for anything, Martha. Please come."

His desire to embrace her, even there, in public was almost more than he could control. This was almost too much for Martha to absorb. Her heart pounded, and her mind was in a whirl. A wife, a pioneer, a dangerous trip out to Indian country, leave her family, her beloved sisters, Mamma. Lindsey had a reputation. There were bandits. Would he protect her or abandon her as soon as another pretty face came along? And babies? Who would be there to help her have her babies? As she was thinking they were dancing, Lindsey gazing at her, waiting hopefully for an answer, holding her as close as he dared.

He could have cried from the confusion he saw in her face. He had assumed she had known how he felt. Hadn't she seen him follow her everywhere?

Martha looked into his eyes, smiled and all doubts vanished, "Yes, Lindsey, I'll go with you as your bride."

Suddenly no one else seemed to be around and they whirled inside their own dream. They came back to earth as snickers caused them to discover they were standing motionless, alone on the dance floor.

Pink with embarrassment, they ducked through the crowd and out onto the front steps where he kissed her gently. It was awkward and obviously her first kiss. She stood rigidly as he kissed her again, pressing her close. They both felt the tingling thrill of that first romantic contact and then the moment was broken by a gruff voice, "Martha, you will return to the chairs inside!"

Startled they jumped apart to see Michael Houser. He wasn't taller than Lindsey, but he appeared gigantic. He stopped Lindsey from following Martha inside.

"I knew you would try to take advantage. This is why you cannot see Martha again. You go to Kansas. Stay there. Good riddance!"

Lindsey said, "Sir, I'll go to Kansas, but I asked Martha to go with me, as my bride."

Color rose in Michael's face. "What? What? You go to Kansas with nothing of your own. Just a boy! A boy who wants a wife? I cannot believe you are serious! Grow up! I'll wager you'll come back. Your drinking and wild carousing show no responsible man to me. I wouldn't trust you to care for my pigs, much less my sister! Go prove yourself responsible then maybe, just maybe . . . if you've proven you are a man, I'll consider you as a suitor for one of my sisters.

"I'm twenty-two in August," is all Lindsey could feebly say to Houser's back.

Shamed, Lindsey went to the wagon. He became angry at being found out and interrupted. Angry that he didn't stand up to Houser now all he could do was think of all he should have said. He also thought of Martha's kiss and how she had said "yes." What was he doing out here? He peeked inside the door looking for his "Chocolate Princess."

She was surrounded by her sisters and her mother. The refreshments were being served, the men had gathered to one side of the room, the women on the other. Margaret saw Lindsey and went to him with a piece of cake.

"What are you doing out here? This is a party for us and you should be in here saying your farewells."

Lindsey said, "I'm leaving now." He ran for his horse, mounted and rode off toward the Johnson farm.

Good-byes must be too much for him, Margaret thought.

Halfway to his grandfather's farm, where Harvey had continued to live, he stopped and went into a grove where the famous Johnson still was hidden. He would rest here and mull things around with the help of a jug. As he sat on the stump drinking, he thought, I'll go to Kansas, I'll be a big success and show that Dutchman! I'll have a spread, ten times as big as Housers. Maybe I'll even strike gold. By gum I could do it, too, if I had Martha.

They would elope! They would get the wagons loaded and ready to go then they would just casually drop by the Housers, and Martha would hop on board and away they would go, leaving old Houser in the dust! This made him feel very self satisfied. Now it was all planned. He took the jug with him as he rode back to town feeling very romantic.

Back at the church he gave a little boy a penny to go tell Miss Martha to come outside. The boy returned to say she had gone home. Lindsey stumbled back to the Pugh's wagon, crawled into the coverlets curled up and cried.

The farewells were harder than Margaret thought they would be. The party, the kind words, the farewell gifts, touched her with the reality. She would be gone from this place and these people, perhaps never to see or hear from them again. "We'll have a fresh start Maggie," Bennett spoke softly endearingly. She smiled

138

hoping the fresh start would not be like Wisconsin's fresh start.

They drove home. Not being able to rouse Lindsey, they left him asleep in the wagon.

A fly buzzed his face as the sun bore down on his heavy, pounding head. Unable to move at first, he finally covered his eyes with a quilt and slowly sat up, totally disoriented. Had he found Harvey last night? Had he found Martha again? Oh he hoped not! What sort of fool had he made of himself? Oh, how could he feel so bad? He crawled out of the wagon making a run to the outhouse, which only hastened making him sick. He came out to wash in the outside basin at the back door. The cold water helped a little. And then he remembered. Today they had to pack!

Inside the house was already a bevy of activity. Margaret was packing dishes in barrels. Bennett was dismantling beds and emptying drawers. Mary and Saphronia had stayed over to help. Lindsey was glad there was no mention of food and he helped himself to the coffee, wishing they would not make so much noise.

Bennett saw him in the kitchen and curtly asked, "Help me with this, Lindsey, and next we'll load the ice box and the dining room set. These all need to be at the depot for the noon train."

Lindsey knew he didn't dare complain about his hangover and began painfully to help. With his hurting head he tried to form a plan on how to elope with Martha.

By afternoon, and hours of hard sweating work, he had recovered a little and took Bennett aside. He would need Bennett's help to carry out the plan to take Martha along.

"What do you think?" he asked.

Bennett smiled indulgently and spoke with sympathy, "I know just how you feel Lindsey, I was also in love at a young age and I don't deny your feelings are deep. But you don't even know if Martha will elope and if she does, you can bet Mike Houser would come after you with the law. He could keep you apart forever by having you jailed so long they'd forget all about you. Or worse, he could kill you in a duel. You know that German is a marksman and dueling isn't a past thing with him!"

"I can't leave Martha behind, Bennett!"

Bennett set his jaw. "Oh, yes you can! I left your mother to do my duty and you can too! You go with us. Return later as a man and take her for your wife then. If she's worthy, she will wait."

Lindsey didn't like to hear that. He felt he was a man already. He brooded all night. By morning he could see some reasoning to it and knew it was a lost cause since Bennett was not going to help.

Lindsey saddled up early the next morning while the rest of the family put last minute things into the wagon. As they prepared to leave, he rode off to say farewell to Martha, but only for now.

Martha was out hanging clothes as the sun came up. Her hair was pulled back with a kerchief, her skirts tied out of her way and her sleeves rolled about her elbows. She was wet all down her front from the wash she had just done. Lindsey had never seen anyone so beautiful. She was so small, yet so strong. She was carrying a basket as large as she was. He quickly dismounted and took the basket from her.

"Martha, you said you'd go with me."

Martha blushed, "I said, yes, I'd be your bride, but you ran off. Where were you? Are you afraid of Michael? Are you leaving now?"

"It isn't fair to take you out there to Kansas when

I don't have anything to offer right now. Will you wait? I'll try not to be too long. I'll homestead a place as soon as I can." His eyes pleaded desperately.

"Yes, Lindsey," a tear slid down her face, "I'll wait, but write once in a while so I know you are still wanting me. Michael will want me married at twenty-one and will promise me to someone if you don't write. Oh, Lin, can't you stay?" Tears openly flowed without sobs.

Lindsey almost cried, too, but he remembered Bennett's counsel. "I'll return and prove to your family that I'm man enough to take care of you. Give me your promise and I give you mine." He leaned over the clothes line and kissed her on the mouth. "Can I have a lock of your hair to carry in my watch?"

Martha came around to his side of the line, her head down to hide the tears, she removed her kerchief and her long dark hair tumbled down like a veil. It had a slight curl on the ends and with his pocket knife, Lindsey snipped off a small piece. He held her to him tightly, "My love, I'll be back. I pledge thee my troth."

"I pledge to thee as well Lindsey, stay safe for me."

Knowing it was time to leave, he mounted and with his tightly twisting heart almost choking him, he rode fast to catch up with Margaret and Bennett. He realized the cool wetness he felt from Martha's embrace.

The trip was reminiscent of the one to Wisconsin as the daily routine was much the same. The roads were far better now and with three men to hunt, the fare was better too. By hanging a pail of cream from the wagon, the day's jostling gave them butter and buttermilk at night.

Margaret knew Lindsey's mind was far away, but did not probe as to why. Jesse was so wound up with the excitement, he didn't notice and the little boys, Li'l

141

Jacob and John, were thoroughly enjoying the adventure of sleeping out of doors and riding in the wagon. They wanted to explore the woods after every stop and it was then the fairy tales served their purpose. The big bad wolf kept them close to camp. Indians and bandits would not have made any impression.

There was a real threat of highway men. Law officers were in short supply and range "justice" was the only deterrent to crime. Margaret and Bennett both thought it greatly exaggerated, but kept rifles close at hand. Lindsey wore a pistol, but Bennett laughed and said, "I'd forget what I had holstered and pull it out and fling it like a sword."

Chapter 10

Going West

St. Louis was a sight to strangers. Every sort of vehicle, from hand drawn carts, covered wagons, drays and buggies to four-in-hand coaches were busy jockeying for street space. There was every type of business, and some Margaret had never dreamed of, like the dentist. Imagine a man specializing and devoting his entire career to taking out teeth! The barber at home always did just fine! There was every sort of dress, plain cottons and homespun, to silks over hoops, tall Indians in beaded leather and blankets. Everyone wore hats from cloth sun bonnets to feathered straws. Men likewise in tams to beaver top hats with a crown that looked like a stove pipe.

"I never cared for those much," Margaret pointed to one, "They look a little silly."

Wagons were loaded with belongings, and people were passing through, which made St. Louis mostly a place of preparation, obviously. Activity was greater as they approached the docks. Steamships and barges waiting to unload and reload. Hustle and bustle and traffic! It looked to Margaret like the whole world was on the move.

And there was the Great River, the Mississippi itself. The current was swift and dark, muddy, brown. It was wide enough to defy anyone to wade across, but Margaret was just a little disappointed in its size. From the stories she had heard she had pictured a river so wide you could not see across to the other side. They parked the wagon and looked about to find how they would cross. Hawkers were on every street corner selling themselves as guides of trains going West, some obviously with no knowledge or experience beyond the city limits. Others they could not quite tell about. It would be difficult to team up with someone and not get bilked out of your money or worse, put your life in danger as your "guide" could also do you in. Margaret suggested they find a church minister and ask about someone he would recommend. They also needed to stock up on final supplies for the trip across Missouri. Margaret tried a new fruit she had never tasted before. Bananas! She loved them!

Lindsey and Jesse were sent out with a list of supplies to buy, while Bennett and Margaret located the Methodist church. The Reverend Peters greeted them and after an exchange of pleasantries and hearing about their search for a trustworthy guide, he said, "I've made the trip myself and have listened intently to others who have returned. You must team up with other travelers and follow the trails. Save your money. Help each other. Elect a leader and go. That's the best way I know. You will all be protecting your own property that way and no hired hand could do as well by you!"

Bennett shook his hand and left a stipend with gratitude for the sound advice. They went back to the docks and introduced themselves to others with wagons. It wasn't an hour before there were five families gathered and talking about the trip and the best way to cross the river, and where to go. They could see some families being loaded onto the steam ships and others on barges. There was also a ferry plying back and forth, also expensive, but less than the steamer. They could see a bridge under construction. Too bad they didn't have time to wait a few years, they could just drive right across.

One of the other men talking to Bennett said, "I thought they had that bridge done by now! I heard way back in 1864 the legislature approved the Illinois and St. Louis Bridge Company! Here it is 1871! Someone told me they weren't going to be satisfied with just any old bridge, it had to be the biggest and finest in the world, one of the wonders of the world." He went on to tell them the bridge was designed by a Captain Eads, and they didn't start building until 1867 and they aren't half done yet.

Bennett said, "That's fine for them to build something so great but you'd think they would put in something to make do until they finished it. Well, fellas, this isn't getting us across. I think I'll take the ferry. Shall we join up now or talk it out on the other side?"

"See you on the other side." The stranger pulled out his wagon ahead of Bennett's.

"This constant milling about is worse than Chicago ever was! Don't people eat or sleep?" Margaret asked the lady in the next wagon.

"Guess not," she hollered over the noise. "Sure stirs up the animals! Did you see that Indian camp on the south side of town? I didn't know they let them on this side of the Mississippi."

"Must be guides, or relatives, or some such." Margaret said. "This heat and dust is awful. Dust in everything, even into what was sealed up in trunks. Things were full of dust when I opened them."

"Must be going to storm, wind's out of the southwest and shifts now and again. Always can tell. Joints, you know." Margaret liked this lady, an understanding wife and mother, a kindred soul.

Margaret called to Bennett, "Looks like we'd better cross before we camp tonight, if it rains the river will be up!"

"We're going now, Margaret. Pull down to the ferry. "Lindsey! Jesse! Get up here, load that stuff on and let's go!"

Lindsey finished his job, mounted and said to Margaret, "Let's get out of here. This dust and the crowds are driving me crazy!"

They pulled into line and had to wait as the ferry moved with the drift of the river down and across, playing out the lines from the eastern shore, poling as well as steering skillfully, using the current to make it to the west bank. Everything had to be unloaded, reloaded with east bound passengers and cargo and slowly winched across back to the east shore. It took hours. The move onto the ferry was a relief, even though Margaret was afraid of the water because she didn't swim. Something about that brown, murky water bothered her unreasonably.

They led the ox drawn wagon, and the horses onto the ferry. The wagon was anchored with blocks and tied down to iron rings put in the floor for the purpose. The oxen were unhitched for the trip in case they fell in. The harnesses were left loose around them. Margaret was slightly nauseous as they shoved off. The dock smells wafting down and the clouds gathering, a low rumble of distant thunder, all assailed her senses at once. It was humid and hot, the breeze they felt midstream felt good. The ferry drifted freely now as it diagonaled to the west bank. It bumped hard, staggering the passengers and it was over. Margaret felt foolish for her fear.

146

Suddenly a steamboat rounded the bend let out a blast on its whistle and simultaneously a bolt of lightening and clap of thunder cracked right above them. The usually docile oxen bolted, dragging harness between them, knocking Margaret down, raking her along under the harness and into the water at the edge of the ferry. The beast jumped from the ferry to the sloping landing site, leaving Margaret clinging to the edge of the deck, floundering about in the shallow water. The men had their hands full controlling the horses and had not had time to assess Margaret's danger. However, she quickly found her footing and stood up, wet, dripping, scratched and bruised, her clothes torn all over. It frightened the little boys who cried in loud wails from the wagon. But insult was added to injury as all the men stood there laughing.

"I'm sorry, Maggie. I'm relieved you are not dead, but you look a sight!" Bennett pulled her from the shallows and tried to caress her. He took a handkerchief, daubed at her scratched neck. She jerked away, whirled around and shot a fierce, scolding look to the others who turned so they would not be seen smiling.

The rest of the unloading went smoothly and they joined a campground full of other travelers just outside of the west bank settlement. It started to rain.

Margaret had changed clothes inside the wagon and poured whiskey on her scratches. Dry, and much cooler now, and hungry, on a little "jerry stove" she started a kerosene fire while the men tended the animals. When they came back, the canvas was tacked down snuggly on both ends and smells of vegetable soup wafted about.

"Margaret! Let us in! We're getting wet out here."

Margaret lifted the flap just enough to push out three quilts and a hard roll of summer sausage and

147

said, "Here you are fellows. You make your beds hard and you'll sleep in 'em. Under the wagon would be my guess, but not in here!"

They huddled under the wagon, wet, hungrily chewing on the hard sausage. Looking at each other they started to giggle again. Lindsey laughed. "She was funny lookin', Guess I'd a laughed even if she had been hurt! I can't help it, weed over one eye, wet and mad. I've never seen her so mad!"

"Hush, Lin. Your mamma will make us sleep outside from here to Indian Territory if she hears you." But he and Jesse chuckled too.

The next morning Margaret looked vainly for the family she had seen on the dock the day before. She hung clothes and wet blankets out on the trees to dry and made a real fire to cook up provisions for the trail. They would stay here for a day or two and push on up the Missouri River road to Jefferson City.

Two days later, getting ready to pull out, Margaret saw the familiar, friendly face from the day before yesterday. However, that face was strained and flushed today.

"Hello!" Margaret ventured, but the lady stared straight ahead and drove by her.

The husband following horseback, stopped briefly, nodded to Margaret, "Excuse the Missus," he said sadly with a crack in his voice. "We 'uns lost our boy yesterday in the crossing."

Margaret recoiled, shocked. "Oh, no. I'm so sorry!" tears welling in her eyes. He nodded, looked off into space and rode on.

The trip was more than Margaret had expected. The scenery went from bare rock to brushy marsh, from wide lush meadows to hills and canyons. Keeping up with two small boys and cooking for six made the trail seem never ending. Bennett wanted to get to Parsons, Kansas and pick up their furniture as soon as possible, so many days they pushed much farther than Margaret wanted to. Little time was left for the evening chores and she was already tired when they stopped. She was at least grateful that the wagon was new and in good shape and so was the tent. There was plenty of traffic, so they didn't worry about bandits or renegade Indians they heard about as stories circulated in the camps at night.

One hot afternoon when everyone was about to choke on the wind and dust, the humidity pressed into their bodies like a hot wet blanket. Weak from perspiring so heavily, they stopped the wagons out on a rocky overlook. The view was breathtaking, stretching out miles into the horizon. The road below snaked out like a faint ribbon obscuring only in spots by brush and trees, yet marked by puffs of dust behind the travelers and their bleached white canvas wagons crawling along westward. The breeze was freshening and it felt so good. Margaret had shed her long petticoats but her dress clung to her sweat soaked pantaloons.

"I think I'll cut them off above the knee," She giggled aloud as she wondered what on earth her mother would say at such daring. She also wondered how her mother had made this same sort of trip from Pennsylvania to Ohio and again from Ohio to Illinois when there wasn't even a road. She had heard her father talk about axing a trail to make way for the wagons. She was too young to remember much except the trip had demanded work from her she had never experienced before, much like little Jacob and John had to do now, looking for wood, water, bringing it to the camp fire every night. The boys who had fanned out to scout for kindling, and four rocks to make a fire

149

pit big enough to balance a pan. She heard the chop of an ax against a dead log for the main fire tonight. Fire! Who needed one? Who even wanted to eat in this heat? Ah well, what they didn't use would be left for the next traveler.

The clouds began to boil about, moving rapidly high across the sky from the west. Back toward the south was a darkening flat rain cloud and the wind shifted and felt cool. Margaret busied preparing a meal and rearranging the wagon.

Bennett came up and spoke to her through the rolled up canvas. "Margaret we've got to move camp and hurry." The urgency in his voice scared her enough not to question, but to move. She jumped out, and quickly gathered up belongings.

There was no need to call the boys. They, and the dog, had been under foot all day fighting constantly, and now they argued about taking the wood they had gathered. "Stop that and get in!"

The horses and the oxen had been restless since they had stopped. The oxen stamped and lunged at the hitch uncharacteristicly, as they were fastened. They were eager to leave camp. Margaret at the reins, looked for Bennett to lead the way on horse back. They waved her ahead. She sensed, rather than saw the reason for the quick move. Storm! It was suddenly silent of any bird song or animal movement. The sky had a yellowish, gold glow, and the air was oppressive. They were the only movement and they headed back down the trail over the hill which they had laboriously climbed just this afternoon. Just at the bottom of the hill they pulled off into a cleared area. Barely dismounted, they heard a roar like a dozen freight trains. Realizing it was a cyclone they started pulling quilts from the wagon. Margaret pulled the boys to the west

150

side of the wagon, wrapped them in quilts and pushed them to the ground against the hill. They all lay like cord wood trying to protect each other as the wind swirled around them. The noise was deafening, wood snapping like rifle shots, debris, gravel, and dirt blasting into their skin like pellets while the air seemed to be sucked from their lungs.

Perfect calm returned as suddenly as the storm. The sky was still black, they looked up and counted one another. Horses were running without direction toward the east and in awe they saw one lifted, twirled high into the black cloud as if on an invisible merry go round. It flipped over and dropped as if spat out and splat onto the earth below. Lindsey moved to go to the horse's aid, but Bennett pulled him back, "Stay here Lin, he's dead and we're still in for the back side of this blow."

About then it hit again. Everything was blowing in the opposite direction from before and then came the hail! It pounded their backs and they huddled under the hot quilts, just glad to be able to hang onto them. The coolness that followed the hail was welcomed. The rain followed. Peeking out to see if the wagon was still there and if they could get into it, they saw it had blown over on its side. All their belongings were strung out for two hundred yards beyond. The oxen were fighting to get out of the traces and rise to their feet. They were so tangled the men had to cut them loose.

Ignoring the rain Margaret ran out to recover some of her clothing and stuff it back into the broken trunks. The deluge quickly soaked them. They huddled inside the overturned wagon bed, and let it rain.

They looked around at each face, and realizing they had lived they started giggling. Margaret laughingly said, "Did you see the look on Jesse's face?"

151

Bennett replied. "The look on your face was pretty strange as you grabbed those blankets! And why did you go back for the compass?"

She laughed, "I didn't want to be left out here and not know which way was west!"

The dog ran in, shook all over and brought more giggles. Who cared! They were soaked already and they were alive. Passing through such awesome power and living to talk about it was worth a celebration! The little boys didn't see what was so terribly funny.

The rain stopped as suddenly as it began, but had dumped so much water in such a short time the road down the hill was running like a stream. Loose tree limbs and rock were washing down into new arrangements all around them. Mud was sliding off the newly denuded hillside and down over some of their scattered belongings.

They sloshed through the red, sticky muck, gathering and piling up their things. Lindsey and Jesse had gone off to find the remaining four horses. Bennett retrieved and checked over the oxen. They had not run far but were still very nervous. The traces had been cut and broken, the far wheels were buried now and they couldn't tell if they were broken or not.

They worked into the twilight and on to dark digging out. Still not dry, even with a fire to huddle around, there was no place to lay down except for the bed Margaret made for the little ones inside the overturned wagon. There was no giggling now. Depression set in over the magnitude of work before them tomorrow.

Inspecting the next morning they saw many ironies. The wind that was able to topple over their wagon, lift a horse and fling it to its death, break trees like dead twigs, had left her fragile China dishes scattered but unbroken! Most of their food had stayed in the barrels, and after they gathered it all up most everything was found.

Once the wagon was righted the wheels inspected and judged sound, they had to reload everything, muddy as it was. They made no attempt to clean it, or themselves until they could make way back to a creek. It was so hot everything was drying out and great chunks of mud caked off their clothes. They slept that night from pure exhaustion in their muddy clothes on the muddy ground. No one had passed by. Everyone must be in the same fix. The road wasn't passable.

Repairs were made and the precious drinking water was saved. "It looks like that Chinese laundry we passed in St. Louis!" Lindsey said. They headed back east for the creek. They left after a quick breakfast of fry cakes and arrived about noon at the creek. Other people had congregated there.

They eased the wagon up close to the creek bank. Every last thing had to be unloaded. Li'l Jacob and John were warned to stay away from other people's camps and wood piles.

Buckets of water were sloshed into the wagon and Margaret brushed and scrubbed it down. The barrels and trunks were washed off and cleaned out. Clothes piled high beside her. Margaret washed on a rock mid stream. She welcomed the cool water that was only to her knees, grateful that it was clear. The storm must not have hit up stream she thought.

Exhausting as their efforts were, they were famished and all pitched in to cook a feast. Clean at last and getting dry! Heaven itself could not have been so welcome as the full meal. Neighbors passed down word that they were having a "gathering" after supper. Hungry for company as well as food, they moved up the

153

line until they saw the bonfire and the fiddlers warming up to play. They mingled, and talked and swapped stories of the trail and the cyclone. Most were too tired to dance, but the music was a welcome reminder of civilization. They listened until the fire died down and returned to their wagons refreshed.

Three wagons pulled out together two days later. Far from rested, but clean, dry and well stocked with fresh milk from the Brown's cow and eggs from the Bartig's chickens, they were ready for the next "push." The respite was highlighted by the cakes Margaret baked in the Dutch oven to bring along. Now on the trail again the oven would be used for stews of rabbit, squirrel, opossum, quail and sometimes biscuits.

Chapter 11

The West 1871

The terrain they covered was anything but monotonous, with rocky hills and sandy marshes, and sticky mud to fine dust. When they reached the rocky overlook where the cyclone had overtaken them, they gave silent thanks for their deliverance. The trees had been set afire by the lightening, and the ones that escaped the fire were scraped away as if by some giant hand. Not even grass remained in long stretches of earth.

Settlements along the trail were usually only a trading post. Some would have five or six establishments. A stop at the public well would be a source of fresh water and directions to the next place. They would pull in and camp next to the store, or off a little way from the train. Occasionally they would stop at a farm where they could get fresh vegetables. Lindsey remarked, "We are eating better now than we did at home!"

They had turned south at Jefferson City, Missouri, and were following what was politely called the road to Springfield. They would not go that far south, but would turn west about fifty miles north of there and go to Fort Scott. They did not want to proceed into southern Kansas without first checking with the Army about the safety of the trails.

The Browns and the Bartigs became close friends as they visited each evening discussing various rumors they had picked up about outlaws like Quantrill and the James Gang. They had been assured that the Indians were no problem in Kansas anymore. Now the Sioux in Colorado and the Ute were something else, as were the Apache in New Mexico. Then they would tell their favorite story about a horrendous Indian raid "Not so long ago . . ." Margaret was not bothered by the talk, she had grown up hearing stories about Indians attacking and then what the white men would do to get back at the "savages." It all sounded like war and injustice for both sides and she prayed fervently that was all behind them forever. Margaret had tried very hard to raise her children free of those prejudices. "Hate only brings grief," she would tell them, "like the war." Besides she had heard that the missionary had been working with the Indians for many years now and found that they also believed in one God and had taken to Christianity right well. All this confirmed her own belief that people are people. Each wanted a good life for himself and his family.

At one stop, after a long day of crossing one rocky hill after another, and finding the water of the well at the general store especially sweet and cold, they spread out bedding and decided this would be a good place to stay over a day or two. It was twilight when they stopped, but real dark when they ate and bedded down. It was so warm they lay out in the open on pallets without covers.

During the night the horses and oxen were stomping. Wakened by a strange itchy feeling, Margaret and Bennett sat up, but could see nothing. Margaret whispered, "I think we must be in some sand fleas!" She shook out her quilt and gown and moved into the wagon.

At daylight she woke them all with her screams! "Ticks! Bennett! Ticks! Lindsey, Jesse! Look at those ticks! Everywhere!" She brushed and picked frantically. "They are in everything! I'm covered and some are dug in! Help me!"

She picked up little John who had been sleeping beside her until she had screamed, now he, too, was screaming, for what he didn't exactly know. For over an hour they brushed, combed and picked each other and still would find ticks reattaching. They hitched and moved the wagons away from where they had camped.

The general store owner had come from his upstairs apartment to see the commotion. "See you folks have made acquaintance with the population of Lemon!" he said casually. "We call it that 'cause them ticks turned us sour on livin' here. Can't go no place else now so we try to live with 'em. I'll sell you some kerosene to soak rags in and tie around your ankles and wrists. That's one way to ward them off. Another is using sulfur powder, but I'm all out of that. Sulfur's not so hot on the skin and it's good for chiggers too."

"What is a chigger?" Bennett asked testily.

"Oh that's a little bug you can't see but he'll eat a hole in your hide bigger than he is and spits in a poison that makes a welt and itches like crazy! Only one thing worse and that's a 'No see 'um. It's the same thing, but it flys!"

"Gnats?"

"Something like a gnat, yes sir, not quite."

Bennett paid for the kerosene and went to work making oily strips of cloth to bind up with. They used rags to wipe down the animals after the boys had brushed and combed them. He was not so confident that the kerosene would kill the nasty blood suckers.

157

It didn't stop the itching much. They pulled out that morning not even stopping to make a meal. Their only thought was to escape the plague of ticks.

Day after long hot day finally brought them to Fort Scott.

Little Jacob peered out the back of the wagon and announced to Margaret, "Ma, what's those darkies doing wearing blankets when it's so hot?"

"Hush Jacob!" she would explain later.

The Indians were camped just outside the fort in a few brush and stick huts. Margaret, Lisa Brown and Dolly Bartig all stared as they passed by and were stared at in return.

"I suppose we look as strange to them as they do to us." Margaret remarked when they stopped.

"Does it make you nervous to see there were only men and women?" Lisa asked, "There are no children." They felt better inside the walls of the fort but learned that they could not stay.

The men went to talk to the commander, who told them, "Rest assured gentlemen, these are Osages back from Washington. They have just made a historic bargain. They have bought deeded land in the Indian Territory. They are getting ready to resettle. They sold their land in Kansas back to the government. They are very progressive, now, instead of taking a government "gift" of land, they want a white man's deed and they are willing to pay for it. Just like civilized people."

Bennett, Ed Brown and Al Bartig motioned the wagons to follow them to a camp ground on the west side of the fort. They stayed for five days. They not only needed the rest, but the animals needed to fill up. Grazing was dry now. July had been like a drought and the black jack and cedar trees so thick there wasn't much grass. They were surprised at the abundance of

158

grass around the fort considering the army stock, the Indians and travelers, too.

Lindsey walked around to the Indian Camp, taking Little Jacob and John with him to show the Indians he was friendly.

An Indian man, looking to be about Lindsey's age, approached and could speak English. Lindsey tried to pass the time of day. The Indian didn't move, nor speak, but still he looked friendly and a glint of amusement showed in his eyes. Lindsey started to move away and the young man said, "You gonna be rude and leave?"

Lindsey said, "What? Why?"

"My name is Strike Axe, in your language. You do not know my language nor my customs and you plan to leave in ignorance."

"Well," Lindsey replied, "I can't learn much if you don't talk to me."

"You don't keep quiet to listen!"

They both laughed together, and they quickly became comfortable with one another. Lindsey stuck out his hand to shake with Strike Axe and said "Touch."

"To say, to say." Strike Axe repeated.

"Teach me?" Lindsey asked, and they spent the next several hours, with Little Jacob listening to the strange words and customs being patiently explained.

"Many of our people would have nothing to do with you, but I know we will be surrounded and outnumbered, and if we are to live, our leader, Pawhuska, has said we must buy this land in the territory and learn to live in harmony. Otherwise we will all be gone from the Earth forever."

Without ceremony, Strike Axe removed a beaded arm band and casually offered the beautiful artwork to Lindsey. "A token to remember our meeting."

159

Lindsey was touched, for he realized the band probably meant more than just a decoration. He took out his own ivory handle pocket knife, knowing now he was expected to be unselfish and exchange gifts, and wondering in the back of his mind what his grandfathers would think of giving an Indian a weapon? Strike Axe was pleased both with the gift, and the fact that his new friend understood the Indian gift ritual. As Lindsey left he said, "I must go now, and if you are to be our neighbors, I hope you will be the one closest."

The little wagon train pulled out and headed southwest along the railroad tracks. They would follow them all the way into Parsons, Kansas. Margaret rejoiced! "We can pick up our furniture and we shall only be one more week out of Cedar Vale! Oh glory! I'll set up my bedstead and sleep in it even if it's right on the open prairie!"

Chapter 12

Arrival

They arrived in Parsons, the first of October, 1871. Three and a half months of living outside, out of a wagon virtually at an end. Dusty and dirty from the trail and sweltering in the awful heat, Margaret was momentarily elated to have reached a destination. They went straight for the depot to claim their freight.

The station master took their claim tickets and looked blank. He shoved them back and said, "Don't have any freight like furniture on this dock."

Bennett patiently explained. "We shipped about four months ago, perhaps it has been put into a warehouse. They knew we would be a while before claiming it."

"Nope, no warehouse here, just the depot."

Margaret asked, "Could it have arrived and someone claimed it?"

"Wouldn't know about that, ma'am. Lots of freight comes in here and it goes out with a claim check. I wouldn't know your furniture from someone elses."

Bennett was getting agitated now, "Look here, would you trace it? Perhaps it was sent to another depot. We have claim checks, surely no one else could claim such a large amount of furniture without proper papers."

"I'm sure I wouldn't allow such a thing, mister, but you see we have to store the freight right here on the premises and, well . . . sometimes it goes astray. Been

161

robbed a couple of times. Course we can check by telegraph and see if it went by mistake to Pierson, or some such place with a similar name. Check back here tomorrow and we'll see if it's out there somewhere."

The freight man tried to sound sympathetic, but he was not hopeful. Margaret sank to the depot steps and cried. Bennett just stood in disbelief. Margaret's tears released the pent up feeling of loss of her family, home, the fatigue and stress of the trip, and from fear of what lay ahead. They were starting over, and now the loss of her furniture, which she had found so comfortable and familiar through the years, most of it with beautiful memories from the past, was all gone. The beautiful carved cherry wood that gleamed to a mirror polish, the link or symbol to her roots. That furniture was the symbol of her family's unity. How could it ever be replaced?

She slowly arose from the steps and went back to the wagon. Staring bleakly at it, it came to her that unless they found the shipment of furniture, she was looking at their entire estate. Everything they owned in the whole world was right here contained in one small wagon — a life time of work.

Strangely, before ever leaving the depot, she knew the furniture had been stolen and it would not be traced. They waited a week trying to get some compensation from the railroad, only to be told someone should have traveled with the furniture to insure its safe arrival, or have someone meet the train at its destination.

Lindsey wanted to fight the station master, the next train engineer, anyone. Jesse was ready to back him up. Cool-headed Bennett talked them out of it.

The Browns and the Bartigs had moved on without them. Bennett had a new map from the surveyor's office and they were relieved to see Cedar Vale was only about 50 or 60 miles more. They would be there in five or six days.

"And then what?" Margaret asked dejectedly.

"Opportunity!" Bennett replied optimistically.

"It wasn't his furniture!" Margaret mumbled bitterly under her breath.

Before leaving Parsons, they were advised to buy necessities and stock up all they could as prices were high because Cedar Vale was beyond the railroad's reach and had to be freighted. They saw to it that salt, flour, sugar, and potatoes filled the wagon. When Margaret spied a can of cocoa, she had to have it at any cost. Lindsey bought lead balls and powder for his gun. Jesse bought a new pair of boots. And the shopping spree spread until they were all outfitted in new but sensible clothes.

They journeyed on into Sedan, and noticed that although they had heard liquor wasn't allowed in Kansas, each town had a wide open saloon and almost every man wore a revolver. It kept them from asking questions until they needed to stop to have the horses shod.

"That will be $2.00 for four horses," the blacksmith said.

"Damn, prices are higher out here," Bennett swore.

"I guess I'll take that remark from an unarmed man. You are joking, aren't you?" the blacksmith smirked.

Bennett asked, "Why do so many arm themselves here?"

"Rattlesnakes, most of them with two legs."

At Sedan they met the Bartigs and Browns again just as they were pulling out. They had camped only yards away. Broken wheels had slowed them down.

163

Pulling into Cedar Vale, they smelled a pleasant, refreshing breeze from the south. It was the sweet, spicy odor of cedar trees. The Caney River was lined with all species of trees, but the cedars were dominant. Nestled at the foot of what was later known as "Lookout Mountain" in a valley, sat a treeless village laid out in so called streets that ran northwest to southwest. Some of the streets were just staked out and cleared, while others more obviously traveled, with buildings of fresh new lumber along them. Most buildings were small and had porches. Others even smaller faced with high false fronts to make it appear to be a substantial business building. As they moved closer to the town there had been more and more farms laid out with fence corner posts made from rock which had been cleared from land.

They stopped at the largest building, a general store. Inside were slabs of lumber affixed to the walls containing merchandise stocked rather randomly. Another slab over barrels served as a counter, behind which a young, mustached man stooped. Beside him on the counter was a small wooden box marked "Post Office."

Bennett inquired about finding William Baird.

The man behind the counter put out his hand and introduced himself. "J. W. Marsh, sir, Welcome to Cedar Vale, hope you like it and stay with us. The Bairds? They live just in the next block, on the corner. It's the house with the new addition. They doubled its size."

He leaned over to Bennett and said in a confidential tone, "If you are looking for a place to stay, take the Baird's offer. The hotel is really just for men, even though the stage stops there, it doesn't accommodate ladies yet."

164

Bennett immediately liked this man. "Thank you for your welcome. We have come at William Baird's invitation, and our nephew Jarome Wilson's testimonies of opportunity. We do plan to stay." Bennett went on to say, "I thought it was less sparsely populated." He explained he was a bit apprehensive about the opportunities, now that he had seen what was here.

"There are plenty of lots and land, and it's by no means settled," J. W. reassured him. "It is just that this summer the whole nation is on the move. And when word got out that the Indians would move out in the spring, well everyone decided to move into Kansas! This summer's influx was something to see. I already have some competition from another general store, we have two doctors that have their own pharmacies, a blacksmith and livery, a mill for grain and another for wood, two boarding houses and a hotel! Actually don't be nervous about anything, you will see they are far from being really established."

Bennett left with some things to think about.

The Bairds welcomed them like long lost relatives. Margaret had not been really well acquainted with them in Illinois, but when she saw a familiar face after so long a time, she was overcome with delight. The Bartigs and Browns were introduced, and Mrs. Baird asked them to stay for "pot luck," which turned out to be buffalo steak, fried potatoes, biscuits and gravy with a beautiful pecan pie and whipping cream. "The first pecans of the year," Mrs. Baird proudly told them.

The women worked together after dinner doing dishes and the men toured the town with Bill Baird. They stopped at the saloon for a drink and met George Lapp, the saloon keeper, who was just as friendly as Mr. Marsh had been. He explained that each town made its own laws, he didn't sell liquor to Indians.

165

Margaret told of her experiences of the trip and was finally able to laugh, after she got proper sympathy, about the loss of her furniture.

Anna Baird empathized with her. "I lost my furniture in the Mississippi! Believe me, no matter how homesick I get, I can get over it by just thinking about having to recross that river!"

Mrs. Bartig chimed in, "We lost our other wagon over the side of a cliff. We recovered lots of our things, but there was no way to put the double load into one wagon. We left things just sitting beside the road. We lost the horses that pulled it."

This was the first time Margaret had heard about any of their losses and made her feel ashamed that she had so selfishly thought that she was the only one who had suffered.

Sarah Brown told of a family that had lost everything and continued the trip alone and on foot! They were going to Oregon. "I wonder if they made it? At least we don't have to worry about Indians scalping us anymore!"

Ellie and Al Bartig were from Ohio. They had no children with them. Edward and Sarah Brown newlyweds from Illinois, were expecting their first child. Margaret learned more about them that night than she had the entire trip.

Back at Marshes, the men talked about the land. J. W. explained, "Because of the dispute over the Kansas State line and the Osage Nation's boundary deeds are not available yet, but we expect to be able to file deeds real soon, after the Indians move. Now Bennett, here's what we are doing around here. The larger tract of land you buy, the cheaper it is per acre, right? So we are all signing up privately here on this agreement, just between us gentlemen, when they open it up for deeds we'll send a representative to make the purchase on the large south and east timber and north and west prairie tract. He will then deed the lots and farms to us as we have agreed."

Bennett swallowed hard, "I thought this was open for homesteading."

"It was, but that was years ago, all the homesteads are further west now. It is flatter and dryer out there than you can imagine. And so far from the railroads there isn't even a promise of progress yet! We are sitting on the next boom, though," he added optimistically. "The railroads have already come out to inspect for right-of-way. There are corridors between the Indian lands that the cattle can be driven through from Texas. We will ship right out of Cedar Vale one day." His excitement was contagious. Bennett found out that Jarome Wilson had over a thousand acres north of town. His father George always was a good speculator, perhaps this was a good idea.

This would certainly be a good trading center. The Indians were eager for anything sold in the stores, especially the blankets and shawls.

Anna Baird told the women, "The Indians do not own anything personally, and they really do not understand that we do. So if a group of Indians come to your house and start to take something, don't argue. Most likely he will use it and bring it back when he is finished. If you refuse to allow him to take it, you will be branded as selfish and bad and they will tease you by stealing you blind! But if you are generous with them, they will bring you gifts that will put you to shame! You see, they measure their wealth by how much they give away, not by what they have. It's foreign to us, but if you learn this quickly you won't have any trouble with them."

Ellie asked, "Do they steal horses and cows like I heard?"

"They hold all things in common. They don't consider it stealing. They take only enough to eat. Don't begrudge them. We have driven out most of their buffalo and the Osages have certain ones of their tribe who cannot eat deer because of their religion."

"Are there still renegades?" Sarah asked.

"The big Chief Pawhuska is peaceable and even has an Indian police force. Keep the liquor away from them and you'll have no trouble. If only we could do the same for the whites." She cast a glance at the dusty group returning from the saloon.

The visit continued past supper and into the cool of the night. They went to the wagons to sleep as usual, but this time the relief of having arrived allowed them to sleep more soundly.

At dawn the smell of a cedar fire and bacon frying, and coffee boiling, woke them to a pleasant, crisp, cool day. Anna Baird had started breakfast and called them as soon as she saw they had returned from the privy.

"You folks can wash up here on the porch and breakfast is ready when you are!" she announced.

Margaret was embarrassed that she had slept in, and was imposing on the Bairds for another meal. She now knew how pampered royalty must feel. She whispered, "Bennett, we have to pay them, there are six of us!"

"We will, Margaret. If they won't take cash we can give them a bolt of material, or something." Mentally checking their funds, "I'll work it out with Bill."

Margaret was overwhelmed at the beauty of the place. The turning leaves were a riot of color, from the red oaks to yellows and oranges of the elms. The white barked sycamores crowned with the light yellow halos in the sunshine, and stands of the cedars with fluffy cone of evergreen branches making the wind sing as it wafted the cedar odor toward them. It cooled like gentle fans. Hills rolled all around and the townsite snuggled in its valley below Lookout Mountain. From here they could see across the tree tops and the Caney River to a ridge of hills.

"Over there," Bill said, "is the Osage Indian Territory, just beyond that ridge. It's seven miles from here. Plenty of room for all of us." He sensed Bennett's reluctance.

Margaret hadn't, but now asked, "How do we pick out our place?"

Bill spoke up, "Most of it is staked out. Just find a place that doesn't have somebody else on it!"

"Oh, Bennett, could we build a house before winter?" Margaret was excited, "Will we buy in town or homestead a quarter section? Or both!" Bennett did not answer.

Lindsey broke into the conversation for the first time, "Is there work for a single man that's not ready to homestead?"

Bill replied, "Sure there is, Lindsey, your cousin Jarome Wilson is looking for ranch hands. He's brought up some of those Texas cattle and is getting ready to ship them next week. You could pick up some work there, but I figured you'd stay and help your folks out?"

Lindsey shuffled around. He didn't know how much Margaret knew about the homesteading situation and he wasn't going to tell her. He didn't want to be a burden on her and wanted to make lots of money quickly. He'd have to work.

That evening they found a campsite by following the directions of Anna Baird, who hated to see them move from their place. "It is so good to have company. I just love feeding people. Do keep in touch. Let me know your plans."

Margaret, who had never been one to show much physical affection put her arms around Anna and told her, "Your warm welcome will keep me in good spirits for a long long time. I'm truly grateful."

The three wagons were together, but tonight they each made a separate fire. They all had some planning to do, now that they knew the lay of the land.

Bennett waited until the children were asleep then they discussed money, "We don't have a lot left. We'll have to replace the cow and chickens, I think, and we spent so much for the new wagon, horses, shipping the furniture." He looked at Margaret.

He went on, "We've lived off this money with nothing coming in for almost four months and now it looks like some of our plans are different. You see, I thought the land would be free and now it is going at a pretty good price. Oh, we'll make a profit if we'll speculate, but I'm speaking of what we can afford. Lindsey, I'd planned to homestead you a place and let you prove it up while I built a home on a corner of it, put in a cabinet shop, eventually build us a boarding house like your mother wants." Another glance at Margaret who was nodding her head. "We just don't have enough to do all we want to do. We have to decide what to do to survive this winter and the . . ."

Lindsey spoke out, "I'm going to work, Bennett. I'll pull my weight."

"Me, too, Uncle Bennett," Jessie added, even though his dreams of free land were dashed.

"Forty-three and starting all over with nothing," Margaret sighed. "Well, we did it before and we'll do it again. God doth provide and it came to pass. We'll

170

go see brother George in the morning and see how he has faired out here. Maybe he'll have a milk cow."

George was living in a soddy on a quarter section south of town about five miles from his northern holdings. He came out to greet the new arrivals, and when he saw it was his sister and her family, his grin spread ear to ear.

"Hello, Margaret! Lindsey! Bennett, Jesse Pugh, I see you've come too! Hey, little guys, aren't you the handsome men! Hey, Lindsey, you being the proper big brother to these little fellows?" He drug up some stumps for them to sit on in a semicircle around his front door. "I'd ask you in, but I'm afraid we would not all fit!"

Margaret, realizing that this was George's house said, "George, what on earth are you living in? I've never seen anything like it. We passed these a few miles back. I thought they were for grain!" She gingerly opened the rough hewn door to peek inside.

"Oh, it's quite the thing out here and there are more out on the prairie west of here. Actually, they can be quite good for a home if they are carefully built, cool in summer and warm in winter, and keeps the weather out. What more can a body ask?"

Margaret saw a small dark room with what amounted to a campfire pit in the middle, a bed constructed from stout tree limbs protruding from the walls and attached to another one up-right which made the corner of the bed a sort of rope hammock that supported hay and a bed roll. Boxes stacked along the wall apparently served as table, dresser, hamper and cabinet.

"It's a place to live in temporarily, Margaret, until I can get a home built. I'm never inside except to sleep, anyway." He was becoming a little apologetic seeing

171

the disbelief in Margaret's eyes. "They are hard work to build. You have to cut this virgin sod and some of it is more than six inches deep and then haul and stack the bricks and mix a mortar of mud, but where there are so few trees — why down in Mexico, Margaret, they have permanent homes made this way."

Margaret asked, "Are you planning to build a home here, south of town? I thought your land was all north?" They had joined the others who had nodded approval of the practical soddy.

George said, "Yes, see that lumber stacked over there to season? We milled that last year and I've been waiting to find someone suitable to build the house. This will be our home and the land to the north is for cattle now and speculation in the future. When the railroad comes they will buy land, not just a place to lay the tracks, but railroad companies speculate too, buying tracts of land even far from the tracks and depots, and as the territory becomes populated, they will make money on the resale. Our cattle operations are hampered some right now, but I'm working it out. We brought in Texas cattle lately and because of the tick fever, they are bringing them in on the Chisholm trail to Wichita. We have a dip pit there, then drive them on over to our land here."

"Do you need a hand, Uncle George?"

"I sure do Lindsey. I can't trust some of these drifters. They'll go out to work your cows and tell you all the calves have disappeared, maybe they have and maybe they haven't. Sometimes the cowboys and the calves disappear together. It can be dangerous, Lindsey, are you sure that's the sort of work you want?"

"I'm up to it Uncle George, and Jesse here, too!" They slapped backs and shook on the deal.

172

Bennett had walked around the lumber piles. It had been milled as good as any back home. "You say you need labor to build a house, George? I have a couple of men in mind for helpers. We could build you a proper house in no time."

"Will you have the time?" George asked. "It will be a lot like father's house back in Olney. We'll start here," he unrolled the plans. "We will add on later. How about your accommodations for the winter? Do you want to build on to my soddy first? It's hard work, but it doesn't take long."

"We will think on that George." Margaret said, pleased that he was being so generous with them and not resenting them being here.

They shared news from home, some jelly Margaret had brought all the way, and of course the story of the trip. George painted her a verbal picture of his plans to have a cattle empire, support their parents, the children, the grand children, into their golden years! It was getting late and they said their good night and returned to camp. Margaret was sure now they would survive at least for the winter, and George has come a far piece from teaching school.

Early next morning Al Bartig and Ed Brown went with Bennett back to George's place, Lindsey and Jesse sleepily trailing behind. They agreed to work for $1.00 a day and a 12 hour day until the job was done. George left Bennett in charge and turned his attention to the boys. "We'll stop in town and pick up my wagon and supplies for the building project. I'm glad we're starting on that house. I'd hate to have to spend another winter in that hole in the ground!

As they rode George filled them in on a little history about the trouble with the farmers and the cattle. "You have to watch those dumb cows now, boys, because

173

they started making us pay for damages and that could ruin an outfit! We have a 'Line Watch' too. There are border patrols that watch for cattle being sneaked over the Territory line. You must pay heed to them, because they are keeping the tick fever out, which is very important or we all will end up in ruin."

Lindsey and Jesse had brought their bed rolls and were looking forward to their first real man-sized jobs. George said, "Boys, I'm not going to tell these cowboys you are relation. They may find out later, but it would go hard on you if they knew, and you're green anyway. You just keep your noses clean, your eyes open and be willing to learn. I'll let you know when it's time to come home."

Since all their best laid plans went awry after they arrived, Bennett and Margaret could do nothing but live one day to the next and take any opportunity that presented itself. Life in the wagon took on a routine. Margaret's day began with braiding her hair into a coil and dressing inside the confines of the wagon. She would then take the chamber pot down stream to dump and wash. Back at the wagon she would stow the pot, grab a bucket and hike upstream for water for the coffee pot. Now she could drop the hinged table, lock the legs in place and go retrieve the butter and milk from the stream where it was kept to cool.

Taking down her pans and a bowl, she started stirring up biscuits. They were placed in a greased dutch oven snuggled deep into the coals of the fire. She balanced another skillet between two rocks and filled it with bacon strips that she had sliced thick from a slab wrapped tightly in cheese cloth. The aroma of coffee, biscuits and frying bacon woke the children. Bennett stirred also and quickly dressed and began to get ready to leave for work.

"You do all this with such ease, Margaret, you can make a home out of the very air," Bennett said.

She was pleased with the compliment, but said, "I'd rather make one inside four walls, thank you, with these boys to watch. I'm either going to have to tie them to the wagon or teach them to swim! And I can't swim!"

"We'll be moving out to George's place as soon as he gets the well dug and you won't have to keep pulling them out of the creek. The soddy is almost finished. Wait till you see it."

After Bennett left for work, Margaret and the boys would tidy up, collect wood for the ever needed fire, and set out to inspect the traps that they had set the day before for small game. Today she didn't find anything in the traps, but had to reset one trap.

When they returned to the wagon, they heard a commotion inside. Margaret grabbed her walking stick as a club and lowered the wagon tail gate. The noise startled a raccoon rummaging in their boxes and they saw each other at the same time. Margaret let out a startled cry, the coon squealed and ran out right over the top of Jacob's head. He, too, squealed and laughed, and tried to whirl and catch it, but he wasn't fast enough. Breathless and heart pounding, Margaret suggested, "Well, that's enough excitement for today, let's go fishing." They needed something for supper. They were all very serious about their efforts and by noon they had fish, caught, cleaned and fried. Some Margaret made into chowder, letting it simmer over the fire so it wouldn't spoil.

After the noon meal, Margaret would have time to go over to visit Sarah and Ellie. They had pretty much the same routine and now was the time for relaxing, quilting, knitting for winter, sewing or whatever project was at hand while they talked. It never occurred

175

to any of them they could just sit, but they were brought up to understand that 'idle hands were the devil's workshop,' and no one with any self-respect would be idle.

On a wash day they all went to the creek together so they could help each other wring and hang the clothes. The wind was a help as well as a problem here in Kansas. It would blow out the wrinkles, but it could also blow away the clothes if not careful. Some of the white things would be spread out on the grass, and anchored with rocks. They sun bleached beautifully spread out like that.

When Margaret baked, she made enough for Sarah and Ellie so she could trade out milk, eggs and butter. Delicious breads, cakes and pies were started from her yeast jar. She had to feed the jar a little sugar every morning. Everything was baked in the dutch oven, one at a time. Pies were made from the fruit bought along the Missouri trail and sun dried in the mesh net bags hung between the wagon stays. They had apples, peaches and apricots. Also, stored away in cotton socks, were prunes and raisins.

The weather eased more into winter from day to day. Margaret was always worried about the children catching the croup or pneumonia on the cool days because, as most boys, they would not stay "bundled up". The occasional rain was good for the men's work. It softened the ground and made digging sod blocks for the soddy easier. As they heaved and hauled the bricks into place, Bennett longed for the time they could work with lumber building George's house.

They converted George's soddy into a much larger room. George had stayed away on business all this time and Bennett began to wonder how he would feel when he saw all the ground that they had to dig up for the sod house. It was almost an acre. They had started where George's new house would be. Digging the foundation would be easier now.

Men from town came to dig the wide, deep well, and Bennett marveled at the speed and skill of the masons laying brick from deep inside this hole to the surface. This was a special talent and these men were much in demand. Folks from town came out to watch the process, admire the well, and taste the water. They also gave Bennett advice about his building, offered to help, but mostly content to chat and get acquainted, and see what was going on.

Ed and Al opted to stay at the creek for the winter when the soddy was finished and Margaret and Bennett moved in. Margaret hated to leave the companionship of Sarah and Ellie, but she was delighted with the soddy. Compared to the wagon, she seemed more secure when she was able to shut a door to the outside. She even had two windows with wood shutters. Opened they created a draft to cool the room quickly after dinner. Bennett put up their little wood stove from the wagon. It was small, but it only used a small amount of wood. They had two sturdy beds made from the jack oaks located south of George's land, and a table some what crudely crafted. They used George's stumps for chairs. The food barrels were brought in, the storage barrels and trunks were stacked outside and covered with one of the canvases from the wagon. Bennett pointed out that now the wagon can be used for hauling lumber, and fire wood that will be needed for winter.

Chapter 13

Cedar Vale, KS

The routine did not change much except now, with the privacy of a bedroom, Margaret felt like a bride again and she and Bennett could make love as passionately as they were both capable. The isolation at night both from the neighbors and their children made them cling to each other as if they were the first two people on earth, both emotionally and physically. They were the whole world to one another at that special moment, and passion was enhanced as never before. After she had weaned Little John and become used to the outdoor work that had hardened her muscles, her body defied her forty-three years.

The actual work on the main house was underway. The men tried hard to finish the roughing in quickly so they could do the finish work inside out of the weather. The most difficult part was hauling rock for the foundation. They had to go south about five miles to cut sandstone, chisel it into blocks and haul it back. They used no mortar but fit the stones carefully together. This was as much a craft as was that of the masons who did the well, but Bennett thought nothing of it. He too was getting rock hard from the labor. He felt good, except for his knee, and was making plans out of this opportunity, determined to make a good life out here in spite of starting from nothing. After all that was what the West was all about.

Storms came and went all during the fall. There

were heavy rains, lots of wind and the soddy leaked some, but no matter, it was still better than the wagon. Mice moved in, big ones. Margaret swatted them with brooms, and even swept them out the door. She was sympathetic in a way. They were also seeking shelter for the winter, so were spiders and snakes, all kinds of varmints bored through the sod and came in to claim a corner until she discovered them and drove them out. Margaret became a fanatic about cleaning every corner every day. The food had to be locked tight in the barrels and the barrels themselves inspected for holes. otherwise they would also be hungry by spring. Not having a garden this year had left them strapped for food supplies. Things were so costly this far west, and they had to use cash money for everything. Not much would be set aside for rebuilding their dream.

During a storm Lindsey arrived, wet and cold. Staggering in, he paused to kiss his mother. Margaret drew back in surprise. "Lindsey you're drunk! What on earth have you been doing? Where have you been?"

"Ma, we got a day off. We been to a party!" He shouted, not able to hear himself, "Old man Weber makes good whiskey. Not as good as Grandpa, but good enough." He negotiated to the bed in the corner and sank into the featherbed, "Ah this is heaven Ma, I been sleeping on the ground for . . . years! Good to see you Ma."

"Lindsey, I'm glad you are home, but you could have come home sober. What will Little Jacob and John think?" But she was talking to a sleeping body. In spite of her annoyance and disappointment, she looked lovingly at her son. He was filling out across the shoulders and had a stubble of beard. She could see a likeness to Ezra. How she would love to cradle him in her arms once again, like she had when he was small.

179

"Hi Ma, who's here?" Her reverie was broken by the little boy's voice she almost thought was Lindsey's.

"Jacob? Look at you! Where have you been to get so dirty? Hush Lindsey's here and he's asleep and so is John." Little Jacob whispered back, "I found a hole Ma, a big hole and it's got little kitties in it. Little yellow kitties!"

Margaret blanched, "Don't you go back again Jacob. Those kitties have a great big mamma and she'll hurt you bad! Beside that, the hole could have caved in on you. You hear? Stay away from that hole." She hated to dash his joy, but the fear of her little one in danger was too much. She gave him a dipper of water and thought of the well. "Stay away from all holes!"

Little Jacob sat beside his big brother quietly and patiently waiting for Lindsey to wake. Margaret tended the fire and the stew.

Another mouse ran behind the wood pile, Margaret picked up a piece of kindling and slapped at it and missed.

"Missed, Ma." Jacob said matter of factly.

"I know, Jacob. I've missed them all, we're getting over-run since the cold hit. They burrow right through the bricks. I plug the hole and they make another one, you'd think we built this house for them!"

"We need to trap them like we do the rabbits."

"That's good thinking, Jacob, why don't you do that for mama." Maybe that will keep him busy during the rainy spell, she thought.

Lindsey woke when Bennett came in for dinner. Bennett smelled the booze, but said nothing. "So, Lindsey, what is going on out on the range? Where is Jesse?"

Lindsey's face reddened and stuttered, "Jesse's in town. Jesse stayed over. Ah . . . ahem, we partied a

180

little and he stayed with . . . ahem, friends." Changing the subject, "I picked up a letter for you." He dug in his pocket and gave Bennett the rumpled water stained letter. "Mr. Marsh said to apologize for the letter, but the rats got in his post office box and took everything, they even ate a packet of stamps and he had to dig the mail out of their hole. Some of it got wet. He sure is sorry, kept apologizing over and over. Said he's going to build a proper tin lined box and hope they can't chew through that."

Bennett was reading hungrily the news from home, "It's from Preston and Mary, they are well."

He handed the letter to Margaret. She turned her face away as she read. The pangs of homesickness swelled in her chest and stung her eyes. She swallowed hard, but she smiled. They were alive and safe. The letter was laid out on the table as a visible display of their family links all the way back home. The pleasure of hearing from them and knowing they were well covered her like a warm blanket. If they couldn't be here this was the next best thing. She read the letter aloud, then reread it over and over.

Dear Mother and Bennett, Brothers,

We are all well and pray daily that word will arrive again soon to assure us that you are still alive, well and happily engaged in a project of satisfaction.

Preston is talking of farming in the West and we are anxious to learn from you any detail that would enlighten us about that part of the country. Uncle George stopped over briefly to report you are living on his property until you finish building his house. Why are you not starting on your own building instead? Is Lindsey also working on Uncle George's house?

181

We send warmest regards and love along with love from Saphronia and John.

Inform Lindsey the Houser girl has announced her engagement to him. I hope he is aware of it!

Your Loving Daughter,

Mary

Lindsey's eyes welled with tears. "Ma, I gotta go home and I ain't got the money."

"You have to get home and you do not have the money." Margaret corrected, a ploy to keep from being overcome with the sympathy she felt for her son. Coughing, she continued biting her lip. "Well, for one thing you could go to work, buy a horse and go home, but then what? Your plans would be no further along than when you left. Right this minute write to Martha with your love and hopes and plans to work diligently at saving a nest egg." She paused leaning over him to emphasize her words, "Instead of going to a party." Her curt reply cut into Lindsey, but he could see Bennett's approving nod.

Margaret put out the pen and ink, brought out some paper carefully stored in a trunk. Even if letters did cost 50-cents apiece she had to write to Mary and Saphronia, and allow Lindsey a word to Martha.

"Mama, how do you know what marks to make on the paper so sister can tell what you say?" Little Jacob asked, reminding Margaret of her neglect to teach him how to read or write. Ashamed she thought how quickly we lose our sense of perspective and priorities out here. She said aloud, "I'll be teaching you very soon, son, we'll find you a school." Lindsey wasn't the only one getting lazy.

The next day Jesse came in looking pale and sickly. Margaret put him to bed and kept the children in front of the house in case he was contagious, but her suspicions were right. He was just sobering up and he snapped out of it after a long sleep. Bennett had no mercy and put both the boys to working hard, long hours for their keep.

Real winter was setting in and wood had to be cut. Lindsey and Jesse could do that and hunt and fish too. With them out in the woods the menu expanded to deer and turkey.

They even cut wood in exchange for a hog with the Holversons. They helped kill and butcher for Mr. Holverson, and he showed them how to smoke the hams and bacon in a mud kiln like the Indians used.

The first day of December a blizzard came about dark, out of the northwest. The hills about their little valley did little to divert the horizontal driving snow. As Margaret closed her shutters, she thanked God all of her family was safe inside in spite of the cramped quarters. It was snug and warm and dry. Outside one could literally not see their hand in front of their face. She comforted herself as usual with her favorite phrase, "And it came to pass."

Bennett fretted about the construction wood getting wet since the windows were not in yet, "Guess I'll just have to let it dry out again and redo if necessary. I sure can't stop anything like this and George hasn't made it back with the windows."

There was an urgent knock on the door. They couldn't believe anyone would be out on a night like this. The wind caught the door and Bennett staggered back. Without waiting to be asked in, four ghostly shapes of snow crowded inside.

"Ed and Sarah, Al and Ellie, you poor dears! What has happened to bring you out?"

183

Ellie sobbed, blowing on her frozen fingers trying with the rest of them to catch her breath.

"Please Margaret can we impose? Our wagons blew over, we were afraid they would break apart and bury us in the snow. Our horses ran off and we were exposed to the elements. Ed and Al thought we could get over here quicker than town and this way the wind was to our back, so here we are, praise be to God. I would have sworn a dozen times we were lost. It must be close to morning."

"No, it's only 10 o'clock." Margaret said as she poured them some hot tea, "Take off your wet clothes and hang them on those pegs over by the door."

"We brought our cow, thought if she died we could eat her, no shelter back at the creek either."

Bennett jumped up, "We'll shelter the cow. We'll put her in the new house. Good as a barn! And we'll have some fresh milk, if she hasn't gone dry."

"You'd best let me do that," Ed said, "She knows me, but I'll need another rope and man to hang onto it."

"What for?"

"You haven't been out there. I'm telling you, I could be lost between here and the house. I've heard of these blizzards, but never seen the like till now. I'll tie one end of the rope to my waist and you hold the other, then I'll feel my way back. May save us both. You won't have to come out looking for me."

"Makes sense." Bennett found his longest rope, bundled himself against the blast and they both were immediately gone into the swirl of storm. Although Bennett stayed close enough to touch the house, he was disoriented. Ed literally fell into the cow and headed into the direction he sensed the house would be. Luck held and he found the structure, but had to feel all around the side to find the steps. The docile cow

184

led up the two steps, across the porch where she and Ed both fell and flopped around slipping on the wet boards. Finding the doorway Ed wondered if the partially constructed house would withstand the wind unfinished as it was. Once again outside, he tugged on his life line and received a tug back. Hand over hand he pulled himself along down the rope blindly and back to the safety of his friend's home.

Margaret had made room for their company, glad that their friends were safe and that they had something to share. What a predicament it would have been with no soddy at all.

The storm continued for two more days. They talked, played with the children, cut strips and braided on a rug, fingers flying. The men got restless, and in spite of the ice and driving snow had to relieve their tensions by going outside to check on the horses and give them some oats to sustain them through the storm.

They shoveled snow away from the door to the outhouse and repeating the chore each trip out, as the snow drifted back over it quickly. Ed milked each morning and evening, relishing the warmth of his head against the cow's side and her warm teats in his hands. The milk was most welcome inside the house as well.

On day three of the blizzard the snow changed into freezing rain, encasing everything in a sheath of ice about an inch thick. Running down between the cut wood in the stack the whole cord became one large block of ice. Now, what should have been a simple task of bringing in wood became a chore of chipping out each piece with a pick, thawing it out and trying to make it burn wet.

In spite of the confinement and worry about the

stock, it was almost a festive time, everyone pitching in to keep clean and warm. They sang songs..."Billy Boy" and "Skip to My Lou," and played games. Lindsey learned to play dice with Bennett, who had learned in the war . . . a revelation for him at how much fun Bennett could be when he relaxed, opening up a whole new dimension in their friendship. Sarah starting teaching Little Jacob his letters and numbers. Margaret smiled at how patient she was with him. I'm too old to go through all that myself. I heard a new school started in October in Cedar Vale. As soon as the weather permits, I'll send him over there, she thought.

They discussed the spring cattle drive, building the house, the railroad coming, getting their land; and that constant tinge of worry, how long would the Indians remain peaceable and on the reservation?

The fourth morning the snow was light, but still falling. The drifts were up to the eaves of the soddy, but it had warmed considerably, so everyone came out to help with chores and get a breath of fresh air. Five men, three women, and two boys in such close quarters created considerable rankness. Everyone pitched in to sweep and scoop the packed snow and accumulated cow manure from inside the new building. A snowball flew, then another, then a full blown snow fight was underway, everyone laughing and giggling, running, ducking behind wood piles until they were exhausted.

Little John had followed outside to join the laughter and fun. Not being able to see over the drifts he had climbed up onto the edge of the well. Dancing with delight, he fell unseen by all except a blanket-wrapped Indian who had also been attracted by the noise. Silently he lowered the bucket, the child grabbed onto it. He was raised up, grabbed by the arm, sputtering, when Ellie spied them standing there, crusted with

186

snow. Not realizing what had happened she screamed alarmingly, and pointed to the apparition holding Little John by one arm.

They had all frozen at the instant of the scream and the Indian grinned, removed his blanket and wrapped the dripping, freezing child as Margaret ran to gather him up. Her heart pounding, she backed away, not sure yet why this man had her child in the first place nor what he wanted of them.

The Indian looked cautiously from face to face, "Fall," he said pointing to the well. He continued to grin and indicated with gestures that John had slipped and fallen into the well and how he had pulled him out. With mutual understanding grins and gratitude poured from the men. The women kept their distance and eased into the house. Margaret shook out the blanket and returned the tightly woven, colorful wool cover to Bennett who passed it back to Drum Maker with a handshake. Then they listened as Drum Maker tried to communicate his problem by sign. Lindsey remembered some of his Osage words and finally realized that the Indian needed help for a companion.

Wary because this man was so far north, and not sure it wasn't a lure to get the men away from the house, they parlayed a while. Jesse and Lindsey finally said they would go with him. They told Bennett and the others, "You stay here with the women and surely it is safe. Why would he have helped Little John only to massacre him later!" The young boys were annoyed with the older men's lack of trust.

Riding double with Lindsey, Drum Maker directed them down the path he had made through the snow and around the drifts. Lindsey wondered at the courage to travel so far on foot during such a storm. The path was evident at first because the wind had about

187

stopped, but as they went on it was difficult to pick out the way. Lindsey realized Drum Maker had walked about two days, maybe three. Had he eaten?

Lindsey pointed to the saddlebags where Drum found some ham and biscuits that Margaret had stuffed in as they were leaving. He laughed, ate and appreciatively slapped Lindsey on the back.

Pointing to a small patch of trees, Drum gulped down his biscuit and dug out another, but instead of eating it he dropped off the horse, ran to a pile of snow covered brush and started digging. Lindsey and Jesse ran also to help. They uncovered an Indian brave inside the brush shelter.

"Strike Axe!" Lindsey exclaimed.

Strike Axe grinned sheepishly and spoke weakly, "Friend Lindsey. God has brought you a long way in bad weather to help me. Welcome to my home." He waved a hand and a look around his little brush cave. "Drum Maker protected me before going for help." Drum Maker shoved the biscuit at Strike Axe who ate it slowly, relishing his first food in four days.

Checking his friend for wounds Lindsey found the flesh of his left leg torn open above the knee.

Strike Axe explained, "I foolishly ran my horse into the trees after a deer. The tree attacked me." He laughed, "I don't know who won, the tree or the horse, but one is over there and the horse is gone. Drum straightened the bone and I don't remember much until today.

Drum said, "Two horses won. Both gone in the blizzard and also the deer." Lindsey pieced the events together in his mind.

The problem at hand was to move Strike Axe without disturbing the broken bone or causing him too much pain. Drum was already busy building a travois.

Lindsey marveled at his dexterity and swiftness using a blanket from his own back and strips of leather from his fringed breeches, he tied through the tightly woven fabric to the poles. Without asking, he used Lindsey's rope for harness to hook the affair to the front of the saddle.

"How far is it to your camp?" Lindsey asked.

"No camp close." Drum replied matter of fact.

Strike Axe nodded, "Our winter camp too quiet, Lindsey, and we were anxious to learn our new territory before spring, so some of us went off in different directions to learn the land. We are scouts. Many days from camp, we were caught by the weather. If we could find our horses, we could eat one and ride home on the other." He looked over at Lindsey's horse.

"Get that notion out of your head friend, you're not going to eat my horse yet!" Lindsey grinned.

The only solution was to take both Indians back to the soddy. Besides Mom could poultice Strike Axe's wound and heal him.

The trip was slow, but thanks to the depth of the snow, not too bad on the patient. They hailed the house and people came out into the bright sunlight from every window opening in the new house. Work was going on inside, and they welcomed the fresh air and sun even though it was nippy. Without the wind it was rather nice.

The travelers had killed several rabbits and Drum had raided a squirrel's den of its pecans, so they didn't arrive famished. Margaret was taken aback by the challenge of two more mouths to feed. Sarah and Ellie stood together stiffly, and the men instinctively gathered in a protective manner.

Lindsey broke the ice. "Look here, Mother! My friend Strike Axe! You met Drum Maker. He saved

189

John's life." He allowed the words to soak in. "They need a little help."

Margaret smiled and added, "My pleasure."

The Indians became uncomfortable as they sensed the awkwardness and faced a custom strange to them of being introduced to the women.

They both grinned as they nodded, to demonstrate they were there as friends, and stretched out both hands, palms open to show friendship.

Margaret warmed quickly when she recognized the man who had saved her son from the well, "You are certainly welcome here," she said through a genuine smile. "We were worried about the drifts. What has happened? Jesse, are you alright?"

Everyone started talking at once. Lindsey explained about Strike Axe's injury, and Margaret inspected the leg. He looked familiar to her but she was not yet aware of him as the person with whom Lindsey had spent time at the Fort.

Strike Axe stoically allowed her to probe and clean the wound. He sensed that she knew what she was doing, besides he was now running a fever and he really didn't care. Drum Maker watched from a corner of the room. Everyone else had stayed outside.

Bennett turned to Lindsey, "Why are you bringing two Indians outside of their reservation? I know they need help but you should have taken them home!"

Lindsey explained the distance and reminded Bennett that the Osages are not on a reservation.

"Same thing. They are supposed to stay on it!"

"Well, they're not," Ed broke in, "and there is no way we are going to stay and impose on you any longer. Bennett, we'll be going to see if we can round up our horses and right our wagons and set up camp again. Since the storm is over we can make it now."

"Why not bring your wagons over here while you work on the house?" Bennett said with a look at the soddy.

Ed understood. There was still mistrust about having Indians around. Even one with a broken leg. "We'll see what we can do."

Lindsey called after him, "Tomorrow we'll help look for your horses, Mr. Bartig."

Right after dinner the Browns and the Bartigs gathered up their things and started through the slush for their wagons. Margaret protested their leaving. As crowded as it was, she hated to see her friends leaving the soddy to live in a wagon on a creek bank. Besides, she'd be losing the only female companions around.

Next day, Lindsey, Jesse and Drum saddled horses and made the rounds of nearby ranches to look for the Bartig's and Brown's animals. They found them at the Connors' place next to Halroyd's, where they had instinctively gathered with other horses in the Connors' corral.

Mr. Connors smiled and welcomed the boys. "I knew someone would want them back!" Then he told them of Severt Hansen's death. "Yes, sir, caught out in the blizzard! This is the first death we've had here. Guess every where's got to have a cemetery, and now Cedar Vale will have to start one. Sure was a bad storm, boys. Killed cattle, too."

They did not know Severt Hansen, but figured he was with the bunch of Norwegians who had come in from Chicago back in '69. Most had left.

After passing the time of day with Mr. Connors, they learned that Ned Wagner had been teaching school there since October and he invited Lindsey to bring his little brothers in next year. No one ques-

191

tioned Drum's presence, but kept an eye on him around the horses.

Mr. Connors whispered to Lindsey as they were mounting, "Keep that Indian ahead of you as long as you have these horses, boy, you want to be sure and get home with them."

Lindsey laughed because here was a man he didn't even know turning horses over to him while at the same time distrusting an Indian just because he was an Indian."

"Yes sir, thank you for the advice, sir!" was all he said aloud. They headed for the Bartig's camp.

Christmas neared and Little Jacob asked about a Christmas tree like they had in Olney.

"Oh Darling, where would we put a tree? There is just no room in here," Margaret explained.

He was disappointed because he knew there would be little else for Christmas. He saw mother inventorying the beans and cornmeal and other foodstuff to calculate if it would last the winter. And he also knew there was nothing to buy at the two general stores beyond food and hardware. Feeling sorry for himself he pouted.

Strike Axe announced to no one in particular, "The Birth of Christ is an event to celebrate. There are many ways to do this. Our priest also put up a Christmas tree with a manger beneath it and statues of white people around the baby. They were not large statues, but they did not fit inside the church so he put them outside the door of the little church. It looked different than we had been taught, but the meaning was the same. A tree is good. The priest taught that it is a symbol of Christ. Evergreen means *everlasting*. Christ is the tree, we are the branches. He explained the tree is also the instrument of our salvation. We understood this. It fit with our own idea of the Great Spirit and how our Spirit lives on after the body dies. Many of my people were baptized Catholics."

Margaret jerked her head around unconsciously. She stared anew at Strike Axe. She had assumed he was heathen, now he reveals he is worse. He is Catholic! She fought to conceal her surprised look, but not much escaped the notice of Drum Maker.

Drum Maker proudly said, "My family has been Catholic since my grandmother lived in Ohio as a child. Her father could read the Bible!" Then he said to Strike Axe in Osage, "Let us make a crib for the children." Without waiting for an answer he left the house. About an hour later he returned with some cedar wood about three inches in diameter.

Margaret had said no more about the conversation but had a lot to think about. She prided herself on her lack of prejudice, but the old stories she had heard as a child about Catholics were about as horrifying as the ones she had heard about Indians. She knew these Indians were not the heathen, devil agents, murderers, nor crazed for blood and white women. She had never quite believed the gossip, but she wasn't so sure about Catholics. They sort of understood to stay aside with their own kind and she had not ever known any, but she finally reasoned the Indians converted to Catholicism because the priests got to them first. As soon as they found out about the priest burning people for heresy, and nuns killing their babies, they will change. "I wonder what they are up to?" She watched them over her knitting.

Jacob forgot to pout and also watched fascinated. Strike Axe welcomed something to do and quickly set about peeling the hairy bark from the wood. He began telling the story of the angel visiting Mary. Margaret was as spellbound as Little Jacob, and now awake from his nap, John. After he told of Joseph taking her as his wife, the story stopped and so did the whittling. "Now, you must help." Strike Axe directed Little Jacob to clean up the shavings but to save them.

After dinner the scene was repeated and the story continued. It was more elaborate than that told in the Bible because Strike Axe would embellish the story with Indian lore as well as some of the historical customs and details the priest had taught them, making the story long and meandering at times, but always the whittling stopped with the story leaving everyone feeling quietly at peace.

Margaret and Bennett had been busy fashioning gifts when the children were not around. So when Christmas Eve arrived, the story finished, and the oiled cedar statues were placed beneath a cedar tree by the front door, a manger was built and filled with the shavings, and the last figure, the infant Christ Child, placed gently in by Little Jacob, who exuded a sense of wonderment and understanding.

Margaret was grateful to these two strangers, now friends, who had enriched them all this Christmas as no church service ever had. Christmas morning the wooden horse and buggy and wooden tops were also in the crib and Margaret brought out new bulky knit sweater jackets for everyone. The children knew the toys were for them, of course, and were surprised to have anything at all.

Bennett went over to invite the Bartigs and Browns over to dinner and they came reluctantly. Ed said, "Bennett, I'm not sure about bringing my wife around those heathen men." This gave Bennett the opportunity to tell him all about the past few days, the Bible stories and the whittling of a crib scene. They marveled together that these men were so well versed about Christianity — but Catholics? Would they have mass? "Not likely," Bennett said. "They need a priest for that I'm sure."

Lindsey provided the wild turkey, Margaret made the cornbread stuffing and at Drum Maker's suggestion, added pecans! They still had potatoes and carrots kept fresh in straw and buried back in the hillside barrel, onions dried had kept well too and although there wasn't much else but the gravy, they ate like kings. The presence of the crib inspired them to sing hymns and to their surprise, Strike Axe and Drum Maker knew some of them, too. Sarah and Ellie lost all fear of the Indians and the men even included them fully in their conversation after dinner.

It turned out, as Drum Maker learned more English, he was quite the story teller and told about the ferocious storms that would sweep away the very grass and trees. Illinois was not without a tornado now and again so they believed every word. He also told about the sweeping fire that was needed each year to give the buffalo grass room to grow. He explained that it was deliberately set to burn off the loco weeds and stinging nettles, then the grass would breathe the fresh air and the sun could beckon out the grasses that the buffalo and horses loved so well. He explained that the fire burned so quickly everyone in the way had to hurry to prepare shelter, like the soddy or make a fire break with plowed ground. People and animals could be saved. The buffalo knew when the grass came up and returned only when it was ready. They grazed it out and moved on. It would now be difficult to get enough meat because the herds would move out of their Indian Nation and they could not follow as they had before.

"We will have to hunt white beef." They laughed, more than half serious.

February approached and it was still cold, but no more heavy storms. Mr. Marsh came out to say the deal was all set for Mr. Davis to buy the land and he needed some more money for the trip for the deed. Lindsey was excited as he signed up for his plot, and Bennett was heartened that it was not taking as long as he had thought it might.

"See you in town on February 12 to transfer the deeds to our names." Mr. Marsh waved as he rode away to tell the others.

With tea and poultices Margaret had staved off infection in Strike Axe's wound. She then kept him busy winding yarn, beating cakes and telling stories to John and Little Jacob. Drum Maker made himself useful by bringing in fresh meat or fish every day and proved himself very adept at learning some carpentry and helping the men with the building. He was fascinated by the tools and wanted to learn each one. Bennett's cabinetmaking especially fascinated him. His language skills also improved and everyone adjusted to their presence. More than that, they were becoming good friends.

Margaret marked off the days on the calendar and when February 12 came, they all rode into Cedar Vale.

Drum Maker stayed with Strike Axe at the soddy as he was just now hobbling around with a crutch getting some strength back after the long forced inactivity.

Everyone else crowded into the wagon in spite of the breeze that made the crisp wind bite into their faces. Even that did not dampen the joy of being out of the house and actually going to get the deed to their very own property. Hopefully Lindsey could get some, too.

A crowd was already assembled at J. R. Marsh's General Store and as they were beginning to filter inside a tense silence fell as Mr. E. W. Davis stepped up beside J. R. "Gentlemen! Thank you for coming today. I have had a long journey from Parsons, but I wanted to personally assure you that each and every investor will receive his money back. You will not be deeded any property today, but it will be for sale again soon at an announced date."

He cast his eyes to the floor and started to leave when J. R. yanked his arm and swung him half around. "Just what the hell does that mean?" Davis was startled as another man stepped in his way and as a group they crowded him back, voices rising to a roar as anger and fear set in.

Raising his one free arm, Davis regained their attention. "Gentlemen," he said assuringly, "I have your money. You will get it all today! You can then see me about purchasing the property you are on. You see, I have purchased several thousand acres from the railroad and I have the deed," he assured them. "As the owner, I will decide to whom I will sell and at what price. It is all perfectly legal!"

J. R. broke into the roar of the crowd, "You were supposed to buy that land for us with our money!"

"I did buy it for you!" Davis yelled back, "I'll sell it to you, but I did not use your money. I was able to get independent financing, so now the land is mine. However, I don't need all of it so I'm willing to sell some, at a profit of course."

The entire room moved forward again. Bennett had not felt such rage since the war. Anger in the crowd demanded action, and the small bulging room

197

gave them no room for action. Davis was bodily maneuvered outside. Margaret had never witnessed such potential for violence, and held the boys tightly. However, she too seethed within, feeling she was being robbed of what was rightfully hers once again. She stood at the door with Annie Marsh, neither speaking.

There were no blows, but a great deal of yelling and shoving toward the blacksmith shop where someone yanked the rope slack from the pay pulley and began making a noose. Davis was pale and finally realizing that these men would not be persuaded to see his point of view, he let them have the deed. On a keg top with three men still holding him tightly he signed over the document to the company.

Sweating in the cold, he kept saying over and over, "It was legal. I was within my rights, it was legal!"

Bennett spat as he looked at him closely, "It was legal, Davis, but it sure as hell wasn't right!"

Lindsey, Jesse and Bennett, along with the rest of the crowd, were still agitated and ready to get things settled. Back inside the store a committee was elected to file the deed to the town company, previously having signed the company contract on the SE 1/4 and the E 1/2 of the SW 1/4 and the NW 1/4 of Section 11. They no longer trusted one person to do it, so on the following day, February 13, 1872, at Sedan, Kansas, it was duly recorded. The town was official. Now they could begin to build in earnest. They were real property owners now, as each cleared his debt to the company and filed his separate deed. Lindsey, Jesse and Bennett each now owned a city lot.

A town lot wasn't much but it was property! How elated they all were on the trip home, "At least we won't be having feud fights over a town lot like some of these ranchers have had. Scholffstead is still having it

198

out with Doc Stewart, and Annie Marsh told me about a man named McClearning going to the penitentiary for killing a man named Jones. It's troublesome, all the violence."

"Unsettled is the word. Happens on every frontier," Bennett replied. "Things have to get settled some way and there's not enough law out here to do it in court. Our folks went through all this back in Ohio, and again in Indiana, but Margaret, I never want to feel that way again. That anger and rage, I guess I didn't realize what this land meant to me or how the fever of an enraged crowd could influence me."

Margaret patted his leg. "I felt it too, Bennett. It was terrifying to know I could have let that man's life be taken away today and have been content with mob justice."

Chapter 14

Strive to Survive

Spring awakened new activity. The warming sun provoked a house cleaning spree when suddenly there was an awareness of the stench of bodies, cooking, and dirty clothes, so Margaret started cleaning house with a passion.

Feather beds hung out on a line she put between the outhouse and the soddy. An iron tub of water boiled the bedding, the clothes, and everyone knew that spring baths would be next.

Strike Axe and Drum Maker took her actions as a signal to leave. With elaborate preparations, but not saying a word, they packed with one eye on Margaret. However, she did not discourage them. Although they had provided food and assistance through the winter it would be a great relief to reduce the crowding. As they mounted she handed them a tea towel wrapped loaf of bread, cheese and pecan muffins. Handshakes made the rounds, and Lindsey promised to visit when he went south.

Little Jacob and John were saddened by their leaving. These men had taught them to make snares and fish lines, and let them whittle with their knives when Margaret wasn't looking. Bennett was "loaning" them a horse thinking it better to do so than to have them think he was "cheap and selfish" and later, well who knows? Besides it was sort of payment for Drum's help during the winter.

Only a week had passed when a buggy came sloshing up the muddy ruts left by the last freight wagon. There was a joyous reunion with George. Dapper, dressed in eastern fashion and passing out gifts, he hugged his sister and the little boys. He marched around looking over the almost finished house and was very pleased.

"Furniture is on its way," and looking at Margaret, "and someone is traveling with it on the train."

She smiled. She had lived without it and survived. There was an unexpected sense of satisfaction in that. She had made do with a bare minimum and now having known the Indians, knew she could do with even less. Yes, there was satisfaction in self-reliance.

After supper George remarked about the town's flurry of building activity. "There's a whole wagon train of lumber and it looks like everyone is buying."

They told George about the trouble everyone had getting the deed from Davis.

"Well," he remarked, "at least you have a deed. I still have to "prove up." Of course the house and the one crop a year will do it for me. Now that the house is up the rest will be easy. My problem is getting my family out here. Jarome is ready but I want him to finish school. Elizabeth isn't convinced he is. And she doesn't want to move Mother Wilson again. We have settled in St. Clair County now and Margaret, it didn't help when you wrote home about living with the Indians! It scared Elizabeth to death!"

"Why, George, I thought it would ease her mind, they were as nice as they could be."

George was thoughtful awhile, "Margaret, I've been thinking. It will be awhile before Elizabeth comes out here, so why don't you go ahead and move into the new house, fix it up a little for us, you know, curtains and such. It will take Bennett a while to build your place, he'll need a shop, too. You'll be doing me a favor because this homestead thing requires me to live on this property for six months of each year. If you are here, who's to know the difference?"

Margaret smiled, "Dear George, you are feeling sorry for me in this soddy, and you don't need to. But I will accept your offer to live in your new house, if you think Elizabeth won't mind. However, do talk her into coming out. Mother will adjust, and it would be so great to have family close again."

George left for a week to round up drovers for the trip south for cattle. If they left now they would be back in the fall. Lindsey and Jesse would be going, but not as trail boss. That required someone with experience. They would not only have to know cattle, but men and how to lead them and how to settle differences. They would even have to know how to do battle with bandits, other drovers or anything the lawless territory could throw at them. They'd be better drovers if they could make peace like Jess Chisholm had done, but he was gone now, a man to remember and exemplify. Many a man tried to do that now. It was obvious that the Indian could not be shoved back any further west. They would all have to live together.

Margaret was amazed at the growth in town. Many new faces driving freight wagons, and things sold right off the tail gates. Bennett bought his lumber and started building his shop the same day, before the lumber was stolen or sold over again by a shyster. He had already set up a tent to live in temporarily.

Margaret was buying items to furnish George's house. A beautiful enamel topped kitchen cabinet; tables and chairs for the kitchen; material for curtains and some rods, even a bedstead. However, she kept to

202

the basics because she knew that Elizabeth would have some of her own things to bring from home. It was hard for Margaret to think of her own beautiful furniture that she had lost. She shook her head, at least we didn't lose a life, she reasoned.

They stopped by to visit the Bairds who were building on another guest room addition and found them so busy they could hardly stop to talk. Margaret came to attention when she heard Mrs. Baird say, "It's all getting out of hand. I'd sure like to find some experienced help. I have to tell these girls every little move to make twice to three times."

Waiting for a pause in the guest traffic at the boarding house, Margaret approached Anna, saying, "I used to own a boarding house, Anna, and now that Bennett is in town and the big boys are on a cattle drive, I'd like to be in town, too, where Little Jacob could go to school."

"Oh, could you? I mean, would you consider working? What a blessing. Oh, Margaret, sweet, sweet girl, you are an answer to a prayer."

Margaret was pleased to know that now she could contribute to the rapidly dwindling cash they had left. She also had a job where she could bring the little boys along.

Bennett wasn't very happy about his wife working again. He had dreamed about being the bread winner out here. However, looking around, he realized that on the frontier every woman worked side by side with their men folk, at any task needed from driving teams, herding cattle, plowing fields, building houses, and he even knew a couple of women out here alone, doing it all. This was truly a time of "pulling the wagon together." Listening to talk after church one Sunday, he even overheard some gossips saying, "A city sissy, she is. Can't even pump her own water. Humpf! Lot of good she'd be if we'd have to defend ourselves. She even hides when it thunders."

Margaret commuted to town in the buggy George left when he returned to Illinois. George being here, and her moving back into a regular house, made Margaret suddenly aware of her appearance, and she began to sew a new spring dress, patching her old one to work in. She bought some moccasins from the Indians and fell in love with them instantly. They were more comfortable than heavy boots, or the high buttoned, tight fitting, high heels, that were good only to look at.

Now she could get more involved in the community and return to church on a regular basis. Margaret once again bloomed. Working hard seemed to give her energy. She enjoyed the hotel as much as Anna Baird. People came and went and enjoyed food as good as they served in St. Louis. Anna was not stingy with the servings or the menu.

Bennett's furniture became popular and orders stacked up waiting for lumber. He was really razzed when George's wagon came to town with his Eastern manufactured furniture on it.

A very early hot, dry, spring kept everyone looking westward for a hint of rain to start the crops. Everyone planted gardens when it was warm enough, but gardens, too, depended on the rainfall. Tender shoots could be coaxed out of the ground by hauling buckets of water to them, but it was an impossible task to irrigate the whole garden that way. The little sprouts dried up and literally fell out of the ground. Hot winds followed as if to brush them away. Bennett cursed, "Seems like only weeds thrive in this weather." Still they must plant again and again. They had to have food.

Smoke drifted across the sky one morning off to the south, heading north. Curious town folks gathered. Smoke could mean many things, and none of them good. A burned home, or even a village, a battle, but as the cloud extended along the horizon and blackened a strange, ominous fear simultaneously gripped the community. Wild fire heading this way! None of them had experienced one before this, but remembered the old cowboy telling stories about the fierce heat-propelled fire that flowed across the densely weeded prairie faster than a horse could run, overtaking everything. The wind, he said, came before the fire and sucked the air from your lungs before the fire itself could touch you.

Wells were pumped furiously and buckets of water doused onto the sides of buildings, weeds yanked from around the foundations and blankets, rugs, and sacks set to soak in the watering troughs. Everyone was hoping that the fire would stay west of the Caney River.

Margaret and Bennett raced for the ranch and remembering Drum Maker's stories, hitched up a team and began to plow back and forth a strip of ground to the south and west of the house. He couldn't let the fire destroy the brand new house. The rock foundation would help. Margaret and the little boys packed water from the well and gathered the horses into the corrals on the north side of the house. They doused the brush that was close to the fences and pulled out what they could.

Suddenly upon them, a forceful gust of hot air blasted them almost to the ground. Bennett grabbed their hands, pulling and partly dragging them into the

205

soddy. They huddled in the far back side and listened to the roar pass around them. Smoke seeped through the cracks of the shutters causing them all to cough and gag. Momentarily they panicked, thinking of being baked from the oppressive heat as the breathing became more difficult, even through the wet towels over their heads.

It passed just about the time they felt they could breathe no more. The boys were crying and coughing, but the noise and the heat subsided telling them it was safe to peer out and see if the house had survived. They heard the horses whinny and knew they were alive.

Stepping out onto the charred ground, the crunch of hot blackened grass under their soft soled shoes. The house still stood. They raced to the corrals to see that the animals had survived unscorched, nervously trotting from one fence to another. The little family hugged each other for long minutes, grateful to have survived.

They had to go to their neighbors now and see if they had fared as well. In town there had also been a plowed strip. They found Anna, who silently pointed out angry town folks milling around, saying, "It's those Indians trying to burn us out."

"Yeah that's how the fire started. If we live through this, we oughta go wipe them out! They're sneaky, it's just like 'em to pull this stunt." Anna fussed, "These silly people don't even know whether the fire was set on purpose." She continued to explain the events that led up to the fire, "A fire watch was set up on Look Out Mountain, and when the fire jumped the river, the watchman rang his bell, the church bell was rung here in town, the children were all taken to the church basement where they had plowed extra ground for their protection. Everyone in town stood with buckets

206

and gunny sacks shoulder to shoulder, waiting. By the time the great gust of heated wind hit with a great force, they threw the gunny sacks over their heads instead of fighting the fire that raced in and out about the buildings. We turned our backs against the force and stood in awe as the fire raced over the earth like an invading sea. When we were released from the grip of the wind, we raced around town ourselves fighting and beating the small remaining spots of flames. A dry outhouse burned, some buildings caught, but were beat out. I was never so quickly exhausted in all my life!

"We brought out the children to reunite with their families, and cheers went up. Everyone was smut streaked and water soaked, but alive!"

Messengers had been sent out to warn the neighbors and some straggled in like Margaret and Bennett to join the spontaneous community street picnic and dance!

As some jugs were passed around to emphasize how grateful folks were for their escape from the fire, there was more talk about the Indians and getting revenge. Bennett's explanation about the Indian custom of burning weeds did not pacify as he had intended, but only confirmed their suspicions that they indeed may have been responsible. Bennett volunteered to go to the agency to talk if they would wait for his return before doing anything. "That Agent Gibson is building a house down at the White Hair Camp. We'll talk to them. Remember they will be our neighbors for a long time and they want to do business with us. Why would they want to burn us out? The Osages like the white man's goods."

"But look at our land now! Black as pitch, so dry it'll probably be nude of grass forever!"

A calm voice spoke out, "I don't know about that.

207

Up 'round St. Louis I saw a burn once that took the weeds and we still had a fine stand of grass. Besides, Silas, you was gonna plow it all anyhow, so what difference do it make?"

Silas, still angry, "I was gonna plow that green under for the ground nourishment, but there's no green out there now."

"Well if'n you wasn't so late plowin' it'd be done by now."

The arguments went on. Bennett saddled up and J. W. Marsh came over and mounted up too. "I'll go with you Bennett. It isn't good for one man to travel alone. Besides, I need to find out first hand if this was a peaceable thing or not."

"Yeah," Bennett replied. "My boys went out through the Indian Territory to Texas with an agreement with Gibson. I need to find out if they made it. Was it with the Indians or just the agent?"

They struck out to the southeast crossing of the Caney River, then south to Bird Creek which they followed. They camped two nights, sparing their horses and staying to the shade and protection of the trees. Early the third day they came into the camp called Pawhuska (White Hair), named for the grandfather of this Osage Chief who had started to scalp a British soldier and instead of real hair, he came up with a handful of white wig. The Indian wore the wig and was forever known as Pawhuska, White Hair. His descendants passed on the name to the present Chief.

This part of the country consisted of rolling hills and valleys, wooded with black jack oak. They stayed to the creek for guidance and were unaware of being followed. Like an apparition, two Indians suddenly appeared before them. Halting abruptly, controlling their instincts to resist reaching for their rifles, they raised their hands in the peace sign. The Indian braves pointed to the rifles and indicated they wanted them. The older Indian pointed to the silver badge on his shirt and again to the rifles.

Bennett looked at J. W. and asked, "Should we turn over our weapons to show them we mean peace, or . . . ?"

J. W. was uneasy, too. Were these renegades who might just turn and use the guns they wanted to murder them? Why do they wear silver badges? Did they kill a Marshal and take it off him? Aloud he said, "I guess we'd better cooperate, but no one is going to take my gun."

Ben said, "Suits me." In Osage he said, "No, we come in peace, but we must keep our rifles. We bring gifts for Gibson, to talk. Which way to Pawhuska?"

The two braves laughed at his attempt to speak Osage and after inspecting the contents of their saddle bags accepted them as an indication they came in peace. They pointed east and rode behind the two white men on into the Camp.

Surprised, J. W. and Bennett saw only a few round thatched huts near the trees along Bird Creek. They had expected a large village of people. Their escorts pointed to a large hill rising east of the creek and the trail that crossed to it. Atop the hill they could see for miles all around and the beginning of a sandstone quarry and construction of a house in progress. "This must be Gibson's place," J. W. offered.

Sure enough a man in white shirt sleeves, blue britches with high laced boots came out of the sandstone structure and with a purposeful stride came to greet them. "See my deputies found you. You come willing or forced?"

"Willing," Bennett smiled. "What sort of deputies

do you have here, Mr. Gibson?"

"Regular Indian Police force. We don't have enough U. S. Marshals to patrol the borders of our new nation, so we have our own police, U. S. Deputies, empowered to confiscate all liquor and fire arms. Here, I forget my manners. Please, get down and rest yourselves."

Quietly speaking to the Indian deputies in Osage, Gibson dismissed them. With trust the Indians turned and rode down the hill. Seated on a huge slab of sandstone rock, they exchanged pleasantries, then told Gibson about the fire and the unrest it had caused.

"Yes, our Indians set the fire. They do it almost every spring. Tell your people it's a natural way to get rid of the weeds and shrubs that crowd the prairie grass. They'd do well to imitate them!" He went on, "However, they'd best do it the Indian way. There are certain days in the spring when the grass isn't up far enough yet to do damage, and the weeds haven't gone to seed. Believe me, I've seen this work over and over in Kansas. Now down here with all this timber, we'll have to wait and see. But gentlemen, these people have no malice for Cedar Vale. Hell, the whole village isn't even here yet. Their main concern is to have good grass when the main body of the tribe arrives this summer. We are waiting for the final deed to arrive at any time now. I'll tell you what. I won't get any work done on my house while I'm gone, but I'll go back with you to Cedar Vale and calm everyone as best I can. I can assess any damage done as well."

They made camp up on the hill with Gibson and readied to return to Cedar Vale immediately, not knowing if the Cedar Vale people had stayed behind or not.

That night Gibson conferred with the Chief and arranged for two braves to escort them back to the border

210

and make sure all was quiet. J. W. and Bennett felt more comfortable returning. Their visit had reassured them all was peaceful, and they also learned that Lindsey, with the other drovers, had gone through safely. "I gave them a Federal letter so they should have safe passage as long as they behave themselves. Can't guarantee anything, but least wise they'll have legal authority to be in the Territory."

A crowd awaited them in Cedar Vale. Someone had calculated the time of return and had the two not appeared, the men were prepared to ride out for a "rescue." Gibson stayed on his horse for visibility and repeated his plea.

"These Osage Indians are only interested in finding a resting place. Their numbers have dwindled so low they realize they can't take on the whole United States! They learned that they cannot divide us as they had hoped during the war, so now their thoughts are only on making a small nation. Actually, right this minute their only thoughts are of moving. This fire was only a way to better the grass. They had no notion of harming anyone. They do this almost every year, and only once a year. Now you know and can see how you can prepare for it. It just might work for you, too!"

He shifted, relaxing as his words pacified the crowd, "Now, while I'm here folks, I want to tell you, the Osages will be making a final move this year and they will be coming through this area. We will have a few braves for escorts. These braves are Deputy U.S. Marshals." He let these words sink in then continued, "The army will tag along behind as well. You can sell the Osages anything they want to buy except liquor and firearms. Dire consequences follow anyone who is in violation of these orders. Now then, no harm will come to you if you will just leave them alone. They are going to be your closest neighbors and they want to get along as much as you do. If there is any grievance you can come into the agency, but if you cross the border without your "Federal Letter" you may be arrested by our bona fide Federal Indian Police!"

There were murmurs from the crowd, but most were satisfied and surprised. Gibson dismounted and went into the saloon to discuss more of the prairie fire and calm a few of those yet concerned, and the rest of the crowd drifted off home.

Bennett went to find Margaret and tell her the news about Lindsey. "Bennett, I can't tell you how worried I was. I kept thinking the men in town would booze until they would go after you, and you would be caught in a cross fire between them and the Indians. Some were so hotheaded, but thank God you've returned. Even the little boys were upset and angry about what was being said."

Business picked up at a fast pace that spring and they discovered that the bridge in St. Louis was now finished, opening a way for a flood of immigrants.

The Osage's exodus to their new nation came through in May. The tribe skirted town, but merchants came out with wagons to trade. One man tried to bring out whiskey, and was angrily descended upon by the white population and he quickly left town.

The medicine man did a brisk business of selling his "Revitalizing Elixir" to the citizens of both nations. A festive picnic atmosphere reigned for two days until a spring thunderstorm rumbled in from the horizon, scattering the population to a variety of shelters. The Indians, wrapped in their blankets, largely ignored the storm, but recognized that the trading was over. They ambled after the wagons, and at the army captain's suggestion, went into town and negotiated with the livery stable owner to allow them shelter until the storm passed. The small army detachment sought shelter in the saloon.

Nowhere on earth does nature display her awesome strength so dramatically. The lightning bolts appear four to six at a time, ripping the darkness in a flash of flourescent brightness and moments later a web of horizontal electricity crackles and spouts between the clouds sitting on opposite horizons. The resulting blasts of thunder send out a forceful vibration that verges on a physical jolt. The wind shifts from west to east, then back again. After the sun sets, one can only guess, listening to the sound of the wind, if a funnel will swoop out of the sky and pluck you and your belongings away. But instead of worry, this was another occasion for the town to have a party. Snug indoors, someone produces a fiddle, opens an organ, or just begins to sing and the feet start stomping.

Every event calls for a dance these days. A baby born at the Rush house, a barn raising at Holroyds, each new floor was an excuse to dance on.

In Cedar Vale the biggest celebration yet was in preparation. The Conklin girls were making a big flag for the Fourth of July, a gazebo had been started for a band to play and everyone was celebrating our Independence as the veterans of both the north and south were joining in one nation, like President Grant was asking.

On the bank of Cedar Creek the big day came with sunshine and heat. The flag raising ceremony was accompanied by the band, some in uniforms brought from their previous home towns. Picnic baskets filled with fried chicken, bread and butter sandwiches, fresh tomatoes, and corn on the cob, watermelons cooling in

213

the flowing eddy of the creek. Youngsters ran freely, climbing trees, playing chase, catching frogs, and teasing girls. Except for the sparse wooden buildings, one would not suspect they lived on the very edge of civilization, a day's ride from the heart of Indian Territory. Mr. Higgins organized a horse race, which a fine Kentucky horse easily won.

Back home after the big day, the exhausted children asleep, Bennett and Margaret embraced in a celebration in life. The giddy feeling of Independence, space, and control of their own destiny was heady and powerful. The sense of security that comes from self sufficiency enveloped them in an ecstasy, and their love making surpassed everything they had ever experienced before. Margaret had very little time to think about her two girls away in Illinois, or Lindsey on the cattle drive.

Margaret's time was occupied with the ever present task of survival. Not that she did any more than any other pioneer woman and realizing that she was not the only pioneer with this feeling, at least made it bearable. There was a garden to dig, plant, hoe, harvest and preserve. The chickens were a handy source of eggs, meat, feathers for beds and pillows, but they had to be fed, watered, and have their house cleaned. The twice a day chore of milking, straining a part of the milk, and giving the rest to the pigs. How nice to have one's own butter and cheese and fresh cream for the oats in the morning. They went ahead and put in the fruit trees, although George and Elizabeth would be the beneficiaries years in the future. Margaret hoped they would have their own place in the four or five years it would take fruit trees to bear.

Little John and Jacob both took to the chores as was expected of them. Everyone had to hold up his part of the load. They were fairly expert at pulling weeds, bringing in wood, fetching water. After the chores each morning came breakfast, and pie making, then the trip into town to work at Mrs. Baird's. Bennett would drop them off and go to his cabinet shop.

Summer's blistering heat was tolerated by fishing on the shaded banks of the Caney River. They would all swim on extremely hot days. The small town, being so much like a family, would be shut down and everyone turn out for a picnic and horse shoe pitch, fish and swim and catch up on the latest gossip.

Fall brought the thunderstorms again. Almost a repeat of the spring, except the heat made the humid air stifling. The cool nights of October and November were welcomed. Wood was purchased as Bennett could not spare the time from his shop. It was expensive to purchase anything, but there was very little wood left after all the building that had been going on this year. The cedar grove was rapidly growing smaller.

Lindsey arrived unannounced in mid November. Margaret was overjoyed and overwhelmed at the relief of seeing him alive and well. She had lived with a motherly anxiety about Lindsey for years, and when he was there once again, tears of relief flowed as she looked him over and noted the development of muscle and his growth of maturity.

"I'm not staying, Mother. We've come from Dallas to Baxter Springs and I'm moving on to Sedalia, Missouri with the herd. I'm going from there back to Olney. I don't know just what I'll do back there, but I've gotta see Martha."

A lump stuck in her throat at the thought of him leaving so soon, but she was still pleased to have him for a little while. The little boys were all over him talking lickety split.

"Whoa, there, slow down and I'll tell you all about it. Come wash up for dinner with me." Lindsey led them out to the wash basin by the back door, just like the one in Olney.

As they ate Lindsey told them all about the cattle drive. He only shared the high points, the outlaws they had run off, the near stampede for water. The broken wagon that left them without food for two days because it was lost off the trail. He skipped over the part about the dust, monotony, heat, thirst and the irritated grumblers who complained constantly about not being able to wash, rest or have a woman. A surprise had come when he realized how fast he wore out his boots even when they were in the saddle so much. Lindsey stuck out his foot and showed them he was near barefoot. "I plan to stop long enough in Baxter Springs to get a pair of boots made. We'll be there about four days resting up for the final push."

"Ma, it sure is good to eat your cooking."

Margaret smiled pleased at the compliment and everything her son had to say. He sounded different. His voice had deepened and he had picked up a drawl from someone.

Letters were hastily written to Mary and Saphronia and put with a packet of jelly, bread, new socks and mittens and a new sweater for Lindsey to take home. No, to Olney. Home was here now. Tears stung her eyes with the thought that she would possibly never see her girls again. Maybe . . . . when the trains get through . . . . she had heard they went clear across the continent now, soon the nation will be a grid of rails and no one would need travel by horse except to and from the train. What a marvelous age we live in.

Lindsey leaving after so short a visit left her

216

wrenched inside. Bennett cradled her and cuddled her and teased her back to her usual self again. He always knew just the right thing to say.

Lindsey collected his wages for the year's work from Uncle George in Sedalia. "You're a grown man now, Lindsey. You've done a good job. Come back in the fall and we'll do it again."

"No, thanks, Uncle George. You and mother can carve out the frontier, but I'm going back to Olney. Kansas wasn't what I expected, and I can cowboy the rest of my life and never earn enough for a place of my own."

"What will you do in Olney, Lin? Set up a saloon? Your grandpa isn't in the bank any more to help you there."

"Well, Uncle George, I'm looking for an opportunity, I can always ride back out to Kansas and live off jack rabbits."

George laughed and slapped him on the back, "I like your attitude. I'll look you up when I get back."

Lindsey had his two horses re-shod and headed east, for home.

Arriving in St. Louis was an experience. If he had thought two years before that it was a big city, it had doubled in size now, and it was a sight to behold. The new St. Louis bridge was finished and the crossing was a whole lot different from the one going west two years ago. He laughed as he recalled their experiences. Lindsey did not stop to enjoy any of the temptations. He had been warned by his fellow cowboys how fast a man could be stripped of his money by the city slickers. Even the women would rob you, they said. Instead he rode around town, gawking at the new buildings, fine carriages, and shops, and wagons lined up to cross the

217

river mouth, all going west. It almost changed his mind. It looked like he was the only one swimming against the tide.

Lindsey rode hard, his excitement mounting as he neared Olney and the familiar countryside. A feeling of belonging came over him, and anticipation grew as he thought about seeing Martha. He refused to admit that she might not have waited for him.

He rode into the Houser farm before going into town. No one was in sight. Mamma Houser answered the door, acting as if she didn't know him. "Yes?" she asked, peering at him with clouded vision.

"Mrs. Houser, it's me, Lindsey Johnson, back from Kansas!"

Her eyes brightened a little, "Good to see you, boy. I didn't recognize you, it's cloudy today," she remarked, looking past him to the sky.

He frowned, it was a sunny day, she must be getting blind, he thought. "Is Miss Martha home?" He peered over her head, but heard no sound from the house.

"No, she's working out, such a sweet girl, comes home every Sunday to take me to church and gives me most of her salary to help out. George and Michael help too, but they are both married. All the girls are hard workers and they all work out for people, except Catherine, of course, she is married."

Impatiently Lindsey interrupted, "Tell me where can I find Martha?"

"She's working for the Foxes, but I don't know where it is any more. It's hard to remember things."

"I'll find it! Good day, Ma'am." Lindsey shot the words over his shoulder as he mounted his horse and rode away.

218

"Rude young man." Elizabeth Houser said to herself.

Riding into town was exciting. Lindsey's western gear set him apart from the local farmers and gathered stares and a following of children. Out of habit, he had left on his chaps and spurs. His working saddle had the customary large, sturdy horn, and had been hand tooled with a beautiful design by a Mexican artisan in Texas. Yes, he was quite a sight for the placid little town as he rode in. He also needed a bath and a shave.

He was surprised at the changes. The boarding house was gone, some of the businesses were changed, and at the livery stable where he had worked, he found strangers. "Old man died and I came from back east. Lots of folks going west, even farther than this," the young man offered without introducing himself.

Lindsey found a boarding house near the depot on the opposite side from their old place. He bathed and shaved and again recognized no one, nor did they know him. He was getting a lesson, nothing stays the same while you are gone, and you are soon forgotten. It left him with a lonely feeling. He needed to find his sisters.

He rode out to George Faulk's place in Clarmont. As he rode in, his sister Mary was on the porch snapping beans. They looked at each other, not quite sure that the familiar face was real, then setting the bowl on the step, Mary ran to embrace Lindsey as he dismounted. "Lindsey! You are so brown, I thought you were an Indian, did you ride in all alone? Is mother coming back too? Are you hungry?"

"Whoa, there, sis. Let me catch my breath. Just look at you. Yes, I'm alone. No, mamma is not coming back, and yes I'm hungry but I can wait until dinner time. Where is Saphronia?"

"She's here. She came to visit just last night, That's

why it is so hard to believe you are here too! She is upstairs putting the children down for a nap. Ona!" She called loudly, "Ona, John, look who's here!" The porch filled with familiar faces, hugs were exchanged and Lindsey finally felt at home.

In the talk after dinner, Lindsey was pressed to tell them every detail of Kansas. The trip, the life, the Indians, all of it. It didn't sound so bad in the telling. He left out about the loneliness and homesickness. He never talked aloud about that. A little whiskey would make that feeling go away, but today he didn't need any whiskey.

He learned that Saphronia, (nicknamed Ona), had moved up to St. Clair County near Uncle George. John was a newspaper man up there. Mary and her husband, Preston Pugh (Bennett's younger brother), were living next door to George. They had leased some of his land to farm on shares. They were all "getting by" but like most folks, they said they would never be wealthy, maybe never even own a piece of property and dreamed, like everyone else, of going west and staking a claim — free land for the homesteading of it.

"Well, you'd have to go farther west than Kansas nowadays." Lindsey told them emphatically. "Homesteads are for buying now. They may sell cheap by someone giving it up, but there is no more free land there. The free land is all out in the Colorado and Oregon territory, and I heard on the trail that you had to plow it with a chisel and wait a hundred years for your crop! They don't call 'em Rocky Mountains for nothing!

"I worked with a fellow that had worked on the railroad across the mountains up there and he told me the air was so thin and cold he couldn't breathe. And talk about Indians, all the resistant ones have been pushed

220

back into the mountains. I heard they'll fight a buzz saw, whites, negroes, and even each other! Now our Plains Indians," he had not realized he had personally identified with them, "they are peaceable. Some are even dressing in our dress instead of blankets. Some are intermarrying!"

Everyone gasped. They had heard of this and had known people even in Illinois who had married with Indians, but they were politely ignored and lived a quiet country life off to themselves. Lindsey had forgotten the "eastern" prejudice and he felt sorry for them. They would never know the loyal friendship, the generosity of having an Indian friend. He told them about Strike Axe. It changed no one's mind.

In all the excitement Lindsey still had not forgotten why he had come home. He finally asked, "Where can I find Martha Houser?"

"Why, Lindsey?" Ona teased, "I thought you came back to the bosom of your family, but you seem to have thoughts of another!"

"Yes, siree, I intend to get married."

"What makes you think she waited?" Mary coyly asked.

Lindsey reddened with emotion, "She said she would."

"Have you written her?" Ona asked.

"Once or twice, but she knows my feelings about her."

The girls' laughter made him embarrassed and uneasy and they enjoyed it immensely. Ona, seeing that they were going too far, finally told him, "She is working for the Fox family between here and Olney. You probably rode right past their place on the way here, but watch out for Michael!" she teased.

It was dark already, but Lindsey could wait no

221

longer and rode out to the Fox place. The road was hard and dry and the night was warm. The Foxes had a two story house and there was only one small light from a back window in what appeared to be the kitchen, so he rode around back, tied the horse and quietly knocked. There was no answer until the second louder knock brought a small voice, "Who's there?"

"Lindsey Johnson to see Miss Martha!" The door flew open and there was Martha, outlined in the lantern light like a halo glow. He gathered her into his arms, her head coming even with his chest, and they clung to each other as the world seemed to stand still.

Lindsey felt her start to sob, "Martha, I'm home, what is wrong? Are you sick?" a horrible thought, "are you married?"

"No, no, no, darling, I'm just happy, I'm overwhelmed by the surprise and you almost got yourself killed." She laughed and held up the pistol she had in her hand. Lindsey's mouth gaped open, "Wha . . ."

She laughed again, "I'm here to care for the Foxes. They are old and alone. The children have hired me to do for them and I manage fine, but being out here in the country with strangers passing all the time, I need to protect myself, and them, as well." She looked down, feeling ridiculous, but said defensively, "I'm a pretty good shot."

"Whew!" Lindsey breathed and helped her put the gun back in the cabinet.

"I should have shot you, Lindsey, for not writing to me. I've wept many a tear fearing you were dead. That left me pining away and getting on past marrying age like any old maid." She pretended to be pouting. He kissed away her anger and was becoming very arduous.

Martha, not wanting to, but firmly determined

222

said, "Stop that now, Lindsey, where is your respect for me? There is no ring on my finger yet."

He backed away, hurt physically and mentally, but she was right. He had come to marry, not disgrace her. They held hands and talked until almost morning. Martha gently whispered, "There's a place out back, an old bunk house. It's clean you can stay there. I'll have to get the Foxes breakfast soon. They get up before dawn."

Lindsey kissed her and went to the wood pile, brought in an armload and helped stoke the stove, kissed her again and went to the bunk house. He didn't think about food as he rolled out his bedroll onto the woven rope bunk. He slept soundly. He was home.

Chapter 15

Kansas Belle

In Kansas, the year 1873 went by much the same as the year before. Margaret was teaching Jacob his letters and they all worked diligently toward a goal of owning their own land and building their own house one day.

George came and went several times, reporting that he could not yet get Elizabeth to move. She was terrified of the Indians living so close. He was very pleased with the home Margaret was making and each time he came, he would bring baskets of fruit, peppermint candy and some cloth. It was always like Christmas when Uncle George arrived.

In July, Cedar Vale had a repeat of the big Fourth of July celebration once again on the Caney River. After the success of last year, the turn out was even bigger. It went on for two whole days and some folks camped out for the night. The children bedded down in the wagons. The adults had a dance that lasted into the wee hours of morning. They played as hard as they worked and it was revitalizing.

In September, a letter arrived from Olney to tell them about Lindsey and Martha getting married. Margaret cried partly with the joy of hearing from her son, at long last, and partly for the joy of his happiness. She carefully marked the date in the Bible, 24 August 1873. He was just 19 years old. "I wonder what he'll do to support them?" She said to herself. Cowboying wasn't for a married man.

One bitter December day, Margaret shook off the snowy blanket wrapped around her and the two little figures huddled beside her on the buckboard. She shivered while collecting the now frozen pies, while the boys scurried into the Baird House. Anna met her halfway across the porch to help her carry the pies.

"Margaret, what on earth are you doing? I did not expect you out in this foul weather." Settled in the kitchen, over a cup of tea they shared the local gossip, the future, the children and then Margaret said, "Anna, if there is nothing much to do during the bad weather perhaps I will stay home. It is time for my confinement soon." She looked down at her expanding mid-line, "Although I haven't noticed anyone around here staying confined, there is too much for a woman to do to stay indoors while she is pregnant." She looked around to see if the boys had heard the word, giggled and said, "I heard Mrs. Holverson almost had her baby in the potato patch!"

After dinner, Anna fixed her a foot warmer for the trip home. "Anna, you are a dear. A visit such as this is well worth the trip into town." They picked up Bennett and rode home in the badly drifting snow.

Bennett continued to go to his shop every day possible, working long hours at his woodwork. Varnish and oils were hard to get, so sometimes the finish work had to wait. Some pieces he finished with only linseed oil and turpentine, actually some people preferred it that way instead of the shiny new varnish.

Evenings Bennett would whittle scraps into toys and figures, while Margaret taught Jacob and John their letters. They talked about the winter spent in the soddy and had many a good laugh about how they had

225

managed. "I thought I'd have to dig another outhouse before spring."

"We sure saved on wood, so many bodies in such a small place heated without a stick of wood some days."

At Christmas, Margaret had made her usual new sweaters and mittens and caps from their sheep's wool. Bennett, however, was keeping a secret in the attic. Climbing down the ladder, he placed the box carefully before Margaret. He checked to see if the children were still in bed asleep and tiptoed back to her, "Open it."

Gingerly she lifted the lid, quite puzzled at the delicate way Bennett was acting. She exclaimed, "Oh Bennett, how elegant and expensive. Real glass ornaments for the tree." There were a dozen, a church, several houses, carolers, trees and a star. They decorated a small cedar tree with popcorn and cranberries looped about its branches. Now, with the new glass ornaments, in the fire light the tree looked like it was bejeweled!

"I thought it was about time to be a little extravagant," Bennett whispered.

Morning brought oohs and ahhs from the boys who wondered what magic had decorated their tree during the night.

There was little snow that spring, but it was very very cold. On the first day of March, Margaret awoke shortly after going to bed with a cramp. "It's too soon," she whispered to herself. She tried to relax, but her body kept contracting, often. "Bennett the baby is coming!"

She had just spoken the words and he was awake and pulling on his boots, "I'll go for Doc Donalson."

"No, there's no time. The baby is early," she paused

to have a contraction, "Get the oilcloth in the cupboard and a clean sheet. Bring it."

Bennett ran to do her bidding.

"Fold it under me, save the featherbed." As she raised she had another contraction and had to wait. "Line the cradle with the big quilt and bring me the baby's quilt." She folded the baby quilt and told Bennett to sit on it to keep it warm after he stoked up the fire. He sat nervously watching as the contractions rhythmatically followed one another.

Margaret tried to relax and allow her belly to ball up and heave at its own pace until the pressure started and an uncontrolled desire overcame her to push. A gush of fluid, a heave, another push of tremendous effort and sudden relief!

Bennett jumped to his feet as Margaret released his hands from her grip. Tears of relief and happiness streamed down his face as he picked up the little wet, blue, shivering baby. He gently laid the tiny girl on her mother's chest. He tied the cord with string and cut it with scissors as Margaret instructed him. He gently cleaned the baby, and wrapped the afterbirth and disposed of it. Margaret wrapped the infant carefully in the warm quilt, and slowly cleaned herself over the wash basin, tied on a clean rag and returned to bed, where, except for the little bundle, one would never have guessed anything extraordinary had happened.

Margaret and Bennett examined the tiny figure between them, all pink now, and perfect, and Margaret cooed, "My little Belle, my little Kansas Belle."

Chapter 16

The Plague

Summer tried men's souls. It came in early, dry and hot. There was no rain for long periods and when it did come it was only a sprinkle, just enough to make the weather miserable and muggy and everyone irritable. The wind blew incessantly and sand and dirt almost smothered them. Some days Margaret would have to put a wet blanket over the crib to keep the dirt from covering the baby. The garden did no good except the okra. It was a weed they had learned to eat the seed pods by boiling them with tomatoes to cut the slimy texture, but this year Margaret rolled them in cornmeal and fried it because there were no tomatoes. It was strangely good to eat that way. Anna Baird pickled some that was also good. Anna could pickle anything! They became concerned about the level of water in the well.

Many farmers, living on the edge of survival anyway, were going hungry, or saw that they'd never make the winter, decided to pull up and move, either back East or go on West to a dream of better land, and milder temperatures. Springs in the Rocky Mountain beckoned that year, and many joined the wagon trains that came through.

The heat, drought, and slack work made everyone restless and irritable. In town they were fighting about dividing up the County, "It's just another way to hire more county workers, we don't need more than one, leave it just as it is," was one argument. "We need a county seat that is more convenient. It's too far to vote, have courts and keep records," said another. Every little town, including Cedar Vale, wanted to be the new County Seat.

Margaret was working during the dinner time and was keeping abreast of every argument from both the discussions at the boarding house and at home, where every evening Bennett would excitedly report it all and get worked up again over the details. This was all more exciting than the 1872 Presidential election when the town was divided about whether Grant was a "savior" from Andrew Jackson's term, or a "military dictator." To Bennett there was no decision. He was both a Union man and an Illinois man. Politics were exciting during this time. Everyone was keenly aware that they were "building a nation." From coast to coast they would soon celebrate 100 years of a "Constitutional Government by the People" and that would validate the fact that they were on the right track. As frontiersmen the sacrifice of living here was just part of the job.

Margaret, always opinionated and outspoken, could not keep her mouth shut when a childish argument among the men at the dinner table broke out at the Baird's House. She interjected into the conversation, "It is only good business sense to have one large county and only pay for one set of clerks, one Court house, and one government. I cannot see the urgency of duplication."

The dining room fell silent and a dozen pair of male eyes scornfully stared at her. She took her point a step further, "Circuit Judges bring the court and justice system to us and they are much cheaper than building court houses and . . . "

She was interrupted with a sneer by a small, pot-bellied salesman. "We hardly think you are an authority on the complex subject of politics. You should not bother your 'emotions' with such a subject." With a lofty tilt of his head he motioned to the table, "Please excuse us now," and the group followed him to the parlor.

Margaret was so angry and embarrassed she stood there with her coffee pot in hand and stared at each man as they turned to leave.

Anna overheard, "Margaret, you know you cannot discuss men's business. You only upset yourself dear."

"Anna, I'm angry and humiliated because he spoke to me like a child! It is not just men's business. Taxes affect me because they take food from my mouth the same as Bennett's. I want law protection before county clerks. I want a better community. I have as good an education as that man does. I probably read twice as much. Afterall, I'm 45 years old, I have a mind. Believe me, if women could vote those men would sit up and listen."

"Well, we can not vote and never will, because men are the lawmakers." Anna added.

"Someday, Anna, someday, somehow, we'll take our place in making decisions about our lives. Men run around making wars and pushing out the frontiers, but look who has stayed to make the home, bring up the children and develop the community. They fought the Indians and we women have stayed behind to make the peace with them. Women have finally proved that they can do anything a man can do, even be educated."

Anna agreed, but to herself she wondered if the time Margaret described would ever come.

The ladies quilting bees had always been a place of female education. Because it was innocent and inconspicuous to the male population, a woman could excuse herself from the home for a day to join the community task of "doing a quilt" for this one or that, sometimes even one of her own. Traditionally, after the local gossip was exchanged, a book would be brought out and one of the group would read. Sometimes it was a newspaper and discussions always followed. To some ladies this was their only exposure to literature or outside opinions. Men actually believed an education, or even knowing how to read and cipher, could put a strain on the female emotional system, so females were "protected" from books. Some ladies were also convinced of this, but since the Civil War when so many females were left at home to fend for themselves, a surge of independence flowed through the female population as a whole and continued to be promoted.

They learned that many previously popular books thought to have been written by men were actually written by women. Then came Harriet Beecher Stowe, and female doctors, and all sorts of examples of female ability. At the quilting bees, they taught each other to read, hoarded books and had a circulating book loaning system. Some were even so bold as to form a Bible study group. After all, how could a good husband object to that? Under these guises they were becoming educated even though some had to disguise their abilities or suffer outburst of rage from their spouse.

By 1876 women began pushing their daughters to go to school at least to learn to read. Surprisingly, many men objected. They argued that boys and girls should not intermingle in the same room for so long a time because it would lead to something sexual before they are ready.

General opinion gradually swayed and society conceded that perhaps it would be good for a female to learn to read, but schooling beyond the age of twelve was frowned on. A child of the male gender should then follow an apprenticeship, and females attend to their hope chest, learning wifely skills of cooking and embroidery and even making her wedding dress that could take years of stitching white on white linen with perhaps some cut work or Brandenberg lace.

Margaret voiced her dismay one day at the quilting bee, "I plow the garden at home but when the single tree broke and I tried to buy a replacement at the hardware store, the clerk asked me to check with my husband before purchasing. I was even stared at for going into the store. It was like saying I was a child, out of place, asking for something I was to ignorant to know anything about." Dozens of similar stories flew around the room. "One day, perhaps our daughters will be recognized as people who have respectable opinions. The key is education," Margaret said.

Little Kansas Belle played with the other children under the quilt frame or in the corners of the room and overheard these discussions and absorbed it all like a sponge. They were being educated on the spot more than Margaret dreamed.

A disastrous blow was the 1874 plague of grasshoppers. In addition to the drought the land was twice devastated. The sky blackened, and every leaf in sight was devoured by the insects. It was absolutely futile to fight them. The sickening sight continued for days as they swarmed like a sea across the landscape. It was the last straw for many farmers, but those who chose to stay were welded into a bonded, unified family.

Now no one was "poor." Everyone lacked something, so each shared what they had, traded and bartered and learned to make do with what was stored from the past year — use it up, wear it out. They also had more parties that year than ever before. It bolstered the spirits, shared the food, and gave everyone a feeling of hope.

A favorite event borrowed from back East, was a Bergoo. A huge pot of stew was made from wild game or whatever could be had. Bread was baked and fry cakes made and a good time was inescapable, with horse races, turtle races, men, women, children dancing and listening to the fiddlers play. It made everyone forget that tomorrow water would have to stretch the thin fish soup, or that the family would all pretend to have eaten enough when in fact they were starving.

Some made it because they had to slaughter and dry the meat from their milk cows and such because there was no grain or hay to feed livestock. They were grateful for that, but wondered how they would plow without horses, and get milk without cows. Sickness moved in behind the malnourishment and many weaker ones died. The fight to get the county seat was forgotten in the struggle for survival.

Howard County was soon divided into three counties, Chautauqua, Elk and Howard. Cedar Vale had lost the fight to Sedan 16 miles east, to get the county seat of the new Chautauqua County. During the previous year there had been squabbles over the possession of the records. Posses stole some of them away during the night, and they were stolen back again and no one could be sure where the county lines were. Many lawsuits were filed over ownership, some of which were not clear to start with. It was thought some of the records were lost "conveniently."

People left in droves, either to return East or to move on further West, but others quickly moved in to buy while the prices were cheap. Still, land of their own was out of reach for Margaret and Bennett. They religiously saved 10% of every penny they earned and they were proud of their progress. They refused to dip into the little brown box when times were tough. Each deposit gave them great satisfaction. Margaret was now going from Baird's, to Mrs. Smith's, and to Luke Phelp's Hotels to bake her pies and bread instead of doing it at home.

At 46 she was considered old by some, but she could outwork any young woman. She supposed the children kept her from thinking of herself as old. Some of these young women dried up in the Kansas sun and hope went out of their eyes and they actually died of "melancholy." Margaret felt as if she had been made just for this task, a surge of determination. A length of iron in her backbone as strong as the railroad rails that were pushing through the territories, reminded her that this life was meaningful and fulfilling.

1876, one hundred years of Independence! The Civil War had been over for some time. The Centennial celebration had a healing effect between the north and the south as they took joint pride in the melding of the nation that was rapidly growing continental in scope. They had a government that, for all its faults, still functioned "By the People" after one hundred years. No nation, not even the Romans and Greeks, had lasted so long.

Every hamlet across the country prepared to celebrate. Expansion to the West was contagious, and whole towns often packed up and moved, following the "Drummer" West.

Indians were still resisting and The Indian War history was being lived. Fear to face the Indians out West resulted in the invention of the Indian Territory. It was believed by the general public that the Indians

234

were contained and being given land just like the homesteaders. They were taken care of. The few that might resist, people were told, had signed treaties to agree passage of wagon trains through their land. These statements were half truths, though. Not all Indians were in Indian Territory. Many of those who were supposed to be there had not moved yet. Most had been offered no voice about going there so some bands resisted strongly. However, that news was not advertised as widely as the tales portraying the land of opportunity the Drummer wanted folks to hear. Business boomed and a wagon train came through Cedar Vale every few days on its way to Wichita.

With the scarcity of law enforcers, outlaws naturally migrated to the area, and U.S. Marshals welcomed those groups of citizens who would help enforce the law. Cedar Vale, like most communities formed an "Anti-Horse Thief" association. They appointed themselves watch dogs against crime and also patrolled the Indian Territory border to prevent cattle from crossing over with their tick infestation. They diverted them into Missouri. Bennett did not approve. He told Margaret, "They'd do better to mind their own business. They just meet to get beered up and then ride hell bent all over the country! They'll get tired of that and cook up mischief someday."

It wasn't long before the group took four prisoners away from Marshal Dick Walters near Arkansas City. They hung them at Grouse Creek. They got little thanks from the general population and most of those involved would not admit the fact they were a part of the deed. The town hired a Sheriff and the "Association" quietly dissolved.

Still, most disputes were settled personally and one area, the road to Hewkins place known as Sky Line

235

Drive between Blue Mound and Possum Trot, was also called Hell's Bend because it was the frequent scene of land disputes, family feuds, and outlaw hideouts. Folks knew to stay clear unless they were looking for trouble.

Chapter 17

Friends and New Friends

Little Jacob started to school decked out in new wool knickers and long stockings with new shoes. Tucked under his arm was his own slate, and he was as rich as any child could be. In the throes of recovering from the drought, these items all came with sacrifice and long, extra hours of work by Bennett and Margaret, but things were looking up. At least there was work to do again, as much as a man (or woman) could stand. This year the garden was good, there would be plenty of grass and that meant birds, game, and wild berries would be plentiful. Even a few fruit trees were bearing.

Without advance notice Preston Pugh, Bennett's brother who became his son-in-law, too, when he married Margaret's daughter Mary, came driving into the farm in their Conestoga wagon with their baby, Marcus. Margaret almost fainted with surprise of seeing her daughter after five long years!

Mary and Margaret clung to each other weeping, laughing, looking and laughing again. Little Marcus and Kannie timidly stood, holding mother's skirts, looking at each other then up at their parents and both started to cry. The women picked up their children, laughing and calming them. "I never thought your children would have aunts and uncles the same age!" Margaret said, "Look at you. You precious darling!"

Bennett and Preston walked up and they all began talking at once. There was so much to catch up on.

Saphronia and John were well, but not inclined to suffer the wild frontiers of Kansas, they sent their love and a letter, which Margaret read, weeping with the emotional release of the reunion.

Lindsey and Martha were expecting a baby, so they could not join them either. Maybe they will come out later, but Lindsey had a good job managing the Faulk farm. Mary and Preston had come with only three wagons and had no trouble. They accumulated a stake from selling out in Illinois. "Mamma, I just couldn't bear the thought of you out here and my children growing up without a Grandmother when they could know you." Margaret allowed the tears to flow again and gave Mary a tight embrace and said, "I do love you for that Mary, I'm so glad you are here!"

Mary explained how Uncle George had told them about some land thirty miles northwest of Cedar Vale near Winfield, Kansas. It was likely to be on the railroad. Uncle George knew all about the lay of the land. Since so much of it was limestone, you had to be careful to get the right piece of property for farming, but they took Uncle George's word and bought it through a lawyer. They were still nervous about seeing it for the first time. Lawyers could not always be trusted.

They stayed a week then packed up to journey on to their own land. The experience started Margaret and Bennett to counting out their savings to see if perhaps some way they could have their own place again, too. It didn't quite stretch. There had been too many lean years in spite of both of them working and the return of good times this past year.

Mary and Preston came back down for Christmas in spite of the cold and possibility of snow.

"We brought our portable stove in the wagon, it wasn't bad." Mary said as she cuddled up to the cook stove. Preston proudly pulled out his deed, to show that it had been signed and recorded. They now owned the N 1/2 of SE 1/4 Sec. 33; T33 of R8E! It was good land and they excitedly went on and on about a cabin that was already there, but they had to repair and it would do until a proper house could be built. The grass was good and first thing in spring they would get a cow, chickens and start a crop and garden. Margaret could see that Mary was in for lots of hard work, but that was the way of this part of the world. There was much satisfaction from being self-sufficient in spite of the work involved. Margaret was reminded of the bind of her work. She was doing all the wifely things and working, too.

"Oh! I almost forgot!" Margaret ran to her sewing box to retrieve a letter. "Look what came last week! A letter from Lindsey and Martha, they have a baby boy! He was born 14 September 1876. A Centennial baby!"

"Oh, Mamma, how could you forget to show us this! Oh, I'm so happy for them, Martha thought she never would get in a family way." Mary read the letter. "They named him William Oscar, William Oscar Johnson, well, I declare." They all laughed at what she didn't say.

Later Margaret cuddled the youngsters, who were enjoying each other as they became reacquainted. She told them stories about her own grandmother Heap, who lived in a fine brick home in Pennsylvania with servants and flowers, and about their Virginia grandparents who had a plantation. She wanted them to be proud of their family and to know they were not always poor and living off the land, but she could see it meant little to them. These children could not imagine what having a servant meant, they related more closely with cowboys and Indians.

As summer came the children were kept busy as usual with tending a few sheep, spinning, milking, picking berries. There was so much to do, and sleep came early even on hot summer nights when everyone moved their beds to the porch. Even cooking outside didn't prevent the house from becoming an oven on these hot July days.

Margaret's brother George sent out a letter that said, "You are most cordially invited to stay, but Jarome and I are moving back to Cedar Vale this summer as soon as he has been graduated from college. We plan to come and stay. Elizabeth has chosen to stay here in Freeburg."

Margaret was disturbed. They had lived mostly in town but after so many years had come to think of the farm as theirs. They cleaned it and made repairs and any time there was a party or festive occasion it was at the farm. She was not prepared to be a housekeeper for her brother, so her practical nature prevailed and she could see that this was an opportunity which would force them into more permanent plans, although there was the dilemma of what?

There was not enough money for a farm of their own even after hoarding every penny for the last eight years. Bennett's business was slack because Eastern furniture was being shipped in, and with people selling out, the coming and going, more furniture was exchanged than was built.

There was railroad work for the able bodied men. They were worked like the machines that ran the rails, long, hot, and constant. If they dropped dead, others waited to replace them and little notice was made of their passing. Margaret hated such employers and had little to say to any that tried to big shot around the boarding house.

Cattle drives were about the thing of the past since the railroad had expanded into Texas through Indian Territory. Now, Preston's offer looked very inviting.

Preston had written that he was having quite a time trying to get in a crop alone. He was too far from town to get someone to help and his neighbors, as good as they were, were busy with their own chores. Would Bennett consider coming up and working on crop shares? They would plant oats, corn and wheat and perhaps get a fall crop. If not they would plow it all under and wait until spring and have early summer crops for sure!

It was a very hard decision to leave Cedar Vale. They had really just begun to put down roots again. They had some dear friends, forged from mutual dependance and isolation from the outside world, but even many of them were getting restless and moving on to different dreams. The whole country was stirring with a feeling of need to move, expand, build. States were joining the Union faster than stars could be sewn onto the flag!

Cedar Vale was growing, even getting its own grist mill now. Davis Tabler and Alenzo Adams are building one on the Caney River, but that did not interest Margaret, having no crops to grind. Besides her mind argued, I could never go into business in competition with my friend Anna Baird.

The decison was made. They set their minds to the business of moving. They cleaned George's house from stem to stern. Having only lived in the main rooms, they had to pack personal belongings and wondered where in the world it had all come from? Being so frugal they were still amazed at the amount of accumulation from eight years. Bennett had a buyer immediately for his building, lot and some of his tools. This he traded for a livery buggy and horses, reasoning that he would need them for transportation in the city. The wagon was almost worn out. They sold their sheep, cows and pigs, leaving the chickens for George. While sorting out and packing, Anna came by to invite her to a gathering at the hotel Saturday evening. Nothing fancy, just a few friends in to say a proper goodbye.

Margaret and Bennett were overwhelmed as they walked into the hotel (as it was now called). It seemed that every one in town had come to the party! The Mills, Akers, Burketts, Dales and Donalsons, Hills, Lyons and Rushes, Drumms, Lemerts, Webbs, the Bartigs, and the Browns, and many more. They all brought superb dishes for the pot luck and some one brought out a fiddle and the party was in full swing until the wee hours. Margaret was so touched. She had not realized how many and what good friends she and Bennett had made in the years here. They made leaving very hard. Were it not for the progress of the move, she might have changed her mind.

Chapter 18

Winfield, KS

The land up here was different. Although just twenty miles from Cedar Vale, the terrain turned from rich black soil into ridges and hills of limestone rock with soil valleys. There were already farms with prosperous homes built from good crops of maize, corn and winter wheat, the new kind that can be planted in the fall, grazed most of the winter then harvested in the spring!

They were greeted with open arms by Preston and Mary. The living quarters were cramped and reminded Margaret of that first winter in the dugout at George's place. Well, Margaret thought, there was George's place, now Preston's place. When will we ever have our place? She said nothing aloud. It will come to pass, she thought confidently to herself.

They received *The Winfield Courier* by mail and kept up with the town's development with lots of interest, especially the establishment of schools, and the railroads. Churches were important and the Women's Christian Temperance League was a power. Every week *The Courier* had an article expounding their ideas and beliefs. The Methodist Church was building a college, to later be called Southwestern Kansas Conference College.

One day Margaret read that the Kansas State Governor was going to be in Winfield to address the town on 19th of February. "Look here Bennett, it says he'll

243

speak twice that one day, once at 2:00 P.M. and again that evening at 7:00 P.M. at the opera house. Citizens will meet him at the train at 11:00 A.M. at the Santa Fe depot and escort the Governor through town. A reception open to all will be at Mr. D. A. Millingtons. Oh, Bennett, could we go?"

"Opportunity for what? He is just speaking about temperance, he's just playing politics. He knows what is in the wind these days."

"He is not! Those temperance ladies can't vote! In fact, they are hurting their cause to get the vote by attaching this temperance issue onto the idea. But I still want to see the Governor! We could go by train!"

"Margaret, read the rest of the paper, Small Pox is on the move again and it plainly says STAY HOME and vaccinate, do not travel!" Bennet replied.

"Yes," and it also says, "Sherman's gold mine is making a showing, and you know Sherman!"

Margaret made preparations to go to Winfield anyway. She made a new black dress, with ruffles across the shoulders and around the throat. Her mother's silver broach was centered and nestled in the throat ruffle. A chiffon net bodice overlay came over the shoulders and made a V drape across the front. The skirt had the "apron" drape in front with the bow pulled around to perch atop a flounced bustle. She made a matching hat of a multitude of small black ribbon roses attached atop her head with a black ribbon tie under her chin. She even spent money to buy a regular pair of shoes, pointed and heeled, which she had not worn since getting used to the moccasins she had learned to make from Strike Axe. With all of the preparation Bennett knew Margaret's heart was set on this event and he could not disappoint her. It would be expensive he argued, and she agreed and went right on sewing. Finally when she cut her hair in front to make curly bangs, he was so shocked, and delighted in her new attractiveness that he could no longer resist.

They could not get on the first train because the cars were so full, but a second train had been dispatched on the line so they waited in the cold for it to arrive, which put them in too late for the Governor's arrival. However, by skipping dinner they did gain admission to the opera house for the afternoon event. The townspeople had been asked to come in the evening so the out of town people could attend the afternoon speech and return to their homes. Still, it was very crowded. Margaret and Bennett had not been in such a crowd in years. Margaret felt so special and elegant! Never had it mattered before, but today a signal was sent to her very soul that something grand was about to happen to her. The excitement mounted.

A prayer was said by Reverend J. E. Platter, a temperance song was sung by the choir, then Senator Hackney introduced his Excellency the Honorable Governor of Kansas, Mr. St. John.

He began, "No greater truth was ever uttered than that by the great Abraham Lincoln, when he said, 'this government cannot exist half slave and half free.' It is no less a truth to say that this Government can no longer exist half drunk and half sober." (applause)

He continued about the exodus of 40,000 to Missouri because of prohibition, but said that the state had gained 100,000 in the last eighteen months of the very finest class of people. "One place where we have lost population is inside of our penitentiary!"

Margaret did not hear everything he said, but was hypnotized with the hum of the crowd's reception of his words and found it uplifting as a sermon. Politics or not, she was moved to agree they were indeed "on the

245

right track to stop crime, violence and save our sanity and country!"

They left the opera house with hundreds of others in attendance, and could not get a jitney. They inquired about directions to the reception and found it was only four or five blocks away. The informer was a photographer, taking pictures for the occasion. Bennett and Margaret both posed for him in their new finery.

Bennett tried to talk Margaret out of going to the reception. "We don't know anyone there! Besides I am ready to find something to eat. And these shoes hurt."

"Well, sir, they can't hurt any more than mine do! And I'm going if I have to go alone! Besides I'm cold and the walk will warm us up, we can get inside and eat there. We'll be warm and well fed to boot. What else is there to do until train time?"

The homes in Winfield were elegant. Small as the town was, the City had tried diligently to encourage growth of a stable and cultural nature. The banks had discouraged oil and gas people as transient. Mr. Mattington and his paper had done a great deal to set the tone of the town with its verbal crusade for education and commerce.

His home was a reflection of his prominence in the community. Margaret had never seen a dwelling so lovely and it brought back memories of her mother's stories about her home in Pennsylvania. Now after all these years she knew what her mother had sacrificed to come out into the Ohio and Illinois wilderness. As nice as her childhood home had been in Olney, it never had the scope of this finery.

Passing through the receiving line she was thrilled with shaking the hand of the Governor, embarrassed because her stomach took that exact moment to growl.

She remembered to curtsy, and she ignored the noise. After they were received by the hosts and guest of honor, she and Bennett headed for the large table of food. A string quartet was playing music and there were no chairs available. They went out to the garden, cool as it was to sit on the porch rail to eat.

"Do you think we took too much food Margaret? Not many people filled their plates like we did. This is sure good but I'd rather be home at my own table, I'm damn uncomfortable!"

"Hush Bennett, something grand is happening, don't spoil it!"

They returned to the ballroom and an orchestra had replaced the quartet and couples were dancing. Margaret could not help sway to the beautiful music. She had never heard such grand music. Beside them stood a gentleman, very well dressed in formal attire but not at all pretentious. He turned to Bennett and shook hands, "Lovely music isn't it?"

Bennett nodded.

"Where are you folks from? I know most every one in town and you are new."

"Yes," Bennett replied and explained their circumstances.

"I am Mr. Robinson of the Read's Bank. Mr. Read is my uncle. Like to farm do you, Mr. Pugh? Perhaps we can be of assistance sometime. Our bank will put up the $200.00 to file a claim in Wichita and accept the new deed as collateral until the debt is paid out on time. If this interests you give me a call. Here is my card. I've made loans as far away as Cedar Vale and never had anyone default on the deal yet." Turning to face Margaret, smiling into her face, he said. "May I have a dance Mrs. Pugh?" Before she could say she could not dance to this music, Mr. Robinson explained the new waltz, "Big step, and two small step, step, quite simple," and away they whirled. It was so fast, and his hand on her back and the other in the air, as strong as she was, she felt like she might swoon from the music and the pace and rhythm of the waltz!

As the music stopped they applauded, she caught her breath, and he thanked her for her company, "You are a delight to dance with, my dear, truly a natural. You must have studied the ballet!"

Margaret flushed at the attention and the compliment, but was poised enough to say, "Oh, but it must have been my very able and graceful instructor!"

Mr. Robinson beamed at the flattery, took her hand placed it in his arm and lead her back to Bennett standing as if glued to the same spot where they left him, seething inside and trying hard to look like a normal civilized human being, but feeling more like a raging wild animal. A nod and bow from Mr. Robinson, who thanked Bennett for the company of his lovely wife, then turned leaving them alone. With clenched teeth Bennett whispered, "We are leaving now."

"But the train doesn't leave for an hour!"

"We are leaving." He took her hand and copying Mr. Robinson's gesture, placed her hand in his arm and holding tightly led the unwilling Margaret out into the street.

"Bennett, you're jealous! Mr. Robinson was only being hospitable. At my age a little flattery is so rare I can't imagine you feeling this way, he is years younger than I!"

"So am I!" Bennett said, "He held you right up in his face. That dance is indecent except for married people!"

"Bennett!"

The train depot was cold in spite of the pot bellied stove they hovered around and the company was colder on the trip home. However, nothing could spoil it for Margaret and she had Bennett soothed with a whispered promise to stop with him in the buggy on the drive to the house. Intimacy was a problem since they began living with Preston and Mary. Bennett grudgingly agreed this may be a fine evening after all.

Every detail of the evening was shared over and over with Preston and Mary. How Margaret wished Mary had been able to share it with her, but being pregnant, Mary could not have gone out in public.

Thinking about moving to the city became almost an obsession to Margaret. She planned her every waking hour about a business of their own. A boarding house was her best dream since she knew that business so well, but a building of that size would cost a fortune and they had such meager means.

They had sold the furniture building in Cedar Vale, but had used almost all of the money to buy a buggy, new wagon and team. However, Margaret had never used her earnings from working at Anna Baird's and it had built to a small nest egg.

"If we could get a building, we could have enough to start up." Margaret confided to Mary. "We need material for baby clothes and a crib. The men need all sorts of supplies for the new house. I am going to Winfield on a shopping trip, everyone make a list."

Something needed to be done to get everyone out of the rut. Mary was getting terribly testy, being pregnant and crowded and she wanted her own home to herself and so did Margaret. Margaret did not tell Bennett her exact plan. She wanted to see if it worked.

Mrs. Green, a neighbor, went with her to Winfield and they had a fine day shopping. They went to the

Williams' Hotel for the night and discovered there was no room.

The Hotel manager called Mr. Williams about the problem and he came over promptly when informed two "lovely ladies" needed a room for the night. His face fell somewhat when he realized they were "older lovely ladies," however he graciously escorted them to the Methodist Church parsonage where Mrs. Earp invited them to stay with her. Margaret explained she was very embarrassed, she should have wired for reservations, but had no idea that the hotels would be so fully occupied. "Oh, yes, my dear, with the traveling salesmen, construction workers, and all in town, finding a room is impossible. That is why I open my doors for the unfortunate, if they are ladies."

The next morning Mrs. Earp gave them breakfast and they discretely placed a "stipend" in an envelope and left it on the buffet. Margaret and Mrs. Green went to the bank at the stroke of 10:00.

Mr. W. C. Robinson was at his desk behind a half wall made up of teller's cages. His familiar face eased some of the gut wrenching tension Margaret felt, but she felt justifed by telling herself she was only making an inquiry.

"Good day to you, Mrs. Pugh! What a pleasant surprise. Have you seen today's paper? This is a good day for bankers. That rascal Jesse James was shot, killed by his own men! The Ford boys they said, Robert and Charles. Some are saying they were agents of the Governor all along, but I don't think so. You have heard about Jesse James? Awful man! Robbed banks and encouraged others to turn to crime. No conscience. He would attack in broad daylight, and kill and maim! But enough rejoicing, what can I do for you today?"

"I am thinking about going into business, that is

my husband and I," Margaret's enthusiasm took hold and her whole plan, carefully thought out unfolded before this attentive stranger. She was so obviously knowledgeable Mr. Robinson was impressed. He jotted numbers as she talked. As she ran out of words, she paused before asking for a loan. After all, she was a woman, and a married woman. She knew her place and what was possible, although she had never wished more than right now to have been born male.

Mr. Robinson read her mind and said, "Mrs. Pugh, I will speak to the board about your proposal, I believe there is a building available near the Santa Fe Depot that you may be able to lease for your business. Have your husband come in to "negotiate the loan" and I think we can do business to everyone's satisfaction."

Margaret's heart soared. "Thank you, thank you very much! My husband doesn't need to know I preceded him here does he?"

"Mrs. Pugh, this entire idea shall be mine. Just have your husband come in soon!"

At home Margaret could hardly contain her information. She talked about shopping, the killing of Jesse James, the train trip, and then casually interjected, "There is a beautiful new empty building just a ways from the Santa Fe Depot. I can think of so many wonderful enterprises that would thrive there, travel bags, clothes, harness, a boarding house would be perfect! But whoever is energetic shall get it, for it won't last long unoccupied. It is my understanding that it is not for sale but lease only, and very negotiable as the owner wants a place to live in the upstairs. By the way, I met Mr. Robinson. He said to give you his regards. He would like to do business with you, Bennett."

Bennett grunted acknowledgement and said some-

251

thing about the cows, got up and left the room. Out of doors, he pondered about the city life versus the rural and admitted to himself that neither he nor Margaret were getting any younger and the hard chores out here were taking a toll. A boarding house wouldn't be easy work, but with hired help it could be a good retirement life. He remembered the closeness they had shared in Olney. But money! He had heard that the Read Bank was generous and stood behind local business. At supper Bennett announced that he had decided to investigate this property in Winfield.

"Oh, Bennett!" Margaret cried out and gave him a hug right there in front of the children. They talked into the night about the possibilities. Winfield was the new county seat, railroads were coming in from every direction, schools were abundant and good and with the exposure to church close at hand, the children might find suitable partners for marriage, rather than cowboys or transients.

Bennett was impressed with all of the brick buildings going up all along Main Street. The street was a broad avenue crossed with another of equal width at 9th Street. Rather than the usual "court house square" the Court House sat a block beyond Main with a park extending east. Another park was located at the end of Main with a beautiful new bridge across the creek that made way to this seven acre wooded island. It was a natural campground.

They stood before the building Margaret had admired. It was of light brown sandstone blocks with an array of windows all across the fifty foot front, both upstairs and down. The two pair of double doors also had glass, all in small square panes. This opened up into a spacious room with fifteen foot ceilings. Upstairs were seventeen rooms built around a stair landing

252

large enough for a sitting room. In the basement was a water pump from a cistern in the corner fed from a well out back. It was not a corner lot, but very handy to everything in town. Bennett and Margaret both began to make plans on the spot as to where "this would be located" and "that would fit there" when in walked a portly gentleman. His walk was somewhat unsteady but dignified.

"I'm Mr. Grose the owner and builder of this fine building, can I help you?"

To Margaret and Bennett's dismay, Mr. Grose did not want to sell his building, but he would lease it. He had also had a boarding house in mind but he was getting on in years and was looking for a place to retire, be taken care of in his old age, and realize a small income. Having no family he was trying to think of his future. He was willing to live in one room, take his meals with the boarders and accept a percentage of the income. "How does that sound?"

Bennett could not believe his ears! For practically board and room this old gentleman would allow them to come in and start business.

"Agreed!" They shook hands before Margaret could finish admiring the building.

Their savings would be enough to begin operating the business, but not enough for furnishings. Margaret gently hinted that the Read Bank had a reputation for helping people invest in the town. Bennett headed that way.

Mr. Robinson gave no hint that he had spoken earlier with Margaret but shaking both their hands he graciously smiled and said, "Oh yes, Mr. and Mrs. Pugh, from the Governor's reception, I believe," and diplomatically turned his full attention to Bennett.

Bennett's animation about the project also impressed Mr. Robinson and was the sort of enthusiasm they were looking for to build Winfield. A loan was negotiated with payments delayed until they had a chance to get ready to open, providing they would open an account with their savings in this Bank. Bennett could not believe it was so easy. He had never quite trusted banks. He surmised that part of the town's growth must be due to this bank's generosity in making loans. Of course they had the right to repossess all one owned if they became delinquent, and that thought made Bennett rather uneasy.

They left the bank as new business people and they relished in a new sense of dignity. They had missed it and had never realized they had missed it until now.

With Margaret's thriftiness and skill in furnishings and Bennett's handiwork, they opened very soon. As they settled into the old familiar routine they realized they were only working half as hard as they had on the farm. With no animals and just one building to clean and repair, "And Bennett, it is ours!"

"Agreed! And if I don't like the looks of any of these fellows, I can just run them off without offending my boss."

Margaret laughed, "Oh, don't you go thinking you don't have a boss around here!" They laughed together and it felt very good.

Winfield was not too different from hundreds of other little towns across the country. Striving to be the biggest and best and invaded by the transient elements from the mass migration to settle the west. This growth, like a pubescent child, plagued all of America right now. Everything had speeded up with the railroads pushing ever west these last 10 years. Connected coast to coast since 1869, the only scarcity in this big country was people. Immigration was solving that quickly. The only thing that set Winfield apart was an overall desire to build a solid future based on education and agriculture. Oil and gas exploration was going on but discouraged, even though $200 was offered for a gas lease and was too much temptation for many. The bank did not extend loans readily to these prospectors.

Chapter 19

The Dream Boarding House

The boarding house was full from the start and they soon had to hire help. Margaret supervised the cooking and cleaning and did all of the baking herself.

The rooms were occupied mostly by single men, traveling salesmen, merchants that had not established a family home yet.

The restaurant was a busy place. Food and pastry odors wafted out the door to entice people in. Salesmen would rent an area to display their wares, and Margaret's training at an elegant table in her mother's home paid off handsomely because her restaurant soon built a reputation for supplying the elegance fit for a luncheon by the Christian Women's Temperance League, and other social functions.

One day Bennett called out to Margaret and the household, "Come in here everybody! You must see this machine. It's amazing!"

The smell of popped corn breezed out over the building bringing them all to the dining room. There they saw an enameled box about five feet square with a glassed compartment, the corn popping out of a kettle with no fire under it! It was like magic. They stood transfixed watching the batch after batch hop out into the glass compartment. A crowd from the street began to gather, each person awed by this new invention.

"I have to have one!" Bennett declared.

Margaret scowled, "How much?" But she recognized that look in his eye. Not very often did he get really determined about something, and she knew that look in his eye when she saw it and said nothing to interfere with his decision. Being a model driven by steam from a fire box the machine could be wheeled to the train station or the park and it would soon pay for itself. They added sandwiches and John and Jacob helped deliver them right onto the train during the regular stops. Their only limitation was running out of popping corn, and that was remedied when a local farmer agreed to plant a crop just for Bennett.

Both boys were sensitive children and being outsiders wished to fit in with their peers. As teens they were keenly aware of what they judged their parents' shortcomings to be. In the light of the times, they saw Bennett's gentle nature as a weakness. They were not yet mature enough to know that courage did not come from carrying a gun and backing people down. Margaret's independent and assertive personality, in contrast, sometimes made Ben appear "hen pecked." The reality was that Bennett was always in control of his family and financial affairs, but in his own gentle and loving way.

One especially hot and humid summer day, the boys were helping Ben set up the pop corn machine in the park east of the court house for an evening performance by the Musical Conservatory School Band. Although still hot, the sun was lowering in the west and a few people had gathered to pick out a seat on the lawn for a picnic supper. A scraggly man in an unkempt wool, grey uniform charged across the lawn, rifle in hand and with the banshee Rebel yell, began firing at random! Ben pushed the boys to the ground behind the corn machine, and in a low, crouching, zig

257

zag run, charged full force into the demented man. He wrestled the gun away. Another man then ran to his side and helped subdue the old soldier who continued to rave and rant, making no sense whatsoever.

The boys lay there stunned. They saw two people dead and others bleeding. The local police arrived and the wounded were carted away in various buggies.

"Dad, are you alright? Are you wounded? What made him do that?"

"I'm fine boys." Dusting himself off, "Poor devil, war nerves. It's been twenty years, but war can do that to a man. Some let it fester in their minds and one day it all boils out, breaks the mind. Now he'll have to live with what he has just done, too, if he ever recovers. Probably be put in an insane asylum for the rest of his life."

Never again did the boys doubt Bennett's courage.

Margaret's life appeared normal once again except for her yearning for her children. Letters were often mailed trying to get them to move out here with them. She wanted to be a part of their lives and get to know her grandchildren as well. Now, as she grew older, she realized that she had deprived her children by moving them away from a stable community environment. On the other hand they had developed an independent nature that gave them the freedom to fit into any social occasion. How would they turn out?

When they spoke about it Bennett would try to ease Margaret's mind, "Margaret, you cannot take every blame for these children's mistakes. We live in terrible unsettled times. Look at the influences children face today. They have a new way of life! It's fast and changing! Look at the trouble they can get into that we never dreamed of. There are gangs of outlaws, transient people by the hundreds, cowboys, freight trains

258

that can go forty miles an hour and more. There is constant fear of Indians, we are just recovering from a Civil War. It's this world we live in. These times! All we can do is bring them up right and pray."

Margaret agreed, "These are hard times on families, all split up from their roots, no grandparents to reinforce the parents, well perhaps things will settle down for our grandchildren! We shall just have to try very hard to make a place here and try to get our family together again."

Jacob, much like Lindsey, loved the trains and would faithfully watch each one come in. He listened to the cowboys and the drummers, the teamsters who hung around the depot waiting for work. It was quite an education that had nothing to do with school. He had a horse now and would race about town to be seen by the girls from their porches and hopefully not by the local constables nor a parent who would report him to his father.

The lovely Carrie Creary was courted on her porch and in his father's buggy as often as her father would allow. He was working on the railroad and was becoming muscular and handsome, but still he sometimes displayed some of the daredevil attitude of the youthful road crews, and Mr. Creary did not wholly approve of his reputation. He had heard the boy was seen in saloons, so courting was mostly limited to the front porch under Carrie's parents' watchful eyes. This special girl was most faithful about being seen every time he rode by. He would tip his hat to her, she would nod, soon he had to stop to check his horses' hoof right in front of her house. She asked, "Is there a tool you may need that we can lend?"

"No, thank you, Ma'am. Very kind of you to offer." The conversations began, then the walks, and Jacob

259

began to "keep company." However it was several years away from making a commitment of marriage. Jacob had no trade nor education and was befuddled yet about the direction he would take.

John, at sixteen, had lots to learn about living in town. There were the boy-type scraps to get into. He had to establish himself among his peers. He kept most of these attempts to himself. Always a very private child he ate, slept and did his chores, but spoke very little with his parents. They, being busy, allowed it, as he caused no trouble for anyone, usually.

One Memorial Day picnic he was "called out" to defend Bennett's being a Union Veteran by a Southern boy. There was such a ruckus the older folks thought the war had broken out again! Another time he was compelled to defend Margaret's reputation. Whispers had it that Margaret's boarding house was something more. Hearing this, John had to set the offender straight! Yelling, "I'll have you know that my mother sits at the head of the stairs and makes sure everyone goes to their rooms without "extra" guests. She is a good and Christian woman!" He spat in the dirt, tears and sweat on his face as he stood over the luckless boy who had implied otherwise. However, John knew where the real "house" was located and would creep down there at night to peek in as the doors opened and shut. He and some other boys had found a partial bottle of whiskey thrown in the alley and sampled it. He liked it. Thus, gradually integrated with the other town boys, he settled into a new way of life, too. He was especially accepted after Bennett bought him a horse. "You're spoiling that boy! He'll be racing up and down the streets, and off to Lord knows where, just like Jacob."

But Bennett knew a boy's need for a horse and

argued, "Now he'll be available to run more errands." Of course he never did because he was seldom home.

Kansas Belle, *Kannie*, was the darling of everyone. She was learning to read from menus, drummers' catalogs and the Bible, although she didn't start school until next year. She was so inquisitive nothing escaped her, and by observation she learned about setting tables, doing laundry, keeping accounts and anything else she could poke her nose into. She could recite at the drop of a hat, knew a hundred rhymes and was getting to be more of a show off than Margaret liked.

Between children and customers, Margaret had quite a busy life style. Gradually her reputation spread. The Methodist minister's wife was a great help when she planned a tea for the Ladies Aides and the W.C.T.L. (Women's Christian Temperance League) at the restaurant. It was served so elegantly, that no one failed to be impressed. Margaret used her mother's tea service she had acquired from brother George. "This," she thought, "will give my daughter a lesson in what a proper elegant home should be even if we are on the frontier." It then dawned on her how she was talking and acting like her own mother did to her years ago.

Margaret still had respectful feelings about the "girls" down the street. She well remembered the miracles the likes of them had performed during the war and how most have been forced by circumstance beyond their control to follow the "profession". With so little available for a woman to earn a living it was easy for them to sell themselves?

Margaret threw aside any caution about her reputation and hired some of "the girls." She knew there would be talk, but her compassion outweighed the risk. She trained waitresses and laundresses, and befriended them all. What they did on their own, she did not ask.

The laundry did especially well down in the cool basement. It was tough to pack out the heavy baskets of wet clothes to pin on the lines, but the girls were young and strong. Other hotels and restaurants began to have their laundry done there and soon there were eight tubs going at a time! As hard as the work was, the girls preferred it to being forced to find a husband to support them. They had heard the stories about the women who went West to live in the desolation and deprivation until they lost their minds. It was said that the dry, hot wind was responsible, but Margaret felt it was living out in the West where there was not a tree, nor a neighbor, nor a hill to change the scene or break up the monotony day in and day out. Others spoke of the hardships and the wind blowing the rain and snow in the darkness of winter with nothing to use as fuel except the buffalo chips and they were getting scarce! Winter or summer everyone agreed that the wind was maddening and wanted no part of it.

Margaret began to write letters to Lindsey about the prosperity of Kansas now and how wonderful it would be to have the family back together. Jacob was learning plumbing, a new trade, to lay pipes that gas would flow through to all of the street lights and the homes so they would have a marvelous source of light. Several gas wells had been discovered and people were leasing their property for almost as much as they could sell it for. Also the limestone quarries were in operation, and the gypsum mine too. All this and farming too.

Reading the letters made Lindsey restless. Olney was also doing fairly well. Being raised here he could always find work through his aunts and uncles, but Mother is getting old now, and as an oldest son, he supposed he should think of being where he could take care of them.

He asked Martha, "How would you like to go to Kansas?"

"Are you crazy? Start completely over? You have no job there and homesteads are gone. You aren't taking me out to the wilderness to lose my mind."

But Lindsey had made up his mind before he had asked Martha and being a "good wife" she packed up her belongings and choked back her tears.

Martha and Lindsey left Olney much the same as Margaret and Bennett had, except all they owned was packed into one wagon. Martha's peony bulbs, pear tree seedlings, and one rose bush were the last things to be packed.

Friends and relatives followed them for most of the first day, first one dropping behind, and then another as sad farewells were said. The last one to leave them was Martha's beloved little sister, Sarah. Five years Martha's junior, she had always been Martha's baby. She called her "little Dutch" and their son, little William Oscar, called her Aunt Dutch. They clung to each other promising to write, saying reassuring things like, "We can visit back and forth now on the train!" Knowing that they probably never would be able to afford it. Martha sobbed most of the day and could not be consoled that night, camped out under the wagon. She refused to make a fire and cook, so Lindsey rummaged through the offerings that had been left with them by those saying farewell.

Hard as the trip was, the road was now at least well defined, way stations were frequent and danger from Indians was replaced with fear of bandits.

The delight of the trip was seeing the St. Louis Bridge! Lindsey was so glad Martha didn't have to cross the way his mother had. Lordy! She would have turned around for sure! When they arrived in St. Louis, they lost some of their fear by signing up with a wagon train heading West. Some were going on to California, but they would leave it in Kansas as it turned south to skirt the Rocky Mountains, and the badlands of Oklahoma.

Lindsey excitedly showed Martha the bridge across the Mississippi and pointed out to her the changes that had taken place since he was last here. He also told her the story about their first crossing and Margaret's dunking. He had a big whoop about it, but Martha failed to see what was so funny. Margaret could have been killed.

The small group of fourteen wagons crawled along at about six miles a day and Martha began to feel they would never get to Kansas. She yearned to be clean again and have the luxury of stopping and rest. They traveled every conceivable road condition in every sort of weather as spring turned from its cool nights and hot days into just plain hot summer time.

Their shoes gave out and Martha limped along for eight days until even the cloth inside fell out through the worn out soles. "They look just the way I feel!" she moaned one night. Lindsey, pulling off his boot, stuck his hand up through the sole of his too, looked at her and began to laugh.

It felt so good to laugh that they almost became hysterical, and fell exhausted onto the wagon pallet. Little Will, sensing that the tension had finally been broken between his parents, jumped in with them, giggling at a joke he knew nothing about.

William Oscar, sometimes called W. O., sometimes

Will, sometimes Bill, really enjoyed this adventure. There were other children to play with. He was with his parents twenty-four hours a day and being only five, had few responsibilities. He was to "look out" for Indians from the wagon seat beside mother, or from the saddle with dad. He was learning to handle the harness of the mule team. They drove awhile and then walked awhile. Walking was more comfortable and then he could run ahead, back and forth. Martha would worry about him, "Don't run between the wagons! You'll get trampled, you'll cause a runaway, don't run up behind those mules, they'll kick you silly!" and "Stay away from Reverend Green's campfire, they have grownup conversations and it's not for you to hear!" Will listened momentarily like most five year olds, and then he was off to some other interest.

Martha had four miscarriages since he was born and it didn't look like she would have any more children. So she concentrated all her mothering and her German discipline on him. She was determined to raise him "right." "Spare the rod and spoil the child." She did not spare the rod.

Except for wearing out the leather soles they had replaced twice, the heat, dirt, rain and weariness of the trip were uneventful. Lindsey was excited to see the changes along the way. Whole towns had grown up where only a farm had been ten years ago, and the road! It was beaten down on both sides to where it took a good deal of searching each night for fire wood. Like as not there were travelers camping in the favorite spots when they arrived and they would meet up and pass each other with regularity.

At Fort Scott the garrison was much the same but enlarged with a town surrounding it now. New maps were obtained and studied and the Fort's Commandant gave them a lecture on the protocol to be used when encountering Indians.

"These people are at peace. They have been for several years." He went on to say, "Keep your rifles and handguns in their scabbards and follow your wagon master's guidance. It is no longer necessary to have an escort across Kansas, but for those going to Oregon, you will check with the Fort Commandant at Fort Hays before progressing, and those headed for California shall stop at Fort Wichita before going further south. You cannot pass into Indian Territory without passes. The United States Marshals patrol that area for your safety, but mostly," and he repeated, "mostly to protect the Indians from YOU. So don't go gettin' any ideas that you can pick out a spot of land and stop and homestead there, cause you can't! There has been some uprisings down in Arizona and with the business of chasing outlaws and running off squatters these Marshals have their hands full.

"You can't expect much help from them, but don't go causing any trouble either. Stay on the trails, mind your own business, and stock up on provisions here or in Wichita. You have a long, long journey. You may prefer to stay in Kansas rather than face the dreadful conditions ahead. That will be fine with us. Read your map carefully, the mileage is NOT exaggerated! It is a long time between water holes and you are entering in the summer."

Listening to the speech made Lindsey very grateful they were so near to their destination, although he played with the possibility of extending the adventure so they could see California. He remembered the cattle drive to Texas and decided there was nothing of beauty out there to attract him.

With cheerful goodbyes and best wishes exchanged

266

with the friends they had made on the trail, they left the train about ten miles out of El Dorado and headed south to Winfield. Farm after farm dotted every 160 acres. So much different from his last trip here. Houses, even orchards had grown up. Gardens looked as if they had been made here for the last 100 years. Only the fences gave notice that this was new to civilization, and it was barbed wire for the most part. "Wicked stuff," Lindsey scowled, "it will tear a horse apart and even chew cow hide if the cow is stupid enough to brave it. Guess they have stopped the cattle drives through here!"

Margaret was once again thrown into a surprised ecstasy! Lindsey just walked in off the street and said, "I'm here, Mother!"

Celebrations were in order and telegrams were sent out to Uncle George, Cousin Jarome and Mary and Preston. LINDSEY HOME, DINNER SUNDAY.

Lindsey was awkward with his siblings after such a long separation. He had still imagined the "little boys" as little boys, yet here was Jacob, not a large man, but a man nonetheless. John, a restless teen, and darling baby Belle, not a baby, but a precocious seven-year-old pixie, obviously jealous of the shift of attention being showered on the more innocent five-year-old William Oscar, clinging to and protected by his mother's skirts.

During the reunion dinner Lindsey became more comfortable and basked in his families' attention. All spoke encouragingly and offered ideas for finding work, buying land and housing. With everything booming Lindsey could not miss success here!

Martha, on the other hand was becoming more and more uncomfortable with their length of stay. Belle and Will were at each other almost constantly. Each

267

jealous of the other's toys, attention, and mother's time. Margaret and Martha each tried hard to be fair, yet each had a mother's protectiveness and each was sure the other child did something provocative first.

Feelings tensed also because Martha was cleaner than Margaret who prided herself on her well kept house and took offense when Martha would sweep and dust where she had just finished, or do dishes while Margaret was trying to have her second cup of coffee. Tension mounted as the first and then the second week ended without Lindsey finding work except as a day labor unloading freight.

One evening Lindsey ventured, "I'm going to Cedar Vale and see what is there. Martha, I want you and Will to stay here with Mother until I get back."

"No."

For the first time in their marriage Martha would not comply.

"If I stay here, there will be bad feelings."

"I don't understand. Mother loves you and Will. I won't be long."

"Lindsey Johnson, I came all this way from Illinois to go to hell and back if necessary, but I won't stay in hell without you. You left me once, and five long years I waited. Well, I wait no more. You go, I go! I'll not live in another woman's house, especially my mother-in-law's. I'll camp with the Indians first!"

Lindsey shook his head. Her German bullheadedness and her feisty nature were tough to overcome, but it was also what made him think she was tough enough to make it out here.

Margaret hated to see them leave again. She had so hoped he would find work in town. She feared for a woman's sanity out in the country all alone. But privately she was also relieved that she would not have Martha "underfoot" either.

"Wire me when you get settled. Stay on the railroad so we can visit often. Watch out for storms and prairie fires," she admonished after them as the wagon lumbered down the partially bricked streets heading south for Arkansas City. If they found no work there they planned to go on to Cedar Vale to the east. Secretly Lindsey did not want to find work in the city. He wanted to run his own herd of cattle and Jarome had given him a hint of how he could do that.

Chapter 20

Temperance

1882-83

The Women's Christian Temperance Union in Winfield was a powerful, driving force. They met on the second Saturday afternoon of each month at 3:00 o'clock sharp.

Margaret was welcomed as a member and felt she had found a just cause. This was a voice to her beliefs in women's right to vote, and liquor as the root of all evil! Wasn't the evidence there? Weekly they published an article on the front page of the *Winfield Courier*, telling of testimony of crime, poverty and cruelty that would never have happened if the perpetrator had not been drunk.

When Margaret and Bennett read the paper and discussed the articles every morning as they usually did, they did not always agree, although Ben was in favor of Women's rights he said, "Why in the world do you women divide your efforts by driving for prohibition? Why don't you concentrate on one issue at a time? This will kill your right to vote! Men want to give up drinking less than they care about the voting issue."

"There are just as many men that believe in Prohibition. Look at the turnout for Governor St. John. Wasn't he elected with a prohibition platform? The right to vote can ride on the prohibition issue!"

"You just wish it so. I say it will defeat it. Just watch! You ladies tried to ride on the Negro's right to vote and that didn't work, now you think it will ride on something else, it just divides your efforts!"

Shifting uncomfortably, changing the subject Margaret coughed and said, "Do you see the story about Yellowstone Park? Do you think that place is really real and strange as they say, or is it all exaggerated?"

"It's in the newspaper, it must be true!" Bennett smiled and Margaret nodded acknowledging a popular belief in the integrity of journalism.

"It also warns that smallpox is spreading and we should not travel and should be vaccinated."

"I'm afraid of the vaccination, Ben."

"Well I'm more afraid of the pox. We go see Dr. Emerson today!"

Speaking with Dr. Emerson while Belle wailed from being scratched with a needle and the vaccine dripped onto her leg where the scar won't show, Ben asked Doc's advice about hooking up to the new city water well. "I'm not sure about this modern idea of pumping water into every home from one well, what if it got tainted? It would kill everyone in town!"

Doctor Emerson patted Belle on the head, "Hush, child, it's all over now, you'll be safe from the pox!" He cocked his head at Ben and said, "You're a Civil War veteran aren't you? You've seen the typhoid."

"That's right, sir, and convenient or not, I'm leery about my water supply."

"Let me assure you, we know more about sanitation today than we did then, and how it effects your health. It is the only good that came out of that War.

Bacteria it is called and every precaution will be made to keep sewage and contamination away from our water supply. In fact it will be much easier controlled than having hundreds of wells all over town.

Just think, people won't be dipping and drinking from it, instead it will be pumped by steam right into your house and nothing will touch it until it reaches you. Can't be more sanitary than that!"

"It will be awfully expensive, but Jacob and John can help lay the lines. Jacob is a plumbing apprentice you know."

"Thank you, Doc." Shaking hands, Ben paid him the $1.00 for the four vaccinations and escorted his family down the street, proud to be so knowledgeable now about "bacteria" and "sanitation." He was retelling to the children about his knowledge as they passed the new well at 9th and Main.

"When Jacob is not so busy with Mr. J. C. Fuller's gas lines, we'll have him plumb our property for gas and water at the same time. Think of it, lights all over the house and water right at the kitchen sink. Maybe we'll have it upstairs too!" Margaret mulled over the wonder of it.

"Ben, where will it all go? The water I mean."

"Drains, my dear, drains right out of the house and into the creek. No more damp back yards from bath and wash water!"

"Marvelous!" Margaret breathed in wonder.

Thanksgiving was becoming a very big holiday. It was more popular since it was promoted by President Lincoln during the Civil War. Margaret would cook the now traditional dinner of turkey and dressing and because of her obligations at the boarding house, her family, Mary and Preston, Brother George and Jarome and his little family would come over to Winfield each year for the celebration. Jarome now had a new wife, Judith Turner, and a lovely little blond girl, Constance. He was also building a very large and beautiful house in the middle of Cedar Vale. Judith had a new baby this year, little Emery, who commanded everyone's attention. Belle particularly enjoyed playing "Little Mother" to the infant.

A State Suffrage Association was formed on the 25th of June 1884, and the W.C.T.U. helped organize a delegation to travel to Washington D.C. to plea for Women's right to vote. Helen Gougar was the main delegate and work was done to enlist the political parties' endorsements. The Populist Party did give their endorsement, but the powerful Republicans did not. Margaret was in a quandary to push Suffrage or Republican! A train came through with the delegates and a quick reception was held at the depot while petitioners signed the petitions and this time allowed the delegates to make speeches and rouse enthusiasm. Margaret and the other W.C.T.U. members were there to meet Susan B. Anthony, Anna Shaw, Rachel Childs, Carrie Calt, Elizabeth Yates, Mary Ellen Lease, Anna Diggs, Doctor Eva Harding, Laura Johns and Anna Wait. Hopes soured for the cause! These ladies spoke eloquently, surely they would be heard.

But nothing happened. Vote after vote was a defeat for women's right to vote until 1887 when a small victory came about. Kansas gave women the right to vote in municipal elections only. Oklahoma, still a Territory, had passed "school vote for females" the year before.

Part of the trepidation was over the fact that if females could vote they would also be able to hold an office and if white women could vote, so could black women. A very disturbing thought to the "superior" white men.

Chapter 21

1885-1886

1885

Suddenly, as usual, Lindsey arrived in with a big cattle drive.

"Where in heaven's name have you been? We haven't heard from you in over a year! Where is Martha and Will?" Margaret admonished and hugged, all at the same time.

Lindsey explained as he washed at the new water closet and sat down to the family table set for dinner. "Me and Martha went to Cedar Vale, met Strike Axe in the bank. We struck a deal for a lease in the Osage Indian Territory.

"You see, the Indians have been forced to partition their land, each Indian allottee getting an acreage. This is against their liking since they believe it all should be held as community property. But no matter, they have to make the best of it, and Strike Axe told me he'd be damned, excuse me Mother, if he was going to be a farmer! Since the Osages can't keep Pawnee slaves anymore everything is topsy-turvy at the Agency. Anyway Strike Axe and his cousins have a lot of combined land and the agency agreed to allow them to lease it for grazing if they don't choose to farm. I can even build me a house! So I talked with Uncle George and he staked me to this cattle drive so I could get some stock. I rode for them for part of the herd. I just picked me out thirty of the prettiest cows and consigned them to Cedar Vale on the Santa Fe line. When I get 'em home I'll get Martha and Will to help me drive them south to the Osage."

"Where has Martha been all this time?" Margaret inquired.

"Oh, she stayed and kept house for Uncle George. That woman loves to clean, Mother you can't believe it! She must have been born with a brush in her hand!"

"Will you be safe? I mean, I know the Indians are friendly, but right there on the reservation?"

"Mother, you just watch. With ownership, I just bet you the Indians will sell off all they own to the whites, why the only thing stopping them now is the agency. Strike Axe thinks it is a joke that I'd pay him for the use of something no one can own. That's the way they think of it just now. When it is all gone, well then there may be trouble because us whites do own what we own. I plan to pay out the lease in cattle and I'll ship out of Cedar Vale. Won't that all be slick?"

"The way things are going I won't be surprised to see a railroad right down through Indian Territory." Bennett injected.

"You're right, Ben, and I'm the one that will try make sure it comes right by my house!" They all laughed together.

Lindsey had to leave to catch his trail. "You always come through like a fresh breeze Lindsey, so fast I wonder later if you have really been here or if I just dreamed it because I wanted it so! I love you! Come again soon! Very soon."

"I will Mother, if I can find a way to leave the cattle."

Shaking Bennett's hand Lindsey noticed for the first time the age in their faces and was shocked to realize it. He counted mentally, noting his mother was fifty-eight years old and her with a child the same age as his.

15 May 1885

It had rained hard for three days and water from the Walnut had begun to overflow its banks. Island Park, only four blocks from the tracks and six from the boarding house, flooded and the water rapidly began to invade Winfield. Another storm struck and water now poured through the streets. Margaret and Ben and all the help took furniture and supplies up to the second floor and prayed the rain would stop before too much damage was done. Since no one had ever seen the water that high before they had no way to know how high it could get. It crested at eighteen inches up on the wall of the main dining room. The water was down in two days and as Margaret shoveled out mud she grumbled, "It's either dust or mud!"

Doctor Emerson came by to warn them all to boil the drinking water and scrub the house down with lye soap, and keep the children out of the mud.

"Oh sure, as if you can keep little ones out of the mud!"

All of the guests left, business was interrupted for repairs and Margaret was so upset Bennett encouraged her to leave. "Go over to Cedar Vale as soon as the trains can run and visit your brother. The two of you may even go see where Lindsey is going to live."

So Margaret packed up a bag for her and Belle, leaving Ben and the boys to work on the repairs, and new plumbing. At the train depot, Margaret bought their tickets and requested a telegram be sent to George so someone would meet them in Cedar Vale. She told Belle, "I certainly hope they don't have a heart attack when they receive the telegram. They may think someone died. Isn't this exciting? We shall be there in only an hour and it once took a whole day by wagon if everything went well. We don't even have to take a lunch."

Inside the train they found a wood slatted seat like a park bench. Another faced their seat. Margaret sat her bags beside her and Belle facing her. She didn't want to take any chance that her bags would be lost like her furniture had been.

The scenery rushing by reminded her of her first train trip, and tears welled into her eyes. Quickly she dismissed the nostalgic thoughts and reminded herself that this was strictly pleasure.

Jarome, her nephew, was there to meet them with a surrey. It was so elegant, with a little trim of red. She felt the stares of everyone in town as they took the main street route so Jarome could point out new businesses and old landmarks.

Margaret and Belle were warmly welcomed and spent two weeks basking in the love and fellowship of her brother and his son and his family. She visited with all of her old friends as well. Anna Baird's son, Arch, at only seventeen, was courting Olive, Jarome's daughter. My, how times did fly.

George told her about his children back in Illinois. "Althea is planning to move out to Kansas soon. No date was set, but it sure will be good to see her."

On the trip back to Winfield, Margaret thought how she had aged. Seeing George, only two years her senior, made her realize she, too, was growing older. With young children, one doesn't think of themself as old. How odd.

She had yearned to see Lindsey, but the rains had

swollen the river to impassable even by horse, and the roads were washed out as well. It was impossible to even think of trying.

1886

"Here's an invitation from Jarome's sister Althea! She is getting married the 26th of March. Oh Bennett, it has been almost a year since we have had a holiday. Could we get away?"

"You could go down on the new Santa Fe line, Margaret, I'll stay and tend to business if you can get one of the girls to cook."

Margaret was excited! She was going alone and would need new dresses. There was a fashion of pleated bodices, puffed sleeves and a high neck collar to which one attached a broach at the throat. The skirt was sewn in panels and hung smoothly over the hips, very revealing, with no bustles.

Jarome had built a new house right in the middle of Cedar Vale. How the town was changing. Adam Mercantile had just opened a new store with everything in it! Johnson Saddlery (no relation) had a fine harness shop and there were brick buildings everywhere, even a bank. Margaret and Jarome chatted all the way to George's house. He was telling her about the expansion of Cedar Vale and she was telling him of the new wonders of gas lights and plumbing and a new process of steam laundry that she was looking into. One could do wool suits. Just think of the trade.

Visiting with George was a pleasure. Althea was very animated about her beau, Joseph Wesley Meldrum. He had a ranch, was so handsome and patient and considerate. She went on until Margaret did not think this man could really be true. She also heard all of the news from Illinois that Althea could give her. It was over a year old now, but still news to Margaret.

Margaret stayed several days after the wedding and she tried to entice some of them to move to Winfield. "We have schools of all sorts, even a Music Conservatory. Stone flagging is all over town. It is reported that we have the most of any town our size in the whole United States. We even have street cars!"

"What are street cars, Aunt Margaret?"

"They are like a train car except they are pulled by mules and go along the streets stopping at intervals to pick up and let off passengers at certain points about town so one does not have to harness the horse and buggy every time they wish to go into town or to school."

"Oh, how wonderful!"

"I hear they plan to have the largest Chautauqua this side of New York by next year, too. I do hope you all plan to come. We'll have some fine educators and Christian teachers making speeches and giving classes. You can stay with me if you'd like, or camp out like most do. You get acquainted with everybody that way, and they come from miles away, even out of state."

Althea was pensively thinking about being tied down as a wife, and probably by next year there would be a baby, but how she would love to attend. George interjected to say they would all try to be there. "We must get our families together more often Margaret. We are so scattered there is much family support being lost."

Word had been sent out to Lindsey and Martha that Margaret was in town and they came in by horse back one cool day late in the evening. Margaret wept for joy, hugged little Will and Martha, and clung as long as she dared to Lindsey. Somehow the older the children became the more she missed them. She worried about his safety and well being, but he looked healthy enough.

Lindsey explained, "It took two days to get here even horse back but it was faster than the wagon now that Will can ride and has his own horse. This was just an outing." Margaret didn't relay her thoughts about Martha's riding astride her horse like a man. It was becoming the usual thing out here but still looked strange to her.

"I suppose she cannot have more children anyway so it probably won't hurt her." She confided to Althea. She and George sat back after dinner and watched with pleasure as the cousins visited and played parlor word games. A favorite was to see how many descriptive adjectives one could find for a common noun. Another was to find rhymes for a word picked out by the moderator, sometimes picked from a book at random. Margaret was pleased to see her son get a little pleasure, she was sure his lonely, hard life in Indian Territory was much as hers had been fifteen years ago. But she heard no word of complaint from either Lindsey or Martha. She was shocked to hear little Will call Constance, "Wha-sha-she-show-pa."

Lindsey explained, "He called her a little Indian girl. I don't know why, with that blond hair she hardly qualifies." Margaret noticed the proud, loving look Lindsey gave his only son.

"Pray to keep him safe," she thought.

Back at home Margaret herself was amazed at Winfield. This year was a turning point. A boom of growth, teachers were being paid $49 a month. "Women only get $36." Margaret snarled. "But look here! It says we have one hundred and ninety-eight teachers employed this year!"

A dam for Bliss' Wood Mill was being constructed and a new bridge. There was the most marvelous invention, just when the gas lights were thought to be the only thing along comes electric ones! There was a new electric light and power company started and everyone was invited to come over and look at the P. H. Albright home lit up at night.

"Mr. Albright would just have to be the first with electric lights!" Margaret quipped. "But mercy on us, gas is bright enough! People are going to blind themselves with anything brighter. One will have to wear colored glasses to protect their eyes. No, I won't have such a thing in my home, even if it becomes available to all."

"Margaret, you must be getting old. You were always the first to want any new fangled thing that came along."

"Well certainly not something that would destroy your health. What if that current burned through the line? There is no telling what electricity does to your system. They haven't tested it long enough to suit me. I'll not be experimented with."

That winter Margaret was so pleased they put in gas heaters in each room. They remained toasty warm all over the house in spite of one of the coldest months anyone ever remembered. The newspaper reported it below zero every day for over a month. Water inside homes froze all over town, but not theirs and the city had the foresight to bury the water lines deep so the main line did not break in the spring. Some people chopped ice from the river and melted it. Of course the ice house was full right off and stored with sawdust to keep it through the next summer.

Chapter 22

Belle's Fall

June of 1887

The Chautauqua movement was started in 1874 in New York to provide education, culture and recreation, plus opportunity for social contacts. It was the first organization to offer college degrees from a four year home study and correspondence work. This was called the Chautauqua Literary and Scientific Circle.

Over 200 Kansas towns participated, but half of the Kansas graduates came from Winfield. This year 1887, it opened with a large auditorium that could seat 2,000, and a round open air Greek styled Hall of Philosophy stood nearby with round tables used for classes. Part of the fun was a week living in tents on the western third of the Island. Some of the campers were even local people. The trolley came into the park and made the circle, in one arched gate and out the other.

Margaret was making Kannie a new dress for the Chautauqua. She was becoming quite grown up. She was still their darling, sweet little girl and a joy to dress her pretty. Her little bouncy steps contained a healthy energy.

Margaret reminded herself that soon she would have to explain marriage to her, but not yet, her interest was on little girl things, not on boys, she doesn't even like boys yet.

Margaret tucked Kannie's Bible in a protective bag and handed it to her. "We'll meet you later at the park with the picnic dinner. I'm sure you'll enjoy the preacher who is speaking to the young people this morning. There is such a crowd we had better plan to meet at the gate at noon or we might not find you."

"Mother! I could eat with my friends! Can't you let me have 25 cents for lunch from a vendor? Everyone else is going to!"

Margaret was conscious that she was probably being a little old-fashioned because she was an older mother, so she relented. "All right, but don't stray out of the park, and be home by sundown. We'll probably see you there anyway."

"If you do, Mother, could you please call me Belle? It is more ladylike than Kannie. Besides everyone wants to know why I have such a name and it is so embarrassing to explain!"

"My, my, since when does it make a difference?"

"Since forever, Mother, please?" She kissed Margaret on the cheek.

"Of course," Margaret smiled, she is growing up.

At the new gate to the Island Park Margaret and Bennett did not see Belle at noon, nor later, but this was such a crowd one could pass close to another and not see them. Margaret forgot about it and enjoyed the speakers. Speeches were mixed with music and singing, and Margaret could not remember having such a good time. The fellowship was warm and joyous and even the weather had cooperated being neither to warm nor to cool.

This differed so much from the political rallies and the election campaigns. There were no axes to grind or causes to fight except against sin and liquor, but it was from a moral basis and not a political fight. Here no one disagreed that liquor was the root of all evil and should be abolished. Glancing around the crowd about sun-

283

down, Margaret thought she saw Belle go by in a canoe, but they were quickly behind the trees and she thought it could not be Belle, as this girl, dressed in white as most others were, had her hair up and was alone with a gentleman rowing the canoe. However, she did not meet Belle by sundown. She and Bennett went the few blocks home expecting to find her there.

Jacob and Carrie were in the dining room having a second piece of cake. John came in just behind them.

"Have any of you seen Belle?" Margaret inquired.

"No, Ma'am." They looked at her blankly.

Bennett took a stern tone, "Boys, you had better go look for your sister. Inquire around and see that she is escorted home. It's dark, take a lantern."

They spread out not needing the lanterns with the gas lights shining along the streets. Bennett retraced their steps back to the park. People were still camped for the one last night before packing to go home. Some quiet inquiries were made of friends who joined the search. Belle was fourteen years old and while this was a religious rally, danger still lurked for one so young. The Mayor, Mr. Hackery, helped as he had a lantern, too. "Don't worry Bennett, these young people are forgetful." But having been to Washington D.C. as a Senator, he was worldly enough to realize a dangerous situation. This was not a girl of courting age. His light caught a golden flash and he heard a mumble from the same direction.

"Kannie Belle, are you there?" A feeble voice replied, "Yes sir, here." He helped her up the slippery slope of damp grass. He could not see all of her in the lantern light but could see she was mussed and had mud in her hair. "Are you all right child? Has someone hurt you?"

"No sir," Kannie said in a mumbled voice with a

284

shiver. Mr. Hackery gave her his coat and led her back to the park gate, telling a man as they passed to tell Bennett his daughter is found and will be at home waiting. He escorted her all the way home. "Your mother's inside, girl, talk to her and explain everything. It is easier now than later." Suspecting what had happened he saw her through the door and left without seeing any of the family to be thanked.

Word had spread rapidly as only it can in a small town and buzzed all night as some of the searchers did not get the word that a girl was lost until daylight. Inside Margaret looked at her rumpled child and an old forgotten pain ripped her body and made her cry out! The memory of her attack as vivid today as it was the morning after it happened. She took Belle upstairs saying to Carrie, "Jacob will be here soon to escort you home, please rest on the sofa, have some tea, I will be down shortly." Carrie had no idea what was wrong with Belle, and stood glued to the carpet, eyes in a fixed disbelieving stare.

Upstairs Margaret urged Belle to tell her what happened.

"Mother, it started out so wonderful. I met Elmer Weber, he is older, and paid a lot of attention to me. He said such nice things. He loved to play with my hair. He joked about it being down my back like a child and said it should be up like a girl courting. When I said I wasn't courting he said I should be, I was woman enough!

"Mamma, I can't tell you what that made me feel like. I kept expecting him to turn his attentions to someone prettier and older, but Mamma, he would just look at me all day. He bought me all sorts of treats, we sang songs and listened to the lectures and then on a whim, he rented a canoe. We went round and round

285

the park, and he talked to me about his future. He said he planned to be wealthy quite young and he wanted to buy me things, anything I could name.

"We played a game, I would name an object and he would fashion it from air and place it on me. We docked the canoe up the creek a ways in an eddy where we got out and sat on a blanket. There were people close by so I wasn't alone exactly like someone courting.

"Anyway, we played this game on and on, and he said he'd buy me undergarments if he knew what to buy. He had never seen any, so he had no idea what a woman wore. He asked if he could have a peek and I didn't think there would be any harm in that, just my chemise. He was real interested wanting to feel the lace, but Mamma I felt sort of cold and he tried to keep me warm, Mamma it felt so strange. I warmed with his arms around me, with my heart racing and felt so weak, I just wanted to keep letting him pleasure me.

"He touched me all over so gently, and kissed me, and stroked my hair. It felt so good I lost track of time. Then he rolled on top of me, and there was a strange feeling that pained me down there. The pain lasted just a minute, then it became mostly pleasure. I asked him to stop, but he said it was me becoming a woman and he made it feel good over and over. But mamma he rumpled my dress and hair, and we rolled off the blanket and onto the mud as the pleasure became greater and greater, and pretty soon it sort of died away. He jerked away from me, and I saw it. Mother do all men have a thing like that? He showed me and said that was what caused the pleasure. He put it away and said he'd be back, but he didn't come back and I was all muddy and didn't want to be seen in the daylight all soiled, so I hid. I think I went to sleep until Mr. Hackery found me. Mamma you look strange, am

286

I changed? Am I a woman now like Elmer said?"

Margaret was weeping. The child had been raped and didn't even know it! How guilty she felt. Kannie did not know enough about sex to even know exactly what the bastard had done to her. She cried and held her baby and rocked her until Belle became alarmed.

"Mother, what are you so upset about?"

"My darling, you are hurt in a way you don't realize and I could have prevented it. I should have told you about men long, long ago. You are so beautiful and so trusting and so outgoing, I should have known and prepared you. But I didn't want to make you afraid of men. I wanted you to think you could do anything they could do and not be intimidated, and now you may have been ruined for life."

They talked into the night. Margaret explaining all of the facts of life. There was no reason to leave anything out now, so Margaret was very plain in her explanations, finally saying, "I will pray to God you are not impregnated."

Margaret left her tucked in bed, went to her basin to wash and discreetly told Bennett, "Everything is alright, I had a talk with her." Bennett relieved of any further responsibility sighed with relief.

Now Belle was in shame. Knowledge, like Eve in the Garden, made her aware of her sin and she felt shame the same as if she had deliberately caused it herself. She reasoned, after all, something that felt so good surely must have been sinful. And dear God, she had been to a religious rally to boot! Would God forgive her? Would she ever see Elmer again? What would she do if she did? Even knowing what she knew now she yearned to see him. She knew he would not come to her house now, so she found an excuse to go alone to the park. Margaret was busy with the laundry and had not forbidden her to leave the house alone. She had only told her how unwise it was to be unchaperoned while courting. Well she wasn't courting, but she was looking and now she knew it had to be a secret.

Unknown to Belle, Elmer was working on the railroad gang and saw her headed for the park. Throwing down his shovel he whispered to his partner, "Lie for me will you? Tell them I got sick." He skirted the back side of the rail yard and scurried down to the creek. He slipped into the water and washed himself off, clothes and all. He swam the short distance to the Island side of the creek. He saw Belle seated on the band stand feeding the ducks. "Belle! Meet me on the far side of the Park." He called in a stage whisper.

"What in the world are you doing here in the water, Elmer?" She laughed at how silly he looked with his hair all wet, and the hair on his chest! Ugh! She ran around while he swam. There was no one in the park today, everyone was at home for the dinner hour and it was a week day.

"I never thought I'd see you here today," she lied. "I never thought I'd see you again." She did not say why, but they both knew.

"Belle, I have to see you again." He came out on the bank and threw his shirt across a bush to dry. "I need to dry these pants too." As he removed them she giggled and turned away. "Don't turn away, look all you please, I don't care. The human body is beautiful. Especially yours, let me see yours."

"Elmer! You go on so, stop it! Put your clothes on!" But she was feeling weak again and really did not want him to, but was afraid of being caught.

"Let's go back up the creek, you know where." She nodded. They found the canoes at the dock and paddled up the creek. This time there was no mud, but no

288

blanket either. Belle turned her dress wrong side out to lay on, and removed her clothes as they played another game Elmer invented.

Afterwards they made plans of how they could keep other rendezvous without being detected.

"My mother and father will force us to get married if they find us together."

"Well, my Darling that will just play right into our hands, because they would not let you marry otherwise because of your age. If they find us, they will have to."

"Oh, Elmer, do you really want to marry me?"

"More than anything."

Belle's activities went undetected, and Margaret thought the problem was solved when Belle's period came on time. However the girl was getting lazy about her chores and could never be found when she was needed. She claimed to be tutoring a friend in math almost every evening after supper, until Margaret told her she would have to inform her friend that there were times when a family needed time together also and if she didn't know her math now she never would. Belle was defensive about being treated like a child, "After all I am out of school now." Margaret didn't like the fact that she had worn her hair up ever since, "then". Belle's reply, "Why not?"

Jacob and Carrie Creary were engaged to be married. Bennett had wanted to give them some sort of start and since business was doing so well decided to build a house for them. Perry McKyger sold him the property in the Monroe addition. Lot 15 Block 94 between 14th and 15th street on Mentor St. He saw it duly recorded in Vol. 23, page 592. He also bought McKygers lots in Block 126 numbers 7, 8 and 9. The thought that one day he and Margaret would build a house on these. It wasn't a large house. After all they were newlyweds and didn't need much room. But it had plumbing built right into the walls, and gas, too. Bennett did not suspect that John was jealous about it. After all Jacob was the oldest and John's turn would come.

John was helping with the construction when he threw down his hammer and announced "I quit!" A quiet person always, it was rare to see him angry.

"Son, what ails you?"

"I am tired of always doing for Jacob, Jacob this and Belle that! To hell with you all! I'll do for myself, nobody else bothers for me!"

"Wait, John, that's not true. We love you!"

John turned with a smirk, "You expect me to believe you now? You never said it before."

"John, Fathers don't say that to sons, often. What are you planning to do?"

"Go home and pack and clear out of this town. I'm going to where there is some action instead of the two bit joints they have here. Prohibition preached and saloons on every corner. I'm tired of the hypocrites that spread gossip around about my mother and my sister! I can't take it anymore!"

Bennett grabbed his shirt, "Just a minute young man, explain yourself!"

"Dad, they talk all over town about Belle and Elmer Weber. He just bought that liquor joint down by the river. And they say Mother has whores working in her laundry so no telling what is going on upstairs! I can't defend them anymore, I don't know but what it's true!"

Bennett hit him hard with his fist, checking at the last minute, but clipping his jaw enough to spin him around. Crying, Bennett stood ashamed at what he had heard and at what he had done. John also in tears ran north to the boarding house. He did not seek

290

Margaret, but left for the station with a cloth bundle of his possessions, bought a ticket to Kansas City. The train was just pulling out, he caught a handle and swung aboard.

Margaret served supper chattering about the work schedule and the girl that won't keep regular hours, and the way she was almost cheated again at the market by a man who assumed she could not read the scales. Bennett was very quiet, but she did not notice. He had said earlier that John would not be to supper and Jacob was working late at the house. And then Belle broke in, "I'm going over to Mary Ann's for her math lesson." But before she could leave Bennett growled at her. "Sit still at this table until we have finished and you are not leaving the house tonight!" His tone shocked both women into silence.

"Bennett!" Margaret breathed, not wanting the other boarders to hear. He leaned forward to say quietly again, "You will not leave this house. You may go upstairs and I will follow to speak to you in a moment."

Belle obediently retreated up the stairs and Bennett's gaze followed her, looking intently he could see a bulging outline of her belly, confirming what John had said.

Alone in the upstairs sitting room Bennett confronted Belle. Margaret standing, had to be seated. She too now saw what she had ignored.

She cried, "No, no, no. Belle, didn't you understand what I told you? Didn't you realize what may happen? I told you!"

Belle said nothing. Caught, she was relieved, now she and Elmer could get married! She had no thought beyond that.

Bennett was livid, barely controlling himself he

291

said to Margaret, "I will see that he makes it right, or kill him tonight."

"Bennett, he's not worth going to jail for. Don't get yourself killed. If you go down there his cronies will gang up on you!"

"I will take care of this."

"Papa, please don't kill him! Papa it's my fault! I wanted to marry him, I knew you'd say no unless I had to! Papa!" She screamed as he walked into the street.

Once again Margaret gathered her baby girl into her arms, both of them frightened of what may be taking place, mother frightened about what consequences are in store for her beloved daughter. "I had such high hopes for you child. Such dreams. Now you've ruined your life. Oh, foolish girl. A moment of pleasure, a life of pain!"

Belle thought Margaret had suddenly lost her mind. Sitting there looking off into space and talking like she had died or something dramatic. For Pete's sake she was only going to have a baby! She would get married and live happily ever after.

Bennett walked into the joint. It was not much more than a shack, a small room with a board bar and a wash basin behind it for washing beer mugs, there was a table with a poker game going and another with dominos waiting for the evening crew to play. Elmer was behind the bar.

"Step around here if you're man enough," Bennett demanded. "I have something to settle that needs to be taken outside."

Elmer knew Bennett and didn't think of him as a fighter and fancied he would be able to take care of himself. In the road beyond the horses Bennett pulled his gun.

"Whoa!" Elmer backed away. "Hold on there! I

thought this was a fair fight! Though I don't know what it's all about!"

The few men that had been inside had followed them out to see the excitement so Bennett did not want to expose his family secret in front of them, but said "You son of a bitch, you know who I am and why I'm here. I'd like to shoot your balls off! But I'll fight you fair. I just wanted to make sure none of your friends help you out."

"Put the gun down and none will interfere." Elmer signaled his buddies, they nodded.

The fight began. Bennett was in surprising good shape from his recent hard labor and the match struggled on and on. Finally Elmer begged off, exhausted. Not having the adrenaline to push as hard as Bennett nor the will to hurt his future father-in-law. The other men had lost interest when they had been told to stay out of it so they were back inside at their poker game long before the two stopped fighting. They sat there in the dirt looking glares at each other, panting, exhausted.

"You'll marry my daughter and make an honest woman of her or I'll kill you here today!"

"Yes, sir, whatever you say."

"You'll marry her and you'll be good to her or I'll kill you any day!"

"Yes, sir, whatever you say."

"You'll say you've been married secretly for a long time."

"Yes, sir."

"You'll find respectable work and support her and the child."

"Yes, sir." Elmer sat panting and sore from the beating but a grin on his face. "This is a hell of a way to get engaged!"

293

Bennett just scowled. "Now go close up that joint and come with me to the house. I have to prove I haven't killed you . . . yet!" He picked up his gun.

Elmer hollered, "Jake tend the bar, I gotta go get married."

Mr. and Mrs. Creary almost called off the wedding between Carrie and Jacob when they heard the gossip that Elmer and Belle had run off and married "several months ago" and now that the baby was on the way they decided they had to make it public. "That is the weakest coverup I ever heard, about as bad as saying a girl has to visit her dying aunt for nine months!" Mrs. Creary said, "I'm not sure that family is the sort we want for grandparents of our grandchildren. I've heard rumors about those working girls at the laundry too. And to think that Weber person has a joint down by the river, he would be an uncle to our grandchildren. No, Carrie, I don't think it will do at all."

"Mother, what about our American belief that every man is judged on his own merits and it doesn't matter who his family is? Jacob is a good hard working man. He is even providing a house before we are married!"

"Well, Jacob wasn't an angel growing up. I remember."

"Mrs. Creary!" her husband interrupted, "Please refrain from any more gossip or you lower yourself to a level of disgrace."

The conversation was ended and no more said about calling off the wedding. But from then on there was a distinct coolness between the Crearys and the Pughs. The wedding went as planned on the 19th September, 1888.

Actually there was a distinct coolness all over town toward the Pughs. First the W.C.T.U. luncheon was called off and replanned at another home, Margaret not being notified "by mistake." There were cool stares and limp congratulations offered at church over Belle's "secret marriage." Margaret could not prevent the blush when asked point blank when and where this "secret marriage" took place. She stammered last spring in Sedan and could not tell the lie looking at her friend's face. She stopped going to church, unable to face the embarrassment.

Margaret saw immediately that was the wrong effect, both on Belle and her reputation. "We are going to go to church. All of us and act as if nothing at all is wrong. We shall hold our heads up and the gossip will die from want of fuel. Belle if anyone asks a personal question that is at all prying for gossip I want you to look past them as if they ceased to exist and leave them standing alone. If they press the matter give them a cold shoulder and say, 'I didn't know you could be so cruel.' Surely they won't press the matter beyond that. Why should we hide? Our daughter is going to have a baby, she is married by our blessings. I've never backed down from anything before, I'll not back down from this. You won't either!"

With Margaret's mind set on a plan no one crossed her and they, as usual, gained strength from her example.

Poor John, had he learned anything from running away?

Chapter 23

The Run, The Osage Nation and The End

Business boomed with the rumors about a part of Indian Territory that was to be opened for homesteading soon. New people began to pour into town.

They had to sign up at the county seat, but would have to go to Arkansas City to get closer to the state line. There was mass confusion because nothing was official yet. No decision was made about how it would be executed, but everyone fancied themselves an expert.

The influx of people brought business, followed by problems such as overcrowded schools, and people who ran out of money waiting for the land to be opened. Men were shot stealing from the markets, tempers flared at the bank when loans were denied for want of collateral.

Mr. Read said, "I'm proud that we have such a solid bank and we'll stake anyone who has good intentions and a plan, but I cannot loan money to be frittered away while these people wait for the government to open a tract of land they said they'd never take from the Indians."

"But these are unassigned lands," Bennett argued. "The Indians on the rolls have been assigned their acres by the courts."

"I know, Mr. Pugh, but that Territory was designated as Indian Territory and we should not crowd them or we're asking for an uprising! There's no peace with the Indians in Arizona nor in the western mountains yet, we could be caught right in the middle! No sir, I don't encourage these people to go into the Territory!"

Another bank patron spoke up. "Something should be decided now that we have elected a new President. Garfield died and Cleveland was so busy admitting states to the union not much was done except beat the British at settling Oregon and Washington States! I bet old Ben Harrison will do something. This country isn't organized! We just go from crisis to crisis!" A second patron added, "It's lasted a hundred years, though! Longer than any other in the world."

Another listening to the discussion in the bank lobby offered. "Yeah! Damned sight better than the British Queen issuing orders to make a bow as she passes."

Plans rapidly developed in the winter months but an opening day was not announced for the "Run" as it was now called. People were to sign up, then line up at the line with their official stakes and make a run for a 160 acre plot. They would stake it, then go file a claim at the land office on the map and it would be theirs if they could hang on to it. Nerves were tense all winter waiting for the announcement of the opening date. Tension was reaching the intensity of an electric current flowing through every man woman and child near the territory.

Beggars were more and more frequent at the kitchen door. Margaret's charity was put to a strain. Her nerves were tense also, waiting for Belle to have her baby, living in the same house with Elmer, the cause

297

of her disgrace, and all the usual day-to-day events became bigger and harder to cope with.

Bennett was making a notation in a diary that on this 4th day of March 1889, Benjamin Harrison was sworn in as President of these United States. Levi Morton would be the Vice-President and they had called a special session of the Senate so the Land Issue could be quickly resolved before full blown riots and anarchy broke out in Kansas involving those waiting for the opening of the Territory. Several had illegally trespassed already and had to be expelled by the Federal Marshals and the Army. It was feared they soon would have to fire upon the citizenry and people would be killed. John Ingalls, President Pro Tempore of the Senate was from the State of Kansas and had a great deal to say about what the chaos was doing to his state.

"Bennett! Go fetch Doctor Emerson!" Startled from his diary, his pen flew to a quick conclusion and he ran out the door laughing nervously. A few that were about on this blustery day looked at the strange man without a coat and wondered if he was daft.

Bennett and the doctor returned in time to hear the cry of an infant.

"It's a boy." Elmer called down the stairs as they were going up.

Bewildered Bennett stood there grinning. Doc went on up to see his patient that had not been so patient, and Elmer and Ben laughed together for the first time.

Elmer had given up the "joint" as promised, but with no livelihood, he was living off his in-laws and there was tension between them.

Now with a baby in the house everyone lacked sleep and tempers were short. It was Margaret's home so she felt a right to make demands of the people living there. Elmer did not feel welcome, nor was he at ease, and he avoided any contact with anyone, so he slept most of every day or stayed in his room. Belle had her hands full learning to cope and care for the baby. Everyone felt put upon.

"You're never going to get rich laying in the bed!" Bennett admonished Elmer.

"Well I can't work at what I know and live with my so called wife!" Elmer retorted.

"Get out and learn something!" Margaret interjected. "Make the run tomorrow! Maybe you'll get trampled!"

"Mother!" Belle cried. "There's enough trouble without creating more here at home. Elmer can't get a bank loan for his business with this bank trouble people are talking about. It's nationwide! Elmer can't help it!"

"He could go into plumbing with Jacob!"

"No he can't, that's not his line of work."

"Oh, you are going to be married to a honky tonk man! Where is your pride?"

"Where is your charity!"

The town emptied overnight. The "Run" was described in every newspaper nation wide. Nothing in all the world had ever happened to compare with it. The nation had expected a few hundred people to make this dash for land. After all, free land could still be homesteaded all over the West, why would anyone want to go into Indian Territory to live on purpose? Yet, thousands signed up. At least five people to every plot of ground. The disappointed would fight, connive, and steal to get "theirs."

"I would not be in that mess for any land even if it had solid gold rocks all over it!" Margaret said.

"There was a day when you would have led the pack," Bennett reminded her.

"Look, it says in the paper the circus is coming to town! A real circus all this way West. They'll set up on the school grounds." She deftly diverted his truth.

Margaret kept the baby while Belle and Elmer went to the circus. They were still such children. Although Elmer was 10 years older, in some ways he was the more childish. He did love to have fun. When they returned breathless from the excitement and the rush to tell all they had seen, they truly entertained Bennett and Margaret with stories about the tigers and bears trained to perform. But the telling could not describe the new invention, the "Ferris Wheel." Finally they all went back to the site to have another ride and personally experience this wild rigging.

"What if it stops? What makes it go? It looks so flimsy! The seats swing!"

"They have to swing, Margaret, or you'd dump out!"

"Oh, I'm not sure. It's awfully high!" And she climbed into the seat afraid and as excited as she had ever been in her life. "Oh, Ben! The whole world is out there visible for miles and miles! Oh, Ben!" She screamed as they crested the top and started down, not able to see any means of support, appearing suspended in air. Her stomach fluttered with a never experienced feeling. The movement of the wheel rushed the night night air towards them, "Oh, I think I shall faint!" Margaret screamed. Others screamed around her and they laughed like children again. "Oh, this is grand!" "Oh, it's going over again!"

Belle had never seen her mother have so much fun before. Suddenly she knew her in a new way.

Elmer stayed another winter. Working again on

300

the railroad, backbreaking hard work. "It's like prisoners on a chain gang. Daylight till dark they expect you to keep moving like a machine!" He refused to give Bennett and Margaret any room and board. When it was mentioned he reminded them, "I am your 'guest' remember. I was told to come here and marry your daughter."

Resentment on both sides grew. He would not give Belle money either for her or the baby's necessities.

The city voted to prohibit all joints and enforced the closing of ones operating illegally.

In the spring of 1891 Elmer Weber left. No explanation, just a note to say he was gone for good. "Do what you want, marry whom you please, I intend to do the same. Elmer."

Belle cried, but was not as heartbroken as Margaret had thought she would be. She had settled into a routine of work at the boarding house and had become as proficient as Margaret in the kitchen, hoping to make up for what her so called husband did not provide. Since tensions had taken the joy out of their sex, they had nothing left to share. Belle was also determined to restore her reputation by being the best at all she did. Except for short visits she and Margaret took together to Cedar Vale and on down to Indian Territory to see Lindsey, they never had a day off. At least they could keep an eye on little Frank.

On one trip out to Lindsey's with Jarome and his sister Constance, they met with a group of Indians coming to Cedar Vale by way of Johnson's Pass. It was Strike Axe and his family. Except for their brown skin and coal black hair they could have been any family going to town for supplies. They halloed each other, then camped and spread out their meal to share with each other. Margaret watched to see if they washed before eating and they all did much more thoroughly than her own boys would have done. The ladies were dressed in cotton dresses much like her own but had beautiful fringed shawls around their shoulders.

There was much to learn about their friend's life. Margaret asked about life on the new reservation. Strike Axe said "You must come to see us in our home someday. We have built a house much like your brother George's. We like it but it is hard to get used to sleeping with so little air. We put the bed against the window. Some ways are better, some ways are not. We go to the agency every so often to collect our supplies. I think the agents just want to make sure we are still around. It would be funny if we all mixed ourselves up, some of us going to Greyhorse, and others to Big Hill Camp, and others to Hominy and when they had us come in we would all be different people than the ones there before. Ha! Do you think they would notice we were different people? Sometimes I don't think the agents know one of us from another."

Margaret found Strike Axe easy to talk with much to the curiosity of the females. They remained very quiet and listened to the loud and harsh sounds of the English words.

"Are there schools on the reservation as were promised?" Margaret asked.

"They are even taking away our names, they are giving us white names. They are sending our children to schools and giving them new names and teaching them white ways. I don't mind the children learning the good new things, but all new things are not good. I don't like them taking our children away from home even when it is as close as St. Louis Girl's School. Did you know that we now have a Catholic Church in Pawhuska? They wanted to take away our Catholic priest but we wouldn't let them. We built a Cathedral and we helped with our own hands. It is one of the finest west of the Mississippi I am told. It opened in 1887 and has stories told in stained glass and marble altars from Italy. It will stay for a long time. We must work hard to keep what is valuable to us and still obey the agency rules," Strike Axe responded.

Jarome told him about how their lives have changed too, and commented that the whole country was changing. "Things are being invented now that we never dreamed about. Man can do anything, now that science has been unleashed." He tried to describe an electric light and could not. They laughed.

"That is for the young," Strike Axe added. "I think I'll go back to my teepee when I'm old and let the young work the new things."

Margaret wondered about his age and could not guess. He was older than Lindsey but . . .

They parted the next morning with directions for finding Lindsey.

A square grey weathered board house stood out like a salt box on a table, sitting firmly planted on the prairie with roses and peonies growing over and around a fence encircling a small yard. Small trees swayed in the wind and Martha was drawing water for the plants. She had nurtured her flowers through heat and cold and was now determined to have fruit trees. The seeds had been hard to come by. There was not another house for five miles.

"HALLOOO!" They called as soon as they were close enough. Martha had seen them coming but could hardly believe her eyes when she saw it was Lindsey's mother. Lindsey had seen them too. Although he was out of their sight, he rode to the house as soon as he saw the dust trail moving toward his home. He too was surprised by the visit.

Martha rushed to straighten her already immaculate home. Margaret was amazed that out here with no neighbors to see Martha had kept such a clean and neat home. Even her apron was starched! And she didn't even know they were coming. Margaret was impressed. There was a neat garden out back. Martha said, "Oh, I can make anything grow here if you give it a chance. Sometimes a little water, other times protection from the sun or the wind, but it will grow."

She picked tomatoes, green beans and some young corn, onions for the beans, with a little ham for seasoning. She picked okra, rolled it in cornmeal and deep-fried it after the bread was fried. "The Indians have taught me to make fry bread. It keeps the kitchen cool in the summer because I don't have to heat up the oven." She gracefully set out a table and cooked the meal over her "summer stove" off the back of the house, which was a pile of stones made into a hearth. She apparently did this every day enjoying her work.

Lindsey said, "Martha can make a feast out of weeds! Course she never knows around here how many will be for dinner."

"Why is that?" Margaret asked, baffled that they would have so much company.

"Neighbors pass here to Cedar Vale, and odd as it looks, this is a stop over station for almost everybody. We have lots of company! Martha doesn't believe it is Christian to turn anyone away, so we feed a hoard every once in a while. They may camp here for days. One thing about it, Martha has a reputation for generosity and some of these folks have been mighty nice to us, too."

The door burst open and there stood Will, dusty, tall and grinning from ear to ear! "Hi, Ma! What's for dinner!"

The long, lanky sixteen-year-old was filling out and looked so much like Ezra it gave Margaret a start! Such broad shoulders even so young.

"Say hello to your grandmother and cousins, and don't be calling me MA!"

"Yes, Ma'am," Will awkwardly pecked her on the cheek, shook hands with Jarome, didn't quite know what to do with Belle until she stood and gave him a peck on the cheek.

"I'm your Aunt Belle, but you don't remember me do you? We used to fight over our toys!" Will turned red. She didn't look like she had ever played with toys and she had a baby there in her lap.

Martha rescued him, "Go wash up, dinner's ready." She turned to the others, "No matter where that boy is he can make it home for dinner. I think he has a hollow leg. He can eat as many portions as all of you put together."

Margaret remembered how it was with her boys at that age and sympathized. Dinner barely over, Martha began to do up the dishes. Finishing, she then turned the chairs over the table, swept, and scrubbed the floor, packed out the dishwater to the pig pens and poured it into the trough with some corn and the plate of scraps. All the left over food was wrapped in towels and put in the cupboard for supper. Then she changed her apron and sat down to visit. Margaret didn't have much to say and neither did Martha so they chatted about the health of the children the need for small pox vaccinations, the garden and the weather.

At bedtime Margaret was once again amazed. A tent was unfolded and set up beside the house, and

305

bedrolls pulled out from under beds. The men folk were to bed down in the tent or in the open if they desired, and the ladies would use the beds in the house. Margaret and Martha had one bed and Connie and Belle the other. Frank slept on a floor pallet, but crept outside during the night to sleep with Will. He had tagged after Will all day after he had been given a ride on his horse. They stayed four days. Margaret going out horseback with Lindsey one day to view the cattle.

The prairie stretched out to the horizon with a tall grass that came to her chin when she stood on the ground. From only a slight knoll one could see for miles, not wholly unlike Kansas, but the ground was more in swells of undulating hills and interspersed with a lacy band of trees which signaled the viewer of a creek or a spring.

"It's just like Washington Irving pictured it in his book, 'Tour of the Prairies" and that was fifty years ago. It seems a shame to ever disturb the calm here. son. It is beautiful and in spite of my feelings they are opening up the Territory for homestead. Are you going to go for some of this yourself?"

"My lease with Strike Axe has worked out very well. My herd will grow. The railroad is going to have a line from Cedar Vale that will cut through Osage territory, probably to Pawnee Villages for shipping. If that happens we won't have to drive the cattle at all, but ship right from here to Kansas City. My only reason to move is to have a house in town for Martha. She seems content, though," Lindsey said. "Now Will, he's another matter. He is wanting to go find some girls! Ha! The nearest ones are in Cedar Vale, 18 miles away. I hear they are eyeing the Cherokee Outlet for homesteading, but I don't want any part of that. Hear tell they have too many cyclones out there."

"You're joking son, something bothers you."

"I want to see integration. I have made a good many Indian friends and they are *good* friends. They, as a nation, have the same problems as any people. They are good people and bad people. Some don't need any control, while others couldn't be controlled by God Himself. But I can see the selling out of their people. Most of them would also like to integrate, but to them that means living peacefully side by side, exchanging trade goods, but to whites it means 'get out of my way, I want what ever you are not using!' I can't be like that. I like my arrangement here. Now Will may want more. If he does let him sell his part of the herd and go homestead. Being American means doing for yourself doesn't it? Beholden to none?"

"I'm proud of you son, and your father would have been very proud, too."

The nineties came in with a bust and made a bang at the same time. The banks were busted and people lost faith in them almost totally. At the same time it was an era of invention and ingenuity as the world had not seen before. Inventions were the order of the day. Carpet sweepers, boxed oatmeal called Quaker Oats for a breakfast cereal. A new undergarment called a brassiere to replace the corset. Corn planters and disc and harrows. Steam powered drills, washing machines, lathes and packaged soaps and bakery bread. Not every invention came to the midwest immediately, but the wonders of it all were advertised in the papers. And, of course, the mail service was expanded coast to coast and was making a reputation for being regular and on time, as well as dependable at least to most regions. However, none of that was as exciting as the day the telegram arrived.

307

"For Mr. and Mrs. Bennett Pugh." The small boy on a bicycle said with his practiced crisp manner.

"Oh, no," Margaret faltered. People only got telegrams when there was a death in the family. She trembled and opened it.

WILL ARRIVE THURSDAY BY TRAIN. LOVE SAPHRONIA.

An excited squeal brought out all the family and the hired girls. She excitedly waved the paper around and danced a perfect highland fling to everyone's amazement. Bennett gave the boy a nickel and retrieved the paper from Margaret.

"That is tomorrow!" She sure didn't give any notice about her arrival. But that is the way these kids are.

They were all at the train when it pulled in and John came down the steps first to turn around and lend his hand to Saphronia, who regally took it and daintily stepped to the platform. Margaret thought, how much like my mother she is. Steel rods in her backbone and proper to the last inch. She greeted her, "Darling, my darling," and embraced her. Saphronia embraced Belle also, but looked her up and down, thinking how small she was for a Wilson lady. But then she wasn't, was she, she was a Pugh, or what? No matter, she was exhausted.

"Even travel by first class coach is tiring. It must be the rapid movement," Saphronia said as she directed the porter to stack her trunks in the depot warehouse and several other bags to be put into the carriage. Thinking that Jacob was one of the jitney drivers, they were all amused when she had to be introduced to her own brother.

Margaret felt very strange. She no longer knew her own daughter. Even her looks had changed so much that a pang of physical pain stabbed through her and she started to cry. She excused her tears as weeping for joy, but they were bittersweet.

Back at the boarding house, having tea, John and Saphronia relaxed more and Carrie broke the ice, "How long a visit are we privileged to have Mrs. Faulk?"

"Oh, please call me Saphronia. We are planning to relocate my dear, with the children grown, we are free to explore other opportunities."

A murmur of wonder circled the group. "Are you serious?" Margaret asked thinking her hearing had failed her.

"Here? In Kansas?"

"Yes, Mamma, we are moving to Kansas. John is retired and we are going to locate over in Pratt County. A friend has located the property and we shall become ranchers." She didn't sound too enthusiastic. "It was terribly difficult to leave the children behind, as you must know Mother, but we have to think of our own future."

"Ranching isn't an easy way of life. Are you sure that is a way to retire?" Margaret asked.

"Quite sure. May I have some more of your delicious tea, Mother?"

The conversation turned to personal events back home, and Margaret basked in the knowledge that her daughter would be within a day's ride by train. Perhaps these older children would come to know their half brothers and sister, if John would come back.

After only a week's stay, John and Saphronia left for Pratt, Kansas.

Events unfolded just as Lindsey predicted. The "Run" of 1889 was only the beginning. People were saying, "All that land is out there and no one is using it and we didn't get a fair shake in the run, there were too many of us." The grumbling went on and on and was encouraged by the settlers who did find a homestead writing to tell of the prosperity they had found overnight.

Whole towns bloomed and the sale of everything was tremendous as everyone was constructing something. Roads, schools, houses, horses, buggies and cattle, just name it and it was in demand. What words to read in the midst of eastern bank failures and unemployment. So the government bent to the people's will and land was opened in 1891. "Just a few more counties next to the Unassigned Lands." Then again in 1892 the Cheyenne and Arapaho reservations were opened for settlement.

The government did not really expect any Indian Nation to survive and have a need for these lands anyway. One could see how drastically their birth rates had dropped off and they succumbed to diseases that only mildly affect whites, so why not develop the land? Finally the Cherokee Outlet was left north of the other invaded lands and the Cherokee was made an offer to move, "So you won't be surrounded by Whites." The buy out was negotiated and the stage was set for the final "run" on September 12, 1893.

Once again everyone was lined up, only on the State line this time. People had signed up in Arkansas City for months and the same scenario played out before each Run. People gathered, went hungry waiting and near and outright riots broke out. Tempers were fanned as their funds became short or non existent. People were forced to beg. Men left families so others could have mercy on their wives and children, so on the final day there were men, women and children all out to get a stake. It was all the Federal

310

Marshals could do to hold them back. No matter that there had been three "runs" before. This was the last chance. Except for some of the eastern Oklahoma lands which were indeed occupied by Indians, this was all there was to have.

Althea and Joe arrived by wagon. Joe was going to make the Run for a hundred and sixty acres in the Cherokee Outlet. He planned to go horseback and make the claim and return for Althea.

"Almost Free land Margaret! Free! Just think, land just for the staking! The $100 fee can be had from the bank with the land as collateral!"

"And just for hard work, you mean. There is nothing free, you'll pay twice the price in sweat and tears," Margaret replied. "But you are young, you can do it, I'm just glad it isn't me having to start all over."

Joe and Althea's little ones toddled into the kitchen from their naps on the back porch. Margaret smiled at their dirty faces. They had fallen asleep without a chance to wash after dinner. She helped Althea pour water in the basin. "I'll wash Josephine and Caroline, you get Everett and Clifford."

The guns sounded. Wagons, horses, buggies and wheel barrows raced for the spots available. Trains, too, were loaded to a groaning point with people, mostly men, waving their stakes, jumping off before the train had come to a full stop, to run wildly for what caught their eye as a desirable place. All of the newspapers were full of news of how it had happened.

Margaret and Bennett, Belle, Althea and the children made a day outing of it by going to Arkansas City. The crowd was unbelievable. They finally crossed the bridge across the Arkansas River south of town and pushed with the crowd to the rise of the hill. As early

311

as it was, every spot was filled with people and their transportation. It was hot and their water was hot, and Margaret was not inclined to stay, but the crowd was such they couldn't move their buggy.

"Belle, remind me never to be so curious again! I may faint." Belle looked closely at her mother to realize again that she was aging. I will be left to take care of father if anything happens to her, Belle thought, Can I fill her shoes?

All at once the gun went off, or did it? The actual sound was obscured by the roar of shouts, rebel yells and thunder of hooves and wheels. They were enveloped in a cloud of dust, later said to have been miles high in the sky and seen as far away as Kansas City, an exaggeration Margaret was sure, but it was literally an earth moving experience.

They dined at an almost empty hotel before going home. They met people heading south. Did they really think they still had a chance to find an empty acreage, or were they following after someone ahead of them?

"There will be many a story to remember and retell from this experience if they find land or not." Margaret said, remembering her own disappointment at not having a homestead after traveling so far to find one.

But her life was and had been filled with satisfaction. There was work to do and a good living to be made. There were her children close by, and new babies being born for the next generation. There was Emmett and Dean, Erma and Florence now, Jacob's little family of precious children, and Belle's Frank, of course. Then the other families (as she thought of them now) grown up children. Let's see, she thought, Belle could just possibly have some more children but that would be about all. She wondered if John had married. Sometimes she had trouble remembering the names of Saphronia's and Mary's children.

A letter came from Lindsey in January and a few days later another from John Higgins in Maple City. "Bennett, look at this. Little John Higgins' child is going to marry our Will! Can you believe it? We were in Wisconsin with the Higgins! We move thousands of miles from there and now they are living in Maple City. He has three girls, and the oldest, Bertha, is going to marry our grandson! They are wanting to have the wedding here in Winfield so the whole family can be here together! Oh, I do love that thoughtful boy!"

"Could be he's wanting a free wedding reception!" Ben added sourly. He did not look forward to the reunion quite as much as Margaret did. He too was getting older and financially pinched at times when he thought about the future.

"Oh, don't be such a penny pincher, Bennett. It is fantastic. It may be the only time we shall all be together."

Belle was excited about the news and planned immediately to start sewing new dresses for them both. The new Gibson Girl was the rage with the huge mutton sleeves to the elbow, the blouson bodice accentuated the waist which was drawn in as tightly as possible with wide belts. Skirts had been raised to the ankle making shoes a more important fashion accessory than ever before.

"Mother you must stop wearing those awful moccasins or your feet will be impossible to fit into a proper shoe," Belle said.

"My feet were always wide and square across the toes and never fit a shoe until I found moccasins, but don't worry, I'll suffer through one afternoon with shoes if you insist on designing my dress with that indecent above the ankle length."

"One day women will get the right idea and start wearing trousers. That would finally be sensible. Skirts get in the way of any sort of work we do," Belle complained.

"Yes, but skirts were apparently designed by men to cover an enticing part of our anatomy from the sight of men who have enough trouble keeping a check on their animal instincts. Actually, a dress is more complimentary and forgiving to a woman's anatomy."

What a prude, Belle thought. Mother is getting more straight laced everyday.

The wedding was planned for March 27, and would be held in the boarding house dining room, the reception immediately afterwards. A. C. Buster, the Justice of the Peace, would officiate. Rooms were scheduled to be vacant so everyone could stay with them. John Higgins and his wife, Martha, brought their other two daughters, Ora and Alice, who stayed with their sister Bertha the night before the wedding. The next morning Bertha was very nervous.

It was a magnificent wedding and reception, and for Margaret, a gift she would never forget. Somehow Belle had contacted John, and he arrived just after the ceremony with his two adorable children, Dean and Rose. There Margaret stood surrounded by her children, Saphronia, Mary, Lindsey, Jacob, John and Belle. Her thoughts included little Sarah and George. Tears filled her eyes and there were no words to describe the fullness, the completeness and joy in her heart that she experienced with them that day.

They all had to go back to their own lives, of course, and the world moved on at an ever faster and faster pace.

314

Margaret would travel to Cedar Vale each time a new baby arrived, which for Bertha was very regularly. Poor Will kept having girls! Rhoda Mae in '96, Sylvia in '98, Ona in '99 and Rose in 1902.

Margaret felt Carrie Nation was ruining the Women's movement with her "Hatchitation of joints."

"She is a madwoman! Destroying property and just causing people to lose respect for the movement." Margaret lamented. "If she keeps this up we will never get to vote."

"I told you. You have to divorce yourselves from all other causes before people will ever consider a woman voting. Carrie Nation is an argument that women are unstable," Ben said.

"She sure does get their attention though," Margaret grinned gleefully.

"Look here, the paper says, she hacked up a saloon in Wichita of one Elmer Weber! Ha! Good for her!"

"I thought you said she was a mad woman destroying property."

"She was until you told me who she hatcheted!"

Belle came in with a tall, very handsome man looking like the cat that ate the canary. The gentleman was impeccably dressed, clean and with a beard and moustache trimmed in the German manner.

"Mother, Father, please meet Reverend Howard Thompson. Reverend Thompson, Mr. and Mrs. Pugh."

"Very pleased to meet you Ma'am, Sir."

"Rev. Thompson is here for the Chautauqua and since we have a dining room, I have invited him to have dinner here with us as there was sure to be far and away enough for an extra guest," Belle fluttered and her face flushed.

"By all means, Reverend Thompson, please join us."

While the men visited Belle helped Margaret in the kitchen, and whispered, "Mother, it's him! I know this is my soul mate! I shall die if he doesn't care for me too! Please make a good impression!"

"Shall I go put on my shoes?" Margaret asked teasing.

"Mother, you must tell him little Frank is your child! I can't let him know I had a child and never really married the Father."

"Now you listen here, young lady. Lies never corrected a sin! He's a minister of God and knows more than most the weaknesses people are subject to. If he is as wonderful and sensitive and caring as you think he must be, he will understand. If not, the truth is the best way in all the world to find out! I shall not lie for you now. I never did before and we all bore the consequences, but we did know who our true friends were when it was over, didn't we? Here!" she firmly slapped the newspaper in Belle's hand, "Have a laugh."

"Wha...?" Belle read about the "hatchitation" Carrie Nation had at Elmer's saloon and almost became hysterical. It was just what she needed to relieve the tension and put an end to that part of her life.

Howard and Kansas Belle were married in the Methodist Church soon after they met. He was assigned in Winfield as a deacon and worked at the new Poor Farm outside of town. Belle derived a great satisfaction working there too. She collected vegetables from homes all over town to take out and cook for the poor unfortunates who lived there. Howard had promised her that if ever her parents could not care for themselves they would not have to resort to living at the poor farm, but would always be welcome to live

316

with them. Each of Margaret's children had the same thing in mind without saying to the other a word about the plan.

It was New Year's Eve of Nineteen Hundred! Little Ona Marie Johnson had been safely delivered to Bertha in Cedar Vale and had returned home with her mother to Lindsey and Martha's house where they all still lived together. (Ona later changed her name to Leona.)

Margaret had taken the train home to be with Bennett on the grand and gala occasion marking the turn of the century. Balls and celebrations were held all over the City. Both, the large and spacious homes, and the more modest, were all hosting open house to welcome in the new century. Everyone dressed in their finest and warmest, going briskly from house to house, greeting their friends and neighbors. Churches were opened for Midnight service. Some were convinced that tonight would be the end of the world as they had computed from their Bible revelations. It was an awesome experience waiting for the new century to begin.

Margaret and Bennett made a few rounds to friends' homes, but retired early to the upstairs parlor and reminisced. Little Frank was sleeping and Belle and Howard were off to church.

"Would you live your life differently?" Bennett asked gently as he curled his arm protectively around her shoulder.

"Not really. It's been hard at times, but for the most part I've . . . we've . . . had a very good life."

"What would you have changed?"

"I would have my Sarah and George grow up. Perhaps I never would have left Olney, but it has all worked out for the best. I'd like to have had a better

317

education for the children. Look at Jarome over in Cedar Vale getting ready to open his own bank this week! My, my his big house, fine furniture. Our children have not done as well."

"I'm surprised at you Margaret. Those are all material goals!"

"It isn't the things I want for my children, Ben. I want them to be comfortable and not have to worry about hunger day to day. Saphronia is out on a farm and will soon use up her nest egg. Mary is in the same fix, scratching out a garden and living on eggs and chickens, and Lindsey, why he doesn't even own his land. He couldn't even get a mortgage to tide him over. An epidemic would wipe out all he owns in a breeze! Jacob at least has a trade. He drinks too much and I don't know why. And John, we don't even know his whereabouts."

"Margaret! Don't be so glum! That's not like you at all. We came West for opportunity, not gold, and we found it. Mary has land and so does Saphronia. Lindsey is running one of the largest cattle herds hereabouts. Jacob has a fine plumbing business and a beautiful little family. His ten-year-old, Emmett is already helping his daddy. He talks like he knows all about the business."

"And Belle, sweet Belle. She is our jewel. She is taking more and more of the load from my shoulders."

"Ah, yes, no raging success for this family, but loving and caring people for the best part and they are all standing on their own two feet, win or lose."

"I'd say they are all successful and they have your strength of training to help them know what is right," Bennett comforted her, "I'm very proud of you and of our children."

318

"Oh, Bennett, I love you more than I ever have before. We won't see much of the 20th Century, but we can welcome it!"

Margaret and Bennett talked about their old age. They had not saved a great deal of money and wondered how long they could have the health to run the boarding house. In fact some of the rooms were not let now and they served dinners to fewer and fewer people. The steam laundry was more lucrative and could be managed without directly doing the work.

In 1903 they all went out to the Meldrum farm to see the phenomenon of a gas well that had been drilled and the gas that came forth would not burn. It was quite a curiosity and people would attempt to set it on fire, half expecting it to suddenly explode. A delicious sense of danger. It was discovered that it was 2% helium. It was located on Althea's place at Dexter.

Joe had proved up his homestead near Newkirk, Oklahoma, and sold it and returned to Cedar Creek, leased 400 acres of land and put sheep on it. Joe died in '97 leaving Althea to raise the four babies alone. She turned the sheep into cash and then to land but struggled to make ends meet.

McKinley had been defeated by Theodore Roosevelt. Winfield had a population of 9,000. Railroads went in nine directions. There were three colleges, a music conservatory, electric trolleys, a marble works, Armour Packing plant out of Chicago and three major hotels, the Copland, Brettun, and the St. James. A book was published by the Commercial Club to promote the city.

The Women's Christian Temperance Union had their National Convention in Wichita, with Carrie Nation as the main speaker.

March 1, 1905 Margaret woke with a terrible headache and chills, a stuffy head, and a tight chest.

"Here, Bennett, this ad in the paper says Sumermiers has Foley's Honey and Tar Compound for pneumonia. Will you go get me some? I don't think it's pneumonia but I sure have a cold."

She tried to read. Russia and Japan are at War, "Oh my! Why do they talk about things a half a world away? Somebody has to be at war with somebody all of the time! The Germans have to fight a war every twenty years or they fight each other!" The next page told about the inauguration preparations for Teddy Roosevelt. "There's a spunky fellow! I just bet we see great things from him."

By March 4, Margaret was bedfast, breathing rapidly in a shallow pant, burning with fever that even aspirin could not bring down, having chills, and her coughs becoming more feeble and weak. Bennett was distraught, never having seen Margaret this ill in this way.

He and Belle and Howard sat at her side, Jacob and Carrie sat in the next room. They all prayed, realizing how much their lives would change without this strong decisive woman.

On March 5, 1905, Sunday afternoon at 2:15 p.m. Margaret breathed no more. Her fevered body cooled. She was at rest.

Unusual for the *Winfield News*, they ran her obituary on the front page Monday morning.

"Mrs. Bennett Pugh Dead"

Mrs. Margaret T. Pugh, wife of Bennett died Sunday afternoon at 2:15. The funeral will be from the home at 614 1/2 Main Street, Tuesday afternoon at 2:30. Mrs. Pugh was 77 years old on the 28th day of September. Her husband and three children, Jacob, John and Belle, survive her. She was born in Ohio, Married in Indiana, coming here with her family 22 years ago.

Belle stamped her foot with tears streaming. "She deserves the obituary, but who wrote it? It's all wrong! She married in Illinois and she had eight children!" Howard comforted her. "It is natural to be angry with someone, the paper will do." He wrapped his arms around her and led her away to the carriage to go to the cemetery.

Margaret was buried in the Union Cemetery. Howard preached her funeral. No marker was put up as the funeral had to be paid for first.

Lindsey returned to the Osage.

Belle followed Howard to Council Bluffs, Iowa.

Bennett went to live in the Veterans Home at Fort Leavenworth, Kansas until his death May 25, 1916. He is buried in Sec. 31 Row 8 grave 12 in the Leavenworth National Cemetery on the south edge of the City off Highway 5.

Margaret didn't accomplish all that she had set out to, and nothing special ever happened to her if she was asked. But her strength and endurance and her pioneer spirit would be remembered and drawn from for generations in the future.

She had truly given the world A Pennyweight More.

❦ ❦ ❦ ❦